Also by Paige Toon

Lucy in the Sky

JOHNNY BE GOOD

Paige Toon

POCKET
BOOKS

LONDON • SYDNEY • NEW YORK • TORONTO

First published in Great Britain by Pocket Books UK, 2008
An imprint of Simon & Schuster UK Ltd
A CBS COMPANY

1 3 5 7 9 10 8 6 4 2

Simon & Schuster UK Ltd
Africa House
64-78 Kingsway
London WC2B 6AH

Simon & Schuster Australia
Sydney

www.simonsays.co.uk

A CIP catalogue record for this book
is available from the British Library

ISBN 978-1-84739-044-8

Typeset in Goudy by M Rules
Printed and bound in Great Britain by
Cox & Wyman Ltd, Reading, Berks

For Indy

My beautiful boy

Be good

Prologue

'Sing! Sing! Sing!'

No. I can't.

'*Sing! Sing! Sing!*'

No! Stop it! And for God's sake, cut that bloody music!

'SING! SING! SING!'

Argh! My palms are so slippery I almost dropped the mic. I'm in bad shape. I can't sing. I can NOT sing. But they won't stop. I know they won't stop until I deliver. And I shouldn't disappoint my audience. Okay, I'm going to sing! Here comes the chorus . . .

> *I'm locked inside us*
> *And I can't find the key*
> *It was under the plant pot*
> *That you nicked from me*

That's not my song, by the way. And when I say I can't sing, I mean I *really* can't sing. When you're as drunk as I am, you could be forgiven for thinking that *if only* Simon Cowell were in the room, he would say, 'Girl, you've got the X Factor.' But I'm under no illusions. I know I'm, in his words, 'distinctly average'.

As for the audience . . . Well, I'm not singing to a 90,000-strong crowd at Wembley, but you've probably guessed that by now. I'm in the living room of my flatshare in London Bridge. And the music comes courtesy of my PlayStation SingStar.

The person who's just grabbed the mic from me is Bess. She's my flatmate and my best friend. She can't sing either. Jeez, she's hurting my ears! Next to her is Sara, a friend of mine from work. And then there are Jo, Jen and Alison, pals from university.

As for me? Well, I'm Meg Stiles. And this is my leaving party. And that song we're making a mockery of? That's written by one of the biggest rock stars on the planet. And I'm moving in with him tomorrow.

Seriously! I am not even joking.

Well, maybe I'm misleading you a little bit. You see, I haven't actually met him yet.

No, I'm not a stalker. I'm his new PA. His Personal Assistant. And I am off to La-La Land. Los Angeles. The City of Angels – whatever you want to call it – and I can't bloody believe it!

Chapter 1

Ouch. My head hurts. What sort of stupid person has a leaving party the night before starting a new job?

I'm not usually this disorganised. In fact, I'm probably the most organised person you're ever likely to meet. Having a leaving party the night before I had to board this plane to LA is very out of character. But then I didn't have much choice. I've only just got the job.

Seven days ago I was a PA at an architects' firm. My boss, Marie Sevenou (early fifties, French, very well-respected in the industry), called me into her office on Monday morning and asked me to shut the door and take a seat. This had never happened in the nine months I'd been working there and my initial reaction was to wonder if I'd done anything wrong. But I was pretty sure I hadn't so, above all, I was curious.

'Meg,' she said, her heavy French accent laced with despair, 'it pains me to tell you this.'

Shit, was she dying?

'I do not want to lose you.'

Shit, was *I* dying? Sorry, that was just me being ridiculous.

She continued, 'All of yesterday I toyed with my conscience. Should I tell her? Could I keep it from her? She is the best PA I have ever had. It would *devastate* me to let her go.'

I do love my boss, right, but she ain't half melodramatic.

'Marie,' I said, 'what are you talking about?'

She stared at me, her face bereft. 'But I said to myself, Marie, think of what you were like thirty years ago. You would have done anything for an opportunity like this. How could you keep it from her?'

What on earth was she going on about?

'On Saturday night I went to a dinner party at a very good friend of mine's. You remember Wendel Redgrove? High-powered solicitor – I designed his house in Hampstead a couple of years ago? Well, anyway, he was telling me how his biggest client had lost his personal assistant recently and was having a terrible time trying to find a new one. Of course I empathised. I told him about you and how I thought I might die if I ever lost you. Honestly, Meg, I don't know how I ever managed before . . .'

But she regained her composure, directing her cool blue eyes straight into my dark-brown ones as she said the words that would change my life forever.

'Meg, Johnny Jefferson needs a new personal assistant.'

Johnny Jefferson. Wild boy of rock. Piercing green eyes, dirty blond hair and a body Brad Pitt would have killed for fifteen years ago.

It was the chance of a lifetime, to go and work in Los Angeles for him and live in his mansion. To become his confidante, his number one, the person he relies on more than anyone else in the world. And my boss, in a moment of madness, had suggested me for the job.

That very afternoon I met up with Wendel Redgrove and Johnny Jefferson's manager, Bill Blakeley, a cockney geezer in his late forties who had managed Johnny's career since he split up with his band, Fence, seven years ago. Wendel drew up a contract, along with a strict confidentiality clause, and Bill asked me to start the following week.

Marie actually cried when I told her it was all done and dusted; they'd offered me the job and I had accepted. Wendel had already persuaded Marie to waive my one-month-notice period, but that left me only six days, which was daunting, to say the least. When I raised my concerns, Bill Blakeley put it bluntly: 'Sorry, love, but if you need time to sort your life out then you're not the right chick for the job. Just pack what you need. We'll cover your rent here for the first three months and after that, if it all works out, you can have some time off to come back and do whatever the hell it is that you need to do. But you've got to start immediately, because frankly, I'm sick to fucking death of buying Johnny's underpants since his last girl left.'

And so here I am, on this plane to LA, with a shocking hangover. I glance out of the window down at the city. Smog hangs over it like a thick black cloud as we fly towards the airport. The distinctive white structure of the Theme Building looks like a flying saucer or a white, four-legged spider. Marie told me to look out for it, and seeing it makes me feel even more spaced-out.

I clear Customs and head out towards the exit where I've been told there will be a driver waiting to collect me. Scanning the crowd, I find a placard with my name on it.

'Ms Stiles! Well! How do you do!' the driver says when I introduce myself. He shakes my hand vigorously as his face breaks out into a pearly white grin. 'Welcome to America! I'm Davey! Pleased to meet you! Here, let me take that bag for you, ma'am! Come on! We're this way!'

I'm not sure I can handle this many exclamation marks on a hangover, but you've got to admire his enthusiasm. Smiling, I follow him out of the terminal. The humidity immediately engulfs me and I start to feel a little faint so it's a relief to reach the car – a long black limo. Climbing into the back, I slump down into the cool, cream leather seats. The air-conditioning kicks in as we exit the car park and my faintness and nausea begin to subside. I put the window down.

Davey is rabbiting on about his lifelong ambition to meet the Queen. I breathe in the outside air, less humid now that we're on the move, and start to feel better. It smells of barbeques here. The tallest palm trees I've ever seen line the wide, wide roads and I'm amazed as I stick my head further out of the window and gaze up at them. I can't believe they haven't snapped in half – their proportions are skinnier than toothpicks. It's the middle of July, but some people still have sad little Christmas decorations hanging out in front of their tired-looking homes. They twinkle in the afternoon sun – no wonder they call this place Tinseltown. I look around but can't see the Hollywood sign.

Yet.

Oh God, how can this be happening to me?

None of my friends can believe it, because I've never been that fussed about Johnny Jefferson. Of course I think he's good-looking – who wouldn't? – but I don't *really* fancy him. And when it comes to rock music, well, I think Avril's pretty hardcore. Give me Take That any day of the week.

Everyone else I know would give their little toe to be in my position. In fact, make that their whole foot. Hell, throw in a hand, while you're at it.

Whereas I would struggle to give up more than my big toenail. I certainly wouldn't relinquish a whole digit.

That's not to say I'm not thrilled about this job. The fact that all my friends fancy Johnny like mad just makes it even more exciting.

Davey drives through the gates into Bel Air, the haven of the rich and famous.

'That's where Elvis used to live,' he points out, as we start to climb the hill via ever-more-impressive mansions. I try to catch a glimpse of the groomed gardens behind the high walls and hedges.

The ache in my head seems to have been replaced by butterflies in my stomach. I wipe the perspiration from my brow and tell myself it's just the side effects of too much alcohol.

We continue climbing upwards, then suddenly Davey is pulling up outside imposing wooden gates. Cameras point ominously down at us from steel pillars on either side of the car. I feel like I'm being watched and have a sudden urge to put my window back up. Davey announces our arrival into a speakerphone and a few seconds later the gates glide open. My hands feel clammy.

The driveway isn't long, but it feels like it goes on forever. Trees obscure the house at first, but then we turn a corner and it appears in front of us.

It's a modern architectural design: two storeys, white concrete, rectangular, structured lines.

Davey pulls up and gets out to open my door. I stand there, trying to control my nerves, as he lifts my suitcase out of the boot. The enormous and heavy wooden front door swings open and a short, plump, pleasantly smiling Hispanic-looking woman is standing beside it.

'Now then! Who have we got here?' She beams and I like her immediately. 'I'm Rosa,' she says, 'and you must be Meg.'

'Hello . . .'

'Come on in!'

Davey wishes me goodbye and good luck and I follow Rosa inside, to a large, bright hallway. We go through another door at the end and I stop in my tracks. Floor-to-ceiling glass looks out onto the most perfect view of the city, hazy in the afternoon sunshine. A swimming pool out on the terrace sparkles cool and blue.

'Pretty spectacular, ain't it?' Rosa smiles as she surveys my face.

'Amazing,' I agree.

I wonder where The Rock Star is.

'Johnny's away on an impromptu writing trip,' Rosa tells me. Oh.

'He won't be back until tomorrow,' she continues, 'so you've got a little time to get yourself unpacked and settled in. Or even better, out there by the pool . . .' She nudges me conspiratorially.

I lift the handle on my suitcase and try to ignore my disappointment as Rosa leads me into the large, double-height open-plan room. The hi-tech stereo system and enormous flatscreen TV in the corner tell me it's the living room. Furniture is minimal, modern and super, super cool.

I'm impressed. In fact, I'm feeling less and less blasé about this job by the minute, and that's not helping my steadily swirling nerves.

'The kitchen is over there,' Rosa says, pointing it out behind a curved, frosted-glass wall. 'That's where I spend most of my time. I'm the cook,' she explains before I get the chance to ask. 'I try to feed that boy up. If I were a bartender I'd have a lot more joy. He likes his booze, that one.' She chuckles good-naturedly as we arrive at the foot of the polished-concrete staircase.

'Are you okay with that, honey?' She glances back over her shoulder at my suitcase.

'Yes, fine!'

'We should really have a butler here, but Johnny don't like a lot of staff,' she continues, as she climbs the stairs ahead of me. 'It's not that he's stingy, mind, he just likes us to be a tight-knit family.' She turns right. 'Your room is over here. Johnny's got the big one at the other end, and behind them doors there you've got your guest rooms and Johnny's music studio.' She points them out as we go past. 'Your offices are downstairs, in between the kitchen and the cinema.'

Sorry, did she just say cinema?

'I'll show you round later,' she adds, slightly out of breath now.

'Do you live here, too?' I ask.

'Oh no, honey, I got a family to go home to. Apart from the security staff, you're the only one who'll be here overnight. And Johnny, of course. Okay,' she says, clapping her hands together as we reach the door at the end. 'This is you.' She turns the stainless-steel knob and pushes the heavy metal door open, standing back to let me pass.'

My room is so bright and white that I want to put my shades on. Windows look out over the leafy trees at the back of the house and a giant super-king-size bed is in the centre, covered by

9

a pure white bedspread. White-lacquer floor-to-ceiling wardrobes line one wall, and there are two doors on the other wall.

'Here you've got your kitchenette, where you can whip your-self up some food if mine ain't good enough for you.' From her jovial tone I'm guessing that's not likely to be the case. 'And here you've got your en-suite.'

Some en-suite. It's enormous, with dazzling white stone lining every surface. A huge stone spa is at the back, and a large open shower is to my right, opposite double basins on my left. White fluffy towels hang on heated chrome towel rails.

'Pretty nice, huh?' Rosa chuckles. She walks to the door. 'I'll leave you to settle in. Why don't you come on down to the kitchen when you're good and ready and I'll get you something to eat?'

As the door closes behind her, I start jumping on the spot like a mad woman, face stretched into a silent scream.

This place is mental! I've seen rock star mansions on *MTV Cribs*, but this is something else.

I kick off my shoes and throw myself onto the enormous bed, laughing as I look up at the ceiling.

If only Bess could see this place . . . It's such a far cry from our dingy flatshare back home. It's getting on for midnight now in England and she will have hit the sack long ago, sleeping off her hangover before work tomorrow. I decide to send her a text to wake up to in the morning. I climb off the bed, smiling at the feel-ing of the thick white shagpile carpet between my toes, and grab my phone from my bag.

Actually, I think I'll send her a picture. I slide open the camera lens instead, snapping the massive room with the (now slightly crumpled) bed in the middle. I punch out a message:

CHECK OUT MY BEDROOM! HAVEN'T MET HIM YET BUT
HOUSE IS AMAZING! WISH YOU WERE HERE X

She is going to die when she sees the outside view. I'll have to send her that tomorrow.

I decide to unpack later and instead go and see Rosa downstairs. I find her in the kitchen, frying chicken, peppers and onions in a pan.

'Hey there! I was just preparing you a quesadilla. You must be starving.'

'Can I help?' I ask.

'No, no, no!' She shoos me away, minutes later delivering the finished product, cheese oozing out of the edges of the triangular-cut tortillas. She's right: I am starving.

'I would offer to make you a margarita, but I think you just need feeding up, judging by the state of those skinny arms.' She laughs and pulls up a chair.

My arms *are* skinny compared to hers. In fact, every part of me is skinny compared to Rosa. She's like a big Mexican momma away from home.

'Where do you live, then?' I ask, and discover that home is an hour's drive away, where she has three teenage sons, one ten-year-old daughter, and a husband who works like mad but loves her like crazy from the way she smiles when she speaks of him. It's a long way for her to travel, but she adores working for Johnny. Her only regret is that she's not often there to see him tuck into the meals she leaves for him. And it breaks her heart when she comes in the next morning and finds the food still in the refrigerator.

'You have got to make that boy eat!' she insists to me now. 'Johnny don't eat enough.'

Hearing her speak about 'Johnny' is strange. I keep thinking of him as 'Johnny Jefferson', but soon he'll just be Johnny to me as well.

I do already feel like I know him, though. It's impossible to live in the UK without knowing about Johnny Jefferson, and after a lunch break of Googling him when I worked at Marie's, I now know even more.

His mother died when he was thirteen so he moved from Newcastle to live with his father in London. He dropped out of school to concentrate on his music and formed a band in his late teens. They signed a record contract and were global superstars by the time Johnny was twenty. But he spiralled out of control at the age of twenty-three when the band broke up, before coming back almost two years later as a solo artist. Now thirty, he's one of the most successful rock stars in the world. Of course there are still rumours of his dodgy lifestyle. Drink, drugs, sex – you name it, Johnny's probably done it. I don't mind the odd drink, and I'm not a prude, even if I have had only three serious boyfriends, but I'm really not into the drug scene, and I've never been attracted to bad boys.

Rosa heads off at six-thirty and urges me to get outside by the pool. Ten minutes later I'm on the terrace, clad in the black bikini that I bought for my recent holiday in Italy with Bess. The sun is still baking hot so I stand on the steps in the shallow end and tilt my head back up to catch the rays. The glittering blue water is cool, but not cold, and I don't flinch as I immerse myself fully. I swim a few laps and decide then and there to swim fifty every morning. I did so much walking in London that keeping fit was effortless, but everybody drives cars here so I might need to work at it.

After a while I climb out and spread my towel on the hot paving stones beside the pool, forgoing the sunloungers so I can trail my fingers in the water. My hangover is long gone, and I lie there feeling blissfully happy, listening to the sound of the water filtering through the swimming pool and the cicadas chirping in the undergrowth. High overhead a distant aeroplane leaves a long white streak in the cloudless sky and out of the corner of my eye I can see little black birds swoop down to drink from the pool. I begin to feel dozy.

'Is this what I pay you for?'

I jolt awake to find a dark figure hovering above me, cutting out my sun. I'm so shocked I almost fall in the pool.

'Whoa, shit!'

I rummage around to try to pull my towel out from under my bum so I can cover myself up, but it drops in the water.

'Bollocks!'

I hastily scramble to my feet, realising all I've done in the last few seconds is curse at my new boss.

'Sorry,' I blurt. His eyes graze over my body and I feel like he's undressing me. Which isn't that difficult, because I've barely got anything on as it is. I cross my arms in front of my chest, desperately wanting to retrieve my soaking towel from the pool. Unfortunately, though, that would involve bending over, which is not something I feel comfortable doing right now. I look up.

He's actually quite tall – about six foot two, I estimate, compared to my five-foot-seven-inch frame – and is wearing skinny black jeans and a black T-shirt with a silver metal-studded belt. His dirty blond hair falls messily around his chin and his green eyes, with the light of the swimming pool reflected in them, look almost luminous.

13

Christ, he *is* gorgeous. Even more so in real life than in pictures.

'Sorry,' I say again, and his mouth curls up slightly as he reaches down behind me to drag my sopping-wet towel out of the pool. I instinctively want to step away from him, but the only way is backwards and into the water, and I think I've made enough of a tit of myself as it is. He straightens himself back up and wrings the towel out, muscles on his bare arms flexing with the movement. I notice his famous tattoos and can't help but feel on edge.

I remember my sarong is hanging on one of the sunloungers behind him, but he makes no attempt to move for me as I awkwardly sidestep him before hurrying over to grab it. I quickly tie the still-way-too-small green piece of material around my waist.

'Meg, right?' he says.

'Yes, hi,' I reply, watching him while shading my eyes from the sun as he rolls the wet towel up into a ball and aims it at a basket six metres away. It goes straight in. 'And you, er, obviously, are Johnny Jefferson.'

He turns back to me. 'Johnny will do.' I note that he has a few freckles across his nose that I've never noticed in photographs.

'I was just, um, taking a break,' I stutter.

'So I figured,' he replies.

'I didn't think you'd be back until tomorrow.'

'I figured that also.' He raises an eyebrow and delves into his jeans pocket, pulling out a crumpled cigarette packet. Sitting down on one of the sunloungers, he lights up and casually pats the space next to him, but with the way my heart is beating, I figure I'd be safer on the sunlounger opposite instead.

'So, Meg . . .' he says, taking a long drag and looking across at me.

'Yes?'

'Do you smoke?' he asks, not offering me a cigarette.

'No.'

'Good.'

Hypocrite. I think it, but I don't have the guts to say it.

'How old are you?' he asks.

'Twenty-four,' I reply.

'You look older.'

'Do I?'

He flicks his ash into a two-foot-high stainless-steel ashtray and narrows his eyes at me. 'There's a lot of pressure with this job, you know.'

Oh, okay, not really a compliment, more a concern.

'I can handle it.' I try to inject some confidence into my voice.

'Bill and Wendel seem to think so.' He sounds quite American, which is surprising considering he spent the first twenty-five years of his life in England. 'Got a boyfriend?' he asks.

Hey, hang on a second . . . 'What's that got to do with anything?'

'Don't get touchy,' he says, looking amused. 'I just want to know what the chances are of you getting homesick and buggering off back to Old Blighty.' *Now* he sounds English . . .

His stare is making me feel uncomfortable so I hold his gaze for only a couple of seconds. He remains silent and I sure as hell don't know what to say to him.

'You haven't answered my question.'

Question? What question? Oh, boyfriend question . . . I'm finding it difficult to focus.

'No, I don't have a boyfriend.'

15

'Why not?' he bats back immediately, before taking another long drag on his cigarette.

'Er, well, I did have one but we broke up six months ago. Why?'

He grins, stubbing out his fag. 'Just curious.' He gets to his feet. 'Want a drink?'

I stand up quickly. 'I'll get it.'

He gives me a wry look over his shoulder as he wanders over to the other side of the terrace where there's an outdoor bar area. 'Chill out, chick, I'm perfectly capable of getting myself a drink. What are you having?'

I opt for a Diet Coke.

He returns with two large whiskies on the rocks and hands one over. I look down at it and back up at him. His expression is blank. Did he hear me?

'Um . . .' I say, but the next thing I know he's dragging his T-shirt over his head. Oh my God, I don't know where to look. I take a large gulp of whisky as he stretches out on a sunlounger.

Right then and there, the ridiculousness of the situation hits me. This is nuts. Johnny Jefferson – *the* Johnny Jefferson! – is here in front of me, so close that I could actually reach out and touch him. I could tweak his nipple, for crying out loud! Imagine if I sent Bess a picture of *this* view. A small snort escapes me at the thought.

'You alright?' He glances over at me.

'Yes,' I answer. But, embarrassingly, I start to giggle.

'What's so funny?'

'Nothing,' I quickly reply, but inside my head my mind is going into overdrive . . .

Nothing? A week ago I was working in an architects' studio in London and now I'm in LA, in a rock star mansion, sitting on a sunlounger next to a half-naked rock star! If that's not surreal, I don't know what is.

He knocks back his whisky in one and I hold out my hand for the glass.

'Another?'

He hesitates for a moment before offering it up. 'Why not.'

About time I start doing my job. I get up and hurry to the bar area, finishing the rest of my drink. I survey the bottles in the cupboard under the bar, searching for the whisky. I spot a can of Diet Coke and consider switching but think better of it. What I need right now is some Dutch courage. And a few shots of tequila wouldn't go amiss . . . Ooh, there *is* a bottle of tequila in here, actually. I glance over at Johnny Jefferson, sprawled out on a sunlounger and facing away from me, oblivious to my beverage dilemma.

No, Meg, no. No tequila for you.

Oh, bugger it, I'll just have one.

I take a quick swig from the bottle and almost spit the booze back out as it sears the back of my throat. I desperately, *desperately* want to cough. Instead I swallow furiously and choke back the tears.

I need water. Water!

Or perhaps another swig of tequila would help?

Oddly, it does.

'You know what you're doing over there?' Johnny calls out.

Whoops, I've been ages.

'Yes, just coming!'

I approach the sunloungers, trying not to get distracted by the sight in front of me.

'Cheers.' Johnny chinks my glass and takes a gulp as I sit down.

His chest is toned and smooth and he has a dark tan. There's a tattoo of some writing right across his trouser line. I can't read what it says, but *phwoar* . . .

Oi! Focus, Meg, focus!

'So Rosa said you were away on a writing trip?'

'Yeah. Trying to get everything together for next week.'

'What's happening next week?' I ask.

He looks a little surprised. 'The Whisky?' he replies.

'More whisky?' I ask. Jesus, he really *does* have a drink problem.

'No, *the* Whisky,' he says.

'I don't understand.' I look at him blankly.

'Girl,' he says, 'don't tell me you don't know about my comeback gig at the Whisky – you know, the *venue*?'

'No, sorry, I don't.' My face heats up. 'Should I have heard about it?'

He laughs in disbelief.

'Sorry,' I say, 'but I don't really know much about you.'

And then I begin to ramble like a lunatic . . .

'I mean, I'm not really a fan.'

Shut up, Meg.

'I don't mind some of your songs but, well, you know, I kind of prefer Kylie, to be honest.'

Why the bloody hell did I admit *that*?

'But at least you haven't ended up with a mad stalker,' I continue. 'I could know anything and everything there is to know about you. I could know your favourite colour, the brand of shampoo you use . . .'

Christ Almighty, ZIP IT! Nope. It just gets worse . . .

'At least I'm not a star-fucker.'

ARGH!

'I should hope not, Meg,' he says, stubbing out his second cigarette in five minutes. 'That would be going above and beyond the call of duty.'

'Another drink?' I offer weakly, the reality of everything I've just said starting to sink in. I'm going to lose my job. I'm going to lose my job before it's even started.

'Nah, I've got to shoot off.' He stands up. 'I'm going to hook up with some pals in town. Ring the Viper Room and reserve us a table for eight.'

'Sure. Er, where . . .'

'In the Rolodex in the office. You'll find all the numbers you'll need in there.'

'Is that eight people or eight p.m.?'

'Eight people. Get them to hold the table. I don't know what time we'll be there.'

So I'm still employed, then? I get up hastily and take his empty glass from him, unable to meet his eyes. I turn away and notice in the reflection of the glass window that he's watching his new PA's departing derrière as she makes her way inside to the office.

Half an hour later Johnny Jefferson comes downstairs and finds me tapping my fingers on one of the two big desks in the office. I'm still feeling nervy, despite the tequila, and I'm not quite sure what to do next.

'Table all booked?' he asks, hooking his thumb casually into his jeans pocket. They're the same ones he was wearing earlier, but he's changed into a fitted cream shirt with silver pinstripe.

'Yes, and champagne chilling on ice. I didn't know if you wanted the car so I called Davey just in case. He's waiting on the driveway.'

'Cool.' He nods. 'Thought I'd have to take the bike.'

At least I got that right.

He stays standing in the doorway for a moment, staring at me, his hair still damp from the shower.

'Right then, I'm off.' He pats the palm of his hand on the door with an air of finality.

I try to resist asking, but can't. 'When will you be back?'

'Tomorrow,' he answers. 'Probably.'

And then he's gone. And suddenly the house feels very empty indeed.

Chapter 2

Bollocks, bollocks, bollocks, bollocks, bollocks.

Bollocks!

Bugger.

I do not fancy Johnny Jefferson.

I don't.

I really, really don't.

I've been telling myself this since I woke up at six o'clock this morning, unable to get Johnny frigging Jefferson out of my mind. He didn't come home last night, and I didn't sleep well. Even with damn jet lag I didn't sleep well, because I was too busy listening for his footsteps on the landing. Now it's three o'clock in the afternoon and I'm still waiting. Where the bloody hell is he?

Rosa says this is quite normal. 'He's a whirlwind, that boy,' is her explanation. She obviously takes it all in her stride, but I'm going to find it hard to get used to.

I made an effort with my appearance today and everything. I even decided to wear high heels. I felt a bit silly at first, with the office being at home and all, but I told myself I had to be professional.

Professional. What a joke. Yesterday he came home to find me lounging around by his fancy pool. Then I got tipsy on his tequila and told him I preferred Kylie's songs to his. Excruciating is not the word.

And now, here I am at three o'clock in an empty house – well, Rosa's in the kitchen and Sandy the maid is upstairs, and Ted, Samuel and Lewis, the burly security guards, are out and about somewhere, but they don't count. I ask again, where the bloody hell is he?

This morning, after I woke up, I decided to keep my resolution and swim fifty laps in the pool. I only got to thirty-three before I felt knackered, but figured that was a good enough start. I went back upstairs, eyes and ears primed for anything resembling a rock star, and had a bath in the enormous, bubble-filled spa. Then I called my parents to let them know I'd arrived safely.

'Barbara says Johnny Jefferson is a bit of a wild boy,' Mum said after barely ten seconds of pleasantries. Barbara is one of my mum's ex-pat bridge buddies. My parents are retired and live in the south of France.

'What do you mean by wild boy?' I'd replied, stalling for time. I had been hoping this topic of conversation wouldn't come up.

'Well, drink, drugs, women . . . That sort of thing. If I'd known any of this I wouldn't have let you take the job.'

'Mum,' I said, 'I'm twenty-four. In the nicest possible way, you couldn't have stopped me. And anyway, you know me better than that. I'm not exactly going to turn into a junkie groupie.'

'Whatever you say, dear. Now, have you called your sister yet?'

'No, Mum. But I will.'

Bess was altogether more enthusiastic. In fact, my ears are still ringing from her screams.

'I can't believe you're actually there! There! In Johnny Jefferson's mansion! When can I come to visit?'

'Soon, I hope.'

Squeal. 'I can't wait! So what does he look like? Is he as gorgeous in real life as he is in pictures?'

'Even more so.'

'*Really?*' Another squeal. 'Do you fancy him?'

'No, of course not.'

'You do! You do! I bloody knew you would!'

'I do not! He's my boss, for God's sake. Don't be ridiculous.'

Then she got frowned at for taking a personal call during work hours so we agreed to touch base on the weekend for a proper chat.

I unpacked after that and actually spent some time putting make-up on.

Not that I should have bloody well bothered.

And now I'm sitting here, behind this big desk, reading the manual left behind by Johnny's last PA, a girl called Paola. It seems pretty straightforward. Book doctor's appointments, manage finances and liaise with accountants, buy everything from shaving foam to zit cream, and obviously book flights, reserve tables and all that other stuff.

Earlier I managed to work out the voicemail system. I listened to the old outgoing message first and it was a bit weird hearing Paola's efficient-sounding voice. She's American. For some reason I assumed she was Italian. I recorded a new message and felt strangely jubilant until I played it back and heard how dreadful I sounded. So I recorded it again. And again, until eventually I gave up and decided to make do.

I also sent out a mass email introducing myself to Johnny and Paola's contacts and my inbox has since been filling up with requests from journalists, business people and countless 'friends' requesting interviews and photoshoots and asking if their names can be put down on the guest list for next week's comeback gig. I've been making a note of everything to run through with Johnny later.

I look at the time on my computer again. Three-fifteen. Hmm. Another message pops up so I click on it.

> hey, meg! pleased to digitally meet you. i'm kitty. i'm a cpa too. you on msn?

cpa . . . cpa . . . Oh! Celebrity Personal Assistant – dur! Exciting. I wonder who she works for?

I quickly reply that I *am* on MSN and we hook up to have a proper chat.

> hi! pleased to meet you too. who do you work for?

> rod freemantle

Rod Freemantle . . . I vaguely recognise the name, but can't place him. Before I have a chance to reply she writes to me again.

> actor. was in grass grows green and the violent light

I still can't picture who she means. Again she hits me back before I can profess ignorance. She sends through a picture of a slightly balding, dark-haired man of about forty, with his arms around two tall leggy blondes. He's leering down at one of their cleavages.

Nice. I tell Kitty I recognise him, before asking if she's one of the girls in the pic. She replies, 'hell no,' and sends through another picture. A gorgeous woman of, I'm guessing, about thirty, beams at the camera. Brilliant white teeth, dark ringletted hair, encased in an embrace with a tall, blond, good-looking man.

Holy shit, it's Brad Pitt!

holy shit, it's brad pitt!

ha ha, that rhymes!

but it's brad pitt! brad pitt!!!!

i can't deny it. sorry, i don't usually show off like that but i just couldn't resist. met him at a party last week and still a bit beside myself with excitement. you'll meet him soon enough though won't you?

will i?!

for sure! you can't work with johnny jefferson and not meet celebs. so what's it like? working with him i mean?

i don't really know yet. only started yesterday

i've been wondering how long it'd be before they'd replace paola. it's been a month. you've got the most coveted job in cpa-land, you know . . .

have I?

oh, yeah. i know a couple of people who went for it. so

where did you come from?

england

no, i mean who did you work for before?

oh sorry! marie sevenou. she's an architect

you didn't work in the business?

no

which agency did you go through?

agency?

yeah, cpa agency

oh, I didn't. my boss just recommended me to johnny's solicitor.

wow! talk about a lucky break. well, we should go for a coffee sometime. can be lonely, this business, especially if you're not from around here

that'd be great!

cool. I'll be in touch – maybe next week? better go now though. the rodster will be back soon and i've got fan mail to get through . . .

Speaking of fan mail . . . There are two giant postbags of it sitting next to my desk. I gaze down at it, mournfully. I've already calculated it's going to take me about a week to sort through it all, let alone any more that comes in. And then there's Johnny's MySpace and Facebook pages to manage. Looks like a royal pain in the arse to me. I avoided Facebook like the plague back in London because I knew I'd probably become addicted and would never get any work done.

Again I listen out for any sound of the rock star and recheck the time on my computer before looking back down at the fan mail. I guess I should get started on it.

The first letter I pull out of the bag nearest to me is pink and decorated with little red hearts.

Johnny baby!
How would you like some of this?

'This', I'm presuming, refers to the woman in the enclosed photograph: a stunning brunette wearing black, lacy knickers, posing doggy-style on a red satin bed-sheet. Her pert arse is in the forefront of the picture, while she looks over her shoulder at the camera.

Charming. I return my attention to the letter.

No strings attached. I don't want to marry you. I don't
want any commitment. But you can have exactly what you
want – wherever you want it. Call me on . . .

Urgh.

I slam the photo down on the desk in disgust and reach for the Rolodex.

Anton Seacroid – accountant

Bill Blakeley – manager

Brad Pitt

Brad Pitt! He's here! He's here, he's here, he's here! Who else, Tom Cruise? Oh my God, Tom Cruise *is* in here! Next to

Penelope Cruz, though. That's a bit out of date, Paola, naughty, naughty. Not for the first time that day, I wonder who Paola was and why she left – before I come across Madonna's name and my jaw hits the desk once more.

'Perusing the Rolodex, hey?'

Johnny's voice makes me jump out of my skin.

'You scared the life out of me!'

He's leaning on the doorframe, wearing the same outfit he had on last night. He looks rough and unshaven. Sigh . . .

'Glad to see someone's made a start on that.' He gestures towards the fan mail. 'It was the bane of Paola's life,' he says, adding, 'well, except for me of course.'

He wanders into the room and stands by my desk. He picks up the photo and studies it with interest, then reaches for the letter.

'You want me to reply to it?' I ask, warily.

'Hmm . . .' He considers my question for a moment. 'No, better not,' he decides eventually, and puts the letter and photograph back down.

'So, I've been reading this manual that Paola left,' I tell him, trying to sound professional. 'And I also have some photoshoot and interview requests for you.'

'Mmmhmm.'

'Oh, and some people want to be put on the guest list for next week.'

'What's happening next week?' he asks.

I'm confused. 'Your gig at the Whisky?'

'Just checking,' he says, straight-faced.

I look back down at the desk and shuffle some papers. Just because yesterday I didn't know about your gig doesn't mean I have a memory like a sieve, I think, annoyed.

'Shall I take you through them now?'

'Fuck, no. Later. I'm knackered.'

'Okay,' I reply. 'Is there anything else you want me to do?'

He pauses for a moment then pulls up a chair beside me. I freeze. He smells of cigarettes and alcohol, and I swear there's a hint of Chanel Nº 5 in there, too.

'Yeah, actually. Check out Samson Sarky.'

I do as he says, logging onto the internet site for the camp celebrity gossip blogger.

'Are you looking for anything in particular?' I ask.

'Scroll down,' he directs me.

I skip past scandalous stories about Britney Spears and Paris Hilton until he calls out, 'Stop.'

'Mandy Periwalker's latest botched boob job?' I ask, mouse hovering over the link for that story.

'No, next one.'

I scan the headline: 'While the cat's away . . .'

If the rumours are true about their relationship, Serengeti Knight had better keep a tighter leash on bad boy Johnny Jefferson, who was last night spotted getting up close and personal with a lithe redhead . . .

Johnny takes a deep breath, because presumably the rumours *are* true.

Serengeti Knight: teen star turned sexy starlet. Tipped for big success this year having scored the leading role in a romantic comedy opposite the gorgeous Timothy Makkeinen. Bess and I have been dying to see the film ever since we saw the trailer a couple of months ago. Mr Makkeinen is hot with a capital H.

But enough about him . . . I've always liked Serengeti Knight. She's talented *and* beautiful; the sort of girl you'd give anything to be. I religiously watched *Highlights & Lowlifes* in my teens, the television show that shot her to fame when she was just fourteen. That was nine years ago, but I still remember the rave reviews she received. She starred in the drama for five years, and the world watched her grow from an adolescent teen into a nineteen-year-old sex bomb. When the show was dropped by the TV channel, Serengeti disappeared off the scene for a year or so, before she started cropping up in indie films, building up her cred until finally she scored a couple of back-to-back supporting roles in big-budget blockbusters. This new film, *Just Juliet*, is her first major part, and the fact that she stars opposite Timothy Makkeinen should surely send her into the stardom stratosphere.

So she's seeing Johnny. Talk about Hollywood power couple. I'm starting to feel a little sick. Who could compete with Serengeti Knight?

Meg! Did you just use the word 'compete'? As if!

I sneak a sideways glance at him. He's peering closely at the computer screen, dark-blond hair partly obscuring his face. His shirt is unbuttoned at the top and I catch a glimpse of his tanned chest. I shudder and tear my eyes away as I recall the sight of him half-naked in the hot afternoon sun yesterday.

'Scroll down,' he orders me again.

He reads the rest of the piece, but it doesn't really say much more apart from touching on Serengeti's whereabouts. She's in Las Vegas, publicising her film, and apparently was shocked and disturbed when she heard about Johnny's supposed infidelity.

He slumps back in his chair.

'Would flowers help?' I suggest, tentatively.

His laugh is laced with sarcasm. 'I don't do flowers, chick. You need to know that.'

I feel my face turn red.

'Oh, that's right, you don't know anything about me,' he says, coolly. 'You're not a star-fucker, right?'

'No,' I bite back. 'But I know where to find one for you if you want.' I prod the photo of the brunette in lacy underwear, irritation searing through me.

He throws his head back and laughs, the first genuine laugh I've heard from him since we met. I look at him, defiantly, still annoyed by the fact that he keeps reducing me to a blushing fool.

'Tempting,' he says, 'but I think I'm in enough trouble as it is.' He grins. 'Better go call her.' He stands up and reaches into his pocket, pulling out a mobile phone. 'Phone ran out of juice last night and she's probably left me a dozen voicemails. You got the charger?'

'Erm . . .' I open desk drawers and hurriedly search through them. He shifts his weight from foot to foot. Feeling useless, I flick through the manual. Where the hell would Paola have left a charger?

'Sorry.' I glance up at his face, which is now a picture of impatience. 'You wouldn't have any idea where it would be?'

'No,' he says, shortly.

I get up and go to the other desk, again opening drawers and riffling through them, my head buzzing with adrenalin.

Calm down, Meg, it's only a bleeding phone charger, for goodness' sake.

A thought suddenly occurs to me. 'Hang on, haven't you charged your phone since Paola left?'

'Oh, yeah,' he says, brow furrowing as he racks his brain for a moment. 'Bedside table,' he informs me and promptly leaves the room.

Bedside bloody table, I mutter inwardly, and set about tidying six now very disorganised drawers.

A couple of hours later I'm still in the office and Johnny hasn't reappeared. Rosa pops her head around the door.

'I'm off, honey. I've left you a couple of pizzas in the fridge.'

'Lovely, thanks!'

'Did I hear Johnny come home?' she asks.

'Yes, a couple of hours ago. He went upstairs to call Serengeti.'

'Aah,' Rosa says, knowingly. I wonder how much attention she pays to the gossip-mongers.

'Have you met her?' I ask, referring to the actress.

'Oh, yes, she's been here a few times.'

I nod, wanting to find out more, but sensing it's not really the done thing to pry.

'Well, then, honey, I'll be off. See you in the morning.'

'Bye, Rosa. Thanks again!'

I call it quits for the day soon after that, and head out of the office. I stand at the foot of the stairs for a moment, listening for Johnny, but can't hear anything. I wonder if I should go upstairs and ask him if he wants any pizza. Should I? Oh, I don't know. I stand there for a moment, wavering. I probably should. I walk up a couple of steps, then pause and go back down again. No, I don't want to bother him. He'll come down if he's hungry.

I go into the kitchen and turn on the oven, taking the pizzas out of the fridge. Rosa has made one with chicken, green peppers and red onion on what looks like a barbeque sauce, and another with buffalo mozzarella, tomatoes and basil. I wonder which one

Johnny would prefer. Is he a vegetarian? I doubt it. But I can't be sure. Did it say anything like that in the manual?

I go to the foot of the stairs again and listen. No sound. This is ridiculous. I walk up the stairs with determination and turn left at the top, but get five paces towards his room and cop out. I meekly return downstairs and look in the fridge to see if there's anything else I could eat to save me making a decision.

I suppose I could just have a jacket potato. I'm not really much of a cook. In fact, maybe I should just go up to my room and use the kitchenette there. I don't want to be in his way.

Yes. That's what I'll do. I'll leave the oven on in case he wants the pizzas. Or maybe I should put them in for him?

I run my hands through my hair with frustration. I'm too tired for this. I'll wait another half an hour and see if he reappears.

An hour and forty minutes later, I've been upstairs to my room and back downstairs to the kitchen about a dozen times. And I'm still no closer to making a decision.

I know it sounds like I'm being a nutcase. After all, it's not exactly a critical question: to eat pizza or not to eat pizza?

Right, that's it. I'm cooking them.

I open the oven and put them inside. A few seconds later I change my mind and take them back out.

'What are you doing?'

Oh, here we go again. Meg looks like idiot in front of new boss. I turn around and plaster a smile on my face.

'Nothing. I was just cooking some pizzas that Rosa left.'

'Or not cooking them, as the case may be,' Johnny says, nodding to the pizzas on the countertop.

I laugh, embarrassed, and pick up the baking tray they're resting on and slide them back into the oven.

'You want one?' I figure it's best to skip over any details that make me look like a moron.

'Sure. What have we got?'

I tell him the options.

'Halves?' he asks.

Johnny suggests we eat out on the terrace, and a short while later I head out there with our dinner. He's sitting on one of the sunloungers, strumming an acoustic guitar. I hold my breath when I realise he's singing, too. He has the most beautiful voice: deep and melodic. I know he can belt them out when he wants to, but here and now he's singing slowly, softly. I'm rooted to the spot.

Please, please, please, let me get what I want . . .

He sees me and stops, resting his guitar next to the sunlounger and looking up at me with those piercing green eyes. Butterflies swoop into my stomach.

'Is that one of your new ones?' I try to keep my voice even as I stand in front of him with two very large plates.

'No, Meg, that one's by The Smiths.'

'Oh, I was gonna say, why don't you look around you, misery guts, haven't you already got enough?' I try to cover up my ignorance.

He chuckles. 'I don't think that sentiment occurred to Morrissey.'

'What's that old git got to do with it?'

'He was the lead singer of The Smiths, Meg. Jesus, you really don't know anything about music, do you?'

'I know that The Spice Girls sold more albums than you when they were at their prime. And that was before they re-formed.'

34

He shakes his head at me in wonder. 'How the hell did you ever come to work for me?'

'Funny you should say that,' I say. 'I was talking to Rod Freemantle's PA earlier—'

'Talking?'

'Well, MSN-ing. Anyway, I was talking to her – Kitty, her name is – and she said it took a month for you to replace Paola.'

'Yep,' he says, getting up and heading to the far right of the terrace where there's a polished-concrete table with bench seating. I follow him.

'Red wine okay?' he asks, going to the outdoor bar.

'Cool,' I say, placing the pizzas on the table. He brings the wine over, along with a couple of glasses and a bottle opener.

'So why *did* Paola leave?' I ask, going to sit down.

'Sit there,' he says, indicating where with the bottle opener. 'See the view.'

I do as he says while he opens the bottle and slides along beside me. I edge away from him a little.

'I'm not going to bite.' He gives me a sidelong glance and pours a couple of glasses of red. We eat in silence for a short while, looking down at the view. The smog has lifted and the sky is changing colour from blue to orange as the sun sets before us.

He still hasn't answered my question.

'So, Paola . . .' I try again.

He takes a large mouthful of pizza.

Oh, I give up. And now I seem to have lost my appetite. Eating pizza is the last thing I feel like doing in front of Johnny Jefferson.

'You done?' he asks, as he finishes his third slice.

'Yes, thanks.' I push my plate away.

He reaches into his pocket and pulls out his fags, tapping the filter end of one on the tabletop before lighting it. He swivels to face me, resting his knee casually on the bench seat. I glance at him nervously.

'You seem tense,' he says.

'I'm not tense,' I lie.

He raises one eyebrow and flicks his ash onto his plate. Yuck. I get up and go to the bar area, bringing back a glass ashtray I spotted in there yesterday. He flicks his ash in it and grins at me. I look away.

'You are definitely tense, chick.'

'I'm not tense,' I deny again, this time a little irritably.

He chuckles softly and slides the ashtray closer to him. I notice his fingertips are rough and calloused, I guess from playing his guitar.

'So what did you get up to today?' he asks.

'Um, just sent out some emails introducing myself. Little bit of fan mail, that sort of thing. And I have a bunch of interview and photoshoot requests which we must go through.'

'You've already told me that.'

'Oh. Sorry.'

'S'okay.'

We fall silent again. I reach for my wine and take a sip.

I wish I didn't feel so jittery. I'm usually quite composed. I sit up straighter with determination.

'Did you get hold of Serengeti?' I ask.

'Yeah.' Pause. 'She's cool.'

'Glad to hear it. I really liked her in *Highlights & Lowlifes*,' I reveal.

'She'll be delighted to hear it,' he says, knocking back half a glass of red wine in one gulp and glugging some more into his glass. 'Top-up?' he offers.

'Thanks.' I slide him my glass. 'Have you seen her new movie yet?'

'No.' He shakes his head. 'Going to the premiere on Thursday.'

'Wow! That must be so cool!'

'I'll get you a ticket. You can come, if you like.'

'*Really?*' I practically squeal.

'Of course,' he calmly confirms.

'I wonder if Kitty's going?' I think aloud.

'Who's Kitty?'

'Rod Freemantle's PA,' I answer.

'Aah, yeah. The one you were MSN-ing earlier.'

I try again. 'You never answered my question about Paola. Why did she leave?'

Johnny shrugs. 'Just wasn't for her, I guess. You're a nosey little thing,' he says, tapping another fag out onto the table.

I don't reply, instead just swirl my wine around in my glass as though I haven't heard him.

'I wanted a Brit,' he explains.

'Someone from Britain?'

'That's what "a Brit" means, yeah.'

'Why?' I ask, undeterred by his sarcasm.

I don't think he's going to answer for a moment, but then he speaks.

'Ah, you know . . . I kinda miss the UK. Nice to have a little piece of it here. Not that I'm calling you a piece,' he adds quickly.

I laugh. 'Do you get home very often?'

'Not often enough,' he replies.

'Why is that?'

'It's a bit of a marathon to organise these days. And the tabloids over there are fucking awful. They won't leave you alone.'

'It must be hard,' I muse.

'Can't really complain. Not when I've got all this.' He motions around him.

'It must still be hard, though.'

He shrugs.

'Do many friends from home come to visit?' I ask.

'Sometimes, yeah. In fact, my mate Christian is coming this weekend.'

'Really? In time for the gig?'

'That's right.'

'That'll be nice.'

Silence. I wish I could think of something more interesting to say.

He takes a long drag and then stubs out his half-finished cigarette, getting up from the table.

'I'm going to hit the town,' he tells me.

'Oh, okay.' I get up and start to clear the plates. 'Do you want me to reserve a table for you anywhere? Call Davey?'

'Nah. Just going to play it by ear,' he calls as he reaches the sunlounger and picks up his guitar, swinging it over his shoulder. 'Catch you later.'

'Okay, bye!' I reply, cheerfully.

As soon as he goes inside and slides the glass door shut behind him, I slump back down on the bench and take a deep breath.

I'm in trouble. I haven't had a crush like this since I was fifteen and in love with my French tutor. He was divine: young – must've been mid-twenties – dark-haired, olive-skinned and devastatingly

38

good-looking. My parents wanted me to take extra lessons because they were considering moving the whole family to France. As it was, they stayed in the UK until I went to university and then retired to Provence, but the lessons paid off anyway. I got an A. Amazing what a crush can do in terms of motivation.

I still remember staring into his dark-brown eyes across the table . . . Mr Dubois. I don't know what his first name was. Funny how it just never occurred to me to ask.

I wonder what he's doing now? He was such a nice man.

Nice men . . . Unlike countless other women out there, I've never really gone for bad boys. Take my ex-boyfriend, Tom, for example. He was lovely and we're still friends. No one could believe it when we broke up six months ago. We got on so well, but we just kind of fell out of love with each other and were more like brother and sister towards the end.

But I digress. My problem now is with Johnny Jefferson. My boss. And I don't quite know what to do about it.

Chapter 3

It's the afternoon of the premiere and I am going stir-crazy with excitement. I've barely seen Johnny these last couple of days and it's taken a superhuman effort to get any work done – I haven't been able to concentrate for buggery. I was convinced he'd forget about his promise, so when he showed up in the kitchen yesterday with tickets to not only the premiere, but the aftershow party as well, I came over all shy like a schoolgirl. It was a bit embarrassing in front of Rosa. Kitty's also going tonight, and we've arranged to meet in the foyer. I won't be sitting with Johnny and Serengeti as they're in the VIP bit, nor am I travelling there with them. I think the film company has arranged Serengeti's transport, but Davey's taking me.

At four o'clock I'm still trying to decide what to wear. The choice is between a cream dress from French Connection or black trousers and silver top combo. The dress shows off my legs, but I can't for the life of me find my cream push-up bra and I look very flat up top without it. Not very helpful in the city of boob jobs.

40

A loud buzzer sounds. I pick up the receiver of the video phone in the office.

'Ms Knight here to see Johnny,' one of the security guards tells me.

Damn. Serengeti Knight is about to make an appearance, and I haven't even got any make-up on. I assumed Johnny would meet her at her house.

I hurry to the front door to let her in, wondering if I should alert Johnny first. I haven't seen him today and I'm not even sure if he's in.

I fling open the door and beam at the beautiful creature before me. Serengeti Knight is petite and perfectly formed: shorter than me by about an inch, and that's when she's wearing heels, whereas I gave up wearing mine in the house days ago. Golden curls cascade around her shoulders and her eyes are the most unusual shade of bronze I've ever seen. They match the colour of her dress, a long sleek number. I'm guessing it's what she's wearing tonight. Either that, or this is a woman who likes to play dress up.

'Who are you?' Her tone is icy and I'm taken aback.

'I'm Meg, Johnny's new PA.'

'He didn't tell me he had a new PA,' she says, accusingly.

'I only started on Sunday.' I try to combat her coldness with the warmth of my smile, but it has no effect. She makes to push past me, so I step back to let her in, feeling disappointed. It never occurred to me that she might not live up to my expectations.

'Excuse me,' she says, annoyed, looking me up and down. I thought I'd left her more than enough room to pass, but I squeeze myself up against the wall so she can wander through with a foot to spare on either side.

I go to close the door, but she spins around.

'Wait!' she commands me, furiously.

I pause, hand on the doorknob.

'Open it! Open it!' she orders.

Confused, I open the door again. Is she a bit bonkers or something?

Impatiently she pushes back past me and stands on the doorstep.

'Footsie!' she calls. 'Footsie, come here, baby!'

Who on earth is Footsie?

I don't have to wait long to find out. A tiny white fluffball of a dog hurls its way towards the door. Then it spots me and starts yapping.

Yippee.

I throw myself back up against the wall once more while Serengeti heads inside. A few moments later, her psycho pooch follows. Closing the door, I make my way with trepidation to the living room.

'Where's Johnny?' Serengeti demands.

'I think he's upstairs.'

'Think? Shouldn't you know?'

'Well . . .'

I hear a door open upstairs, followed by footsteps along the landing. Johnny appears above us.

'Hey,' he says.

'Hey, baby,' she coos, smiling warmly at him.

'Are you coming up or am I coming down?' he asks.

'I'll come up, shall I?'

'Sure.'

Footsie starts sniffing me as Serengeti makes her way up the stairs. Go on, I urge the dog with my eyes. Go with your mistress . . . But he doesn't, choosing to stay and rub his wet little nose all over my bare legs instead.

I go back into the office, pooch in tow. It's only ten past four. Davey's coming for me at six, so between now and then I've got to make a wardrobe decision. And I suppose I should do *some* work . . . I pick up another fan letter and try to pay attention.

At five o'clock I decide to call it a day and go and get ready. Just as I'm clearing my desk, Serengeti walks into the room.

'Oh! Hi!' I exclaim, surprised.

'We're off soon,' she informs me. 'Johnny says you're going to the premiere, too?'

'Yes,' I reply. 'I can't wait!'

She flashes me a tight smile. 'I was thinking you'd be able to keep an eye on Footsie, but I guess . . .'

My face falls just as Johnny appears in the doorway.

'He'll be alright,' Johnny says, motioning to the dog. 'Meg was a big fan of *Highlights & Lowlifes*, you know. She's been looking forward to this.'

Serengeti considers this fact for a moment before crouching down and patting Footsie's curly, white head. 'I suppose you'll be okay, won't you, baby?'

'Is the car coming to collect you from here?' I ask them both.

'Yeah.' Johnny doesn't sound too happy. He looks at Serengeti. 'I think I'm going to take the bike.'

'You know I don't like the bike,' she snaps. 'It messes up my hair.'

'I mean I'll meet you there.'

'Baby, can't you just do this one thing for me? On my premiere night?'

43

Johnny doesn't answer.

Serengeti glances at me and irritation floods her face as she realises I'm eavesdropping on their 'domestic'. I quickly busy myself with the papers again and pretend to be hearing impaired.

'Look,' Johnny says. 'I don't want to do all that corny Hollywood red-carpet crap anyway.'

'But baby, we agreed to make our relationship public!'

'No, Serengeti, *you* agreed with your publicist. I never did. I'm taking the bike,' he decides conclusively.

The buzzer announces the arrival of Serengeti's limo. Footsie simultaneously cocks his leg and urinates over the table leg.

'Argh!' I gasp.

Serengeti glares at me, then at her dog, before turning and flouncing out of the office.

I study the yellow puddle on the floor. I guess that means I'm clearing up the dog piss, then.

I look back up and see Johnny still standing in the doorway.

'What time's Davey arriving?' he asks.

'Six o'clock,' I answer. 'Better go and get ready. Well, after I clean up this . . .'

The corner of his mouth turns up. 'Okay, chick.'

By the time I've found the cleaning stuff in the laundry and tidied away the present Footsie left me, I have only half an hour to get ready. Like a true Libran, I've changed my mind again and have now decided to wear a long black dress. I'm accessorising with a sparkly, red, costume-jewellery necklace that my grandmother gave me from her heydays. I already have a glow from a few days in the LA sunshine, so for make-up, I opt for a summery sheen: rosy cream blusher and just a hint of gold across my eyelids, finished off with black mascara and sheer lipgloss. My blonde hair is naturally straight anyway, but I run the hot irons through it to smooth it down. Finally I slip my feet into killer high heels and survey my reflection. Not bad.

I exit my room and head towards the stairs. Johnny comes out of the door at the far end of the landing.

'Cor, sexy,' he says.

'Yeah, yeah,' I reply, jokily brushing him off.

'You're going to make Serengeti jealous looking like that, you know,' he continues.

'Yeah, right.' I roll my eyes and start to walk down the stairs.

'I'm not actually joking,' he warns.

I look back up at him, a couple of steps behind me on the stairs. 'Are you serious?' I ask. 'Do you want me to go and change?'

He laughs wholeheartedly. 'Fuck no, Meg. Who gives a shit if Serengeti gets jealous or not?'

'Well, okay, then,' I say hesitantly, and continue to walk down the stairs. The buzzer goes as we reach the bottom.

'That'll be Davey,' I say. 'Are you really not going to join Serengeti on the red carpet?'

'Nope.'

'She's going to be disappointed.'

'Do you think I'm a bad boyfriend?' he asks, attempting to look grave, but unable to hide the twinkle in his eye.

I give him a wry look and don't answer, continuing towards the door. He follows me, opening up a cupboard in the hallway and pulling out a black-leather biker jacket and shiny black helmet.

'Want to blow off Davey and come with me on the bike instead?' he asks, shrugging himself into his jacket and zipping it up.

I laugh. 'Oh sure, I bet that would really delight your girl-friend!'

He grins at me cheekily and goes to the door, holding it open for me to walk through.

'You sure?' he asks. 'Last chance.'

I hesitate. God, I would really love to turn up at the premiere with him on his motorbike, but I know it's a bad idea. A *terrible* idea. What is he *thinking*?

'No, I don't think so.' I attempt to sound serious. 'I'm not sure that would be a good look for Serengeti, you turning up to her big night with another woman. Not that it's like that,' I add quickly. 'I mean it just might look like that, you know, to the tabloids . . .'

He raises one eyebrow at me in amusement. 'Suit yourself,' he says as we arrive at the car. 'Maybe catch you later.'

Davey steps out onto the driveway and opens up the door for me, waving his hand towards the back seat with a flourish. I glance over my shoulder to see Johnny reach the large garage, partly obscured by trees, at the other side of the property.

Back in the car, Davey starts up the ignition and slowly drives towards the gates. We wind our way back down through the hills of Bel Air, and then suddenly there's an almighty roar and a motorbike zooms past us.

I feel numb as I realise I turned down the chance to ride with Johnny Jefferson. Bess would hit me on the back of my head with a hammer if she found out. Why does my common sense always kick in like that? Out of all my friends, I'm the biggest pragma-tist.

Well, at least my hair won't get messed up. And I'm wearing a long dress – that wouldn't have worked on a bike. Plus, high heels would've been a nightmare, too.

Nope. Common sense isn't working this time. I still feel like rubbish.

The crowds down Hollywood Boulevard are overwhelming. Davey drives right to the front of the barriers and gets out to open my door. Flashbulbs are going off left, right and centre, and people crane their necks to see who I am. Of course, they soon realise I'm Nobody and turn their attention to the next car to pull up. This doesn't matter to me. I feel like a star as I hand over my ticket. There are screams everywhere as I step through the barriers and I'm vaguely aware of other people on the red carpet signing autographs and having their pictures taken. But I'm so nervous I don't pause to see who they are: I just keep walking towards the entrance. My red-carpet experience is over before I know it, and once inside I deeply regret not making more of it. I stand just inside the doors for a moment and look back.

Is that . . . Is that *Lindsay Lohan*?

'Miss, can you move along, please?' one of the security guards says to me.

'Yes, of course, sorry,' I apologise and hurry up the stairs into the foyer. I look around for Kitty.

I spot her after a moment, ringletted black hair recognisable from her photo with Brad Pitt. I catch her eye, smile and wave, and we manoeuvre our ways through the crowds to get to each other.

'Hi!' she exclaims. 'So nice to finally meet you!'

'You too,' I beam.

'Wow! I love your dress,' she gushes. 'That necklace is amazing!'

It's then that I notice she's wearing jeans. Am I overdressed?

'I wasn't really sure what to wear . . .' My voice peters off.

'I know what you mean. Imagine being a celebrity! Thank goodness no one cares what we mere mortals are wearing.' She gasps, suddenly looking mortified. 'But you look great! If we go to another one of these dos together, I promise I'll make an effort, too! I'm a bit blasé about it all, these days.'

I smile gratefully, but still feel a bit silly.

'Shall we go in?' she asks, changing the subject.

The film is okay. Timothy Makkeinen plays a posh British knight who sweeps Serengeti's character off her feet – literally at one point. I didn't think much of his British accent, though. Much as I adore him, I thought someone like Jude Law would have been better in the role.

Anyway, when we arrive at the aftershow party, which is being held in a mock castle up in the Hollywood Hills, we're immediately greeted by themed knights in shining armour, holding trays of glittering beverages. Kitty opts for a green concoction while I go for a red number because I like the idea of it matching my necklace.

I know, what an idiot, right? On the plus side, it tastes very nice.

Three yummy little red numbers later, Kitty and I are feeling tipsy on our empty stomachs. We've only managed to nab one canapé so far and we're both starving. The place is heaving, but there's still no sign of Serengeti and co. Apparently, turning up too early is decidedly uncool.

The crowd literally parts when the stars of the film do arrive. I'm struck once again by Serengeti's beauty and feel on edge as I study the door to see if Johnny appears. He doesn't.

'Where *is* Johnny tonight?' Kitty asks me.

'He should be here,' I reply, confused. We didn't see him at the movie, either.

'Hi, Kitty.' I hear a voice behind us and turn around to see a skinny girl, about five foot five, with long, dead-straight chestnut hair and a sprinkling of freckles across her nose and cheeks.

It's not often that this happens, but I take an immediate dislike to the girl. There's something nasty about her eyes.

'Hello, Charlie,' Kitty answers, a little wearily.

'Where's Rod tonight?' Charlie asks, her back to me.

'He's away on business,' Kitty replies.

'What sort of business? Not cheating on his wife again, is he?'

'Well, his divorce has come through now, so no, he's not cheating on his wife. Charlie, this is Meg.'

She turns around, letting her blue eyes scan my profile. 'Hello,' she says. 'And what do you do?'

'She's Johnny Jefferson's new PA,' Kitty interjects.

Charlie's eyes narrow. 'Well, well, well. So *you* got the job?'

'Yes.' I really don't want to get into conversation with this girl.

'How?' she asks.

'My boss recommended me,' I tell her, reluctantly.

'Who was your boss?'

'Marie Sevenou.'

Blank expression.

'She's an architect in London. No one you know.'

'Oh.' She turns her nose up.

Kitty taps a passing waiter on the shoulder. He stops and holds a tray full of canapés in front of us. Kitty grabs a serviette and starts to load it up with smoked salmon blinis.

'When did you start?' Charlie enquires, but this time I have a mouth full of blini. She looks at me impatiently while I try to swallow most of it.

Kitty answers for me. 'Sunday.'

'Oh. Very wet behind the ears, then.'

'Have another blini, Meg,' Kitty suggests, offering me her serviette full of them.

I grin at her as I take one. 'Thanks.'

She gives me a mischievous look as I pop it into my mouth.

'Have you met Serengeti yet?' Charlie asks.

I nod, merrily munching away.

Charlie looks at my mouth distastefully before continuing her interrogation.

'I have, too. She's lovely, isn't she?'

'Mmmhmm,' is all I can muster.

'So beautiful.'

I take my time swallowing. Kitty looks like she's struggling not to laugh.

'How's Isla?' Kitty asks Charlie, giving me a break from the inquisition. I use it as an excuse to nick another blini from her.

'She's great, thank you. She's in the VIP area.' Charlie turns back to me. 'Is Johnny in there?'

I shrug, my mouth full. Now Charlie looks annoyed.

'Goodness me, I can't get a word in edgeways with those things!' she exclaims.

'You should have one,' I suggest, helpfully. 'They're tasty.'

'No, thank you. They'd go straight to my hips,' she says, before giving mine the once-over. I tap another passing waiter on the shoulder and help myself to chicken satays.

She sighs impatiently. 'I'll catch you later, then,' she says, 'when you're able to talk perhaps.'

'Okay!' I say cheerfully.

'Okay!' Kitty echoes.

Charlie walks over to two other girls sitting on stools on the other side of the bar. They all turn around and look at us as Charlie no doubt fills them in on what little information we've divulged.

'Can't stand her,' Kitty says to me.

'Can't think why,' I answer.

She looks at me in surprise. 'Sorry, I got the impression you didn't like her either.'

'I don't,' I answer, confused, then realise the problem. 'I was being sarcastic,' I explain.

'Oh.' She giggles. 'I've just been a typical American, haven't I? Forgetting about the British and their sarcasm.'

I smile. 'Who does Charlie work for?'

'Isla Montagne. She's . . .'

I nod in recognition. 'I know her. Well, know *of* her.'

Isla Montagne is the spoilt daughter of very wealthy and very famous film producer Kerry Montagne. Kerry is a man, by the way. All Isla seems to do is get wasted and sleep around with rich young men. The tabloids back home are full of her exploits.

'Always thought she was a silly cow,' I add.

'Charlie thinks she's the bee's knees,' Kitty says.

'Now why doesn't that surprise me?'

We cut short our chat for a little while just to take in the scene around us. Serengeti's nowhere to be seen.

'All the stars will be in the VIP area now,' Kitty tells me when I bring it up.

'I'm surprised they even have a VIP area considering this is a private party.'

'Yeah, they almost always have VIP areas as well. I know, it's crazy, isn't it?'

'Yeah. And disappointing,' I admit. 'What's the point of having tickets to a big premiere aftershow party when you can't even mingle with the rich and famous?'

'At least the drinks are free.'

'True.' I giggle and pick up another from the bar top behind us.

'If Rod were here, he'd get us in. Maybe Johnny can?' Kitty suggests eagerly.

'*If* he ever turns up,' I say, gloomily.

'Yay! Speak of the devil!' Kitty's looking at the entrance.

I spot him, wading through the crowd. He's still wearing his biker jacket.

'Oh my God, it's Johnny Jefferson!'

I hear an excited gaggle of girls next to us whisper frenetically and I quickly become conscious that Johnny is the focus of attention for almost everyone in the room. Partygoers and hangers-on stop him as he slowly progresses through the room, saying hi and shaking hands with people.

'Call him over!' Kitty nudges me gleefully.

'No,' I say, shaking my head and turning back to her.

'Why not?' she practically squeals.

'I don't know him well enough to do that.'

'Don't know him well enough? What are you saying? You work with him!'

'Work *for* him, you mean. No, sorry,' I say, glancing back in his direction and tearing my eyes away again as I see him kissing a stunning brunette in a green dress. 'I can't.'

Kitty's face is steeped with disappointment.

'I thought you were blasé about this sort of thing now.' I give her a knowing look.

She smiles at me shyly. 'I know,' she says. 'I've just got a bit of a crush on Johnny Jefferson, that's all.'

'Have you?' I squeak.

'Yeah,' she nods. 'Don't you?'

'No,' I fib. 'He's not my type.'

'Yeah, but you'd still go to bed with him.'

'No!' My face must look quite shocked.

'Come on.' She giggles. 'Just one night of passion . . . I bet you would.'

'Bet you would what?'

I spin around to see him, standing there in front of us. The gaggle of girls to his right nudge each other like maniacs.

'Hi,' I say, weakly.

'Introduce me to your friend,' he responds.

Kitty's face positively glows. 'This is Kitty.' They shake hands.

'I recognise you,' Johnny says. 'I've seen you around.'

'*Have you?*' Kitty looks like she's going to pass out with delight.

'What were you talking about?' Johnny enquires.

'Nothing,' I state hurriedly. 'I didn't see you at the film?'

'I didn't go,' he tells me.

'Oh. Really?'

'Yeah. Serengeti's going to be pissed.' He grins. 'Was it any good? Do you reckon I can get away with pretending to have sat with you if you fill me in on the details?'

'I'm not lying for you, Johnny Jefferson.' I pull a mock stern face.

'Fat lot of good you are,' he says, jokily. 'I knew I should have gone with that Iranian chick . . .'

We smile at each other for a moment before I remember Kitty and realise we're leaving her out. I step back and am about to try to include her in our conversation when I see a flash of bronze behind Johnny and notice Serengeti approaching. I nod in her direction to warn him. He turns around, spots her, then glances back at me and raises an eyebrow.

'Hi, honey!' she gushes, clearly for the benefit of all those around them, because as she leans in to kiss him I hear her hiss, 'Where the hell have you been?'

'Hey,' he says. 'Just talking business.'

'Sure you were, baby. Now, are you coming into the VIP section?'

'Nah, I think I'll just hang here.'

'What? Why?' she asks, confused.

He shrugs.

'Johnny,' she says through clenched, albeit brilliantly white, teeth. 'You didn't make the screening so perhaps you can help me with this?'

'I did make the screening, didn't I?' He stares at me, daring me not to lie for him.

'Um . . .'

Serengeti whips around and notices me for the first time.

'Hi.' She smiles graciously and holds out her hand. 'I don't think we've been introduced.'

Johnny laughs and leans back on the bar top, folding his arms. 'Serengeti, this is Meg. My PA. You met her earlier.'

'Oh.' She gives me the once-over, looking enormously unamused. 'I didn't recognise you.'

'I'm wearing make-up,' I say, stupidly.

'And Versace?' She nods at my dress.

'No, TopShop.'

'Top what?'

'TopShop. It's a shop in England . . .'

She ignores me. 'Are you coming or not?' she asks Johnny.

'I'll meet you in there,' he says, reaching backwards and grabbing one of the red cocktails from the bar. 'Any good?' he asks me, holding up his glass.

'Very,' I tell him.

'Suit yourself,' Serengeti says in a huff, staring first at my necklace, then at my ever-so-slightly revealing neckline. Finally she glares up at my face and storms off.

'Told you she'd be jealous,' Johnny leans in and whispers in my ear, before lifting up his hand to get the attention of one of the hot bartenders. 'I want something stronger,' he demands. 'A whisky?'

I look at Kitty, whose face is still lit up like Regent Street at Christmas. 'You okay?'

She nods her head vigorously.

A random guy behind me drunkenly shouts out, 'Heeeeeeeerrrre's Johnny!' before cracking up laughing.

'Fucking wanker,' Johnny says, turning back to us and swirling caramel-coloured liquid around in his glass. 'I hate it when people say that.' He rests one elbow on the bar top. 'So what was the film like? You're going to have to fill me in now so I can pretend.' He downs half his glass.

I give him my best unimpressed-schoolmistress look and hold my nerve, but Kitty jumps at the chance.

'Well, it was about . . .' she starts to fill him in while I watch on with amusement. Johnny keeps glancing at me as Kitty gives him a blow-by-blow account.

'Timothy Makkeinen's English accent was awful,' she says, which is funny because she didn't really have a problem with it when we discussed the film earlier. Now she seems to be quite down on the guy.

Johnny motions to the bartender again for a top-up.

'Nice necklace,' he says to me. Kitty's voice falters.

'Thanks,' I reply, feeling a bit guilty about the interruption. 'My grandmother gave it to me years ago.'

'Cool.' He downs his whisky.

Kitty reaches behind her for another green concoction.

'Want another, Meg?' she asks.

'Sure. Thanks.'

'You can finish mine, if you like,' Johnny offers. 'Or have a new one, whatever,' he adds.

'Didn't like it, then?' I hold out my hand for it.

He shakes his head and passes it over, wrinkling his nose. He looks surprisingly adorable considering he's supposed to be a hip rock star. We grin at each other for a few seconds. He is a bit of a flirt, isn't he? Is he always like this with normal girls? Probably.

Oops. I suddenly remember Kitty standing there, sipping her drink quietly. I look at her quickly and smile. 'So what else happened in the film?' I ask.

'Don't worry,' Johnny chips in. 'I reckon I'm in for it, anyways.'

'Hey!' A tall, good-looking guy in a fitted, light-grey suit and white shirt slaps Johnny on the back.

'Hey, mate!' Johnny turns around and they do that manly handclasp, back pat, half-hug thing that cool guys do. 'I haven't seen you for ages! Where the fuck have you been, man?'

'Oh, here and there. Hey . . .' He leans in and says something in Johnny's ear that we can't hear.

'Yeah, yeah, cool, man,' Johnny answers. 'Catch you later.' He gives us a half-wave and follows the guy through the crowd, looking down so as to avoid eye contact with anyone.

'Nice meeting you!' Kitty calls after him, then exclaims, 'Darn! We forgot to ask if he could get us into the VIP section!'

She starts to dissect her liaison with the gorgeous Johnny Jefferson, and I really try to concentrate. But it's hard when I'm distractedly studying the glass he gave me to see if I can find the imprint of his lips.

Chapter 4

Johnny has been 'poked' seven thousand nine hundred and eighty-one times and has had four hundred and fifty-nine requests to be a 'pirate' since anyone last checked his Facebook page. What the hell am I supposed to do about *that*?

It's Saturday morning and I'm in the office for want of anything better to do. I didn't see Johnny at all yesterday. I'd assumed he finally caught up with Serengeti and one look at samson-sarky.com confirmed it. There was a picture of them both coming out of the aftershow venue together at four o'clock in the morning. I had wondered if Johnny managed to persuade Serengeti to go on his motorbike with him, but yesterday late afternoon I got a call from him, groggily asking me to track his bike down. He'd left it in a valet car park near the party venue, but wasn't sure which one. After calling four garages and waiting on hold while the valet attendants searched the place for a bike of Johnny's description – a description I first had to hunt out by interrogating Samuel, one of Johnny's security guards – someone finally remembered Johnny Jefferson riding in.

Samuel went to collect the bike for me. He's a bit of a motor-bike buff, I'd discovered, when Rosa pointed me in his direction. Just as well she did, because Paola's manual mentions nothing about Johnny's modes of transport. Tut tut.

But back to Facebook. What am I supposed to do here? Poke seven thousand nine hundred and eighty-one people back? Join four hundred and fifty-nine pirate ships? What the hell does being a 'pirate' mean, anyway? I bloody knew I should have signed up to Facebook when I worked for Marie. But then, I suppose, if I had, I might not have been so efficient, and therefore might not have got this job. See? Told you I was a pragmatist.

I know: I'll call Bess. She's a Facebook nut.

'Hey, how are you?' I ask.

'Terrible. Some bloody bastard just gave me his seat on the tube,' she replies.

'Why does that make him a bastard?'

'He thought I was pregnant, the wanker!'

'Oh. Bugger.'

'*Yes*, bugger,' she says.

'What did you do?'

'I took the seat,' she says, flippantly.

'Did you really?'

'Anyway, enough about me, goddammit! Tell me about Johnny! Do you still fancy him?'

'I never said I fancied him in the first place!' I respond, voice rising an octave or so.

'Yeah, yeah. Have you met his girlfriend yet?'

'Serengeti Knight? God, yes.'

'What's she like?' she asks excitedly. 'Is she as much of a diva as the papers make out?'

'Much, much worse,' I respond. 'I've had to clean up her dog's poo on several occasions.'

'No!' Bess gasps.

'Yeah, gross.'

'Not all glamour, then?'

'No. Well, saying that, I did go to her premiere the other night . . .'

Scream. 'No way! Ohmigodwhatwasitlike?'

I laugh and fill her in. She's not very impressed with me turning down the chance to ride on Johnny's bike for fear of Serengeti getting annoyed.

'That is such BULLSHIT! Whogivesacrapaboutserengeti knightanyway! You are NUTS to say no!'

'Bess, keep your voice down! I have to keep holding the phone away from my ear! Aa-nyway,' I continue, keen to move on, 'he came and chatted to us at the aftershow party, so that was cool.'

'Wow. I bet everyone in the room was staring at you.'

'Yeah, I think they were,' I agree with delight.

'What about Timothy Makkeinen? Did you talk to him?'

'I didn't, actually.' In fact, I'd forgotten all about my Timothy Makkeinen crush that night. I was too distracted with someone else.

'Now, Bess,' I say. 'I need your advice about Facebook.'

'What about it?'

'Johnny has these Facebook and MySpace sites which I'm responsible for managing and I don't have the foggiest idea where to start.'

'I told you to sign up for it.'

'I know, I know,' I brush her off. 'Just explain to me now, what the hell is a "pirate"?'

'It's just a bit of fun. You can have battles with other pirate ships and stuff like that. I bet he's had requests to become a "ninja" too, hasn't he?'

I look more closely. 'Yes, there are about two hundred of those. And a whole bunch of "vampires".'

'Has he got a Hotness rating?'

'A what?'

'Go to applications and add Hotness to Johnny's page. It's really cool. People can rate how hot you are. He'd do really well.'

'Okay . . .'

'And I bet loads of people have bought him gifts, too.'

'Gifts? What are you on about?'

'Hang on, I'm going to log onto his page myself. You're hopeless. Yep,' she says, moments later. 'Tons of gifts. Aah, look, someone's bought him an electric guitar.'

'Really? Wow, that's generous.'

'Not a real one, you idiot.' She laughs. 'It's just a cartoon picture of one.'

'What's the point in that?' I ask, following her directions to look at the gifts myself.

'You're not supposed to take it seriously.' She giggles. 'Ooh, you should make him do a FilthBook test.'

'What's that?' I ask.

'It's a really rude quiz. Check it out on my page. You have to click on it to add it to Johnny's. I bet his purity ranking is really low.'

Ten minutes later, I wrap up the conversation. 'I'd better go. Should get on.'

She sighs. 'I still can't believe you've wangled that job, you lucky B. I bet you're actually on holiday in Croatia or something and you're just pretending to work with Johnny Jefferson.'

I hang up, laughing, and click back on Johnny's Facebook page, where I immediately get two more 'pirate' requests and a couple of offers to buy Johnny a drink. Hang on – I look more closely – he's already been bought over seven thousand drinks. What is that about? No, I can't call Bess back. I'll email her later.

I start poking people and then give up. *Surely* we shouldn't encourage this sort of behaviour. Hasn't Johnny 'poked' enough girls as it is?

I hear the front door shut and stand up, ears straining to hear if it's Johnny returning. It is.

'Hi.' I pop my head out of the office and smile at him.

'Hey.' He smiles back, and then Serengeti appears in his wake.

'Hello!' I say, cheerfully. 'How are you?'

'Fine. Where's Footsie?' she asks.

Uh-oh. Where *is* Footsie? He was here yesterday. Poor Rosa moaned about having to clean up after I let him sleep in the kitchen on Thursday night. She arrived at work on Friday morning before I came downstairs, which was a bit naughty of me, but I had knocked back about ten of those little red beverages the night before. Anyway, last night I put the fluffball in the laundry to sleep.

'I'll go get him, shall I?' I smile, trying to cover up the fact that I've neglected her pooch for going on ten hours now.

She doesn't answer, so I hurry past her in the direction of the laundry. I open the door and the smell assaults my nostrils.

Shit!

Literally.

'Has he been in here all night?' Serengeti demands from right behind me.

'Um . . .'

'He has, hasn't he?' She pushes past me to get in the room. Footsie goes bonkers with excitement.

'Sorry,' I say, and genuinely mean it when I see how delighted the critter is to finally have company.

'You should be!' she says, angrily. 'Poor, poor baby!'

'It's only a dog,' Johnny helpfully interjects.

'Only a dog? *Only* a dog, Johnny?'

'Okay, okay. Well, he's alright now,' Johnny soothes, before discreetly rolling his eyes at me.

My guilt immediately evaporates and is replaced with glee. I can't believe he keeps dissing his A-List girlfriend to me.

In the early evening, after I've whiled away the day reading and writing emails to my friends in the UK, Johnny comes into the office.

'Did you get my bike back?' he asks me.

'Yes! Samuel went to pick it up. I hope that's okay . . .'

'Yeah, yeah, cool, man.'

'Johnny,' Serengeti interrupts, 'can we get something to eat? I'm famished.'

'Sure. Did Rosa leave anything?' Johnny turns to me.

'Yes, she's left some chilli, I think. Do you want me to heat it up? It can be ready in ten.'

'Fine.'

Forty minutes later I'm still alone in the kitchen. I've had to turn the heat on the stove right down, and have been unhappily surveying the contents of the pan, convinced it's going to spoil.

'Going to have to put a hold on the chilli, I'm afraid,' Johnny says, emerging at last. 'Serengeti wants to eat out instead.'

'At Asia de Cuba,' she says, coming into the kitchen behind him.

'Okay.' I keep my voice upbeat.

'Inside,' Serengeti adds, plonking Footsie down at my feet. 'By the window.'

'Oh.' I get it. 'Do you want me to book it for you?' I ask.

'Er, *yeah* . . .' she replies, stressing the 'yeah' in a way that implies she thinks I'm really quite dim.

'Sure thing. I'll do that right away.' I switch the stove off and go to leave the room.

'Don't you want to sit outside on the terrace?' Johnny asks Serengeti. 'It's much nicer out there.'

I pause by the door.

'No, JJ, you know I get too cold.'

'Don't call me JJ,' Johnny grumbles.

'But it's so cute!' Serengeti cries, putting her hands on his waist.

'So's Cathy, but do I call you that?'

She detaches herself from him, sulkily. I'm guessing Cathy is her real name.

'Inside is fine, Meg.' He walks out of the kitchen. Serengeti – aka Cathy – totters after him, closely followed by Footsie.

I manage to make a last-minute reservation thanks only to my diners' star status, and line Davey up. Serengeti leaves me Footsie for company. Company for Footsie, not me, you understand, and after three hours of walkies, din-dins and cleaning up yet more yellow puddles, I finally call it a night and hit the sack. Footsie sits outside my door and howls for a while, but eventually shuts up. An hour later I'm woken by a different kind of howling.

'Poor, poor baby!' It sounds like Serengeti is actually inside my bedroom. 'How could she leave Footsie outside again?'

'Okay, okay, come on, let's go to bed.'

I hear Serengeti's voice get quieter as she follows Johnny back down the landing. 'I can't believe she did that again'.

I roll over, groan and struggle to fall asleep again.

Chapter 5

Serengeti Knight. Serengeti Nightmare, more like. It's Sunday morning and I'm outside in the pool doing my laps. Theoretically I don't have to work today, although I'm always on call, and anyway, I don't have any other plans.

It's another hot, sunny day, and I pause for a minute by the side of the pool. I hear the glass door slide open behind me and turn around just in time to see Serengeti plonk Footsie down on the terrace and slide the door shut behind her. She doesn't say anything to me, but I'd bet my passport that there's a doggy surprise waiting for me somewhere inside.

I get out of the pool and dry myself off, then tie my sarong around my waist and slip on my flip-flops. Footsie runs over to me and gives me five short, sharp barks.

'Come on, then,' I say. 'Let's take you for a wander around the garden.'

He follows me quite happily, piddling here, piddling there, as we make our way around to the other side of the house. The large wooden gates start to open.

I watch, confused for a moment, as an old green Chevvy truck pulls into the driveway. A young, Latino-looking guy is behind the wheel. He raises his hand at me and smiles, and then it clicks. The gardener, the pool-boy. Santiago, that's right, that's his name. I remember reading about him in Paola's manual.

'Hi.' I smile warmly as he gets out of the car. 'I'm Meg. You must be Santiago?'

'Hey, pleased to meet you.' He shakes my hand.

He's actually quite cute. Lovely white smile, nice body. A little bit on the short side, but seems sweet.

'Don't you usually work on Saturdays?' I ask.

'Yeah, but sometimes I have to switch if my mum's working. She's a nurse,' he explains. 'I have to babysit my little brother when that happens.'

'Oh, right.'

'Hello, Footsie,' he says, reaching down to calm the yapping dog.

'Ah, you've met before,' I say.

'Mmm. We're very well acquainted . . .'

I immediately sense we're on the same wavelength regarding a certain blonde movie starlet.

'So when did you start?' He begins to unload a few tools from the back of the truck.

'Last Sunday,' I reply.

'Glad to see someone's using the pool.' He motions to my outfit.

'I'm trying to do fifty laps each morning.'

'That's pretty cool,' he replies.

'Well, I've only been managing about thirty, if I'm being honest, but hey ho.'

We wander together to the pool.

'Want me to help you carry something?' I ask, as he opens up the pool shed and starts rummaging around inside.

'Hey, thanks, but I can manage.'

'Have you worked for Johnny long?' I go to sit on a sunlounger and bask in the heat while Santiago kicks off his Nikes, hoiks up his beige calf-length shorts and makes his way down the pool steps with some sort of robotic cleaning machine. I hope he doesn't mind me hanging around, but it's nice to see another friendly young face.

'About two years,' he replies. 'What about you? How's your first week been so far?'

'Good. Went to Serengeti's premiere on Thursday night, which was pretty mental.'

'Wow,' he says, in awe. 'What was that like?'

I fill him in while he steps back out of the pool and rolls his shorts legs down again.

'Hey, I need to see to the hedges round the front,' he says after a while. 'You wanna come keep me company?'

'Sure.'

'Do you work for any other celebrities?' I ask, opening up a black bin bag, ready for cuttings from the hedges.

'I have a few on my books now, but Johnny's my biggest client. I've worked for him since I was nineteen.'

That makes him twenty-one if he's been here two years.

'So,' he whispers conspiratorially, 'what do you think to Serengeti, eh?'

'Erm . . .' I reply.

'Don't worry, I don't think he can talk.' Santiago grins, indicating the dog.

'I haven't really had a lot to do with her, to be honest,' I answer.

'Now you're just being polite,' he says. 'If I have to clean up one more doggy do-do, I'm going to go mad.'

'Do you know how long they've been together?' I enquire, as he gets started on clipping the hedges.

'She's been on the scene for a month or so, now. Quite a long relationship for Johnny.'

'Is it?'

'Oh, yeah.' He nods vigorously. 'All I'm saying is the sex must be good.'

Ew, what a thought. I move on. 'She doesn't really seem like his type.'

'Nor he hers,' he replies.

'Oh?'

'She usually goes for much older guys,' Santiago explains. 'Her last boyfriend? He was a fifty-year-old film mogul. And what's more,' he adds, excitedly, nudging me on my arm, 'he was the one who gave her Footsie – called Footsie because he had a foot fetish!'

'Now you're just pulling my leg.' I laugh.

'No, no! I'm serious!' he insists.

'That's hilarious!'

'FOOTSIE!' The sound of Serengeti's voice cuts our laughter short.

'Better go,' I say. 'Nice to meet you, if I don't catch you later.'

'Yeah, you too.'

Footsie follows me around to the back of the house where his mistress is waiting.

'I need the car,' Serengeti demands.

'Sure. Where do you want Davey to take you?'

'Home,' she says, picking up Footsie and kissing him on the top of his head. 'Then the airport.'

'Going anywhere nice?' I ask as I open the door and stand back to let her pass.

'New York,' she says shortly. 'Then London. More premieres,' she explains, her voice softening.

'Cool! I really liked the film, by the way,' I tell her. Well, it's half true.

'Thanks.'

She puts Footsie down and he runs in front of me into the office.

'I'll let you know when the car's here,' I tell her and go in to call Davey.

When that job's done, I go back out into the living room and find her there, sitting alone on one of the dark-brown-leather designer sofas, watching TV.

'Where's Johnny?' I ask, surprised.

'Upstairs in the studio.' Her attention is focused on the telly, a documentary about lemurs.

'The car will be here in twenty.'

I wait for acknowledgement but don't get any, so I go to leave.

'Oh,' she calls. 'Meg?'

'Yes?' I turn back.

'Did you really like the film?'

'Yeah, I thought it was good fun. I loved it when you forced Timothy's character to eat a peanut butter and jam sandwich.'

'Jam?'

'Jelly. Whatever you call it. And the bit where he was trying to teach you how to drive and ended up on the wrong side of the road was really funny, too.' I laugh, lamely, before adding, 'I guess you taught him in the end, hey!'

God, can I not think of anything more interesting to say?

She smiles and nods. 'Want to watch telly?'

I'm about to make an excuse and say I've got work to do, but then I see some lemurs skipping through a forest on two legs, arms up in front of them.

'Aren't they funny?' I look on in wonder as I sit down next to her.

'What are they?' she asks. Clearly she hasn't been paying attention.

'Lemurs.'

'Huh.'

We sit there in silence for a minute or so, watching.

'I'd love a pet lemur,' I say, eventually.

She giggles. 'You should ask Johnny. He'd probably get one for you.'

'You reckon? I can just see a lemur skipping around this joint. Bit of a bugger to clean up after, though.' I can't help it; I glance at Footsie.

Serengeti shifts uncomfortably on the sofa.

A door opens above our heads and Johnny bounces down the stairs.

'What the fuck are they?' he asks, coming over to us.

'Lemurs,' Serengeti and I say in unison.

'Hmm. So anyway, I reckon I'll hitch a ride with you after all.'

Serengeti beams. 'Great!'

The buzzer goes. 'That'll be Davey now,' I say.

'Perfect timing.' Serengeti gets up and casually takes Johnny's hand as they walk in the direction of the door.

'When will you be back?' I call after Johnny. 'Do you want me to do anything while you're gone?'

'Nope,' he tells me. 'Just chill.'

'Okay. See you later!'

Serengeti stops and looks around as she reaches the door. 'Thanks for looking after Footsie.'

'You're welcome.'

And then she actually smiles at me. Maybe she's not so bad after all.

When they've gone, I return to the office. I know Johnny said not to do any work, but I don't have a whole lot else to do without a car. I wonder if I should try to rent one while I'm here?

I sit down and log onto MySpace. As usual, loads of girls want to know if it's the real Johnny Jefferson's page or not. It's a pain in the butt reassuring them all the time.

Johnny returns later that afternoon. 'What you up to?' he asks, slumping down onto the black Eames chair beside my desk. His T-shirt rides up over his stomach.

Concentrate, Meg!

'Just trying to organise your MySpace page.'

'It's Sunday,' he says, 'you shouldn't be working.' He wriggles around in his chair and pulls his T-shirt down.

Phew.

'I don't really know else what to do.' I glance back at the computer screen. Someone's just posted a message.

'Go for a swim?' he suggests, helpfully.

'Santiago's just treated the pool.' I strain to read what it says.

'Go for a drive?'

'I don't have a car.' Something about his gig next week.

'You can take one of my cars.'

'Really?' Now he has my full attention.

'Sure. The Porsche 911 would be okay to use.'

'The Porsche?' I'm flabbergasted.

'Sure. Why not? You can drive, can't you?'

'Yes, but are you really going to let me drive your Porsche?'

'Maybe not the Carrera GT, but the 911 is fine.'

I don't actually know what he's talking about. 'Porsche' is 'Porsche' to me, although it does sound like he has two.

'Wicked!' I reply with delight. 'Maybe I'll do that next weekend?'

'Suit yourself.' He stands up and pokes his head out of the door.

'Christian, what the hell are you doing? Get your arse in here!'

'Alright, fuckwit, I was just talking to Davey.'

A man who I can only assume to be Christian enters the room. He has straight, black hair, cut indie-boy style.

'Hi.' He comes around to my side of the desk to shake my hand. 'I'm this tosser's mate from back home,' he informs me in a Geordie accent. He's about the same height as Johnny, but not as lean, and his skin is positively pasty in comparison.

'Christian's going to be using the office a bit,' Johnny explains. 'You can use that desk,' he tells his friend, making a poor attempt to tidy up a messy pile of paperwork. I get up and take the papers from him, relocating them to my desk.

'Christian's writing my biography, aren't you, mate? Going to tell it like it is, eh?'

'Yep. About time the world knew what a wanker you are.' They both laugh and play-punch each other.

'That chilli still okay to eat?' Johnny asks me.

73

'Um, I don't think so.' I rack my brains. 'There's some spaghetti Bolognese in the freezer. I could defrost it if you like?'

'Cool. You want some, too, Meg?'

'So how are the preparations for Thursday going?' Christian's dark-brown eyes flick between Johnny and me once we're all seated outside on the terrace. I'm facing away from the view this time so Christian can have the pleasure.

Johnny stares across at me. 'Don't ask her, she didn't even know I had a gig coming up.'

'No shit?' Christian's eyes widen in shock.

I feel my face heat up.

Johnny grins. 'Preparations are going fine, mate. Record company have it in hand. Nothing left to do except write some fucking songs.'

'Have you got any new material?' Christian asks.

'A few songs, yeah, but it's still a work in progress.'

I'd like to know more about the gig, but I'm too embarrassed to ask in case I get ridiculed again. I turn to Christian instead.

'Have you written much of your book?'

'No,' he answers. 'I'm kicking it off with the comeback on Thursday.'

'So, mate,' Johnny interrupts. 'Up for a big one tonight?'

'No way,' Christian moans. 'I'm fucking jet-lagged.'

'Yeah, yeah.' Johnny waves his hand dismissively and Christian gives him a wry look.

'How's Serengeti? You still seeing her?' Christian continues.

'You should know,' Johnny answers. 'Fucking journo,' he elaborates, tapping a fag out onto the tabletop and lighting up.

Christian chuckles. 'I don't believe anything I read unless I'm the one who wrote it.' He stands up and starts to clear the plates.

'Don't worry, I'll get those,' I say.

'Thanks.' He hands me his empty plate and Johnny's almost full one. 'I'm gonna take my bag up,' he says. 'Am I in the gold room?' he asks Johnny.

'You're in whichever room you like,' Johnny replies, reaching across the table and flicking his ash onto his pile of half-eaten spaghetti. 'Except for Meg's, of course. Keep your hands off my staff.'

Christian rolls his eyes and heads back indoors.

'See you downstairs in twenty,' Johnny calls after him.

'I'm telling you now, I'm not having a late one,' Christian calls back.

'Sure you're not, mate.' Johnny grins at me. 'Can you book Davey?' He discards his cigarette onto the ground and gets up.

'Sure,' I reply. 'Guest list anywhere?'

'Nah. We're kicking off round TJ's place.'

'TJ . . .'

'Member of my band,' he explains.

'Oh.' Should I have known that?

After they've left I try to get enthusiastic about going for another swim in the pool or watching a film in the private cinema, but in the end I just wander upstairs to bed.

Chapter 6

Thirty-one . . . Oh, I give up.

It's seven o'clock in the morning and I'm out in the pool doing my laps. I reach the shallow end and stand up, wringing my hair out as I climb up the steps.

It's another glorious day. I wrap a towel around myself and stand there on the stone terrace, looking down at the city. The smog has lifted and it's just blue, blue skies as far as I can see.

I hear a loud yawn from behind me and turn around to find Christian, in boxer shorts and a T-shirt, stretching his arms above his head.

'Hi.' He smiles, sleepily. 'Nice day.'

'Sure is.' I smile back.

'How's the water?' He motions towards the pool.

'Gorgeous. You going in?'

'Nah.' He shakes his head and yawns again. 'Maybe later.'

'You're up early.'

'Jet lag,' he explains.

'What time did you guys come in last night?' I didn't hear them.

'I cracked at about midnight. Fuck knows about Johnny. He'll probably walk in the door at any moment.'

Hmm, so Johnny *doesn't* always get his own way, then.

'You hungry?' he asks me, pointing his thumb towards the house.

'A little.'

He waits outside the door for me while I quickly dry off with the towel and put on the fluffy bathrobe that I found in my bathroom. He slides the door closed behind us and follows me to the kitchen. It's Monday morning and Rosa will be here soon.

'Toast? Fruit? Cereal?' he asks.

'Cereal sounds good.'

Christian starts opening cupboards and pulling out boxes.

'What is *that*?' I point at a colourful box, standing out amongst the more muted tones of mueslis and fibre-based cereals.

'Fruity Pebbles,' he reads from the box. It's decorated with cartoon drawings of Fred and Barney from *The Flintstones*.

'Are you going for the kiddie cereal?' He asks the question as though he's speaking to a small child.

'Hell, yeah!' I reply and he laughs, taking two bowls out of a cupboard and pouring Pebbles, followed by milk, into both. He grabs a couple of spoons from a drawer and brings everything to the table.

I peer inside the bowl. It's full of flat, little rice crispy-style things, brightly decorated in all the colours of the rainbow. We both scoop up spoonfuls and shove them into our mouths. It's *really* sweet. I start to giggle.

'I fucking love kids' cereal,' he tells me between mouthfuls.

'It's the best,' I agree.

'So how did you get this job?' he asks, adding, 'If you don't know anything about Johnny . . .'

I fill him in.

'So you had to pack up and leave, just like that?' he looks at me, wide-eyed.

'Yeah.' I laugh, slightly in disbelief. It still seems so unreal.

'I love that you don't know anything about Johnny,' he says. 'He's got way too big an ego as it is.'

I shrug. 'So what about your book?' I ask. 'How did that come about?'

'Um, well, he pretty much just asked me if I wanted to write one and I thought, why the fuck not?'

'What have we got here, then?' Rosa appears at the door.

'Hi, Rosa!' we both chorus. Christian stands up.

'Hello, my boy,' she says warmly, coming round the table to give Christian a hug. 'Good to have you back.' Then she frowns, looking down at the remnants of our cereal. 'What are you two eating?'

'Fruity Pebbles!' I tell her, enthusiastically.

'They rock!' Christian adds.

Rosa rolls her eyes and starts to put the boxes of cereal away. 'I could make you a nice omelette or something, if you'd prefer?' she says. 'Or a full English breakfast? I know how to do those.'

'No, no, it's okay.' I get up. 'I'd better go and get showered.'

'Yeah, me too,' Christian says. We take our bowls to the dishwasher, but she snatches them from us and shoos us away. Christian follows me up the stairs.

'No doubt see you in the office,' he says, breaking off at the top of the stairs to turn left as I go right.

'Absolutely.'

Half an hour later I walk into the office to find him already in there, tapping away at the keyboard. He smiles and says hi, but his expression is distracted.

I log onto Facebook. A crazy number of girls have written 'I love Johnny' on his wall. Yawn.

The two gigantic post bags to the side of my desk have been taunting me for days now. I know I should tackle some actual fan mail instead of this online nonsense, but it's just so addictive. I reluctantly close down the window on my computer and reach for a handful of fan mail. The first envelope I open is plain white with black, spidery handwriting.

Dear Mr Jefferson,
I am your biggest fan.

Yeah, yeah, heard it all before.

I have listened to your songs on the radio since I was
twenty years old. Now, like you, I have just turned thirty. I
am sure you will go on to sell many more records. But,
sadly, I will not be around to hear them. I am dying of
cancer.

Oh.

And the only thing that would make me truly happy as I lie
on my deathbed, would be to meet you in person and
shake your hand . . .

I breathe in, sharply.

'You alright?' Christian peers at me over the top of his screen.

'Hey? Oh yeah, just a horrible fan letter. He's dying of cancer and wants to meet Johnny.'

To my surprise, Christian casts his eyes to the heavens.

'What? You think he's lying?' I ask.

'No. I mean, he probably *is* ill. But do you know how many letters Johnny must get like that?'

I shake my head.

'Hundreds. *Thousands*. He can't meet everyone.'

'True,' I concede. 'So what do I do? Do I show him this one?'

'I wouldn't,' Christian says. 'I'd put it to one side and see how many you get, then decide what to do. There *will* be ones that you should show him, but you can't show him everything. That would really do his head in.'

However horrible it seems, I know Christian's right. I open another envelope as Christian goes back to tapping on his keyboard.

As the morning wears on, with Rosa bringing us in regular cups of coffee and freshly baked peanut butter cookies, there's still no sign of Johnny.

'Did he even come home last night?' I ask eventually.

'I think so,' Christian replies, before finally succumbing to his curiosity and my concern. He pushes his chair out from under the desk and stands up. 'I'll go check on him.'

He returns after a couple of minutes. 'He's coming down now.' Ten minutes later, a shirtless, sleepy Johnny stumbles into the office and slumps down in the Eames chair. He's wearing dark shades.

'Good night?' I ask brightly, struggling to look at his face and not his chest. It isn't easy.

'I don't really remember so I reckon it must've been pretty good. You are *such* a pussy,' he says to Christian.

'Fuck off,' his mate replies and keeps on typing.

'Can you stop doing that for a minute?' Johnny asks.

'Why?' Christian answers.

'I want to talk to you.'

Christian's tapping comes slowly to a stop. 'What?' he asks, a little irritably.

'What's your problem?' Johnny asks.

'What do you mean, what's my problem?' Christian snaps.

'Chill out, mate.' Johnny grins. 'Has he been in this mood all morning?' he asks me.

'Erm,' I say hesitantly, 'I think he might just be in the Zone.'

'The fucking Zone.' Johnny laughs.

Christian goes back to his keyboard.

'Oh, whatever,' Johnny says, getting to his feet and ambling towards the door. I follow him.

'Johnny, could we sit down and talk about those photoshoot and interview requests?'

'Yeah, yeah. In a while, crocodile,' he replies, heading into the kitchen. Rosa greets him with her usual gusto, vigorously grabbing his upper arms with her chubby hands and making 'grr' noises. He seems to like it.

'What are you up to today?' she asks, setting about making coffee.

'Today, Rosa, my gorgeous girl, I've got the band coming over. Anytime now, in fact.'

It's two o'clock.

'Is there anything I can do?' I ask.

'Nope, Meg. I just got to get myself in 'the Zone', that's all,' he answers sarcastically.

The buzzer goes.

'That'll be them now,' Johnny says, staying put.

I head towards the front door. Four scruffy-looking individuals stand behind it, all wearing shades. I stand aside to let them pass. Two carry guitar cases, one has a keyboard, and the last guy is carrying a pair of drumsticks, so I figure the drum kit is already upstairs in the studio. I say hi and introduce myself and they all nod and grunt. I don't get an introduction back.

Johnny is at the top of the stairs as they traipse up in the direction of the studio.

'Be with you in a minute, guys,' he calls out, and heads towards his room at the end of the landing. I watch from the bottom of the stairs as they enter the studio and slam the door shut behind them.

'They were a chatty bunch,' I say to Christian as I re-enter the office.

He chuckles. 'They turned up at the club as I left last night,' he explains. 'Late night, I'm guessing. Right.' He stands up and grabs a pad and pen from his desk. 'I'm off to take some notes. Catch you later.'

A couple of hours pass and I manage to put a dent in the fan mail. Occasionally I can hear music coming from the studio upstairs, but it sounds muffled. At 4.30, Christian pops his head around the door. 'Come up and have a listen,' he says.

The music gets louder as we get closer to the studio. He opens the door and ushers me inside. Johnny and the band are behind a glass screen. Johnny is shouting out instructions and the four guys are nodding their acknowledgement. Christian pulls out a chair for me behind the mixing desk and sits down beside me. His notepad in front of him is full of messy scribblings.

'Have you heard any new stuff?' I ask.

'Not yet.'

'Who are the band?'

'The drummer's Lee, TJ is on bass, Mike's on rhythm and Bri is on keyboards. On tour there's a much bigger team – backing singers, sax, violins, the lot, but this is more of an acoustic set. Johnny's playing a couple unaccompanied.'

I look at Johnny's side-profile now as he talks to his band, guitar strap stretched across his chest. He's wearing a tight, faded grey T-shirt. A cord trails from the acoustic guitar hanging behind him, leading to an unseen amp. The band nod at what he's saying and he turns to face the glass, swinging the guitar around into his hands. He starts to strum and Christian turns up the sound on one of the dials in front of him.

I recognise the tune; it's an acoustic version of one of his more upbeat hits. Johnny steps up close to the mic, lips touching it as he starts to sing. His voice fills me up, warm and soulful, and I'm mesmerised, rooted to the spot.

And then he looks up and it's like an electric shock as his green eyes penetrate me. He's singing to me and I'm frozen, unable to tear my gaze away. I'm locked in a stare with him.

And then he looks down, back at his guitar, and doesn't meet my eyes again. The song finishes and he turns back to his band. It's as though I was never there.

I suddenly feel overwhelmed. Tears prick my eyes, and I'm aware of how crazy that sounds, how bizarre it is.

I glance at Christian and am surprised to find him calmly watching me.

I stand up, nervy with embarrassment. 'I should get back to work,' I say, fidgeting with thin air.

'Right you are,' he says, and looks down at his hand, pen hovering over a blank sheet in his notepad.

I walk to the door and glance back at Johnny for a moment, and in that very same instant he meets my eyes again, his expression grave.

I try to keep my legs steady as I walk out the door.

Chapter 7

I reach the end of my length to find a large pair of pale, hairy feet before me.

'Argh!' I splutter and hang on to the side of the pool, looking up to see Christian grinning down at me.

'Pebbles time?'

I laugh and tell him I'll meet him in the kitchen. Twenty-eight will do. I seem to be getting further and further away from my goal of fifty.

'Another late one?' I ask as I sit down.

'Not too bad, actually,' he answers. 'Gig tomorrow night so Johnny's a bit stressed.'

'What the hell is that?' Johnny asks as he comes into the kitchen, again wearing dark shades.

'Pebbles,' I tell him, my heart flipping. I feel like I haven't seen him for ages. 'Want some?'

'No way. Looks technicolour vomit.'

'I could get you something else to eat?'

It's seven forty-five and Rosa's not here yet. In fact, it's strange to find Johnny in the kitchen at this hour.

'Just a coffee would be good.'

'Band coming over again today?' I ask.

'Yeah, any minute. Meg, bring the coffee up. I'm going to get cracking.'

'He's in a bad mood,' a happily-munching Christian muses as Johnny exits the kitchen. He reaches for his notepad and starts to scribble.

Five minutes later I take Johnny's coffee upstairs to the studio, black, no sugar, just how I know he likes it.

'Cheers, babe,' he says, taking it from me. He eyes me up and down. I'm still wearing my bathrobe.

'Sorry, I'll go and get changed. I've just been for a swim,' I explain, feeling jittery.

'Aah. Got that skimpy little bikini on under there, hey?' He raises one eyebrow at me. The buzzer goes and I start. Johnny chuckles softly as I leave the room.

'I'll get it,' Christian calls up the stairs to me.

'Thanks.' I hurriedly make my way to the safety of my bedroom.

A couple of hours tick by and the phone is ringing off the hook in the office. I catch sight of Rosa passing by outside with a tray and pluck some courage from God knows where.

'Rosa, I'll take that up for you,' I call. 'I need to chat to Johnny about a couple of things anyway.'

Christian is still sitting at the mixing desk, although the only dial he's touching is the volume. He gets up quickly to hold back the door as I budge it open with my left shoulder.

Johnny looks annoyed behind the glass. He nods at me,

acknowledging my presence, and swings his guitar off his shoulder. The band stay behind the glass as Johnny enters the room.

'I'm fed up with this,' he growls as he grabs his mug of coffee. 'Want to take that in to them?' he says to me, so I pick up the tray and go through to the band. I get a couple of grunts but no actual thank yous.

'I think it's sounding good,' Christian is saying as I return to the mixing room.

'It sounds like shit,' Johnny snaps. Christian reaches for his notepad.

'Don't piss me off,' Johnny warns.

'What, you want to censor me?' Christian asks with a hint of sarcasm.

'No! Oh, for fuck's sake. I can't concentrate!'

I stand awkwardly by the door, my own notepad in hand. Johnny notices me suddenly.

'Do you want something, Meg?'

'Erm, I really need an answer about those interviews.'

'What interviews?'

'You know, the ones I've mentioned to you a couple of times.'

'Remind me.'

'Well, *Rolling Stone* want to speak to you backstage, just before you go on. A journalist from the *NME* is in town and he's coming to the gig, wondering if he can—'

He interrupts. 'You sort it. You decide.'

'But—'

'*What?*'

'Okay,' I say. I'll have to ask Bill. I don't know Johnny well enough yet to know what is the right thing to do. It's a bit bloody stressful, to be honest.

Christian is still writing on his pad.

'Mate, will you cut that out?' Johnny says.

'Look!' Christian responds, angrily. 'What do you want me to do, write your fucking biography or kiss your arse?'

Johnny looks furious for a moment, but then his face relaxes.

'Sorry, I'm just feeling a bit harassed with all this.' He runs his hand through his hair and looks in at his band.

'Yeah, I know, mate.' Christian's voice softens too. 'Is there anything I can do?'

I'm still standing awkwardly by the door, not sure whether to stay or leave.

'No, you're alright. And Meg,' he says to me, 'sorry for snapping at you. Speak to Bill. He'll know what to do about the interviews.'

'Okay,' I say. 'Thanks.'

'Hey,' Johnny says, suddenly, 'why don't you two take the afternoon off? Go somewhere, down to Santa Monica or something. You've got enough of me being in a foul mood for the book, haven't you, Christian?' He smiles, weakly.

'Er, yeah,' Christian says, considering the suggestion. 'That's not a bad idea. You up for that, Meg?'

'Um . . .' I don't really want to leave the house while Johnny's in it, but it would be a shame to pass up a sightseeing opportunity.

'Go on,' Christian urges.

'Okay, but I'd better ring Bill first and get back to these journalists.'

'Cool!' Christian enthuses. Johnny heads back into the glass room. 'Hey, mate,' Christian calls after him. 'Can we take a car?'

Johnny waves his hand, distractedly. 'Sure, sure, whatever.'

Christian gives me a look of unadulterated excitement and

pushes me out of the room. 'Quick! Before he changes his mind.'

I don't know what all the fuss is about until forty minutes later when I arrive at the bottom of the stairs to see Christian still looking like a kid who's about to go to Disneyland.

'Come on, come on!'

I can't help but laugh as I follow him outside to the garage.

Christian waves at one of the security guards – I think it's Lewis – who comes over to the garage and types in an eight-digit security code.

'Keys are in the cars. Have a good day,' Lewis says, ushering us inside with brusque authority.

'Are they always that cool about letting people take Johnny's cars?'

'No. I arranged it with Lewis a little while ago. Johnny's let me use them before.'

Christian flicks a switch inside the garage and the large white room is illuminated. Lined up in front of us are six differently coloured cars, gleaming in the overhead lights. There are a couple of motorcycles at the end.

'What do you reckon, Meg? Which one shall we go for?'

'I don't know. The blue one?'

He laughs. 'You can't just say the blue one.'

'The red one, then?'

'Meg! That's practically blasphemy. Stop talking in colours.'

'Sorry, I don't know that much about cars.'

'Right, then, you're going to have to learn, otherwise this will be a totally wasted experience for you. Come on.' He beckons me to follow him and we head over to the first car on the left. It's sleek, shiny and charcoal grey.

'This is a Mercedes Gullwing. It's a 1950s classic car. The doors lift out to the sides, so it looks a bit like a seagull – hence the name Gullwing.'

'Cool,' I say, peering in at the red-leather interior.

He moves on to the next one. It's electric blue.

'And this is a Porsche 911 turbo. Good run-around, every day kinda car. Only costs around £110,000.'

'Sorry, did you just say *only*?' I ask, taken aback. I can't believe Johnny said I can drive this one.

'Those two at the end will set you back more than a million bucks.'

'*What?!*'

'Hang on, we'll get to them in a minute,' he says moving along to the next one. It's silver.

'Here you've got another Porsche, but this is a Carrera GT. It's one of the fastest cars Porsche ever produced.'

'Nice,' I admit.

The next car is red.

'Ferrari Enzo. They only built four hundred and you had to be invited to buy one. Johnny was one of the lucky few.'

'Wicked!'

'Don't make up your mind yet,' he tells me, sternly, moving on to the penultimate vehicle. It's black.

'Now, this sexy little beast is a McLaren F1. It was the fastest production car ever built for a while.'

'Oh, I like it . . .'

'Yeah, it's also Johnny's favourite because it's got three seats.' I look at him inquisitively. 'Good for pulling two groupies when he's in that sort of mood,' Christian explains.

On second thoughts, I don't like it very much at all.

'The seats are tiny,' I point out, trying to sound nonchalant.

'That's the way he likes his girls,' is Christian's reply.

'So what about this one?' I hurry on to the silver and cream creation at the end.

'Now *this* is a Bugatti Veyron. It is currently the world's fastest supercar. Nought to sixty in three seconds, and it changes shape to reach its top speed. Johnny bought it only six months ago.'

The reverence with which he speaks is quite amusing.

'Let's take it!' I decide.

'Why? Why do you want to go for this one?'

Oh bugger, now he's challenging me. 'Well, you just implied it was the best. Isn't it?'

'Yes, it is,' he concedes. 'But I want you to fully appreciate *why*. Have a look inside,' he encourages, opening the passenger door.

'It is really nice,' I tell him, before realising that won't quite suffice. 'I like the dash,' I improvise. 'I bet that looks amazing when it's all lit up.'

That seems to do the trick. Christian leaps into the driver's seat.

'Are you ready?' he asks. I solemnly nod that I am. He turns the ignition on and presses a switch to start the engine. The car roars into life. 'Listen to that,' he says, opening his eyes and looking across at me.

'Wow.' Okay, it does sound pretty impressive, but I'm not going to climax or anything. 'Ooh, look,' I say, pointing at the lights on the dashboard.

Christian smiles and leans back in his seat, listening for a minute.

'Are we off, then?' I press.

'So you definitely, definitely want to take the Bug, right?' He looks across at me.

'Bug? Oh, Bugatti. Yes. The Bug is clearly the cream of the crop.'

That seems to settle it once and for all. He adjusts his seat and mirrors, puts his belt on, and gently eases the car out of the garage.

'THIS SPEED LIMIT IS REALLY FUCKING ANNOYING!' he shouts to me, fifteen minutes later. We're on the freeway, heading towards Santa Monica. 'I REALLY WANT TO GIVE IT SOME WELLY!'

I give him my best sympathetic look but don't attempt to compete with the noise of the engine.

The ocean stretches out in front of us, clear and blue, the afternoon sun hitting it and sending up billions of glittering sparks. We pull up at the super-swish Viceroy hotel, which Christian thinks is the safest option for local valet parking.

'We should go for a drink at the poolside bar later,' he tells me. 'It's really nice in there.'

It's not as hot now as it has been, although I'm sure the cool breeze from the ocean has a lot to do with that. We wander along the dusty pavement in the direction of the water.

Santa Monica beach is long with boardwalks running through white-as-snow sand. Palm trees line the pavement at the highest point of the beach, and off in the distance there's a pier with a Ferris wheel. Christian moves me out of the way of a passing rollerblader and I look back to see six more coming. We approach a skates-for-hire shop, and I'm kind of tempted even though I can't skate for buggery. It just seems like an appropriate thing to do.

'Fuck off, you're not going to get me on those things,' Christian says when I suggest it. 'I'll have a go on that, though.' He points to an area called 'The Original Muscle Beach', according to a sign. It looks like an adult-sized kids' playground.

'Go on, then,' I say, smiling.

We take off our shoes and step onto the warm sand, which is packed with sunbathers. To our left a group of super-fit people are playing volleyball and I also spot a couple of lifeguard watch towers. It's like we're on the set of *Baywatch* or something. Except I'm distinctly lacking in the boob department, and Christian's not exactly the Hoff in his prime, either. He launches himself at the rings and starts to swing from one to another. He gets to four in and then stops, hanging there, panting. He looks so ridiculous I start to laugh.

A large, muscular man with an orange tan and oily limbs stands by, watching as Christian attempts another couple of rings. It soon becomes clear he's waiting for Christian to get off, so I go to the end and start to offer encouragement.

'Come on, Christian, you can do it!' I shout, enthusiastically. He swings a couple more.

'Come on, boy, come on!' I shout again, this time patting my knees like he's a dog. He doesn't look very amused, but he makes it to the end eventually.

'Fuck me, that was hard,' he pants, doubled over, as he glances back to see Oily Man swing along all of the rings in five seconds flat. He flashes me a cheeky grin and I start to giggle.

'Wanna go on the Ferris wheel?' he asks.

'Yeah!'

He does have a lovely smile.

The Ferris wheel is followed quickly by the rollercoaster, but Christian refuses to go on the old-fashioned carousel. 'Do I look like a little girl to you?'

'No, but you *do* eat kiddie cereal.'

It's remarkable how relaxed I feel in Christian's company, considering we've only just met. I wonder if he has a girlfriend?

He'd be an ideal boyfriend. Not for me. For Bess. Or Kitty. Someone, anyway. It would be a shame to waste him.

As the afternoon wears on and the sun starts to dip in the sky and cast shadows over the footprints in the sand, we wander along the pier towards the end. There's a mobile candy shop along the way and my sweet tooth gets the better of me, so I pull on Christian's T-shirt to get him to stop. His eyes widen in wonder as we stand and survey row upon row of brightly coloured sweets. He hastily grabs a plastic bag and passes it to me, hanging on to the scoop himself. I point at some soft mini watermelons and he digs in while I hold the bag open in front of him.

'How 'bout some bananas?' he suggests. 'Can never go wrong with a sweetie banana.'

'Definitely,' I agree. 'And get some of those grape-flavoured chewy-looking things.'

As we continue along the pier, munching away, I muse, 'I've never before met a guy who has as sweet a tooth as me.'

'Fuck yeah, I have a sweetie age of about seven.'

'Sweetie age?' I look at him, inquisitively.

'Yeah, you know, the sort of sweets you go for – who they're mainly aimed at. This is little kids' stuff.' He lifts up the bag. 'Terry's Chocolate Orange I would say is a sweetie age of about thirty-five. And then you've got things like your After Eight Mints. We're talking ninety plus.'

'Well, I reckon I must have a sweetie age of about seven, too,' I decide. 'Maybe eight, because girls are more mature than boys.'

We reach the end of the pier as the sun starts to slide down below the horizon. There's a Mexican restaurant with an outdoor bar area, full of people.

Christian turns to me. 'Shall we say bollocks to the posh bar and go in here instead?'

Soon we're seated outside with frozen margaritas.

'Cheers,' Christian says, and we chink glasses.

'How do you know Johnny?' I ask, as Christian starts to devour the complimentary nachos.

'We met at school, donkey's years ago.'

'Was that in Newcastle?'

'Yeah. We lived on the same street, went to the same school. I've known him practically all my life.'

'It's so nice that you're still mates after all this time.'

'Mmm.' Munch, munch, munch.

'Johnny moved down to London eventually, didn't he?' I tuck my hair behind my ears and lean in.

'After his mum died, yeah,' Christian confirms. 'We were thirteen.'

'That must've been hard,' I say.

'Yeah. But when I went down to London for university we hooked up again. It was just like old times. Got a flat together. Then the band took off, and that's it really.'

'Wow. Must've been pretty mental to see that happen to your best mate.'

'Yeah . . . Hey, shall we order some food?' he asks, abruptly.

I pick up my menu, understanding that, for now at least, that's enough about Christian and Johnny. I'm just deciding between a fajita and a burrito when the cool new iPhone that Johnny gave me when I started begins to ring.

'Where are you?' It's Johnny and he doesn't sound very happy.

'Erm, Santa Monica?' My feeble reply sounds like a question.

'Where's Christian?' Johnny demands.

'He's right here.'

'Put him on.'

I pass the phone over with a worried look. Christian seems unfazed.

'Alright, mate?' he says. 'Ah, shit,' he continues, rummaging around in his jeans and pulling out his mobile. 'Got it on silent.' He plunges the phone back into his pocket. 'We were just about to order some food . . .' Christian says, shortly followed by, 'Oh, okay. Yeah, of course.' He looks at me and pulls a face before Johnny fires his next question. 'The Bug,' Christian answers, then, 'You said we could!' Pause. 'The Viceroy.' Another pause. 'Yeah, okay, we'll head home now.'

'Was he okay?' I ask, hesitantly, when the call ends.

'Yeah. Just miffed we've been gone so long.'

'Eek! I don't want to piss him off.'

'You haven't, don't worry. Anyway, it's me he's annoyed at for taking his prized Bugatti.' Christian grins, but I feel concerned. 'Honestly, Meg, it's fine. He didn't say we couldn't take it – it's his own fault for not being more specific.'

I'm obviously not looking convinced because he adds, chuckling, 'Seriously, he gets like this all the time. You just learn to ignore it.'

The waiter brings the bill over and Christian throws down a note, steadfastly refusing to let me go halves. Then we get up and make our way quietly back along the pier in the direction of the car.

Chapter 8

The interviews have been organised, the guest list has been sorted and Samuel has just buzzed me to let me know Davey is on the driveway. I turn to Johnny.

'You ready?'

'As I'll ever be.'

Johnny, Christian, Bill and I are all travelling together to the gig and I am *beyond* excited. This is the gig that everyone is talking about and I'm going to be there, right in the middle of the action. Okay, so I know my friends would whinge that this opportunity is entirely wasted on me but I don't care. Woohoo!

Johnny was nowhere to be seen when we arrived home last night, and I was worried that I'd annoyed him. Today, though, he's been in a great mood.

Before we've even passed through the property's gates, Bill has delved into the car's minibar. I prepare four glasses with ice while Bill reaches for the whisky. He pours generous servings into two of the glasses and hands one to Johnny.

'You having whisky, Chris?' he asks Christian.

'I'll have a beer.'

Bill passes Christian a bottle of Becks and turns to me.

'What about you?'

'Do you have any Baileys?'

He sniggers and looks at Johnny, who's sitting opposite us, next to Christian. 'Fuckin' Baileys. Get this down ya, girl.' He hands me a whisky and pours himself another one, before collapsing back in his seat. I sneakily pour Christian's ice from his unused glass into mine in an attempt to water my drink down. Christian looks at me in amusement before raising his beer bottle.

'Here's to a good comeback gig, mate.'

'Cheers,' Johnny replies.

The Whisky is situated on the Sunset Strip and the queue is already snaking out and around the building regardless of the fact that the gig isn't due to kick off for another couple of hours.

A group of girls near the front begin to scream hysterically as they spot the limo. The queue dissolves as people break away and run after the car. Their faces are actually quite terrifying as they bash on the windows, trying to get in. I glance at Johnny in alarm, but he seems completely unfazed by this attack of the zombies.

Davey drives on. 'I think we'd better go round the block,' he shouts from the front.

Bill sighs and looks at me. 'You gonna call security and let them know we're here, or what?'

'Yes, sorry,' I say, rummaging for my phone. It's not like anyone has told me what to do in these circumstances, but I'll know better next time. So much of it is a case of learning on the job.

A short while later, after the backstage entrance has been secured, Davey pulls up and we file out of the car. A crowd of about fifty people are waiting on the off chance that we come through this way, but, boy, can they make some noise. Flailing hands try to get to Johnny despite the bulky security guards holding back the tide as we hurry into the venue. The door is secured behind us and a tall, blonde woman with an earpiece and a clipboard leads us to the backstage dressing area. I enter the room in a daze.

'That was a bit mental, hey?' Christian says.

'Gonna be a good one.' Bill claps his hands together in anticipation.

Johnny bounces on the spot energetically a few times.

'You alright, Meg?' he asks.

'Fucking look at her, she can't believe her eyes!' Bill laughs. 'I think she needs another drink.'

'Yeah, I'm up for that,' Johnny says and grabs a bottle of whisky from a tabletop which is bulging with booze and snacks. He cracks it open and swigs straight from the bottle before offering it to Christian with a grin. Christian passes it straight to Bill and gets himself a beer from a bucket of ice.

'What're you drinking, Meg?' Christian asks me.

'I'll go for a beer, too.' I figure it'd be preferable to more whisky.

'You should crack open the champers, love,' Bill suggests.

There's an idea . . .

Hmm, little bit silly. The whisky and champagne have gone straight to my head and I feel tipsy. Well, okay, drunk. Johnny's off doing an interview with *Rolling Stone* and Christian and I are lounging on a sofa. I think he's a bit pissed, too. The room is bustling with the hip and fashionable. Some of the guys seem to be wearing even more make-up than the girls. I don't know who these people are, but they're all down on the list. Friends of the band and Johnny, I presume. Christian has been telling me that the Whisky – actually called Whisky a Go Go – has played host to some of rock 'n' roll's most important bands, from The Doors, to Janis Joplin, Led Zeppelin and Nirvana. It's smaller than I thought it would be. I guess I'm used to hearing about Johnny playing stadiums.

'It's the first time he's played live in over a year,' Christian says to me.

'Is it?' I'm distracted. Johnny has just entered the room. I watch as he's greeted by cheers and a few slaps on the back before he finally materialises in front of us.

'Come and watch from backstage,' he says.

We follow him to the backstage area. A roadie rushes past with a mic stand and Johnny puts both his palms on my arms to manoeuvre me out of the way. His touch leaves my skin burning.

'Nervous, mate?' Christian asks him.

'Nope,' Johnny responds, shaking his head.

I haven't seen him like this before: full of energy and verve.

He lights up a cigarette and I sneak a sideways peek at him.

'So Meg,' Johnny glances at me, blowing smoke out of the corner of his mouth. 'Would you rather be at a Kylie concert?'

I laugh a little too loudly. He grins at me. Oh God, I fancy him.

He throws his fag down on the floor and stamps on it.

'Back in a sec,' he says.

Christian closes the gap between us. I take a deep breath.

Ten minutes later Johnny still hasn't returned and I can't think straight. The lights on the stage have gone out and the girls in the audience have started to scream. The band files past us and take their positions. Then Johnny appears at my side, guitar hanging behind him.

I watch him in the darkness as a soundman hooks up an amp to his instrument and tells him he's good to go.

'Good luck, pal,' Christian says.

'Yeah, good luck,' I echo.

'Thanks, mate,' he says to Christian. He looks down at me. 'Cheers, chick.'

The noise from the crowd is deafening as Johnny bounds onstage and launches straight into one of his hits.

'Wicked, isn't it?' Christian shouts above the music. 'Getting to watch from so close?'

'Amazing!' I shout back.

The room is dark and grungy, smoke filling the air. The audience is made up of competition winners and press and I walk a few steps to my left so I can peek out at them. They've gone wild and are jumping up and down as one. Exhilaration soars through me as it finally sinks in. I am a lucky, lucky girl. I never want to stop working for Johnny. In fact, I'm going to work so hard for him he's going to wonder how he ever did without me.

After two songs, my boss addresses the crowd. He tells them he's going to quieten things down a little. The members of the band relinquish their instruments and leave the stage and a roadie brings Johnny a stool. He sits atop it and starts to strum his acoustic guitar. The audience falls silent. I immediately recognise the song as the same one he sang to me in the studio. His voice fills the room and I stare at him, willing him to look backstage at me.

'Check this out,' Christian says from beside me. He's wandered over so he can see the audience, too.

'Those lasses in the front row,' he says, leaning his head in close to me and pointing.

I drag my eyes away from Johnny and follow Christian's finger. I immediately spot who he's talking about. There are two gorgeous girls in the middle at the front, staring up at Johnny, transfixed. One has long, dark wavy hair and is wearing a low-cut top to show off her ample cleavage, and the other is blonde with a pixie crop.

My eyes flit back to Johnny. He's looking down as he strums his guitar. I feel a wave of relief, and then, all of a sudden, Johnny looks straight at the girls as he sings.

I feel a white spike of jealousy shoot through me as I look back at Johnny and see him raise one eyebrow at the girls. I can't bear to think which one he's most interested in. And then it occurs to me it's probably both.

I turn to Christian and try to sound flippant. 'Bet Johnny wouldn't mind getting them in his McLaren F1.'

Christian laughs. 'I was just thinking the same thing. Watch. That guy over there? I bet you a bag of sweets Johnny tells him to give those two slappers aftershow passes before the next song is out.'

'That's a bet I'm not sure I want to take,' I respond, feeling sick to the pit of my stomach.

'It's only a bag of sweets, Meg. Let's say Skittles, to be specific. And I'll share 'em with you.'

'Okay,' I force a laugh. 'You're on.'

Sure enough, by the time the song is finished, I see Johnny nod at the roadie, who clocks the girls. The roadie beckons to a weedy-looking guy dressed in black and wearing an earpiece.

'Watch! Watch!' Christian nudges me.

A few seconds later the second guy makes his way through the gap between the stage and the crowd and discreetly hands the girls passes. They smile demurely at Johnny, and my eyes dart back to him just in time to catch him wink at them.

I try to tell myself this is the reality check I need. I *know* Johnny shags groupies. And he's probably been off doing drugs tonight as well.

He's trouble with a capital T.

So why does he have to be so sexy?

'Told you!' Christian jovially elbows me in the ribs. 'You owe me Skittles, girl!'

'Yeah.' I force a smile and watch the rest of the set with a lot less enthusiasm than I started out with.

The aftershow party is being held at the Standard Downtown, a hotel with a rooftop bar in downtown LA. Johnny is travelling there with the band in their minibus, so Christian, Bill and I arrive alone in the limo. Bill excuses himself immediately and goes to talk to a skinny dude who's manically smoking a cigarette. Christian and I grab a couple of beers from a passing waitress who is dressed in a sexy red and white uniform with short shorts and looks like she should be on rollerskates.

We move out of the way of the lift, which continues to spew out partygoers, and head past the bar and up a few steps. It's quieter around here. There's a long swimming pool, lit up in the darkness, and we have a perfect view of the city's tallest buildings. It's not like New York, skyscraper upon skyscraper packed into the smallest square mileage, but it's still an impressive sight. Considering the earthquakes LA is subjected to, it's amazing they have any skyscrapers at all. There are a few strange-looking large, red, round fibreglass pods to the side of the pool, and as I watch a couple vacate one, I notice that the mattress they were lying on is undulating. I look at Christian excitedly and point.

'Waterbeds!'

He laughs and leads the way. We slip off our shoes and he waits for me as I climb up through one of the four entrance holes onto the heaving mattress. I'm glad I'm wearing trousers and not a skirt because there is no gracious way to get onto this thing. I feel like I'm crawling through quicksand and start to giggle as I eventually give up and collapse onto my back.

'Budge out the way, you silly girl!' Christian pushes at my hip as he tries to get on. He doesn't seem to have mastered the art of the waterbed either, and soon he's collapsing in fits of laughter as well. I'm glad the music's loud up here, because I don't think the trendy types would find us very funny.

'Oh, fuck, I've left our beers out there,' Christian exclaims, and then has to go through the rigmarole of exiting the damn thing and getting back on again. I'm laughing even harder by this stage, and can barely hold up my hands to take the beers from him as he hobbles on his knees, trying not to spill any alcohol.

'Take them, you wench!'

I grab the drinks just in time for him to collapse on his stomach in front of me. The water underneath us swells and falls with every movement.

'I feel seasick,' Christian moans, his face pressed into the white mattress.

'I think it's far more likely you feel pissed,' I say.

He flips over onto his back and attempts to ease himself backwards.

'What the hell are you doing now?' I ask.

'Trying to sit up.'

Eventually he makes it to one of the edges and squeezes himself rather unceremoniously up against the red fibreglass wall surrounding us. It's curved, so it forces his chin downwards until it's practically resting on his chest. He doesn't look very comfortable. I start to giggle again.

'Whose bloody stupid idea was this?' he asks, unimpressed. 'I hope you're happy with yourself, missy.'

I'm currently lying flat out on my back and it's not easy to drink in this position. I prop my head up with one hand as the water moves beneath me. I'm not very comfortable either, but I'm buggered if I'm going to tell him that, so I take a swig of beer and try to look cool.

'Happy there, are you?' he asks, wryly.

'Perfectly, thank you. How's your neck?'

'Really fucking uncomfortable.'

I tell him to stop moaning. He prods me in the ribs with a sock-encased toe and I squeal, which only makes him do it again.

'Don't! I'll wet myself!' I manage to spit out.

'Oh, now that would be a really pretty sight.' Christian laughs, but stops for a moment while I take a swig of beer. Then he prods me in the ribs again and I splutter as the beer goes down the wrong way. All this just makes him laugh harder.

'You. Are. Such. A. Git,' I manage to say, through coughing. I manoeuvre myself around so my feet are facing him, and kick him on his thigh with my right foot. He bats my foot away easily and glugs his beer down.

'What's going on here, hey?' Johnny's face appears at the side of the pod. 'Playing footsies?' He looks amused.

'Hey, mate!' Christian grabs my offending foot and holds it up and out of the way, forcing me to fall back on the mattress again. 'She's a kicker, this one, you'd better watch out.'

Tears have been streaming down my face and I quickly wipe

them away and study my fingers. Shit. They're covered with wet mascara, which means my make-up is currently halfway down my face. As Christian releases my foot, I try to compose myself and clean away what I can as fast as possible.

Johnny passes Christian a whole bottle of whisky and steps up onto the fibreglass frame. He doesn't take his shoes off. He falls down onto his back next to me, and Christian and I both groan as the mattress moves beneath us again. Johnny holds out his hand for the whisky and grins.

'Cheers!' He chinks our bottles and takes a swig from his before passing the bottle to me.

'Urgh, no thanks,' I respond. 'I don't know how you can drink it straight like that.'

'I'm hardcore.' He grins. 'So what did you think of the gig?'

'Fucking excellent, mate,' Christian says.

'Really, really good,' I add.

'Yeah? You liked it?' Johnny turns to face me. He pushes Christian's sock out from in between us. 'Mate, get your smelly foot out of the way,'

Christian instead presses it onto Johnny's nose.

'Ew, that's disgusting!' Johnny exclaims, violently shoving it away. Christian does the same to me. His sock is now slightly sweaty and I squawk in disgust as it brushes my lips. Christian finds that more hilarious than ever and soon Johnny starts laughing too. Christian prods me in the ribs with his foot again and I squeal, which is all the encouragement Johnny needs to get involved. Propped up on one elbow with the whisky bottle in his right hand, he hovers above me and starts to tickle me in the ribs with his left. I scream and bat him away as hard as I can as my top starts to ride up. He and Christian guffaw like a couple of teenagers as opposed to the grown men that they actually are while I lie there panting, trying to recover. Johnny stays propped up on one side and looks down at me, his green eyes laughing.

'Whisky, Meg?' He offers me the bottle.

'Fuck off,' I tell him. Both he and Christian laugh again. I adjust my top and wipe my eyes to rid myself of more mascara smudges.

It's then that I notice the crowd outside. The bar is absolutely packed now – all around the pool area, people are standing and sitting – and the vast majority of them are looking at us. Humiliation washes over me and I hurriedly try to sit up. Johnny's still lying down and seems unbothered about the fact that he's the centre of every guest's attention. I glance back out at the crowd and watch as dozens of pairs of eyes dart away from us and surreptitiously dart back again. It's obvious they're trying not to look. It's not cool to stare. Like a bolt out of nowhere, my feelings of embarrassment are replaced with pride. I'm where every single one of those people is dying to be. I look back at Christian, happily.

'You need another beer, Meg?' he asks.

'I'll get them,' I reply. 'You look so comfortable, I can't bear to make you move,' I add, jokingly. 'Anyway, I need the loo.'

Johnny holds out his hand to take my empty bottle while I crawl across to the opening. He pushes on my bum.

'Oi!' I shout at him.

'I'm just trying to help!' he exclaims. I carry on with my crawling and he pushes my bum again.

'Stop it!' I laugh. I reach the fibreglass opening and ungraciously climb out, sliding my feet into my high heels. I turn back to take the empties.

'You want anything else?' I ask Johnny.

'Nah. Still going.'

As I try to walk with confidence from the shiny red pod, I make eye contact with a couple of gorgeous girls and can't help but feel smug as their lips purse with jealousy.

This is fun!

I arrive at the loos and check my reflection as I wait in the queue. The mascara damage isn't too bad, thankfully. I smooth down my hair and apply some lipgloss.

On my way out I notice the two groupies that Johnny gave passes to. They're hovering a few metres away from the pod. *Our* pod. I feel a wave of dislike for them as I grab another couple of beers from a waitress and make my way back to Johnny and Christian. I'm annoyed to find a couple of moody members of the band have encroached on our little party. But they nod at me and even manage a half-smile of recognition as I slip off my shoes and hand Christian our beers before climbing back up onto the waterbed. Johnny is still lying in the middle of the mattress, while Lee and TJ, the drummer and bassist, are leaning against the side, like Christian. I suddenly feel a little uncomfortable about placing myself in the centre with Johnny, so I crawl across to Christian and he edges himself right to make room for me. He hands me back one of the beers.

'Your groupies are just outside,' I say to Johnny.

What the hell? WHY did I just tell him that?

'Really?' He raises an eyebrow in mild interest, then adds, 'What do you mean? What groupies?'

I'm sure he knows exactly who I'm talking about, but I play along. 'The ones you gave passes to at the gig.'

'Oh, you saw that, did you?' he asks, amusement lacing his voice.

'It was pretty hard to miss, mate,' Christian chips in. 'In fact, I bet Meg a bag of sweeties that you'd give them aftershow tickets.'

'Did you, now,' Johnny says, sardonically, and takes a swig from his whisky. He cranes his neck and glances outside. I follow his gaze. Sure enough, the girls are still standing a few metres away, trying to look sexy. Johnny collapses back down onto the mattress, ignoring them.

'Shouldn't really have done that,' he says, grinning at the four of us in the pod.

'Yeah, where is Serengeti?' Christian asks. 'I thought she was coming tonight.'

'She's doing publicity for her new flick,' Johnny answers. 'She's back on Saturday.'

'I'll miss her, then,' Christian says.

'Why?' I ask.

'I fly back to Britain tomorrow.' He looks down at me.

Oh. I was getting used to Christian's company. I don't like the thought of him leaving.

'That was a short trip,' I comment, unable to keep the disappointment from my voice.

'Short and sweet,' he replies.

'Did you get enough material for your book?' I ask.

'Enough to make a solid start, yeah.'

'And now he's got to get back to his girlfriend,' Johnny adds, in a sing-song voice.

'And my job, mate,' Christian is quick to point out.

I want to ask about the girlfriend, but settle on a job question instead. 'I thought this was your job? Writing the book?'

'No, this is a spare time jobbie,' he replies, and laughs at

Johnny's mock offended face. He turns back to me. 'I'm a journalist. Music journo. Freelance now, but I do still have deadlines to meet.'

'So how is Clare?' Johnny interrupts.

'Fine,' Christian replies, a touch abruptly.

'Say hi to her from me,' Johnny adds.

Christian's response is to yawn loudly. 'Fuck me, I'm jetlagged,' he says. 'How're you feeling, Meg?'

'Not too bad, actually,' I reply.

'Hey, Lola!' Johnny's attention is suddenly distracted by a girl walking by. She turns around and pokes her head inside the pod.

'Hey, Johnny,' she drawls in an American accent. 'Been a while.'

Lola's dark hair is tied up into a high ponytail and her fringe has been backcombed and pinned back. She's absolutely stunning.

Johnny pats the mattress next to him and asks her to get in, but she hesitates.

'Come on,' he urges. 'Come and meet my best mate, Christian. I've known him all my life. He's flying back to the UK tomorrow. And this is my new PA, Meg,' he adds about me, almost as an afterthought. 'You know TJ and Lee.'

She scans the rest of us and a small smile forms on her dark-red lips.

'Come on,' Johnny urges again.

Why is he so desperate for her to join us? I think to myself, irritably. We were having such fun just the three of us. Well, okay, five of us, but TJ and Lee have barely said a word since I got back so they don't really count. Actually, are they stoned?

Never mind that now, it appears Lola has been swayed.

Johnny gets up onto his knees, looking a million times cooler than Christian or I did when we tried to do that earlier, and edges his way towards the pod's opening while Lola takes off her shoes. Johnny holds out his hands to her and gently helps her into the pod. She doesn't laugh like we did, and she doesn't look ungainly getting in, either.

I feel intimidated by her.

'Come and lie in the middle with me,' Johnny says.

'No, I'll sit up against the wall,' she replies, crawling – actually quite sexily, goddammit – to the side and turning around to face us. Johnny follows her and settles himself beside her.

'So, how do you like LA?' Lola asks Christian. 'Have you been here before?'

'Loads of times,' he replies.

'Can't get rid of ya, can I, mate!' Johnny jokes.

Lola doesn't laugh. 'Have you worked for Johnny long?' she asks me.

'Only about a week and a half,' I reply.

'Good luck with that,' she says, drily.

'Oi!' Johnny slaps her thigh. 'Enough of that. Did you watch the gig?'

'No. Had band practice.'

He narrows his eyes jokingly, but I can tell he's disappointed. 'Lola's the lead singer of Spooky Girl,' he explains to Christian and me.

'Ah,' Christian nods, impressed. 'I thought I recognised you. I've heard some of your stuff. Really cool.'

'Thanks,' she replies. 'You should come to a gig next time you're over.'

'I'd love to,' he says.

111

'You too,' she says to me. 'Anytime you want.'

'Great!' I reply, overenthusiastically. Did that sound as forced as it felt?

Johnny laughs. 'Meg, you're hilarious,' he says, shaking his head. 'You wouldn't know a Spooky Girl song if it leapt out of the stereo and whacked you round the bazookas.'

I blush, furiously.

'That's not very fair,' Lola says, defending me. 'We haven't really taken off overseas yet . . .'

'Even if you had, Meg wouldn't know about it. She's into Kylie.'

'Kylie's cool,' Lola replies, nonchalantly. 'Nothing wrong with that.'

Hmm, maybe she's not so bad after all.

'Can we smoke in here?' she asks.

'Dunno,' Johnny replies, but digs into his pocket and pulls out a crumpled packet of fags anyway. He offers her one, but she declines.

'Got my roll-ups,' she says.

'Suit yourself,' Johnny responds, shaking out one of his own cigarettes and popping it into his mouth. It hangs on his lower lip as he turns to light her roll-up first, before seeing to his own. He shoves the packet and lighter back into his pocket.

I watch as Lola smokes her cigarette. Her fingernails are cut short and painted the darkest red. I glance down at her toenails and notice they match. Her feet are slim and tanned, and she's wearing a short, metallic silver dress with a belt wrapped around the middle.

I realise I'm staring and quickly look away, hoping she hasn't noticed.

'I think I'm going to call it a night soon,' Christian says to me. 'You want to hitch a ride? Save Davey doing two trips?'

'Mate, you're not talking about leaving, are you?' Johnny moans, eavesdropping.

'Yep, I'm ready to call it a night.'

'Hey, hey!' Bill's face appears at one of the entrances to the pod. 'This is where the party's at, is it? Room for a little one?' He grins, patting his rotund stomach with both hands.

I really don't want to stay without Christian. But I'm not sure I'm ready to leave yet.

Christian exits the pod and turns back. 'You sticking around?' he asks me.

'Um . . .' I look over at Johnny, who has twisted himself slightly to face Lola. I'll only feel left out if I stay.

'Yes, I'm coming,' I decide.

There are not as many eyes on me as I leave the pod behind this time. Most people are staring in at Johnny. And Lola, I realise. The groupies are standing by too, looking a little desperate now, and I feel a wave of pity for them. I don't think they're going to get what they came here for. Not tonight, at least. Although I might be wrong. I still don't really know Johnny at all.

Chapter 9

Bollocks to swimming. And bollocks to Fruity Pebbles. But yay to
Ibuprofen! Lots of it!

Yes, I have a stonking hangover. And what did I expect?
Whisky, beer, champagne . . . Whoops. The thought of any alcohol at all makes me want to throw up.

We didn't get home until 3 a.m. last night. And at six, I got a
call from Johnny asking me to get him a suite at the Standard. I
felt like my eyes had been doused in vinegar so I went back to
sleep. Now it's ten o'clock and I've just woken up. I don't know
how I'll get any work done today.

Somehow I manage to drag myself downstairs to the kitchen.
Rosa's cheerful voice hurts my head, but her coffee helps it. I go
into the office and get started on my emails.

Christian appears an hour later.

'Is your head as fucked as mine?' he asks.

'Yeah. Do you know what?' I laugh. 'I've never known anyone
to swear as much as you.'

He chuckles, then grimaces. 'Ouch, don't make me do that. I

used to work in a magazine office and we swore like troopers,' he explains. 'My favourite swearword is cu—'

'ARGH! Don't say that one!'

He laughs at my outburst. 'No, the girlfriend doesn't like that one, either.'

I smile. 'So, are you all packed?'

'Yep. Well, I never unpacked in the first place,' he admits. 'Too bloody lazy for that.'

'Johnny stayed at the Standard last night,' I tell him.

'Really?' He gives me a knowing look. 'I might not catch him before I leave, then. I'll come and say bye before I go. I'm going to give Johnny a call.'

He doesn't come down again for some time, and when he does, his notepad is in his hand.

'He alright?' I ask.

'Bit rough.' Christian grins. 'I don't think he'll be making an appearance here anytime soon. Right, kiddo, you look after yourself.' Christian comes round to the side of my desk with his arms open. I stand up and he engulfs me in a warm hug. 'Don't let that boy push you around. If he does, he'll have me to answer to.' He smiles down at me. Reaching into his pocket, he pulls out his wallet and flips it open, easing out a business card.

'My contact numbers and email address are on there. Get in touch if you ever need anything.'

'Aw, thank you,' I say.

'I mean it,' he insists. 'Anything at all. And I mean it about Johnny, too. Don't let him push you around. Keep your feet on the ground. Don't get swept up in any showbiz crap.'

'Don't worry, I won't.'

The buzzer goes.

'There's my ride. Take care. And see you soon!' He leans down and gives me another quick hug, and walks out of the office. I hear him call out his goodbyes to Rosa and then he's gone.

I feel surprisingly sad. The place just won't be the same without him.

Oh no! I forgot to buy him that bag of sweets! Next time.

The day passes by slowly. I've got a better idea now about which publications Johnny approves of and which to avoid. As journalists call about last night's gig, I'm able to decipher which photoshoot and interview requests to tentatively accept, and which ones to gently let down.

At six o'clock I get a call from the man himself.

'Hi!' I say. 'How's it going?'

His voice sounds as rough as sandpaper. 'Would you call room service and order me bacon and eggs? And some fresh towels would be good, too.'

'Of course,' I tell him. 'You want me to book you in for another night?'

'No, I'll be home soon. In fact, can you get Davey here for eight?'

'Consider it done.'

'Thanks.' He hangs up.

He doesn't actually arrive home until ten o'clock that night, after keeping Davey waiting for two hours. I'm struggling to keep my eyes open, but I stay up in case he needs me to microwave something from Rosa's meal stash.

'No, you're alright, Meg. I'm having an early one,' he says, making his way groggily up the stairs, still in his outfit from the night before, but with the addition of sunglasses. I feel anxious as I watch him leave, and then hit the sack soon afterwards myself.

The next morning is Saturday and, according to the manual, that means I'm entitled to a lie-in. All being well, of course.

The house is silent – Rosa doesn't work on weekends and I presume Johnny is still in bed, recovering. I wonder if Christian had a good flight home.

I can't be bothered to swim my laps this morning so I try calling Bess, instead.

'Did you go to his gig, or what?' she immediately butts in.

'Yep. *And* the aftershow party. Oh, it was such a laugh. There were these waterbeds and Johnny and Christian were tickling me and everyone was looking . . .' My voice trails off. It sounds like I'm boasting.

'Who's Christian?' she asks.

I tell her.

'Nice?' she queries.

'Very. Not like that,' I quickly add. 'I mean, he's nice-looking and stuff, but I don't fancy him.'

'Just like you don't fancy Johnny,' she says, teasingly.

'Oi! Will you stop it? He's my boss. I don't fancy him. And anyway, even if I did it's not like anything would ever, ever happen. God, this is so embarrassing – imagine if he overheard me talking like this. I'd bloody well die! Anyway, he's a bit bizarre at times.'

'Go on . . .'

'Yesterday evening he called me from the hotel he was staying at, asking for room service and fresh towels.'

'So?' Bess queries.

'He called *me* rather than the front desk,' I explain.

'Oh, right,' she says. 'How funny. So come on, then, when can I come and visit?'

'Ohhh,' I moan, 'I really don't know. Maybe if he goes away sometime you could?'

'What's the point in that? I want to meet the sex god!'

'You can come and visit soon,' I answer, a little uncomfortably.

After we hang up, I head downstairs to the kitchen. Rosa has left enough food to feed a small army for the weekend and I check the fridge now to see if there's anything I fancy for a fast-approaching lunch. I hear a noise and turn around to find Johnny at the doorway.

'You alright?' he asks, yawning. He's wearing only a white T-shirt and boxer shorts.

'Yeah, good thanks.' I look away. 'Just thinking about lunch. You want anything?'

'What is there? I haven't even had breakfast yet,' he says.

'I could make you something? Bacon and eggs? Cereal?'

'Don't give me any of that crap you and Christian were eating.' He grins at me, sleepily.

I smile. 'How the hell did it end up in your house anyway, if you don't like it?'

'Dunno,' he replies. 'Paola probably bought it. She was into freaky shit like that.'

I don't like the thought of Paola and me having the same taste. I already feel a bit like her ghost is hanging over me every time I read her manual. I want to make changes and put my own stamp on the job, but apart from forgetting to cross out Penelope Cruz's name under Tom Cruise's entry in the Rolodex and adding Katie Holmes and Suri instead, Paola seems to be the epitome of organisation.

'So did Christian get off okay?' Johnny asks. 'No, don't worry, Meg, I'll just have whatever you're having,' he adds, seeing me opening cupboards to check what other cereal might be on offer.

'I was thinking I'd have some of Rosa's lamb stew,' I say.

'Sounds good.'

'Yes, Christian got off okay,' I answer his earlier question.

'Was he pissed I wasn't here to say goodbye in person?'

'No, I don't think so,' I reply. 'I forgot to buy him his Skittles.'

Johnny looks confused for a moment then realises what I'm talking about.

'Ah, your little groupie bet.'

'Yes, our little groupie bet.' I smile. 'So did you get lucky that night?' I don't know why I suddenly feel comfortable enough to have this conversation with him, but for some reason I do.

'Nope.' He shakes his head and scratches his stomach, showing off his navel again.

'Not even with Lola?' I stir the stew and attempt to look indifferent.

'Ha!' He lets out a little laugh. 'Not bloody likely. She wouldn't go near me with a bargepole. Sadly . . .' he adds, cocking his head to one side.

I feel a spike of jealousy again.

'So when's Christian coming back?'

'Why?' He eyes me somewhat suspiciously.

'I'm just curious.'

'Dunno,' he shrugs. 'Depends on his work, I guess. And whether Clare lets him out of her sight.'

'Has he been with his girlfriend long?' I ask, leaning against the countertop.

'Couple of years. Why?' Again, suspicion.

'I'm just curious!' I overemphasise. Surely Johnny doesn't think I fancy Christian, does he?

'Humph,' he responds.

I serve up the stew and slice some bread, bringing it and the plates to the table, along with some butter.

'What's she like?' I ask.

'Who? Clare?'

'Yeah.'

'Why do you want to know so much about Christian's girlfriend?' His green eyes confront me across the table.

'I liked him,' I tell Johnny, pedantically. 'No, not like *that*,' I add when I see his face.

'I don't know,' Johnny answers. 'I haven't met her.'

'You haven't met your best mate's girlfriend and he's been with her for two years?' I'm incredulous.

'No.' His reply is blunt.

'Why not?'

'Jesus, Meg, quit with the questions!'

I'm about to challenge him, but then I remember my place, which is not to argue.

'Sorry.'

We eat in grumpy silence for a few minutes. Finally Johnny speaks. 'So what are you up to today?'

'I don't know.'

My iPhone rings.

'Excuse me,' I say to Johnny and put it to my ear. 'Meg Stiles?'

'Meg! It's Kitty!' comes the reply.

'Hello! How are you?' I put my fork down on my plate and turn away from Johnny. He continues to eat his food.

'Great! Can you talk?'

'Um . . .' I glance across at my boss. 'We're just having some lunch.'

'Lunch with Johnny?'

'Mmmhmm.'

'You are soooo lucky . . .'

'Anyway!'

'Anyway, anyway, I won't keep you from him, I just wanted to ask if you were up to anything tonight?'

'Oh. No, I don't think I am.'

'It's just that Rod's out of town and I kinda fancy a night out. Do you want to come?'

'Let me check that's okay.'

Johnny looks up at me, enquiringly. I cover the phone's receiver with my hand and tell him. He nods.

When I hang up. Johnny's looking at me with interest.

'Where are you going?'

'Oh. I forgot to ask.'

'I'm sure she'll know all the hip places,' he comments.

And she does. Kitty is taking me to the Skybar, which is the residents' bar at the Mondrian hotel – but it's not just any hotel bar. It's a hang-out for countless celebs and is up in the hills with spectacular views overlooking the city. It also has a swimming pool and is conjoined with Asia de Cuba, the restaurant Johnny took Serengeti to the other night. I agree with Johnny: they should have sat out on the terrace. It's much nicer.

The doorman recognises Kitty immediately and ushers us in. It's still warm and sunny, and we head in the direction of the pool, past a group of gorgeous young socialites, who are chilling out on sunloungers, even though they're fully dressed.

Kitty and I perch upon a gigantic cream ten-foot-square beanbag, and a waitress comes over and takes our order. We opt for Mojito cocktails.

This city clearly has an inclination towards vertically challenged furniture, because, just like the waterbed the other night, it's not easy to sit upright on this beanbag thing. But the atmosphere is relaxed, so we lie back and prop ourselves up on our elbows to talk.

There are three guys sitting opposite us who look like they could be in a rock band. One of the guys strips off his white vest to reveal a tattooed, tanned torso.

Kitty sighs. 'You've gotta love LA,' she says.

'Is this where you're from?' I ask.

'No.' She rummages around in her Gucci handbag and pulls out a pair of designer sunglasses, slipping them onto her face. 'I grew up in Chicago. My family are all still there.'

'Do you miss them?'

'Sometimes.' She shrugs. 'But Rod keeps me so busy it's hard to miss anyone or anything.'

'What's he like to work with?' I ask.

'He's good fun. He bought me this bag,' she says, lifting it up.

'Wow!' I exclaim. 'Was it your Christmas present or something?'

'No, for Christmas he got me a car.'

'No way!'

'Yes way. He got me this,' she holds up the bag again, 'because I fibbed to his fourth wife for him.'

'Oh.' I giggle, awkwardly.

She shrugs. 'I knew she'd find out about his latest affair sooner or later, anyway. And she did,' she adds. 'They just got divorced.'

That's right. I remember her telling Charlie this at Serengeti's premiere party.

'Is he a bit of a lech, then?' I ask.

'No, not a lech. He's always been the perfect gentleman to me,' she clarifies, just in case I was wondering, which I was . . . 'He just loves women. And can't keep his hands off them.'

A busty Asian girl in a skimpy gold bikini and heavy dark eye make-up walks down the steps into the pool. She submerges herself, tilting her head so her long black hair falls slick and wet down her back.

'I can't imagine going for a swim here in front of all these people,' I remark.

'No, me neither,' Kitty replies. 'But if I had a body like that, I would.'

'You're not far off,' I say. I'm not actually lying. She's super-slim.

She laughs. 'Thanks.' She turns to me, eagerly. 'Hey, shall we order some nachos?'

I always thought everyone in LA would be a diet nut and gym freak, so it's refreshing to meet someone who's actually normal when it comes to food.

We call the waitress over and order a couple more Mojitos to go with our nachos. Then we lie back and enjoy the scenery in the last of the day's sunshine. The Asian babe is now leaning out of the side of the pool flirting with the shirtless rock star guy.

'Hello, hello.'

I follow Kitty's gaze towards the door. Isla Montagne has just walked in, closely followed by a group of girls, one of whom I recognise to be Charlie.

'Great,' Kitty sighs.

I'm not pleased to see Charlie, and I don't think much of Isla Montagne either, but it's still quite exciting to be at the same bar as her.

Isla and her group stand at the entrance for a moment and scan the venue. Charlie spots us and turns to say something to Isla.

'Wonder what that was about?' I murmur.

'We're about to find out,' Kitty replies.

Isla and her friends strut past the sunloungers towards some comfy-looking seats with an outlook over the city, but Charlie breaks off and comes to talk to us.

Kitty pops her sunglasses on top of her head and sits up a bit. 'Where's Johnny tonight?'

Straight in with the direct question.

'I don't know,' I say.

'Some PA, you are,' she jokes, unpleasantly. She's tied her hair back into a tight ponytail and it highlights her sharp features.

The waitress appears with our nachos and places them down between Kitty and me on the giant beanbag. She hands over our Mojitos.

'Can I get you anything?' she asks Charlie.

'No,' Charlie glares at her. 'I'm with Isla Montagne.' She stresses the name as though the waitress should know much, much better.

Kitty and I tuck in.

'Is Serengeti still out of town?' she asks me.

My mouth is full and I make no attempt to hurry before answering.

'Yes,' I say, and pop another nacho into my mouth. This tactic seemed to work at Serengeti's premiere with the canapés, and if it ain't broke, right?

'When's she back?' Charlie asks.

I shake my head and continue to chew.

'God, every time I talk to you two you seem to be stuffing your faces!' Charlie explodes.

Kitty, unperturbed, lifts up the bowl of nachos and offers it to her. 'Want one?'

'No thanks,' Charlie says, spitefully. 'I'd only end up like you – throwing my guts up in the toilets later.'

The smile falls from Kitty's face. Charlie storms off.

I turn to my friend. 'What a total bitch!'

Kitty doesn't say anything, but her face is red with anger.

'I can't believe she just said that,' I say.

Again silence from Kitty.

'It's not true, is it?' I ask, startled.

'No!' she hotly denies. But she seems to lose her appetite after that.

At about ten o'clock that night, Kitty suddenly bolts upright on the beanbag.

'Hey,' she nudges me, excitedly. 'Johnny's here!'

My stomach involuntarily tightens when I spot him, sauntering through the crowd.

'Johnny boy!' I hear someone nearby shout. I turn to see who it was and realise it's the rock star type with his top off. Johnny goes straight to him and his mates and they greet each other warmly. The Asian babe, who's still wearing her now-dry bikini, stands up demurely and goes to shake Johnny's hand.

'Who *is* that girl?' Kitty wonders aloud.

'Looks like a porn star to me,' I observe.

'Probably is.' Kitty giggles. 'Call him over,' she says.

'No.' I shake my head.

'Why not?' Kitty demands, and I detect a little frustration.

'It's my night off and he didn't know we were coming here.' I try to sound casual. 'Maybe he wants some time to himsel—' My voice trails off as Johnny turns around and spots us.

'Hey!' he says, coming over.

Kitty beams. 'Hello, again!'

'I didn't know you two were coming here.' He bends down and gives Kitty a peck on the cheek. Even in the darkness of the outdoor bar I can see her blushing. She tries to keep her cool.

'You alright?' Johnny asks me.

'Yeah, good,' I say. I don't get a kiss and try not to look like it bothers me.

The waitress re-emerges and looks a darn sight happier than she did when taking *our* orders.

'What're you drinking?' Johnny motions down at our glasses.

'Mojitos,' I tell him.

'We'll get a couple of those and I'll take a vodka tonic,' he tells her. 'Hey, what are you guys drinking?' he calls across to his rock buddies and the babe.

'Bubbles!' the girl shouts back, merrily lifting up a bottle of champagne to prove it.

'Yeah, make it a few bottles,' he tells the waitress. Then he leans down and flicks me on my bare leg – I'm wearing a short skirt and heels. 'Budge over, Meg.'

I do as he says and he collapses back on the beanbag in between us. Kitty, I know, will be beside herself about this.

'What do you reckon?' He looks over at me. 'Comfier than the waterbed?'

'Just a bit,' I tell him, smiling. 'The Standard Downtown,' I explain to Kitty. 'Where we went after the gig last Thursday.'

'Oh, *those* waterbeds,' she says, then she looks at Johnny and pouts. 'I didn't get an invite to your gig.'

'Aw, sorry, babe,' he says, grinning and slapping her on her thigh. 'Next time.'

I don't like the way they're looking at each other so I'm grateful when the waitress turns up with our drinks.

'Johnny, Johnny! Come over, man!' Hot Shirtless Guy says.

'Gotta go.' Johnny stands up. 'Duty calls.'

We watch Johnny take a bottle of champagne from one of his mates and swig straight from it. I soon remember it's rude to stare and look elsewhere. Charlie, on the other hand, doesn't follow that particular rule of human etiquette because I notice she's staring at us from across the other side of the pool.

'I bet she thinks we lied about not knowing Johnny was coming here tonight,' Kitty says, clocking Charlie herself.

'Mmm, probably,' I say. 'Oh, well.'

Johnny doesn't pay us any attention again for about another hour, and it's a painful sixty minutes, trying to act indifferent as a gold bikini-clad potential porn star hangs off his every word.

I'm convinced Kitty is also trying to seem unfazed, and I wonder if I'm that transparent to her.

When Johnny does eventually come back over to us, we must visibly brighten up.

'Hey, Meg,' he says, half-empty champagne bottle hanging in his right hand, along with a lit cigarette. 'Can you get me a suite?'

'Sure.' I stand up. 'Any particular one you want?'

'No, no, any's cool,' he says, taking a drag of his smoke and wandering back over to his mates. The Asian babe puts her hand intimately on his waist and he bends down as she says something in his ear. His expression is blank as he stands up straight again, but she giggles.

'Somebody's in the mood to party,' Kitty comments, drily.

I glance at her, annoyed. What does she mean by that?

I go to reception and book Johnny a suite, taking the key back out to him. The five of them file off together, and as I watch them go, I feel increasingly hollow. When someone has the ability to light up your insides and just as quickly snuff them out, all by his mere presence, it's not good. Crushes like this hurt. And I don't want to have a crush like this on my boss.

Kitty turns to me. 'I should probably head home,' she says, dully. 'You want a lift?'

'Yes,' I answer. 'That would be good.'

As we walk through reception towards the exit, I feel a pincer-like grip on my upper arm and turn around to see Charlie. She looks wasted. Her eyeliner is smudged and the pupils in her eyes are large and hazy. The sight is not pleasant.

'Is it true Johnny fucked Paola?' she slurs.

'Sorry?' I answer, feeling dizzy.

'Did he fuck her? Is that why she left?' Charlie persists.

I look around and spot Isla and her friends standing on the other side of reception. A couple of them glance over at us.

'I'm sorry, I don't know.' I shudder.

'Have you fucked him yet?' she demands to know.

I reel backwards. 'No! Of course not!'

Then she collapses into a fit of drunken giggles and stumbles over to her group.

Kitty pulls me towards the door.

'I just asked her if she'd fucked Johnny!' we hear Charlie squeal behind us, on the verge of hysteria. The other girls scream with laughter. I follow Kitty out as quickly as I can. The incident leaves a nasty taste in my mouth and I'm quiet on the journey home.

'Don't take any notice of her,' Kitty tries to tell me. 'No one listens to a word she says, anyway.'

I just know I'll be keeping as far away from Charlie as I possibly can in future.

Chapter 10

It's Sunday and I'm sunbathing by the pool when Santiago arrives for his weekly gardening session.

'You're not wanting to swim anytime soon, I hope?' he says to me, kneeling down and pouring chemicals into the pool's filter system.

Actually, it is so hot that I could do with a dip, but never mind. My fifty laps have fallen by the wayside. I think I only ever got as far as thirty-five.

'Have you had a good week?' he asks. 'Been to any more premieres?'

'Sadly not.' I lean behind me and pull the back of the sun-lounger up a notch so I can see him properly. 'I did go to the Skybar last night, though. That was fun.'

'Cool, man. Did you see any celebs?'

'Only Isla Montagne. And Johnny.'

'Isla Montagne. Jeez . . . She's a piece of work, isn't she? A mate of mine used to do the gardening at her daddy's place and he swears she tried to seduce him in the bushes.'

'That's some claim to fame,' I comment. 'Did he go for it?'

'He says he didn't – he's got a girlfriend – but I don't know . . .' he adds with a grin. 'God, it's hot today!' He wipes the sweat from his brow and drags his T-shirt over his head. 'Where's Johnny? He home?'

'No,' I answer. 'He stayed at the Mondrian last night.'

'Do you think I could grab a glass of water from the bar?'

'Of course,' I say. 'I'll get one for you.'

Santiago is sitting on the pool steps with his feet in the water when I get back. I hand him the glass.

'Thanks. You mind if I smoke?'

'Um, no.' I'm hesitant, but I don't suppose it matters if he takes a breather.

'You want one?' he offers.

'No, thanks. I don't smoke.'

Pretty much as soon as Santiago lights up, Johnny slides the glass door open and comes out. Santiago leaps to his feet and stubs his cigarette out in one of the tall steel cylindrical ashtrays.

'Sorry,' he blurts. 'I was just taking a quick break!'

'Sure you were,' Johnny comments drily and gives me an un-amused look.

Santiago hurries off to the other side of the house to do some gardening, I presume, and I stand up.

'I'll get out of your way,' I say, thinking I'll go up to my room and leave him to chill out in peace.

'Why? You don't have to do that,' he says, frowning.

'I don't want to encroach on your space.' I wrap my sarong around me and start to tie it up, but he comes over and puts his hand on my arm, making me look up, sharply.

'Meg, don't be ridiculous. This is your house too, now.' He lets go of my arm. 'In fact,' he says, looking around at the sunny day before us, 'I think I'll join you. Back in a tick.'

He goes inside and I tie my sarong up anyway, feeling too exposed lying there in a bikini. I perch on my sunlounger again, wanting to sit up, but knowing I'll look better if I'm lying down with one leg slightly raised, like they tell you in women's magazines. I reach behind and adjust the back of the sunlounger again so I'm able to lie flatter and avoid any unnecessary creases in my stomach. But as I'm doing it, my fingers slip and the back crashes down, right onto my hand.

'OW OW OW OW OW OW OW!' I yell, trying to pull my hand out.

Johnny appears in a flash and whips the sunlounger back up.

'OW!' Tears prick my eyes as I study my hand. There's an indent across it where it was trapped and it's gone bright red.

Johnny gingerly takes my hand. He's wearing swimming trunks and nothing else. The sight is a nice distraction from the bluish tinge that I now see is starting to appear.

'Are you okay?' he asks, concerned.

'Mmm,' I nod, wiping away my tears with my good hand, while he nurses my swollen one.

'Aw,' he says, gently.

I sniff.

'I'll get you some ice.'

He comes back from the outdoor bar, ice wrapped in a tea towel. I flinch as he presses it onto my hand. If it was anyone else, I'd rather hold the ice myself, but right now I'd rather suffer the pain just to be close to him.

'That better?' he asks after a while.

'Much better, thank you.'

He lets go of my hand and lifts his sunglasses up on top of his head. His eyes look red and sore.

'Big night last night?' I ask.

'Yeah,' he says, glancing at me. 'How was yours?'

'Okay, thanks.'

'Did you stay long?'

'No, we left shortly after you went upstairs. Were those guys you were with in a rock band?'

'Hey? Oh, yeah,' he answers distractedly, lying back on his sun-lounger.

I want to ask him about the Asian girl, but he doesn't appear to be in the mood to talk, so we soak up the sun's rays in silence for a while. It's boiling hot. A thought occurs to me.

'Have you got suncream on?' I ask.

'Um . . .'

'Johnny, you're going to get burnt.'

'No, I won't.'

'Don't argue with me,' I say, reaching under my sunlounger and pulling my factor 30 out of my beach bag. I hold it out for him. 'I don't want you getting skin cancer.'

'Do my back, then,' he says, turning over.

'Er, sure . . .'

His back is warm and tanned, and he has a tattoo etched into his left shoulder blade. There's a noticeable white line just below his swimming trunks and I try to get suncream as close to it as I can, without actually sticking my hand down the back of his pants. He wriggles and pulls his trunks down a little so I can get to his exposed bits. I quickly smooth suncream there and go to sit back down on my sunlounger.

'Right, there you go.'

'What about my front?' he asks, turning over.

'You're perfectly capable of reaching your own chest.'

'Bet you wouldn't mind doing it if I was a member of Take That,' he remarks.

The thought makes me laugh loudly.

'You wouldn't, would you?' he asks, huffily.

'Only if it was Jason Orange,' I answer.

'Which one's he? The little short bastard?'

'No!' I exclaim. 'Jason's the . . . Oh, stop winding me up,' I say when I see him smiling. 'Put your bloody suncream on and stop moaning.'

'How's your hand? Is it any better?' He reaches over and takes it once again.

'Much better, thanks.'

At that moment, Santiago appears from around the side of the house. I instinctively snatch my hand away and Santiago freezes.

Johnny casually puts his sunglasses back on and continues to sunbathe.

As Santiago approaches the pool, he gives me a sneaky, knowing look.

'I hurt my hand,' I explain, but somehow it sounds lame. He sets about taking the pool robot out, ignoring us.

I lie back on my sunlounger and try not to let on how awkward I feel. Eventually Santiago finishes up and leaves for the day.

It's almost unbearably hot, now. I really want to go inside, but I don't want to leave Johnny. I'm sure I'll get burnt if I stay here much longer, though.

'Wanna go to the Ivy with me tonight?' he says out of the blue. I must look surprised because he adds, 'I just really fancy one of their pizzas.'

133

'At the Ivy? Won't we get photographed there?' I ask, heart pounding hard in my chest.

'So?'

'I can't imagine Serengeti would be too pleased to see us splashed across the tabloids. Not that anyone would want to photograph me,' I quickly add.

'Who cares? It's all bullshit.'

'Alright, I'll book a table.'

'Cool.'

Am I really going out for dinner with Johnny Jefferson?

I hurry inside to call the restaurant before he changes his mind. The maître d' assures me he'll have a nice, romantic table waiting for us. I try to tell him that a romantic one won't be necessary, but don't want it to seem like I'm making a bigger deal out of it than it actually is.

When I return outside, Johnny's sunlounger's empty. I assume he'll be back soon, so carry on sunbathing, but when he doesn't return, I decide to go and tell him what time I've made the reservation for.

After living here for two weeks, I finally pluck up the courage to knock on his bedroom door.

'Come in,' he calls from somewhere inside. I tentatively obey.

His room is enormous, and unlike the other bedrooms which look out over the trees in the back garden, Johnny's room runs from the back to the front of the house, giving him a perfect, floor-to-ceiling vista of the city. Black and white photographs of famous rock icons – everyone from Jim Morrison to Mick Jagger – line the walls, and many of them are signed. An enormous bed is in the centre of the room.

'Table booked?' I turn around to see Johnny standing in the

doorway of his en-suite, wearing nothing but a white towel wrapped around his slim waist.

'Yes, for eight-thirty. Is that okay?' I try to keep my voice stable.

'Perfect,' he answers.

I look away from him and, for want of something better to say, comment on his amazing room.

He doesn't answer.

'Okay, then. I'd better go and get changed myself.' I hurry out of the room and close the door behind me.

Then I remember I meant to ask him about booking the car. Damn.

I turn around and knock again. He opens the door this time. He's still wet from the shower and I swear I can feel heat radiating out from his naked torso.

'Sorry, I forgot to ask whether you want me to book Davey?'

Don't blush, don't blush, don't blush, I tell myself as I feel my face heat up again. Bollocks.

He looks amused. 'Why don't we go on the bike?'

'The motorbike?' I ask, stupidly. Of *course* the motorbike, Meg.

'Yeah.' He leans up against the doorframe. 'Unless you're worried it will mess up your hair,' he says, wryly.

'No, no, no, that's fine!' I say brightly and turn to walk down the landing towards my room.

Bess is going to kill me!

After about fifteen minutes spent deciding between two dresses it eventually dawns on me that a dress might not be such a good look on a motorbike. Flashing my knickers at waiting paps . . . That really would give Serengeti something to moan about.

Yes. Serengeti, Meg. You remember her. Johnny's girlfriend.

God, I am being so stupid. As if he would ever bloody well fancy me in any case. I'm just his PA, for crying out loud.

Right, I'm wearing jeans, and I'm not going to look like I've made too much of an effort.

It's amazing how much of an effort it takes to make it look like you haven't made an effort, though, isn't it?

At eight o'clock I exit my room to see Johnny doing the same thing at the other end of the landing.

'Am I alright in this?' I ask, motioning to my outfit.

'You'll need a warmer jacket,' he tells me.

'I'm not sure if I've got one.'

'Actually, I think there's a spare in the garage.'

There is. Riffling through a cupboard, he pulls out a helmet and a dark-brown leather jacket. I try the jacket on. It's a snug fit. I wonder who it belonged to.

Johnny is already wearing his biker gear and he mounts his bike, a shiny black beast of a machine. Pushing his blond hair back off his face, he tugs on his helmet, then he kicks down on a lever and the engine roars into life. He looks at me and pats the seat behind him with a glove-encased hand. I throw my leg over the back and climb on.

'You alright?' he shouts over the noise of the engine.

'Yes!' I shout back.

He takes my damaged hand and wraps it around his waist. I jump because it hurts.

'Sorry!' he shouts.

'It's okay!'

'Hold on tight!'

Hold on tight . . . As if I have any choice in the matter. I feel like I'm gripping on for dear life as he shoots off down the road as though he's just pressed a button to send us into light speed. I'm too terrified even to scream as he takes another corner.

Actually, I take that back. Did that scream really just come from me? I swear I can feel his stomach muscles tighten as he laughs.

As soon as we arrive at the Ivy, flashbulbs start to go off in our faces. Johnny hops off the bike and turns to help me, and I'm mortified as I take my helmet off to reveal that I'm not Serengeti, or indeed anyone famous or worthy of being here with Johnny Jefferson. Johnny calmly takes my helmet from me and hands it and the bike's keys to the waiting valet attendant. I try to smooth down my hair as best as I can, while the paparazzi snap away. I'd dearly love the ground to open up and swallow me.

A picket fence fronts the outdoor terrace of the Ivy and the whole place is twinkling with fairy lights. We manoeuvre our way through the crammed tables to meet the maître d', who takes my coat and leads us to a secluded, candlelit table inside. Johnny takes off his jacket and sits down.

'Alright?' he asks.

'No!' I all but hiss. 'That was really embarrassing!'

He chuckles. 'You'll get used to it.'

I open up a menu and bury my head in it, while he tucks into some freshly baked bread. My mind is racing and I can't take in the words in front of me. Finally I give up and decide to get the same as him.

'What are you drinking?' Johnny asks.

'I don't know, a Diet Coke?'

'You can't come to the Ivy and order a Diet Coke.'

'Why not? You're ordering a pizza.'

'Don't argue with me, Meg. Let's get a bottle of red.'

'You're driving.' I state the obvious.

'You can drive home,' he says.

'No! I can't drive that!' I splutter.

He grins at me. 'Joke, Meg. I won't drink much, I promise. You can get hammered for both of us.'

We place our order, the wine arrives and after a few mouthfuls I start to relax. I'm desperate for our conversation to flow, but I'm struggling to think of what to talk about. I settle on Christian.

'Have you heard from Christian recently?' I ask.

'Yeah, he called this morning actually. Wanted to know if I got up to no good with a hot chick at the Mondrian.'

I'm surprised. 'How did he know you'd stayed there?'

'It was on some tawdry website.'

'Well, he should know you better than that,' I graciously point out.

'He *does* know me better than that. That's why he wanted to check.'

'Oh, okay.' Pause. 'So, did you . . .'

'Of course not, chick.' He looks at me like butter wouldn't melt in his mouth. 'I'm a good boy.'

'Sure you are,' I say, drily. 'So back to Christian. Have you guys really known each other since childhood?'

'Yep.'

'Wow. It must've been weird for him when you became famous.'

He shrugs and leans back in his chair.

I giggle. 'I don't know how I'd cope with seeing my best mate become a worldwide sex symbol . . .'

He chuckles and reaches out to finger the stem of his wine glass. He's not being very chatty.

'It must be so nice, though, to have that sort of history with someone. Have you always been best mates?'

He turns down his mouth and nods his head, then lifts up his wine glass and swirls the wine around. He takes a sip.

He clearly doesn't want to talk about Christian. I don't know why.

'Nice wine,' I remark, changing the subject.

'Yeah,' he agrees. 'So what about you?' he asks. 'Got any friends since childhood?'

'Just one,' I answer. 'My friend, Bess. We met at secondary school, though, so I haven't know her as long as you've known Christian.'

'Tell me about your ex-boyfriend.' He smirks.

I smile and lean backwards in my chair. He leans forward and puts his elbows on the table.

'What do you want to know?'

'Why did you split up? Six months ago, was it?'

'That's right.' I take a mouthful of wine.

'Who called it off?'

'It was kind of mutual.'

'Bullshit.' He grins. 'You finished it, didn't you?'

I laugh, outraged. 'No, it was mutual!' I insist, and lean forward again, reaching for the bread. I can see he doesn't believe me. 'We just ended up being more like brother and sister,' I explain.

He looks at me, his green eyes sparkling in the candlelight.

'It was mutual,' I state again.

'I can't imagine any hot-blooded male having brotherly feelings towards you, Meg. Maybe he's gay.' He winks and pours us more wine.

'Tom is not gay.' I sigh. 'He was a nice guy. He *is* a nice guy. We're still friends,' I tell him, determinedly.

'Friends,' he humphs. 'Poor old Tom is probably just waiting on the sidelines, hoping you'll take him back.'

'Stop it!' I laugh.

'How old is he?'

'Twenty-four.'

'Just a baby. You need a real man,' he jests.

'*I'm* only twenty-four, remember.'

He shakes his head. 'I still don't believe it.'

I don't answer, but inside I'm pleased.

'When was the last time you spoke to him?' Johnny asks.

'Just before I came over here,' I reply. 'I must give him a call to touch base soon.'

'You tease,' Johnny says.

'I am not a tease! He doesn't fancy me anymore!' I insist.

'Whatever you say, Nutmeg, whatever you say.'

'Nutmeg?'

'Yep, Nutmeg. It suits you. In fact, I think that's what I'll call you from now on.'

'Shall I call you JJ, then?' I hit back.

'Not if you want me to answer.'

I laugh. 'Okay, enough about my love life. What about yours?'

'I don't talk about my love life, Nutmeg. You should know that. A celebrity like oneself should never divulge personal details.'

'That's so not fair.'

'Life isn't fair,' he says, melodramatically and sits back to make room for the waiter who has just emerged with our food.

Johnny sticks to his word about not drinking more than a couple of glasses, so by the time we finish our meal, I'm feeling quite warm and fuzzy.

On our way out, I'm determined to see if I can spot any celebs.

She looks a bit like . . . No.

Is that? No.

Wait! Yes! It *is* Ben Affleck!

Before I can stop myself, I nudge Johnny eagerly.

'What?'

'Is that Ben Affleck over there?'

He peers through the crowded tables. 'Uh-huh.'

At that moment Ben glances up and sees Johnny. He lifts up his hand in recognition and Johnny does the same.

The paparazzi are out in force as we walk down the steps, but this time I don't care: the wine has tripled my confidence.

One of the valet attendants brings the bike around and Johnny climbs on, pulling his helmet over his head. I do the same, then he kicks the bike into action and we roar off, flashbulbs popping in our faces. I actually find myself laughing.

'What?' He tilts his head back to hear me.

'Nuts!' I shout.

He laughs and pulls up at a red light. I see a flash go off out of the corner of my eye and spy a photographer pointing his lens at us from a black people carrier.

'We've got company,' I say.

'I know,' Johnny answers. 'Hang on.'

The light turns green and he speeds across the intersection, leaving the photographer standing. I hear the car wheels squeal as he sets off in pursuit of us. At the next intersection Johnny runs through an amber light. I look back to see the driver slam on his brakes. He skids halfway across the pedestrian crossing, but is fortunately clear of oncoming vehicles.

'Bloody hell!' I screech.

'Wanker!' Johnny shouts. He takes a right at the next junction and heads down some quieter back streets, just to make sure we've lost him. It seems we have.

I relax into him as he rides out of the city and joins the highway. I press my face into his leather jacket, the scent of it filling my nostrils. I wrap my arms tighter around his waist.

'Where are we going?' I shout.

'I want to show you something,' he shouts back.

We take an exit and start winding up into the hills. A sign tells me we're on Mulholland Drive, and then I look to my left and get a clear view of the city; the multicoloured lights sparkle in the darkness.

After a while Johnny pulls up in a lay-by and kicks his bike stand down. He hops off and removes his helmet, hanging it over his handlebars. I swivel my legs across and he stands in front of me, smiling as he unbuckles my helmet. He puts his hands on my waist and helps me down, then steps over a low wall and climbs a few metres down the slope. There's a big boulder off to one side and he sits down on it, patting the space beside him.

We sit side by side in comfortable silence for a minute or so, staring down at the lights.

'Sometimes I come up here to write,' he says, eventually.

'Do you?' I ask. 'Doesn't anyone spot you?'

'Not so far. It's quite amazing,' he comments.

'How is the writing going?' I ask.

'Not bad.'

'Will you play me some of it sometime?'

He glances across at me and I wonder if he's going to make a crack about my taste in music, but he looks away again.

'Maybe,' he answers. 'In fact I've been thinking we should get away. Go to Big Sur or somewhere, just take a break from the city.

I need to put my head down and crack on with the writing now, and I can't concentrate round here.'

'Sure, okay.' My voice is calm, but inside I feel a rush of excitement at the prospect of going away with him.

'Maybe Christian would be up for coming over, too,' he muses.

'That'd be nice,' I say. I'd really like to see him again. 'Do you think he'll bring his girlfriend?' I ask.

'I doubt it.' Johnny's tone hardens.

'Why not?' I press.

He remains silent.

'You're a funny one,' I say, smiling. 'Why don't you just tell me?'

He sighs. Finally he glances sideways at me, studying my face. 'Christian and I have a bit of bad blood when it comes to women.'

'You didn't shag one of his girlfriends, did you?' I blurt out.

Johnny doesn't answer.

'You did, didn't you?'

'Mmm,' he replies.

'Bugger,' I say, trying to play it down a little. 'How did that happen?'

'Ah, it was fucking stupid,' he says, running his hands through his hair. 'We had this flirty thing going on. It never seemed to bother Christian.'

Because he trusted you, I'm thinking.

'Then one night I got pissed and came on to her.'

'She could have turned you down,' I point out, trying to make him feel better.

'She did. I was pretty persistent. It was just as Fence were really starting to make waves in the industry. I had a big head. Even bigger than I have now,' he says, self-deprecatingly. 'I thought I could have anything I wanted.'

143

'And you wanted her,' I add, simply.

Silence.

'Well, she obviously wanted you too if she went along with it.'

'Guess so.' He scratches his chin. 'But she seriously regretted it. I tried to apologise the next day, but the guilt was too much for her. She came clean to Christian and that was it. I lost my best mate.'

He reaches down and picks up a stone from on top of the boulder and hurls it down the slope. Then he continues. 'I came back from band practice to find he'd moved all his stuff out of the flat.'

'Where did he go?'

'I don't know. He and his girlfriend broke up. I tried calling him, but he never answered his phone and eventually he changed his contact details.'

'What, he never talked to you about it? Shouted at you? Beat you up?' I ask in disbelief.

'Nope. Nothing. He just disappeared off the face of the earth.'

'Bloody hell,' I say.

'I tried to get hold of him through his parents, but they effectively told me to go fuck myself.'

'*Really?*'

'Well, not quite. But his mum did say I should leave Christian alone. Give him some space. And then things with Fence really took off, we went on tour and I just kind of moved on.'

'God,' I say. 'So when did you get back in contact?'

'Well, you know about my breakdown.' He gives me a wry look.

'I've read a little about it.'

'Well, after the band split I kind of fell into a black hole. It took a couple of years for me to climb back out again.' He says it so matter-of-factly. 'And then when my solo career took off I just always felt like something was missing. I lost contact with the band – that was messy,' he explains. 'And I didn't feel like I had any friends.'

'It must've been lonely,' I say.

'Yeah, well, I brought it on myself, Nutmeg,' he responds, flippantly. 'Anyway, eventually I saw a piece Christian had written for the *NME*.'

'About you?' I ask, warily.

'No. He never wrote about me,' he states. 'But I followed his work for a while and after a really long time, I plucked up the courage to email him.'

'Did he email you back?'

'Yeah.'

'So what happened? How did he come to forgive you?'

'Hmm. I still don't think he has.'

'Seriously?' I ask. 'What, even after you apologised?'

He shifts on the boulder, uncomfortably. 'I never actually apologised.'

'Oh.' I say.

'I know. It's shit of me,' he admits. 'But it really *was* weird. We never talked about it. He was cool straight away, and seemed genuinely pleased to hear from me. And I was so happy to have my mate back that I didn't want to rock the boat by bringing up the past.'

'I can understand that,' I say. 'When was this?'

'A couple of years ago.'

'Wow. That recent? Well, at least you're friends now.'

'Yeah. He's the only person who I truly trust.' I hear sadness in his voice.

'Is he really the only person you trust?' I don't believe it. Surely it's just one of those things famous people like to say. 'What about your family?' I ask. 'Blood being thicker than water, and all that.'

'I don't have any family. My dad always was a fuck-up and a half. My mum's dead. My aunty – my mum's sister – died of breast cancer two years before Mum did. Dad was adopted. Grandparents passed away. Only had them on Mum's side because Dad ran away from home at the age of fifteen. And that's it, really. Christian was the closest thing to a brother I ever had.'

We sit in silence for a while as I take this in. My heart goes out to him.

'Anyway, fuck!' he says, suddenly. 'What are you doing, getting me to talk about all this bullshit. Come on.' He gets up and stretches, looking away at the city lights. I stand up. I want to say something to comfort him, but find I don't have the words, so in the end we walk silently back to his bike and he takes us home.

Chapter 11

The next morning I lie in bed for a while, contemplating the events of the night before. I feel differently about Johnny after he opened his heart to me, and at the moment I don't think there's anything I want more than for him to trust me the way he trusts Christian. I want to feel closer to him. It's not just a silly physical attraction thing anymore. I actually care for him. I'm desperate to see him today.

I go down to the office feeling like I'm in a dream state, unable to concentrate. A call from a journalist snaps me out of it. He wants to know who Johnny was with at the Ivy last night. I laugh and tell him it was me, just his PA. That Johnny fancied a pizza and Serengeti was out of town so I went along to keep him company. It all sounds very fair to me, so I hope the gossip columnists see it like that. I wonder what the protocol is for this sort of thing. Should I put out a statement or wait for people to ask? I Google Johnny Jefferson and am surprisingly under-prepared to see pictures of myself getting off his bike. 'Who's that girl?' one person has written. I clap my hand over my mouth in shock and peer closely at the screen.

'What's the damage?' Johnny asks from the doorway.

My head shoots up to look at him. I suddenly feel shy.

He comes into the office and puts his hand on my shoulder. 'You alright, Nutmeg?'

'Oh, yeah, yeah, I'm fine!' I answer, overenthusiastically in an attempt to mask my discomfort. I'm glad he's remembered the nickname he gave me.

He calmly pulls up a chair and I budge across for him. He's wearing his trademark sunnies in the house again.

'Chuck us that,' he says.

I pass him the mouse and he starts to click. He chuckles at the sight of the first picture, one of me walking into the restaurant behind him.

'You look like a rabbit caught in the headlights.' He turns to me and grins, but I can't see his eyes behind his dark glasses.

'You make me laugh with your sunglasses,' I tell him.

'Hey?'

'You. Wearing your sunnies in the house.'

He moves them to the top of his head. 'Better?'

'Ooh, no, not from the state of those bloodshot eyes,' I say in an overly camp fashion.

He grins and slides them back down again, continuing to browse the gossip sites.

'That is so embarrassing,' I say eventually, and rest my head on my hands.

'Don't be embarrassed,' he says. 'It's fucking funny when you think about it.'

'I hope Serengeti thinks so.'

His mobile starts to ring. He glances down at the caller ID and laughs. 'We're going to have to see about that.' He flips his phone open.

Serengeti is clearly furious.

'Yeah, I fancied a pizza,' he tells her, calmly. 'She's my PA. It's her job to accompany me.' He looks across at me and winks. I smile back at him, feeling like a naughty schoolgirl. If he's not bothered, why should I be? We haven't done anything wrong, so if Serengeti has a problem with it, big deal.

After he's hung up, he leans back in his chair and surveys me. I reach for my diary.

'So, don't forget you've got a check-up at the doctor's at one o'clock today, and a soundcheck for MTV at three.' He's recording an acoustic set for them next week.

'Mmmhmm,' he says, looking at me calmly.

There's a knock at the door and we look up to see Rosa standing there, smiling warmly at us.

'Coffee for my kids?'

'Yes, please,' we chorus.

'Come on, let's go and join her in the kitchen,' Johnny suggests as soon as she leaves.

He takes his sunnies off as we stand up.

'Your eyes really do look a bit painful,' I say. They've been looking like this since yesterday morning. 'Shall I get you some drops?'

'Er, sure, okay,' he replies.

I go and hunt some out in the medicine cabinet and head to the kitchen. Johnny is sitting at the table and Rosa is fiddling with the coffee machine.

'Tilt your head back.'

He does. I hold his face still as I apply a couple of drops to one red-tinged eye.

'Ouch,' he says, blinking furiously. I dab at the corner with a tissue and then attend to the other eye. His face is warm and tanned, and the two-day-old stubble on his jaw rubs against my palm. I look back into his eyes to find him staring at me.

I let go of his jaw and turn around to see Rosa watching us quietly.

'Here you go,' she says, putting our coffees on the table.

I pull up a chair and sit down. I feel nervous for some reason.

Johnny taps his long, tanned fingers on the table and doesn't say anything. I find I'm a bit lost for words, too. I take a sip of coffee.

Rosa breaks the silence. 'How did your concert go?'

I realise Rosa hasn't seen Johnny since the day of his comeback gig.

'Yeah, yeah, really well, thanks,' Johnny answers.

'Did a lot of people turn up?'

'We had a good crowd. Shit, Meg,' he says abruptly.

'What?'

'I forgot. I can't go to the doctor's today because I promised TJ I'd drop round before the MTV gig. Can you rearrange for later in the week?'

'Sure, I'll sort it.' I stand up.

'Thanks,' he says.

I leave the room, feeling Rosa's eyes boring into my back.

When Davey turns up later that afternoon, Johnny's nowhere to be seen.

'Do you know where Johnny is?' I ask Rosa. She's chopping onions in the kitchen and has her back to me.

'He went out on his bike,' she says, shortly.

'What do you mean? Davey's here to pick him up for his MTV soundcheck.'

'You'd better send him away, then.'

'Is everything alright, Rosa?' I'm a touch anxious now. The tone in her voice is making me feel uncomfortable.

'Look, Meg.' She turns around, waggling a large chopping knife. 'It's none of my business, but you be careful.'

'What do you mean?' I play dumb.

'All's I'm saying is, that Johnny, oh I love him an' all, but you don't want to get involved.'

'Rosa, I would never—'

She gives me a look that stops me dead in my tracks.

'Alright,' I say. 'Alright.'

Johnny doesn't come back that night, and the next morning Rosa comes to tell me that he's gone away.

'How long for?'

'Shouldn't be more than a few days. Hard to tell with that boy.'

'Why didn't he call me?' I ask, feebly.

'I don't know, Meg.'

'But he's got an interview tomorrow, will he be back for that?' I feel like a moody teenager, complaining to her mother.

'I don't know,' she admits. 'Perhaps you'd better reschedule.'

I don't understand. Why would he just go off like that? And why didn't he tell me? I feel quite ill.

On Wednesday, there's still no sign of Johnny. After I've cancelled his interview and the journalist has made sure I'm fully aware of how much of an inconvenience it is, I sit there staring into space for a while. I try to pull myself together and do some work, so I log onto Facebook. Johnny's Hotness rating has gone through the roof. I should be delighted, but my heart's not in it. For the first time since I arrived in LA, I feel a pang of homesickness. I wish Bess was here. I decide to call her. It's Wednesday night in the UK.

'We were just talking about you!'

'Really?' My mood immediately improves at the sound of her bubbly voice. 'Who's "we"?'

'Serena and me. I was just saying there's no way—'

'Who's Serena?' I interrupt.

'Oh, sorry, I forgot you don't know her. She's new at work. Anyway, I was just saying there's no way you'd go for a romantic dinner with Johnny Jefferson at the Ivy without calling me to chat about it afterwards.'

'Er . . .'

'You DIDN'T!'

'Well, not a romantic dinner. He just wanted some company because Serengeti was out of town.'

'MEG!'

'What?'

'Why didn't you tell me?'

'There wasn't anything to tell.'

I really don't want to talk about this. Johnny leaving has taken the shine off the whole event.

'So what happened? Serena said you went on his motor-bike?'

'How does Serena know about it?'

'She saw it on Samson Sarky and recognised you from your photo.'

'What photo?'

'The one of you and me by the pool in Italy that's on your dressing table. So what was the motorbike—'

'Why was Serena in my bedroom?' I butt in.

'Oh.' Bess falls quiet. 'Sorry, I forgot to tell you. She was looking for somewhere to live. I hope you don't mind, but I told her she could move in on the weekend.'

'Of course I don't mind,' I assure her, although it's not exactly how I feel. We were always going to rent my room out temporarily, but I didn't expect it to happen quite so soon after I left. 'If she wants to use my sheets and things to get her by until she buys some, that's cool,' I say, feeling generous.

'Sure, okay,' Bess says, and I detect something in her voice.

'Oh, do you mean she's already moved in?'

'Yes, this weekend just gone.'

'Oh, right! Sorry, I thought you meant this weekend coming.'

'Yeah. That's okay, isn't it?' she asks.

'Of course!' I try to sound light-hearted. 'She's already been using my sheets, then!'

'Erm, yes. Sorry,' Bess says uncomfortably, 'I honestly didn't think you'd mind.'

'Not at all. Bess, seriously, it's alright. Why didn't you mention it when we spoke on Saturday, though?'

'Sorry,' she says again. 'I just forgot. Are you sure it's okay?'

'Yes, it's fine. Listen, I'd better go. I should be working.'

'You still haven't told me about the Ivy!' she gripes.

'Some other time.'

I hang up feeling worse than I did before I called her. Sorry, but *no*. I *don't* like the thought of some other girl who I've never met sleeping in *my* bed, using *my* sheets, only two and a half weeks after I've left the bloody country! The more I think about it, the more worked up I feel.

Oh, maybe I'm overreacting. It's not that big a deal. Bess was always going to get a new flatmate. I'm just feeling a little out of sorts at the moment.

I wonder when Johnny will be home.

On impulse I pick up the phone and dial a number. The person at the other end picks up on the second ring.

'Hi, Tom, it's Meg.'

'Meg!'

'Hi! How are you?' I ask, feeling better again.

'I'm really good. How are you? How's your job?'

'It's cool.'

'Are you all settled in now?'

'Yeah, pretty much.'

'I was just talking to Lucy the other day. She said to say hi to you.'

Lucy is Tom's stepsister.

'Did she? That's nice.'

'Yeah, she can't believe you're working for Johnny Jefferson. She didn't want to seem cheeky by asking, but if there's any way you could get her a signed pic, I know she'd really love it.'

I still feel a tinge of sadness after speaking to Bess, but Tom's warm voice is going a long way towards cheering me up.

'Of course,' I reply. 'What's she up to these days, anyway?'

'Well, you know she's back with James . . .'

'What? *No!*'

'No, I'm only kidding.'

'You bastard!' I laugh. James was Lucy's old boyfriend. He was a nasty piece of work.

'She and Nathan have just been over,' Tom tells me.

I met Nathan the Christmas before last. He is a lovely guy.

'Are they still property-developing in Oz?' I ask.

'Yeah. And here, too. In fact, they've just finished a barn conversion in Somerset, and now they're back in Australia, ready to tackle the next project. Anyway, you didn't call me to talk about my stepsister, did you?'

'No, sorry. I just felt like a chat.'

'You're not homesick already?'

'Is it really that obvious?'

'Yes, Meg, I can hear it in your voice.'

'What do you mean? I've been really chirpy!'

'You think you have, but you can't fool me.'

Dear Tom, he knows me so well.

'I hope that rock star is being nice to you,' he warns.

'He is,' I say. 'Everything's been good. It's been amazing, in fact. Oh, you know . . . I guess I just feel a long way from home sometimes. But I don't want to talk about me. How are you? What have you been up to? How's your love life?' I force extra verve into my voice for the last question.

'Funny you should say that . . .' he says, and I can tell he's smiling.

'What? You haven't got a girlfriend!'

'I've just started seeing someone, yes,' he replies, sounding a bit too pleased with himself.

'Oh wow, Tom, that's great. Do I know her?'

'No. We met at Nick's birthday bash. She goes to university with him.' Nick is Tom's younger brother. 'You'd really like her,' he adds.

'What's her name?' I can't help but feel a little empty inside.

'Caroline. Carrie for short. I'll introduce you next time you're over.'

Not a flash-in-the-pan kind of relationship, then.

'When *are* you coming over?' he asks.

'I don't know,' I answer, truthfully.

Bill said I could go back in three months to sort my flat out, but with our trip to Big Sur, recording the new album and going on tour later in the year, I don't actually know if I'll be able to get away.

'Listen, Tom, I'd better get on with some work.'

'Hey, are you okay?'

'Yes, yes, I'm fine!'

'You don't sound fine, Meg. You don't mind me getting another girlfriend, do you?' he asks, concerned.

'Of course not!' I reply hotly.

'Well, okay, then . . .' He sounds unsure. 'I mean, it was always going to happen at some point, wasn't it?'

'Yes, Tom! Seriously, it's fine.'

I know I sound aggravated now, and if I'm being truly honest with myself, I am. It's not that I want him back. I'm not even jealous of his new girlfriend. But I did think I'd be first to find someone else.

Dammit, I must stop feeling sorry for myself! Look where I am! Look what I'm doing! Think of all the people who would kill . . .

I sigh. I guess I'd better get some work done.

I log onto MySpace and start trawling through Johnny's comments.

Someone called Terri says:

Hey, thanks for the friendship! I love you, Johnny!

Jim remarks:

Loved your comeback gig, dude. When are you going on
tour?

Nika says:

Saturday night rocked, babe. When can we hook up
again?

Eh?

I scrutinise the picture. Oh my God, it's the Asian girl from the
Skybar.

When can we hook up again?

This day is just getting better and better.

I'm at my desk as usual the following afternoon when the buzzer
makes me jump.

'Serengeti Knight here,' one of the security guards informs me.

'Johnny's out,' I tell him.

'No, he's not. He came back over an hour ago.'

Did he? Then why didn't he come to say hello?

I hurry out of the office and spot him straight away. He's outside by the pool softly strumming on his guitar. I slide the glass
door open. He stops when he sees me.

'Hi,' I say, cautiously.

'Alright?'

'I didn't know you were home.'

'Yeah.'

'When did you get back?'

'Couple of hours ago.'

'Where did you go?'

'Here and there.'

Okay, now I'm getting annoyed. Is he not going to be more specific?

'Johnny, I don't want to make a fuss, but I'm your PA. You can't just disappear without telling me. How do you think it looks when I have to cancel appointments or people ring up for you and I can't even tell them when you'll be back or where you've gone? I feel like a fool. I can't work like this,' I tell him, reasonably.

'Er, *hello?*'

I turn around to see Serengeti standing at the open door, hand on her hip.

'I've been waiting at the front door for ages! Rosa had to let me in.'

Johnny puts his guitar down and goes over to give her a kiss on the cheek. She gives him an enormously grumpy look, and when he tries to take her hand, she resists, pressing it to her hip. She reminds me of 'The Little Teapot'.

Footsie runs out from behind her, his mouth jammed open with a bone Rosa must've given him from the kitchen. He collapses at my feet and gnaws at it, manically.

Serengeti's glare switches from Johnny to me and back again. I decide to make a hasty exit.

'I'd better get back to work,' I say, walking towards the house. The doorway is still occupied by Serengeti's body. She doesn't move for me immediately, but rather makes me stand in front of her for what seems like ages, but is probably only a couple of seconds. Then she steps aside, hand still firmly glued to her hip.

I head back to the office and take my seat, but I'm still irritated with Johnny. I am, quite frankly, being a shit PA. And I'm *not* a shit PA. He's going to have to keep me better informed.

And yes, I know I'm going to have to sort myself out, too.

'Sorry, Nutmeg.'

I look up to see Johnny at the door.

'It's okay,' I say, both surprised and pleased.

He grins and winks, and then he's gone again.

Chapter 12

Because he's been out of contact for over three days, Johnny and I have a lot to catch up on. I need to know about rescheduling Wednesday's interview, I had to cancel his second doctor's appointment on Thursday morning and need to rebook that for some time next week, and I have a list as long as my arm to run through with him about everything from financing the shoot for his album's artwork to which hotel room he wants to stay in when we go to Big Sur in a few weeks.

I'm also debating whether to show him Nika-the-Asian-babe's MySpace comment.

The problem is, it's gradually becoming apparent to me that Johnny has the patience of a fly, so I have to keep going away and coming back again each time he gets distracted. Today Serengeti's the distraction, and after the third time I've had to interrupt their sunbathing session to ask him to approve a photographer for a forthcoming photoshoot, she sighs melo-dramatically.

'Does he really have to do this now?' She looks at me, wearily.

'Babe,' Johnny warns.

'But seriously,' she says. 'I haven't seen you for a week and a half, can't we have some peace?'

Is this a good time to bring up Nika?

Ooh, let me think.

No, probably not.

'Why don't you give her the day off?' Serengeti suggests.

I really had no idea I had invisible powers, but apparently they can't see me standing here, right in front of them.

'Let her go and do some sightseeing,' Serengeti adds. 'Has she been shopping yet?'

'Do you want the day off, Meg?' Johnny asks.

'Erm, sure . . .'

'Well, then, off you go,' Serengeti says. 'Make sure you check out Rodeo Drive. And go have a look at the Hollywood sign, see a movie, that sort of thing.'

'Okay,' I say. Jeez, she really does want me out of the house today. 'Is that definitely okay?' I look at Johnny.

'Yeah, of course, Meg. Go enjoy yourself.'

'Okay, thanks.'

'Take the Porsche, if you like.'

'The 911?' I ask, grinning.

'Yeah.' He grins back.

'Okay, then!' I turn and walk back into the house.

'Johnny, you can't lend her the Porsche!' I hear Serengeti hiss as I go indoors.

'Why not?' Johnny asks.

After that I'm out of earshot, but I take my time getting ready, just in case he changes his mind. I don't want the pressure of something happening to one of his beloved cars if he's not totally happy about me borrowing it. But Johnny doesn't change his mind. So it looks like he won that particular battle.

I decide to call Kitty, on the off chance that she's free.

'I am *never* free on Fridays, but would you believe it, today I actually am!' She sounds absolutely delighted. 'Rod's on holiday in Australia, of all places, and I've been up half the night at his beck and call. They're like, nineteen hours ahead of us, or something crazy like that.'

'Oh dear,' I empathise.

'Yeah. I'm pretty weary. But I could really do with some fresh air and a break. I think I've worked my fill already today. Why are you allowed the day off?' she asks, curiously. 'Where's Johnny?'

'Oh, he's here. Serengeti just wants me out of the house.'

'He's still seeing her, then?'

'Yes.'

'Shame.'

I laugh.

'So do you want me to come and pick you up?' she asks.

'No, I'm driving today. I'll come and get you . . .'

'I CAN'T BELIEVE HE LET YOU BORROW HIS PORSCHE!' Kitty is screaming in the passenger seat beside me.

'Cool, hey?' Actually, I'm pretty nervous, especially as they drive on the right side of the road here. I'm trying not to show it, and the car is surprisingly easy to drive.

We've got the radio turned right up and the windows down. It's a baking hot day and the skies are blue as far as you can see. I pull up at some traffic lights and the scent from the recently-watered grass on the side of the road fills the car. I feel so happy.

Kitty's taking me on a tour of LA, and the first stop is the Hollywood sign.

'Take a right, here,' she directs me. 'We're going up the private roads to it. It's much better than the tourist route.'

We wind up through the narrow residential roads, the Porsche taking the corners like a dream. And then there, in front of us, is the famous sign, gleaming white on a hilltop.

'I can get us even closer,' Kitty says. 'Keep driving.'

'Wow!' I gasp, a few minutes later. 'Do you think I can pull up here? I want to take a photo.'

She glances behind us. 'I don't know. Let's be quick,' she urges.

I hurriedly unbuckle my seatbelt and leap out of the car. Kitty does the same.

'Here.' I hand her the camera. 'Can you get the Porsche in, too?'

As soon as she points the camera at me I spy a police car coming up the hill.

'Oh, shit,' I say.

Kitty gives me a worried look as the cop car slows right down and then pulls up in front of us. Two hefty policemen in their late forties, I'd guess, get out of the car and approach us.

'Sorry, we were just taking a photo,' I smile at them, innocently.

'I can see that, ma'am.'

'Hey, ain't this Johnny Jefferson's reg?' the other cop says.

'He's my boss,' I quickly tell them.

'Well, well, well . . .'

Is his tone an indication of Good Cop or Bad Cop?

'My daughter is his biggest fan.'

Good Cop! Yay!

'I can get you an autograph, if you like?' I chirp.

The other cop chuckles. 'That'll make up for forgetting her birthday.'

'I'll say.' He turns to me. 'Yes, ma'am. You would be doing me the biggest favour.' He flips over his notepad and scribbles down his address and his daughter Charlene's name and hands it over. Then he says, 'Now, back to business. Do you want me to take a picture of you two, or what?'

No wonder they call this place La-La Land . . .

We cruise down Rodeo Drive after that, windows up, air-con on and Ashlee Simpson blaring out of the stereo. I drive as slowly as I can to take in the sights. This street is so pristine that it could be part of a theme park. There's a horde of paparazzi photographers waiting outside Gucci.

'I wonder who's inside?' Kitty says.

'Could be Victoria Beckham,' I remark.

Suddenly one of them glances round and his face lights up as he spots us. The split second he starts snapping, the others whip around and do the same.

'What the hell?' I say, looking back in my rear-view mirror as a few of them leap into parked vehicles and squeal away from the kerb.

'They think you're Johnny,' Kitty says, excitedly.

'What shall I do?' I ask.

'Nothing.' She giggles. 'They'll find out soon enough.'

The Porsche windows have been tinted so no one can see inside. I carry on driving.

'Where shall we go next?'

'Shopping?'

'Wasn't that Rodeo Drive?'

'Goodness, how much does Johnny pay you?' She laughs. 'I mean proper shops. *Affordable* shops. Let's go to Melrose Avenue.'

'Sounds good.'

'So tell me about your romantic dinner with Johnny on Sunday night?'

'Hey? Oh, the Ivy. It wasn't a romantic dinner,' I scoff. 'Serengeti was out of town and he just fancied a piz—'

'Yeah, I read the press release.' She rolls her eyes. 'Tell me what *really* happened.'

'What do you mean?' I glance over at her, hoping I look suitably confused.

'What did you talk about, what did he eat, is he really in love with Serengeti, do you fancy him . . .'

That last one makes me look back at her in alarm.

'No,' I say, firmly.

I'm getting a bit tired of this question, what with Bess going on about it every time we speak.

'No you won't tell me what he ate, or no you don't fancy him?' She tries to keep her voice light and airy, but there's an edge there.

'He had some sort of chicken pizza, and *no*, I don't fancy him. Sorry, I can't concentrate with these guys behind me.' I pull over on the side of the road and unbuckle my seatbelt. They're on the pavement outside the car before I even open my door. Gosh, they move quickly.

The look on their faces when they realise I'm not Johnny is comical. One throws up his arms in irritation, shouting, 'Jeez! She just cost me three thousand bucks!' The others visibly slump their shoulders and traipse back to their vehicles, driving off again. I get back into the car.

'That's better.' I sigh. 'Now, where were we?'

'Johnny,' Kitty says.

'Oh, yeah.' I look across at her. 'Sorry. It's my day off. Can we talk about something other than my boss?'

She's disappointed, but lets it be.

A thought occurs to me. 'Did you know Paola?' I ask.

'Hmm?'

'Johnny's old PA. Paola. Did you know her?'

'Kind of.' Kitty shifts in her seat.

'What was she like?'

'She was nice,' Kitty replies, non-committally.

'What did she look like? Was she pretty?'

'She was tall. Taller than you. Long, dark-brown hair. And yes, she was pretty.' Kitty shrugs. 'She only lasted eight months, though, which was a bit strange.'

'Yes, that is strange,' I agree. 'Do you know why?'

'Nope. There were rumours, of course.'

'What, that Johnny slept with her?' I remember what Charlie said that time at the Skybar.

'Yeah. I don't believe it, though. Surely Johnny wouldn't be that stupid.'

'What do you mean? Stupid enough to sleep with his PA?'

'Yeah,' she replies.

I raise an eyebrow, but she doesn't notice.

'Take a left here,' she says.

After I've spent the equivalent of two week's wages in the funky vintage-clothing shops on Melrose Avenue, I decide I'd better go home. I would like to save *some* money while I'm working here. It's pretty well paid – maybe not as well paid as you would think, considering my boss is a multimillionaire – but with free board and free food, my earnings will hopefully be breaking my piggy bank before too long.

Johnny and Serengeti are lounging around in front of the telly when I get back and I'm made to feel distinctly uncomfortable by the latter. I go upstairs to my room and cook baked beans on toast in my little kitchenette before going to bed for an early night.

The next day Serengeti is still there, so even though it's my official day off, I don't feel I can just chill out by the pool. I'm reading a book in my bedroom when there's a knock on the door.

'Come in,' I call, and am perplexed to find it's Serengeti.

'I need you to do something for me,' she says quickly, Footsie clutched tightly in her grasp.

'Oh?'

'I can't do it myself because I might get papped. I know it's your day off,' she adds, dismissively. 'But you had the day off yesterday so . . .'

'Okay.' I could tell her to bugger off because I don't work for her. In fact, doesn't she have a PA?

'Don't you have a PA?' I ask.

'No,' she says, raising her chin defiantly. 'Not yet.'

Footsie wriggles in her arms, so she puts him on the floor. He runs to me, yapping and wagging his tail. Serengeti looks uncomfortable. Okay, now I'm curious.

'What do you need?' I ask.

She takes a deep breath. 'A pregnancy test.'

I practically feel the blood drain out of my face.

'Please don't tell anyone,' she pleads.

'Of course I won't!' I reply vehemently, getting up.

'Especially not Johnny.'

'Okay,' I say, hesitantly. 'Where is he?'

'He's in the studio, so I don't have a lot of time.'

'I'll go and get you one right away.'

It's probably not worth calling Davey so I decide to take the Porsche out again. I call security and ask them to get it ready.

Half an hour later, laden with three different types of tests, I return to the house. There's muffled music coming from the studio. I find Serengeti up in Johnny's room, sitting on the bed and staring out into space. I feel a surge of compassion for her as she gets up, pale-faced, and takes the tests from me. She doesn't say a word, but heads into the bathroom, shutting the door in my face.

'Do you want me to wait?' I call.

She doesn't answer so I don't know what to do. I pace around outside Johnny's en-suite for ten minutes before I can stand it no longer. She must know the results by now. These things only take a minute or two, don't they?

I knock on the door. 'Serengeti,' I say, 'are you alright?'

I hear the toilet flush inside. A moment later the door opens and a rush of air comes out with a whoosh. I step backwards in surprise. She dumps the paper bag from the chemist into my arms.

'Get rid of this,' she says. 'Not in the bins outside.'

'Where do you want me to put it?' I ask.

She glares at me. 'You know journalists root through celebrities' trash, don't you?'

'Er, yes, I – I know,' I stammer.

'Well, put it somewhere else, then, a public bin or something. Just make sure no one sees you.'

I turn to walk out of the room.

'Oh, for fuck's sake,' she erupts. 'Give it here.'

I turn back around. Now I'm really confused.

'What?' I ask.

'You can't bloody bin them, can you? Now you've been papped having a cosy dinner at the Ivy with my fucking boyfriend, the fucking journalists will think they're *your* pregnancy tests. And I don't trust you to dump them without being seen.'

I stand there in a stupor for a moment. I decide not to point out that I've already been to the chemist and bought them for her. I don't think anyone saw me.

'Give them here!' she snaps, impatiently, roughly grabbing the bag from out of my arms. '*Stupid,*' she adds under her breath.

I don't know what to say. I don't even have the energy to tell her not to talk to me like that.

'Leave, now,' she instructs me.

I look at her in alarm, then turn and walk out.

'And clean up Footsie's shit outside the laundry!' she shouts after me.

I grudgingly deal with Footsie's accident, mind ticking over ten to the dozen. I can still hear music coming from Johnny's studio, but as soon as it stops I assume Serengeti is responsible.

I listen at the foot of the stairs for a moment, but all is quiet. Then, as I turn to walk into the kitchen to make myself a tea, I hear Serengeti's raised voice. Soon it turns into full-on screaming.

I can't hear what they're saying, but Johnny's voice is raised, too. I try to tear myself away and not eavesdrop, when suddenly I hear the studio door open and slam shut upstairs. Johnny stomps down the stairs looking absolutely furious. His eyes are hard as they meet mine and he holds my stare for all of three seconds before he turns right at the bottom and walks out through the front door. I stand there, unsure what to do next, then go to the front door myself. Moments later I see his motorbike zoom out of the front gates at high speed.

I go back inside.

The door to the studio is shut, and from the sight of Footsie sitting outside it on the landing, I'm assuming Serengeti is still inside. I go back through to the kitchen, heart pounding.

Serengeti doesn't come down again, so I feed Footsie and sit in the living room in front of the flatscreen TV, on full alert. There's no point in me leaving Footsie alone and going upstairs to watch telly in my bedroom. I don't know if Serengeti is going to make an appearance anytime soon.

Johnny rings me at eight o'clock.

'Hi!' I say.

'Is she still there?' he asks.

'Yes.'

'Can you get me a table at the Lounge?'

'What, now?' I ask.

'Yes, now,' he tells me.

'Sure thing.'

'Tell them I'll be there in ten. Better put me plus five down on the guest list.'

'Will do,' I answer. He hangs up.

'Was that Johnny?' Serengeti calls from the top of the stairs. 'What did he want?'

I walk to the bottom of the stairs to talk to her. 'He wanted me to make him a reservation at the Lounge.'

'What, at the Standard?'

'Yes, the one on Sunset Boulevard.'

'Yes, I know where the Lounge is, Meg,' she says, condescendingly. Then she goes into Johnny's room and slams the door shut behind her.

He calls me again just after eleven, asking me to put him on the guest list for Bar Marmont.

'Johnny, are you alright?'

'I'm fine, Nutmeg.'

'You're not still riding your bike, are you?'

'Meg, I told you, I'm fine. Is she still there?'

'Yes.'

Once again Serengeti ventures out of Johnny's room for an update, and once again she goes back inside.

The next time he calls is at two o'clock in the morning. I'm in bed by this stage.

'The Viper Room, Meg. Table for . . . How many?' I hear him ask someone. A girl in the background starts to count and then collapses into giggles once she reaches eight.

'Make it for ten!' Johnny shouts down the phone to me. He sounds absolutely wasted.

'Where are you now?'

'Where are we now?' he shouts to the people he's with.

'Outside Bar Marmont!' another girl's voice shouts back.

Okay, he's still at the same place.

'Johnny, I'm getting Davey to come and get you. Stay where you are. Don't ride the bike!'

'You're a good girl, Nutmeg,' he slurs, and the phone line goes dead.

I have to raise poor Davey from a very deep sleep, but he does his best to sound alert. He promises me he'll be there in twenty minutes. I try to call Johnny back to let him know not to leave the bar yet, but he doesn't answer his phone. Eventually I call Davey again.

'Don't worry, I've got him,' Davey assures me.

Relieved, I drift back into a disturbed sleep.

Johnny calls me again at about 4.30 a.m.

'Is she still there?' he slurs.

'I think so,' I answer, sleepily.

He hangs up.

Forty-five minutes later I hear him come home. Thank God for that. I leap out of bed and hurriedly put on my dressing gown. Before I reach my bedroom door, I hear the sound of a girl giggling inside the house. And it isn't Serengeti.

I quietly open the door and peer out. Johnny is halfway up the stairs with a petite platinum blonde, who's wearing a tiny miniskirt and vest top. She's giggling as he puts his hands on her face and kisses her. I watch, feeling bile seep up my throat, as he puts his right hand onto her breast and then pulls her body tight into him with his left hand. I can hear her moaning as he presses himself up against her.

Christ. Serengeti is only metres away.

Johnny pulls away and they stumble up the stairs, her laughing, him chuckling. He almost trips at the top of the stairs, but he grabs hold of her to steady himself, then pushes her up against the wall and presses himself back into her as he kisses her passionately once more. He raises her top and roughly tugs at her bra to release her breasts. I feel absolutely sick watching, but I can't move away. His mouth moves down to her right nipple and she throws her head back and gasps. Seconds later he roughly pushes her skirt up and unzips his jeans. Oh God, no. Please don't have sex with her right outside the bedroom where your girlfriend is. I want to scream, to tell him that Serengeti is inside. To stop him from doing what he's about to do with this girl. Oh hell, how can I stop this?

Turns out it's not me who has to.

The door to Johnny's bedroom opens and Serengeti, fully dressed and pale-faced, comes out.

'Oops,' I hear the girl giggle, and she tries to tug down her skirt.

But Johnny stays where he is, doesn't move away from the girl, doesn't let go of her right breast with his hand. I see him make eye contact with Serengeti momentarily as she rushes past him and runs down the stairs, and then seconds later Johnny takes the girl's hand and leads her into his bedroom, slamming the door shut behind him.

Oh, poor Serengeti. I run out of my room and down the stairs after her. She's searching through the coat cupboard.

'Serengeti!' I cry. 'I'm so sorry.'

She doesn't look at me, just grabs her things. Tears are streaming down her face.

'Please,' I beg, 'is there anything I can do?'

'I need – need to get rid of this,' Serengeti stammers through her tears.

She's clutching the chemist bag in her right hand.

'I won't be seen,' I promise her. She hands it over and at that moment I feel overwhelmingly sorry for her. She goes to walk out of the door.

'Wait! Let me call Davey,' I insist. 'He won't have gone far.'

She stops in the doorway, her back facing me, and nods. I run back into the office and call him. He's only down the road.

'I'm so sorry,' I say to Serengeti, still standing there in the open doorway. 'Please call if I can help in any way . . .' My voice trails off.

The headlights from Davey's car come streaming through the early morning light. Serengeti walks forward to meet him. He gets out quickly and opens the door for her, raising his hand in acknowledgement of me. He gets back into the front seat and shuts the door behind him.

Shit! Footsie!

I run after the car in a panic and bash on the window. Davey stops and winds his front window down.

'Footsie!' I gasp. Davey looks confused. 'Wait!' I hold up my hand.

I run back into the house in search of the little white dog and find him asleep under the table in the kitchen, blissfully unaware of his mistress's distress.

'Come here, Footsie!' I call. He rouses himself and wanders over to me. I pick him up, soft and fluffy in my arms, and hurry back outside. Serengeti's door opens.

'My baby!' she wails. I hand over the dog as she collapses into full-blown sobs. I gently close the door and stand there as Davey drives away.

As I turn right at the top of the stairs to go back to bed, I hear the girl inside Johnny's room experience what sounds very much like an orgasm. The nausea in my stomach rises up again and threatens to overcome me as I go into my bedroom.

Chapter 13

I wake up feeling exhausted and desperately needing a lie-in, but as soon as my mind starts to tick over I know there's no way I'll be falling asleep again.

I wonder if the girl is still in Johnny's bedroom. I wonder how he's feeling this morning. Probably still wasted.

Is Serengeti pregnant? Will she keep the baby? My head aches even thinking about it. I glance down at the little white bag from the chemist, sitting on my bedroom floor. I haven't looked inside.

I consider calling Bess for a chat, but I don't think I have the energy to talk. And anyway, I'm not allowed to talk about this. Not to her, not to anyone. That would be in breach of my confidentiality agreement. The thought makes me feel quite lonely.

My laps have completely fallen by the wayside since Christian left and I really can't be bothered to go for a swim now. But I know that I should, that it will make me feel better, and even if it's only marginally better, it's worth doing. I get out of bed and drag on my bikini, heading downstairs in a daze.

There's no noise coming from Johnny's room and I wouldn't

expect there to be at this time in the morning. It's after ten, but that's early, all things considered.

By the time Santiago arrives for his weekly pool cleaning/ gardening session, my arms are aching from swimming. I've kept pushing myself on, revelling in the feeling of pain and have got as far as forty-three laps. When I see him I'm relieved to have an excuse to give up.

'Don't stop on my account,' he says cheerfully, pearly white smile practically glinting in the sunlight.

'I've had enough,' I say, just about managing to stifle a groan.

I climb out of the pool and he hands me my towel. I wrap it around myself.

'Wow, you look like you've had a late one,' he says, surveying my face.

I know I look rough. No amount of concealer would be able to cover up the dark circles under my eyes, so it's just as well I don't have to go anywhere today.

My thoughts turn to Serengeti and how she must be feeling this morning.

'Not out again with Johnny, were you?' Santiago asks, cheekily.

'What? No!' I answer, annoyed.

'I saw you in the papers,' he teases. 'Nice, romantic evening at the Ivy last weekend. Get you, girlfriend!'

I look at him, unamused. His playful expression rapidly changes to one of concern. 'Hey, are you okay?'

'Yeah, fine,' I brush him off. 'My arms are killing me from all that swimming, though.'

'How many laps did you manage today?' He goes along with my change of subject until I take my leave and go and have a shower.

The girl emerges from Johnny's room shortly afterwards. I'm in the kitchen when I hear her footsteps on the stairs. She looks sheepish when she sees me.

'Are you okay?' I ask. 'Do you want me to call you a car to take you home?'

'That would be great,' she says, eyes darting around to take in her surroundings.

'Wow, look at that view.' She walks into the living room while I dash into the office to call a taxi company. I can't bear to wake Davey again, not after the night he's just had.

I come out of the office to see the girl standing out on the terrace, talking to Santiago. She's giggling and looking up at him, coyly tucking her long blonde hair behind her ears. I listen, but there's still no sound coming from Johnny's room. I poke my head out of the door.

'Car will be here in ten.'

'Cool, thanks!' She beams at me. 'We went to the same school,' she gushes, indicating Santiago. 'I had such a crush on him!'

Santiago grins, enjoying the flattery.

Later, when the car has arrived to pick her up, Santiago asks about Serengeti. 'Is she off the scene at last?' he whispers, loudly.

I shrug my shoulders.

'She is, isn't she?' he presses. I say nothing. 'Yay! No more cleaning up doggie poo!' he enthuses.

I leave him then and go back inside.

I'm in the kitchen having an afternoon cuppa when Johnny eventually appears.

'Hi!' I say, still surprised to see him even though I knew he'd emerge sooner or later. I get to my feet. 'Want a coffee? Tea?'

'Might have a tea.' His voice sounds hoarse. He pulls up a chair, scraping it along the tiles noisily. The sound of it hurts my head.

'Ouch,' he says himself, as he sits down.

I turn to look at him. He rests his head on one of his palms as he gazes at me woefully.

I give him a rueful smile. He smiles back, sorrowfully.

'That was a bit of a cock-up,' he says.

'You could say that,' I agree.

He sighs, while I pour boiling water from the kettle into a mug for him.

'Milk? Sugar?' I haven't made him tea before.

'Just milk. No, I will have sugar, actually,' he changes his mind. 'One.'

I bring his mug to the table and lift a chair out so it doesn't scrape and hurt both our heads. I sit down and nurse my own cup.

'Want to talk about it?'

He sighs again. 'Not really. Where did she go?'

'A taxi took her home. Oh,' I suddenly say, 'who do you mean? Serengeti or . . .'

He shakes his head, unsmiling. 'I don't know her name.'

'Santiago went to school with her if you want me to find out.'

'Fuck, did he? No, thanks.' He gives me a wry look. 'I don't think we'll be seeing each other again.'

'Anyway,' I move on. 'Davey took Serengeti home, if that's what you were asking.'

'Okay. Cool.'

Neither of us says anything for a little while; we just sip on our tea, then I speak.

'Do you want me to do anything?'

'About what?'

'Serengeti.'

'No.'

'Are you sure? I mean, I know it's not your style to send flowers, but—'

'I'm sure,' he interrupts.

'Oh. Okay, then.'

'Look,' he explains, 'it's over. She was getting too clingy. It had to come to an end sooner or later.'

I get up, feeling disappointed in him even though I didn't particularly like Serengeti.

'What's up with you?' he asks, a little irritably.

'Nothing,' I reply, putting my mug in the dishwasher. It's not my job to judge him.

'Yes, there is,' he says.

'No, there's not.' I turn to him and force a smile. 'Now, more tea? Anything else?'

'No.' He pushes his chair out noisily and rises to his feet. 'Nutmeg,' he says, 'this is just the way I am. I ain't going to change, not for you, not for Serengeti, not for anyone.'

I nod. 'I know.'

'I'm going out on the bike,' he tells me.

'Where is your motorbike?' I ask, remembering he had to leave it last night.

'Hmm. I don't know. One of the clubs we went to should have an idea. Used valets nearby.'

'I'll sort it,' I say, as he knew I would.

'I'll take the Hellcat,' he decides, referring to the other motorbike in the garage.

I go back up to my room after that. The little white bag from

179

the chemist is still on the floor by the wardrobes. I sit on the bed and stare at it, fixated. I know I shouldn't look inside, but the curiosity is killing me. I need to get rid of it.

I pick it up and head downstairs, buzzing security to ask them to get the Porsche ready. I drive it for a few miles, checking my rear-view mirror often to make sure I'm not being tailed. Finally I see a bin on the side of the road and pull over.

I glance down at the bag. Should I take a peek? No. It's none of my business.

But wait a second. Surely if Johnny is going to be a father, it *is* my business. As his PA, I need to know these things, right?

I pick up the bag and shake it. The contents rattle inside.

I need to make a decision and fast. This looks well dodgy parking on the side of the road in a Porsche.

Bugger it, I'm looking.

I open the bag and pull out the first box I lay my hands on. Oh. It's unopened. I pull out the next one. Again, the plastic wrapping is intact. What on earth is going on?

But the third and final box has been unwrapped and I'm guessing now that Serengeti was satisfied with its result. I open it up and slide out the pregnancy test. I hold it facing away from me for a moment, as though *I'm* the possible mother-to-be. And then I flip it over.

Nothing.

The digital display is blank. The test has been used, but the display has gone blank after all this time has elapsed. I violated Serengeti's trust and I'm still none the wiser. And that doesn't make me feel very proud of myself at all.

Chapter 14

Over the next few weeks, I try to force Johnny's potential fatherhood to the back of my mind. It's not easy, even though I'm kept ridiculously busy. The MTV recording gets in the highest ratings it's ever had, and everywhere in the press there's talk of Johnny's upcoming tour and forthcoming new album. I have my hands full, organising everything from photoshoots for the album's artwork, to liaising with Johnny's record company about tour rehearsals, and that's on top of my usual day-to-day running about, keeping my boss well-stocked with everything from booze to shaving foam.

The press haven't stopped speculating about Serengeti and Johnny's break-up. Most have implied it's because Johnny was sleeping around, but there haven't been any pregnancy rumours. I've personally been keeping an eye on Serengeti's profile in pictures, studying the outfits she wears to see if she's covering up a bump, but of course it's far too early to tell yet anyway.

I catch up with Kitty a couple of times for coffee, but luckily haven't run into Charlie again. Kitty and I have become closer, which is lovely, although I do feel like my life in England is slipping further away. I always mean to speak to Bess every week, but somehow the days just fly by, and it's always difficult to find a time when it's okay for both of us to speak and not the middle of the night in one country or the other.

My other friends and Tom have dropped me the occasional email to fill me in on their lives. They've been having an August heatwave in England and everyone has been making plans for the bank holiday weekend at the end of the month. I feel nostalgic when I remember going to Tom's place in Somerset last year. I can remember the taste of the bright orange cider from the local pubs and the cream teas from his parents' teashop as if it were only yesterday.

One day I get an email from Christian, bringing up the subject of Big Sur. It's the first time I've heard from him since he returned to England and it's nice to see his name flash up on my computer. Johnny and I are already booked in to go the weekend after next, but Christian had so far been unable to confirm if he could make it. Now he says he can, so I call the Post Ranch Inn, where we're staying, and ask if they can fit another person in. They have a Tree House available, so I book it for Christian. Johnny and I are both staying in Ocean Houses, overlooking the Pacific Ocean, and after I hang up, I realise I should let Christian take my room and I'll stay in a less expensive Tree House. I ring back the resort to ensure our names are swapped over to avoid any embarrassment when we arrive, then I email Christian back to tell him the plans. I also request his ideal flying dates so I can book his ticket.

His reply email is warmer and friendlier than the last one, having made contact after all these weeks. He thanks me in advance for booking his flights, knowing that he'll receive even better First Class treatment if the flight is booked by Johnny Jefferson's representative. He signs off, teasing me about paying up on my bet. I make a note in my diary to buy some Skittles the next time I'm out at the shops. They have loads of different versions here, too.

Johnny's worldwide tour kicks off in November, so Big Sur will be the last chance he'll have to relax for a while. Bill has told him – and me – that he's not to write any more songs for the tour because 'it'll be a pain in the arse to incorporate them at this stage', but Johnny's bringing his guitar in any case. I don't much fancy being on the receiving end of Bill's wrath if inspiration does strike.

Davey's all set to take the three of us, but the day we're due to set off, our plans change. One, Christian's flight is delayed as a result of a security alert at Heathrow. We have no idea at this stage if it will be several hours or even several days before he can fly. And two, Johnny decides that he wants to drive. He hasn't got behind the wheel of his McLaren for months, apparently. So we agree to leave as originally planned, with instructions for Davey to keep checking up on Christian's flight and bring him along as soon as he possibly can. Johnny and I, meanwhile, try to squeeze as much of our luggage into the very minimal boot of the car and leave the rest for Davey to bring along later. Johnny's guitar goes on the second passenger seat, the one usually reserved for an extra groupie, 'when he's in that sort of mood', as I remember Christian saying. I shudder at the memory of him groping that girl up against the wall. I've been doing my utmost not to think about it, but easier said than done.

Unlike Christian, Johnny is quite happy to break the speed limit, knowing that as long as he doesn't go too crazy, he'll be able to afford to pay the fines. I'm on cop car look-out duty in any case.

We speed along Highway One, a twisting, dramatic two-lane road, bordered by dense pine forests and steep rock cliffs. The music is turned right up, so we don't really talk; Johnny's too busy singing along to a shed-load of artists that I don't have a clue about. I don't know the words to any of the songs, and even if I did, I wouldn't sing. A year of playing SingStar with Bess back home and never getting a score above 'Wannabe' is all the proof I need to tell me I should keep my lips zipped.

After we've been driving for a few hours and the music is starting to give me a headache, I gently suggest we put on some Robbie Williams. Johnny finds this enormously amusing, but after a while he turns the sound off. My expression must've been seriously pained.

'You alright, Nutmeg?'

'Yeah, yeah, I'm fine,' I answer, trying to sound breezy.

'Had enough of my tunes?'

'Erm . . . Maybe just a little.'

He chuckles. 'We'll have a break.'

We're driving along a winding road with green fields on our right and the ocean off to our left. The surf crashes violently onto the shore and there are white caps further out on the dark blue water. Seagulls swoop and glide above the rocky beaches. It looks windy out there. A couple of cars up ahead of us turn left into a car park by the ocean.

'I meant to tell you,' I say, 'I saved you ten thousand dollars on your car insurance yesterday.'

'Cool,' Johnny replies, distracted. He slows down and follows the other cars into the car park.

'What are you doing?' I ask, trying not to feel disappointed at his mediocre reaction. I was super-impressed with myself for shopping around like I did.

'I want to show you something,' he says. 'You'll love it.'

I perk up. A few people turn to look at us as we get out of the car, but no one seems to recognise Johnny, possibly due to his sunglasses.

'What?' I ask.

'Elephant seals,' he says, grinning and helping me out of the car. 'Come and check them out.'

But before we have time to get to the viewing area for the seals, I spot a family group feeding a horde of squirrel-type creatures. A little girl of about seven or eight holds out a cookie and one of the critters stands up on its hind legs and stretches upwards to take it straight from her hand.

'What are *they*?' My voice rises in my excitement.

'Chipmunks,' Johnny replies.

'Chipmunks? They're so cute!' I squeal. 'I want to feed them, too!'

'Do you want me to get you your crisps from the car?' he asks, humouring me.

'Yes, please!' I beam, totally forgetting about elephant seals for the moment.

He returns a minute later with my half-eaten bag of cheesy Doritos and hands them to me. I crouch down on the ground, the chipmunks immediately taking notice of the rustling bag. Three of them break away from the family still feeding them and run over towards me. They stand up on their hind legs, arms stretched high like little children. I hand one a Dorito and it huddles over and munches away happily. Suddenly another chipmunk jumps up onto my lap and I look up at Johnny in delight. He's standing a few feet away, watching. I can't see his expression behind his glasses. The chipmunk on my lap tries to get into the bag, but I gently ease him away and get out another Dorito. The third one bounces up onto my lap.

I look at Johnny again and start to giggle. His mouth turns up at the corners as he crosses his arms.

A few minutes later I'm still there, feeding the chipmunks.

'Okay, shall we go and see the elephant seals now?' Johnny finally speaks.

I really, *really* don't want to stop feeding the chipmunks. That one just put his hand on my finger!

'Um,' I say, hesitantly.

Johnny sighs.

I laugh again as another chipmunk tries to get into my handbag.

'Meg?' Johnny presses.

'They're so cute!' I say for about the twentieth time since we arrived.

'Yeah, I know, but elephant seals?'

I'm so torn, I can't even tell you.

'God, you're a bloody nightmare,' Johnny says.

'Okay,' I say, reluctantly. 'Sorry, little guys,' I tell my furry friends, 'the mean man says I've got to go and look at elephant seals.'

Johnny walks a few feet in the direction of the seals and turns back to wait for me, arms still crossed. He doesn't look amused.

I nudge two chipmunks gently off my lap and stand up. My legs ache from crouching for so long. The chipmunks stand up on their hind legs again, holding their little arms out to me.

'I'm sorry,' I tell them again. 'I'll be back in a minute, okay?'

Johnny leads the way to the viewing platform and stands there looking at the beach. He turns to me and smiles.

'Check 'em out.'

I'm confused. 'Check what out?' I ask.

'The seals,' he says, pointedly.

'Where are they? I can't see any seals,' I tell him.

He takes a deep breath and points. 'There. On the sand.'

I peer closely. I'm still confused.

'Where?'

'There!' he says, frustrated now.

'What, those rocks?' I ask.

'They're not bloody rocks, Meg, they're elephant seals.'

'Ohhh,' I say. Sorry, but I'm completely unimpressed. They look like rocks to me. Or lumps of wood. I glance back regretfully at the cute little chipmunks. They've moved on to another group of people now. I look back at Johnny. He's staring at me, irritably.

'Sorry!' I say, trying to look more interested. 'Wow. They really are something,' I add for dramatic effect.

'Fine. Let's go, then,' he says, turning away.

'Can we feed the chipmunks again?' I bleat, running after him.

He turns back and looks at me in disbelief. 'Haven't you fed them enough?'

I look up at him, meekly. 'No.'

His face breaks into a grin. 'Bloody women,' he says. 'Have you got any Doritos left?'

I peer into the bag. 'Not many.' I shake my head, woefully.

'Come on, then,' he says. 'Let's go and feed the shitmunks again.'

Another car pulls up and a family of five get out. A young boy of about three and a girl of about five spy the feeding frenzy and run towards us in excitement. They're followed soon afterwards by two weary-looking parents and a spotty-looking girl in her early teens. The younger kids immediately scare the chipmunks off my lap, greedy little fingers reaching out for my crisps so they can feed the critters themselves. I look up at Johnny and pull a face. He grins.

'Let the children feed the chipmunks, Meg.' He puts on his most patronising voice. I am so not impressed. Bloody kids.

The chipmunks haven't gone far, their craving for crisps over-taking their survival instinct as the children scream with delight and grab at my crisp packet. I let go, grudgingly, and stand up. But then something to my left catches my eye. The teenage girl resembles a statue, mouth gaping open, eyes wide in disbelief. She's staring at Johnny. I suppress the urge to giggle.

'Mum . . . Mum . . .' she starts to say, arm rising from beside her waist, finger outstretched in the direction of Johnny. Her mum and dad turn to look at what – or who – has got her attention. Her mouth opens and shuts like a goldfish as her finger contin-ues to rise until it's pointing right at Johnny's face.

'Time to go,' Johnny mouths at me.

'It's . . . It's . . . It's . . .' She tries to get the words out. 'JOHNNY JEFFERSON!'

Bummer, too late.

'IT'S JOHNNY JEFFERSON!' she screams again.

The other people in the vicinity turn to look as Johnny stands there, embarrassed.

The girl jumps on the spot in a state of full-on hysteria as tears begin to roll down her now-red face. Her parents look com-pletely baffled; her mum tries to calm her as her dad studies

Johnny in alarm, trying to place him. Johnny attempts an awkward smile.

'Would you like an autograph?' he suggests to her, finally. She nods her head, robustly, still crying.

'I'll go and get some paper,' I tell him.

'No, I'll get it,' he assures me quickly, obviously in no hurry to be left alone with one of his slightly crazed fans. He turns to leave, but the girl grabs him by his jacket.

'Angela, let go!' her dad shouts.

'No! No!' she shouts back.

'I'll go,' I tell Johnny as he turns back to her.

'I was just going to get some paper for an autograph,' I hear him tell her calmly as I rush off towards the car. It's locked, of course.

'Johnny!' I call. 'Can you unlock the car?'

He hastily aims his key at the car and it unlocks. By the time I get back to him he's surrounded by all twenty people in the car park, give or take a couple of very perplexed-looking pensioners.

It takes us another twenty minutes to get out of there, after he's signed his autograph repeatedly for friends, relatives and friends of friends and relatives, plus posed for a few photographs.

Eventually I play bad cop, telling people this is the last photo and autograph, and drag him away.

'Bloody hell,' I say when we get into the car.

'Mmm,' he answers.

'Bet you wish you hadn't stopped for chipmunks now.'

'I didn't stop for chipmunks, Nutmeg,' he says drily as we squeal out of the car park, kicking up grey dust in our wake.

Chapter 15

We arrive at the Post Ranch Inn just after six o'clock in the evening, after winding our way into the cliffs of Big Sur, Johnny taking the corners like a Formula One driver. I've been feeling carsick for a while now, but haven't been able to bring myself to say anything that may quash the look of glee on his face.

I called Davey an hour ago to find out how he's getting on with Christian. He's airborne, apparently, although by the time his plane lands at LAX airport, it will be too late to set off for Big Sur. Davey promises they'll be on their way first thing in the morning.

We have a dinner reservation at eight, so set off to our rooms to settle in. A staff member takes us there in an electric hydro-vehicle, and as we head up the hill and round the corner, the sight takes my breath away. We're high up on a cliff overlooking the ocean. Behind us in the distance are mountains and, in between, rolling grassy meadows and forests. I'm excited about staying here.

I almost don't see the Ocean Houses where Johnny and Christian are staying because their curved roofs are covered with a soft carpet of grass and wildflowers. I wait while Johnny and his luggage are seen to his room, and then it's my turn.

I'm in a Tree House situated just across the pathway. It's a triangular wooden structure on stilts, built right underneath a group of mature trees. My view is of the mountains, and it's spectacular.

I follow my host up some stairs and along a wooden walkway into the house. He tells me the fridge is replenished daily and everything is included in the price, so after he's gone that's the first place I look. Goat's cheese and posh crackers, crisps, nuts, chocolate . . . Ooh, and some wine. I open up a bottle and pour myself a glass of white, before exploring. Priorities, priorities.

The bed is very high and very cosy-looking, and a window in the roof overhead gives me a view of the tree branches, coated with mossy bark. There's a fireplace, with a fire built, ready to be lit, and a window seat at the end overlooking the dappled green trees and the distant mountains. At the other end of the Tree House is the bathroom, hosting a deep spa bath with views reaching, again, to the mountains. I wonder how long it will be until sundown, and decide to take a wander with my wine to watch the sunset.

I come out of the Tree House armed with glass and bottle and turn right, ambling along the path. To my left is the ocean, far down below. I spot a hot tub near the cliff edge, full to the brim with steaming water, and can barely contain my joy at the idea of venturing into it tomorrow. This is by far the nicest place I have ever been to.

There are a couple of people in the tub, but to the left of that is a wooden bench. I make my way to it and sit down.

The departing sun is still so bright that it turns the ocean white. I feel like I'm up in an aeroplane looking down over cotton-wool clouds, or in Antarctica with miles and miles of snowy plains stretching out before me.

'Had the same idea,' I hear a familiar voice behind me say. I turn around to see Johnny, clutching a bottle of red in one hand and a half-empty glass in the other. I hold up my bottle of white.

He wanders towards me and perches himself down on the bench.

'Cheers.' We chink glasses.

'This place is amazing,' I say.

'I love it here.'

'Do you come here a lot?'

'Every so often. Been coming here for a few years now. It clears my head.'

'It's so peaceful,' I say.

'It is, isn't it? Good to get away from the city sometimes. And I love driving on Highway One,' he adds.

'You don't say,' I tease.

'I didn't go too quickly for you, did I?' he asks, surprised.

'No, it was alright,' I brush him off. 'You could have given Lewis Hamilton a run for his money on some of those bends, though.'

'Always wanted to be a racing driver,' he says, at the mention of Lewis's name.

'You're a bit past it now, aren't you?' I helpfully point out.

'Jesus, Meg, I'm only thirty.'

'Yeah, like I say, past it.'

He cuffs me round the top of my head gently.

'Oi!' I berate him. 'You'll mess up my hair.'

He leans across and brushes a strand away from my face.

'Nah, it's fine,' he says.

I look away to the ocean and take a sip of wine, wondering why I feel shy all of a sudden.

I haven't felt close to him since that night at the Ivy. What happened with Serengeti forced me to see him in a different light, but he's been distant with me anyway. Okay, so he's been busy, but I've felt more like an employee than I ever did during the first two weeks after I arrived. I look back at him to find he's still watching me. Then a movement behind him makes me freeze. Three deer quietly make their way through the undergrowth to the meadow grass overlooking this part of the ocean.

'Look!' I whisper. He turns around to follow my gaze.

Two of the deer start at the sound of my voice, running back towards the forest from which they came, but the third, not sensing any danger, continues as he was, nibbling on grass. We watch him silently for a while, until he has his fill and disappears out of sight.

'Wow,' I say in awe.

Johnny looks back at me and smiles.

'You hungry?' he asks.

I consider his question. 'Yeah, I am a bit. Shall I go and get some cheese and crackers?'

'Yeah!' he enthuses, holding out his hand to take my glass. I head off back to my room, and return laden with snacks from the fridge.

I open up the crackers and goat's cheese and cut a slice with a small knife, handing it to him. He, meanwhile, tops up my wine.

'So Christian's coming tomorrow, then,' I say.

'What time did Davey reckon he'd make it here?' Johnny asks.

'Well, he said they'd set off early so I guess the afternoon some-time,' I reply.

'What the hell is that?' he says suddenly, pointing down at the ocean. 'No way . . .'

'What is it?' I ask.

'It's a whale,' he says, nodding. 'Yes, it is, it's a blue whale.'

'No!'

'Seriously, look!' He leans his head in close to me so we're touching. I follow the line of his outstretched finger.

'Oh my God!' I gasp. A surge of water spouts out of the whale. Then another one follows close behind it. 'There are two!'

'Wow,' he says. 'I've been coming here for years and I have never seen a blue whale. They migrate at this time of year,' he explains, glancing at me sideways.

'Are you a bit of a nature buff?'

'No!' he says, shaking his head quickly.

'You are, aren't you?' I tease. 'Super-cool rock god, Johnny Jefferson, at one with nature.'

'Meg, did you just call me a super-cool rock god?'

'No.'

'Yes, you did.'

'No, you must have misheard me. I never said any such thing.'

He chuckles. 'Give me another piece of cheese, chick.'

'You're going to spoil your dinner,' I say, handing it to him and cutting myself a slice.

'Oh, well,' he says. 'Chuck us those crisps.'

We sit there for another forty-five minutes, polishing off our snacks and wine until it's time to either cancel the reservation or go to dinner.

'Cancel it,' Johnny decides. 'Let's go for a swim in the hot tub instead!'

'Okay!'

'We're out of wine. You happy on white?' he asks.

'Yeah. You happy on red?'

'Yeah. So you grab me your bottle of red and I'll bring out my white. Meet you back here in five.'

We set off to our rooms. The wine has gone straight to my head, I realise, as I walk up the stairs to my Tree House. I dump the empty bottles and snack packaging and put my complimentary bottle of red wine by the door, then I dig out my bikini. I put on my white towelling guest robe and slippers and call to cancel our dinner reservation before setting off back to the spa. There are no other guests around – they're probably all in the restaurant.

Johnny is already in the water. He's leaning against the edge, looking down at the ocean. His arms are resting on the sides of the tub, the light from the underwater bulb casting a warm glow across his back.

He turns around, sensing me, and watches as I put his bottle of red next to my bottle of white at the side of the pool and slip my robe off.

'I've just seen another whale,' he tells me, as I walk around to the steps.

'Have you?' I ask, brightly. 'God, it's hot,' I say as my foot hits the water.

He wades over to the other side to pour our wine, turning back to hand a glass to me once I'm submerged up to my shoulders.

'Thanks.'

We both move back to the far side of the pool, overlooking the ocean. The sun has almost set and it's beautiful. We watch silently for a while, my body taking to the heat. The water is as warm as a bath.

'This is nice,' he says, finally, letting out a deep breath.

'It's amazing,' I agree. 'Thank you for letting me come.'

'Of course.' He pulls a face then turns to me, chinking my glass for the second time that evening. 'Cheers.'

'Cheers,' I respond. 'How are you feeling about the tour?'

'Aah, Nutmeg, let's not talk about work . . .'

'Okay.' I look at him sideways. 'What do you want to talk about, then?'

'Do you reckon I could get away with smoking in here?'

'Well, there's no one around . . .'

He gives me a cheeky wink then passes me his glass to hold while he gets out. He's wearing just-above-knee-length dark-blue swimming trunks. He dries his hands on one of the many towels freshly washed and waiting poolside, then rummages around in his robe. He pulls out a packet of fags and lights one. His toned body is slick with water, his tattoos dark upon his tanned skin. I realise I've turned my back on the sunset to watch him and have to force myself to look away as he gets back into the pool.

He holds out his hand for his glass, lit cigarette hanging from his lips. Suddenly I really fancy a smoke.

'Can I have a drag?' I ask.

He sucks in deeply and shakes his head, frowning at me.

'No,' he answers, before exhaling.

'Why not?' I'm a little hurt.

'You don't smoke,' he says.

'I do sometimes,' I tell him.

'When was the last time you had a fag?'

'I don't know, university?'

'Exactly. You don't smoke,' he says, inhaling deeply and blowing the smoke away from me.

I look away from him, annoyed.

'Aw, are you sulking now?'

I look back at him, meeting his green eyes. 'No.'

'Yes you are.' He grins and pats my head.

'Get off!' I brush him away. 'I'm not a bloody dog!'

He laughs and flicks his ash over the side.

'Drink up, girlfriend,' he says, leaning his back against the pool edge and kicking his legs up in front of him.

'I'm not your girlfriend,' I say, mimicking his body language.

'Thank fuck for that,' he says.

'Oi!' I poke him in the ribs. 'I should be saying that. Judging by past behaviour . . .' I add, ominously.

He sucks the air through his teeth. 'Jeez, Nutmeg, go easy on a guy.'

'You don't deserve anyone to go easy on you,' I tell him in my best schoolmarm voice. 'You're a scallywag.'

'A scallywag?' He laughs.

'Yes. A scallywag.'

'That's harsh, Nutmeg. Harsh.'

'Just finish your cigarette before I splash you.'

'You better not splash me, girl . . .' he warns.

'Why?'

'I will make sure you regret it.'

'Will you now.' Oh my God, I am *so* tempted. Do I dare?

'I'm warning you.'

I push myself off the side of the pool and swivel round to face him from the other side, kicking my legs up again. It would be so easy . . .

In a flash, he stubs his cigarette out on a rock beside the pool and puts his wine glass down on a ledge, kicking off from the side to get to me.

'Argh!' I flinch, and quickly put my glass on the side, expecting him to drench me. But he doesn't. Instead he pins my arms to my side, powerfully, so I'm unable to move.

'Try and splash me now, little girl,' he teases.

'Ow! Let go!' I squeal, trying to wriggle free. It's impossible. He's too strong. 'I'll kick you in the goolies,' I threaten.

His response is to wrap one of his legs around my bum, pulling himself into me close, so I'm pressed up against the side, and he's pressed up against me. His face is inches away.

Now I'm lost for words. All I can do is breathe.

He looks into my eyes, unsmiling. He's so close I could count the freckles on his nose. A bolt of desire zips through me and I swear I feel him stiffen between my legs. A split second later he lets go and pushes himself backwards to the other side of the pool. We both laugh, awkwardly.

I turn around and pick up my wine glass, while he leans his arm backwards to pick up his. I think I've had too much to drink. In fact, I know I have, but I'll just keep going for the hell of it.

'Dirty girl,' he says, when he's facing me again.

'*Me?*' I respond, outraged. 'I'm a good girl,' I tell him.

He raises one eyebrow, flirtatiously.

'I am!' I insist.

'Sure you are,' he says. 'I bet no one's ever tried to corrupt you.'

'Hey, I didn't say no one had tried . . .'

'Ha! The boys you've been with wouldn't have a clue about corruption,' he says, knocking back his drink in one. He kicks himself over to my side and pours himself another glass, his left arm brushing against my right as he does so. It takes everything in me to stay where I am. My instinct is telling me to go to the other side of the pool immediately. He picks up the bottle of white and tops up my glass, then returns to the other side himself.

Phew.

I think.

'I dread to think how many girls you've corrupted.' My tone is mocking.

He shrugs. 'I haven't had any complaints.'

'You don't open your own fan mail, though, do you?' I joke.

His head shoots up to look at me. 'You haven't had any letters about that sort of thing, have you?' he asks.

I just laugh.

'Wait till we go on tour . . .' he says.

'Oh, *nice*!' I exclaim.

He chuckles.

'Have you heard from Serengeti recently?' Where did that question come from?

He looks down into the water. 'No.'

I don't say anything and he doesn't either for a little while. Finally, he speaks. 'I think she's seeing someone new.'

'That's good,' I say. 'Isn't it?' Well, I'd better double-check.

'Yeah,' he nods. 'Yeah, it is good.'

'She wasn't pregnant, then?'

I don't know where I'm getting the courage to interrogate him. Oh, yes I do: Hi, there, Mr Pinot Grigio!

'Fuck, no, Meg! Christ. I'm not that much of an idiot.'

The relief is immense.

'Always use a condom,' he instructs, giving me a knowing look.

'Alright, boss, I'll keep that in mind,' I reply. 'So what went wrong, exactly?'

'Good point. One broke.'

Is he really telling me this?

'Bummer,' I say.

'Yeah, bummer,' he agrees.

I suddenly remember the girl he was with on the landing. He didn't look much like he was going to use a condom then. The memory of the sight of him pressed up against her right outside the room where his girlfriend was sleeping sobers me up momentarily.

'What's up?' he asks, seeing my expression.

'Nothing,' I reply.

'Yeah, there is. Tell me.'

'Well, it didn't look like you were about to slip a johnny on little Johnny when you were with the girl that Serengeti caught you with.'

'Nutmeg, were you watching us?' he asks, grinning.

Shit! I walked right into that one. My face heats up so fast I feel like I'm going to boil over.

'No!' I quickly reply.

'You were, weren't you?' he teases.

'Johnny, stop looking so goddamn pleased with yourself. It's nothing to be proud of, you know.'

His face falls. 'No, I know. You're right. Fuck.'

Phew. Good save, Meg. I turn round to the wine. Actually, I decide, I don't feel like anymore. I put my glass down. 'Do you want a top-up?' I offer. 'I've had enough,' I tell him.

'Yeah, we're probably turning into prunes in this heat. Christian won't recognise us tomorrow.'

The reminder that I'll see Christian again soon immediately brightens my mood. 'It's so nice that he's coming!'

'Yeah,' Johnny replies, with less enthusiasm. He wades towards the steps. I follow him out, trying, but failing, not to look at his really rather lovely bottom. He hands me a towel and we quickly dry ourselves off before putting our robes back on.

'Aah, if your fans could see you now,' I tease. 'Super-cool rock god Johnny Jefferson wearing a fluffy robe and slippers.'

'Look, even super-cool rock gods need home comforts sometimes.'

We wander back along the path towards our rooms.

'This is me,' I say, as we reach my steps.

'Cool. Sleep well, Nutmeg.' He reaches over to squeeze my arm.

'Thanks.' I look up at him. 'You too.'

'Early night for a change,' he calls over his shoulder as he heads across the path.

'It will do you good!' I call back, watching him go inside his room, before I walk, feeling a touch dejected, into mine.

Chapter 16

Knock, knock, knock.

Who's that? Can't be housekeeping. I came back from breakfast this morning to find the Tree House spotless and the fridge magically restocked. It was as if little gnomes had been in. I've already decided I want to live here for the rest of my life. Here with the little gnomes.

Knock, knock, knock.

Oh, better get it.

'Hang on!' I shout, pushing my chair away from the desk in the corner. I've been trying to get some work done. Johnny is clearly having one hell of a lie-in because he didn't emerge in time for breakfast. I snuck him out some pastries. Christian is going to love the spread they put on in the restaurant.

I fling open the door to find Christian, the man himself, standing on my doorstep.

'Hello!' I exclaim.

'Meg!' He wraps his right arm around me and pulls me in for

a hug, then lets go, looking down at me. I beam back up into his dark-brown eyes.

'You're here already!'

His hair is a little longer and he hasn't shaved his overnight stubble.

'Just got in,' he explains.

'That was quick! Didn't think you'd be here until after lunch.'

'Well, it's two o'clock,' he says.

'Is it that time already?' I've been so busy working I didn't realise. I'm trying to keep a handle on all of Johnny's emails so I don't have a million to go back to.

'Hey, can I see your room?' he asks, eagerly peering past me.

'Sure.' I step aside.

'That view is amazing.' He stands there, shaking his head at the mountains. 'This is really cool.' He looks around. 'Bloody hell, high bed!'

'I know!' I laugh. 'I could barely get onto it last night.'

He climbs up onto the bed and turns around to plonk himself down on his bum. Then he bounces up and down a few times. He looks like an excited five-year-old.

'Fuck me, mate, I turn my back for one minute and you're in Meg's bed!' Johnny says from the doorway. 'How many times do I have to tell you to keep your hands off my staff?'

Christian jumps off the bed and they engulf each other in a big bear hug, laughing.

'Hey,' Johnny says. 'Good to see you. Journey okay?'

'Yeah, in the end. Fucking queues at Heathrow. Nightmare.'

'Nightmare,' Johnny agrees, then his face breaks into a grin. 'Private jet when we go on tour in six weeks.' He nudges Christian on the shoulder.

'Wicked.' Then Christian says excitedly, 'Hey, did you check out the elephant seals on the way here?'

Johnny gives me a pointed look. 'Did we check out the elephant seals on our way here, Meg?'

'Um,' I answer, comically looking left, right and left again.

'Nah,' Johnny says, 'we didn't get to fully appreciate the elephant seals because this one 'ere was too busy feeding the fucking chipmunks.'

Christian laughs. 'They were pretty cute, too.'

'See? See?' I say to Johnny.

'Mate!' Johnny berates. 'You're letting the side down!'

'Ah, sorry,' Christian responds.

'Fuck me, Meg, high bed,' Johnny says suddenly.

'I know!' Christian practically shouts.

Johnny goes and climbs onto it and Christian follows, both turning around and bouncing up and down like little boys.

'Sorry, how old are you?' I ask.

They laugh and get off.

'Have you had lunch yet?' Christian asks us.

'I haven't even had fucking breakfast yet,' Johnny responds.

'You never have breakfast,' I chide.

'Good point.'

'I did get you some pastries, though,' I offer.

He smiles at me, warmly. 'No thanks, Nutmeg. Shall we go and get a bite to eat?' he says to Christian.

'Yeah, that'd be great,' his friend replies.

'You coming, Meg?' Johnny asks.

'Um, I might just carry on with some work here,' I respond, figuring it might be nice to let them have some time alone before I gatecrash their party.

'Okay. You sure?' he checks.

'Yes. Thank you.'

They head out through the door.

I carry on working for a couple of hours and then picture approval comes in from one of the magazines Johnny had done a photoshoot for recently. The art editor has sent PDFs of the page. We've already approved the copy, but it always interests me to see the pages laid out.

The photographs are amazing. The first shot is of Johnny standing front on, staring moodily into the camera. You can clearly see the definition of his torso underneath his vest. I click down a page. This one is a close-up. I feel like his clear green eyes are infiltrating me, and I sit there for a moment just studying them. His lips are perfectly shaped, not too thin, not too full.

Oh God, I fancy him. I still do. Even though he's a total bastard to women. I just can't help it.

Hey, where are his freckles? There are none on his nose. When I first met him I wondered why I'd never noticed them in photos.

Anyway, where are those boys? I haven't seen them since they left for lunch a couple of hours ago.

I don't have to get back to the art editor about approval until tomorrow, so I decide to take a break and go for a wander, see if I can spot Johnny and Christian.

I find them down on the bench that Johnny and I were sitting on last night. Christian has his notepad in front of him and is writing. Johnny is leaning forward on the bench, elbows resting on his knees, smoking a cigarette. I wonder if I should bother them, but Johnny looks up and nods at me. Christian turns around and smiles, so I wander over.

'How's it going?' I ask.

'Good, good,' Christian responds. 'Just catching up on what's been happening lately.'

'Cool,' I reply. 'I was just going to go for a walk. Johnny, that picture approval has come in. Shall I bring it along to dinner?'

'Yeah, yeah. That's fine, Meg.'

I head off around the corner where there's a forest full of enormous redwood pines, situated on a steep decline. I venture into the darkness and am soon lost in my own thoughts again.

I didn't sleep well last night. My head was spinning and I was more drunk than I'd realised. I couldn't get Johnny out of my mind. The sight of him almost naked in the pool, the feeling of his body pressed up against mine . . . I went down to breakfast this morning feeling on edge, turning my head every time another person entered the room. But he never showed up. I didn't know how he'd be with me, but when he appeared in my room he was fine. Totally normal. Just like he was with Christian.

I feel a bit foolish. He probably didn't think twice about our hot-tub encounter. I'm sure I'm making more out of it than I ever should.

But I am so attracted to him.

I stand there in the forest for a moment and close my eyes, listening to the far-off chirping of birds.

He was so close. I imagine putting my hands on his chest, slick and wet from the water. Touching his bare stomach. I open my eyes, feeling feverish and off balance. I wave my hand in front of my face to cool myself down, and keep walking.

That evening I spend extra time on my appearance. I decide on a black dress and tie my hair partially away from my face. I don't overdo my make-up, but keep it soft and simple, just vamping up my eyes with a little black kohl.

I don't want to be the first person to arrive at the table, but by the time seven twenty-five appears on my watch, I can stand it no longer. I'm completely anal when it comes to punctuality. I can just about handle other people being late, but I can't bear it if I'm the offender.

Of course, I *am* the first to arrive. The waiter seats me in the middle, leaving chairs for each of the boys on either side of me. We're on a square table, facing the water, with the cliff dropping away beneath us.

I study the ocean in case I can spot another whale, while the waiter brings over the wine menu and suggests some options for tonight.

Christian appears next.

'You look nice,' he remarks as he sits down.

'Thanks. You too.' A waiter appears to pour the wine. 'So what have you been up to?' he asks.

Soon I relax back into his company, which is just as well, because Johnny doesn't appear for another half an hour. By that time, Christian and I have made our way through half a bottle of wine and a basket of bread and butter.

He doesn't explain why he's late and we don't ask.

We place our food order because Christian claims he's starving, and then Johnny asks me if I've brought the pictures. I have. I pull my laptop out of my bag.

He studies them for a minute, while Christian and I wait patiently, and then finally nods and says, 'Cool.'

'Can I have a look?' Christian asks. Johnny passes over the laptop.

'What's happened to your freckles?' I ask Johnny, motioning towards the computer. 'Where are they?'

He looks a little embarrassed.

'Airbrushing,' Christian says. 'You know, touching up. Getting rid of any little imperfections, clearing up skin tone, making Johnny look hotter than he actually is . . .'

He says 'hotter than he actually is' in a joking tone.

'But why get rid of your freckles?' I press.

Johnny shrugs.

'Do you like his freckles, Meg?' Christian teases.

'Yeah,' I say in a small voice. 'I do.'

'Aah . . .' Johnny leans across and rubs my arm affectionately. Christian just laughs and closes the laptop.

The night wears on. I'm stuffed by the third course (there are five in total) but still manage to squeeze in dessert, whereas Christian has been tucking in with gusto and Johnny has been tasting each dish, happy to leave at least half of it on his plate.

I know I should head off to my room and leave the two friends alone, but when I flag up that idea, they're having none of it.

'Fuck that, Meg,' Christian says, 'let's go to the hot tub!'

'Um . . .' I hesitate. Out of the corner of my eye I see Johnny glance at me.

'Go on,' Christian urges. 'She can't go to bed, can she, mate?'

Johnny shrugs.

'No, really.' I try to be strong. 'I could do with an early night. Anyway, it's too cold for the hot tub tonight.'

It *is* colder tonight. I think we were lucky yesterday.

'It's called a "hot tub" for a reason, you know,' Christian says.

'I know,' I reply. 'But, sorry, the idea of going back to my room, lighting the fire and climbing into bed with a book is very inviting indeed.'

'Alright,' Johnny says, putting an end to the discussion and turning to his mate. 'What are we drinking?'

I set off for my room, leaving them to it.

An hour and a half later, I'm lying in bed on my side, watching the log fire crackling. The hearth doesn't pass out much heat, but the scent of the burning wood fills the room and I'm so relaxed and content that I can hardly concentrate on my book.

A knock on my door snaps me out of my reverie.

'Hello?' I call, reluctant to get out of my nice, warm and very high bed.

'Open up!' comes the sound of Christian's voice.

What does he want at this hour?

'Open up!' comes Johnny's voice.

Oh dear, they both sound a bit pissed. This could be funny. I get out of bed and look for my dressing gown, realising I've left it in the bathroom at the other end of the Tree House. I quickly unlatch the door wearing only my pyjamas and run back to my bed, shouting over my shoulder, 'Quick! I'm freezing!'

'Sorry, Nutmeg.' Johnny tries to sound sober as he leans against the doorframe to my bedroom. 'Didn't think you'd be in bed already.'

Christian pushes past him, clutching a bottle of champagne and three glasses. 'Have a drink with us!' he all but shouts.

I'm pretty sober now, so having a couple of piss-heads crash my solo slumber party could be considered annoying. But, truthfully, I'm thrilled that they're here.

'Come on, then.' I pat the bed.

Christian tries to get a leg up, but stumbles backwards and almost bashes into the fireplace.

'Give 'em here.' I hold out my hands for the bottle and glasses.

Unencumbered, he has more luck, but he's still remarkably ungainly. I watch, laughing, while Johnny just stands in the doorway, looking amused. He seems a bit more together than his pal.

'Come on, mate,' Christian beckons for Johnny to get up. He does so with substantially more grace, lying down on his side behind Christian and alongside me, and propping his head up with his arm. I'm sitting up against the wall, cross-legged, under the covers, and Christian is sitting at my feet with his legs hanging off the side.

'Nice swim?' I ask, nodding towards Christian's fluffy robe. I glance at Johnny – his has fallen open at the chest. I look away quickly.

'Yep, yep,' Christian says, waggling his hands at me and looking eagerly at the champagne bottle I'm still holding.

'Don't you pop that cork and get it all over my bedspread,' I warn, handing it over.

'I will endeavour not to pop my cork all over your bedspread . . .' Christian assures me with a grin as Johnny starts to guffaw.

'Oh, for God's sake,' I berate, 'you two are like teenagers.'

Still looking pleased at his own wit, Christian cracks open the champagne and starts to pour it, deftly, into the three glasses. I've already cleaned my teeth. Oh, well.

'You look different without make-up on,' Christian observes.

'You've seen me without my make-up on before,' I remind him. 'Last time, when I was doing my laps in the morning.'

'Oh, yeah,' he says. 'Have you finished the box of Fruity Pebbles yet? I could really do with some of those right now, actually,' he continues, not waiting for me to answer the question.

'You two and your Fruity Pebbles,' Johnny chips in.

'Hey, what about my bet?' Christian exclaims, suddenly.

'I haven't forgotten,' I reply. 'In fact, if you pass me my bag over there I can settle up immediately.'

Christian groans. 'Bag over where?'

'Over there,' I point. 'That one.'

'Can't get down,' he says, sorrowfully.

'Oh, for goodness' sake,' I huff and get out of bed, bringing two bags of sweets back with me. I chuck them on Christian's lap and climb back up under the covers.

Johnny sits up beside me, moving closer and pulling his robe across his chest. 'Brr.'

'Are you cold?' I ask.

He nods, quickly. 'Can I get under the covers, too?' he asks.

'Oi, oi!' Christian grins.

'Fuck off, mate,' Johnny replies.

'Are your swimming trunks dry?' I ask.

He nods.

'Go on, then.'

Johnny jumps off the bed, strips out of his robe and climbs back in again.

'That is so not fair,' Christian says, shaking his head, unimpressed at the sight of us both, warm and dry under the covers.

I'm struck again by how different these two friends are. Johnny is so gorgeous, I wonder if it's hard being friends with him. Christian's not bad-looking, but he's kind of ordinary. He doesn't look like he's ever seen the inside of a gym in his life, and he certainly hasn't spent any time lying in the sun recently, judging by those pasty-coloured forearms. Bless him.

'Are you sure you're dry?' I ask Johnny again, trying to sound like I'm not in the least bit fazed about the fact that he's moved quite a bit closer to me.

'Yeah,' he nods. 'Have a feel.' He takes my hand and slips it under the covers to touch the fabric of his swimming trunks. I'm so taken aback that I don't even register if they're damp or not.

'Jesus, mate!' Christian shouts. 'Get off her!'

Johnny laughs and lets go and I attempt to laugh too as I put my hand back up above the bedspread. I'm glad this room is lit by firelight; at least no one will notice me blushing.

Christian studies the two bags of Skittles I've bought him.

'Tropical and Original,' he muses. 'Good choice, Megan.'

I laugh. 'My name's not Megan.'

'It's not Nutmeg, either,' he says, 'but you let him get away with it.'

I say nothing. Christian busies himself opening the packets. I feel Johnny edge a little closer to me in the bed. His warm arm brushes against mine, sending a shiver ricocheting through me.

Christian pours the sweets from the two bags out onto the bedspread in two neat little piles.

'Strawberry,' he notes, munching away.

'Pass me one.' I lean forward. He does.

'Johnny?' I ask. He shakes his head.

'Johnny doesn't *get* sweets,' Christian says, rummaging around for a purple one.

'I do,' Johnny says.

'Favourite confectionery?' Christian challenges him.

Johnny considers this for a moment before answering, 'After Eight Mints.'

This sends Christian into hysterics. 'I forgot you loved those things. Man, your sweetie age is ninety. You are such a grandma.'

I suppress a giggle. 'Favourite flavour?' I ask Christian, not wanting to make fun of Johnny.

He calms down surprisingly quickly considering the mayhem, then answers, 'In order of favourite to least favourite, I'd have to say . . . Okay, Original Skittles: grape, strawberry, lime, orange and lemon.'

'Me too!' I sit forward. 'Well, maybe strawberry before grape, but close. What about Tropical?'

He picks one up and starts to chew. 'I can't work out the flavours for these ones.'

'Give me the packet,' I say.

'That's cheating!' But he complies.

'Kiwi lime, banana berry, what the hell is mango tangelo?' I ask.

'Fuck knows.'

'Just do colours,' I decide.

'Right,' he says, sampling each one. Johnny yawns beside me. 'Yellow, blue, pink, green and orange.'

'Let me have a go,' I say. He passes me a handful.

'Yeah,' I say a minute later. 'I'd have to agree. Banana first . . .'

I hear Johnny sigh behind me and realise we're leaving him out.

'Anyway, enough sweetie talk,' I say, leaning back against my pillows again. My arm rubs hard against Johnny's warm bicep – he appears to have moved in even closer. He wriggles a little to make room for me, but snuggles back in close. How strange.

Christian lies on his back, looking up at the ceiling.

'Want a top-up?' Johnny asks me quietly.

'Sure.' He pours in more fizzing champagne.

'Yep!' Christian enthuses, propping himself up slightly and offering up his glass.

'So, mate,' Johnny says. 'How's Clare?'

Christian looks down at his glass and takes a big gulp. 'Wouldn't know,' he replies. 'We split up.'

Johnny sits up straighter. 'Have you?'

'Yep.' Christian hiccups.

'Shit,' Johnny says.

'Yep.' Christian hiccups again, then takes another gulp.

'Why . . . How did that happen?' Johnny asks.

His friend just shrugs.

'Sorry to hear that,' I say, gently, for want of something better to say.

'Why? You never met her,' Christian points out. 'Nor, for that matter, did you,' he says to Johnny.

Neither of us says anything. Christian laughs, awkwardly. 'Ah, it was just one of those things,' he explains. 'Wasn't meant to be.' He hiccups again. 'We should go to bed,' he says to Johnny. 'Let Meg get some sleep.'

'Can't I just sleep here?' Johnny wriggles further down underneath the covers. His leg brushes mine.

'No!' Christian insists. 'Get your arse out of poor Megan's bed.'

I giggle. 'My name's not Megan!' I tell him again.

'Can I sleep here, Nutmeg?' Johnny looks up at me pleadingly with his beautiful green eyes.

Oh my God, he is such a flirt. Is he like this with everyone? Probably.

'No, you can't,' I tell him, laughing.

'Please?' He wriggles closer to me and drapes his leg over my leg under the covers. Christian leaps off the bed and pulls the covers back.

'For fuck's sake, mate, get off her!'

'No!' Johnny protests, jokingly.

Christian all but drags him out of the bed, while Johnny tries not to spill the remaining dregs in his champagne glass.

'Apologise to your PA!' Christian insists.

Johnny looks comically repentant.

'Apologise, I said!' Christian shouts again. I'm giggling now.

'I'm cold,' Johnny moans, hopping from foot to foot at the side of my bed, wearing nothing but swimming trunks. 'Please can I get back in?'

'No!' Christian shouts. 'Put your fucking robe on, you git.'

Johnny grudgingly puts it back on and looks mournfully at the space he's just exited.

It's funny how all of a sudden you can be struck with the absurdity of a situation. Johnny Jefferson wants to sleep in my bed. With me! How nuts is that?

Christian drags Johnny around to the other side of the bed in the direction of the door.

'We'll leave you in peace,' he tells me, pushing Johnny out in front of him.

'Okay. Night,' I say, smiling.

'Night night,' Johnny calls from the doorway.

'Oh.' Christian comes back and sweeps the remaining Skittles off my bed and into his hands. He pulls out a few yellow ones and puts them on my bedside table.

'Come on, then!' Johnny calls from behind him.

'I hope they're banana and not lemon,' he says.

'I hope so too,' I say, super-seriously.

'Night.' He smiles down at me and I up at him.

Johnny comes back into the room and tugs Christian away from the bed, pushing him out into the hall.

'Bye, Nutmeg,' he says, looking down at me.

'Bye!' I reply, cheerfully.

Then he bends down and gives me a kiss right on my lips, eyes twinkling as he turns and leaves, slamming the door shut behind him.

'I'm wasted!' I hear Christian exclaim, as they set off down the steps outside my Tree House.

Shocked, I put my finger on the place where I can still feel Johnny's lips, and lie there, unsmiling, looking at the leaves rustling in the moonlight through the window above my bed.

Chapter 17

I knew Johnny was famous – of course I did – but it's clear I've been living in a bubble for the last few months because this, my friends, is ridiculous.

We're in Vienna to kick off the European leg of his tour, and the crowds that have gathered to see him arrive at the airport are nothing short of phenomenal. This is like nothing I've ever experienced before – and I would say ever will again, but no doubt it will be the same in the next city.

Johnny is big in America. He's big everywhere in the world. But in Los Angeles, the general public are so much more accustomed to seeing major celebrities that they don't tend to go completely and utterly bonkers on the street.

In Europe, though, it's a different story. The flashbulbs going off are enough to blind me, and as for the screams, industrial earplugs wouldn't help. I'm being thrust through the gangway by security guards who are three times my width. Johnny is up ahead, looking cool as a cucumber in Lapland with his dark shades and rock star swagger.

When I see him like this, I can scarcely believe I know him. It's a reality check of the highest order. I see him at home, out by the pool with his guitar or in the kitchen in his boxer shorts, and then he's just Johnny, a thirty-year-old bloke from Newcastle who happens to be my, albeit very attractive, boss.

He's been distant with me since we got back from Big Sur a month and a half ago. My memory of the night that we were in the hot tub together has a strange surreal quality, and I remember the next night, the one when he kissed me goodnight, almost as though I'd imagined it.

The following day it had been business as usual. He was preoccupied with Christian and the book, and I cracked on with work. We left the day after. Davey came to collect me, and Johnny decided to head to San Francisco for a couple of days with Christian. It was a bizarre end to a bizarre stay, all in all. And when he came back it was like he was another person, professional and to the point. Very weird. I just put my head down and worked hard to help get things ready for the tour.

We're staying in a five-star hotel in Vienna city centre. I've gone on ahead in another car to make sure the security team is in place and to ensure Johnny is able to go straight to his room. The location is supposed to be private, but that is an absolute joke. There must be at least two hundred fans waiting outside. They scream as we pull up. Johnny's not even here so I can't imagine the frenzy that will arise when he does appear. I call his security team to warn them and then go inside, but I know now we can't stay here for long. I'll need to find us another hotel and fast.

Security do their best to hold back the hordes when Johnny arrives ten minutes later, but I can see from inside that he's getting bashed from all sides as fans reach out and try to grab a piece of him, whether that be his hair, shades, T-shirt, anything. I watch and cringe, wanting to do something to help, but it's impossible. He's seriously pissed off by the time he reaches the lobby, which thankfully is secure.

'We're going to have to move to another hotel,' he tells me.

'I've already sorted it.'

He nods, curtly.

'Come up to your room now, though,' I say. 'We can't move yet without getting tailed.'

He follows me without speaking as I lead the way.

The screams down on the street below are deafening.

'*Johnny, Johnny, JOHNNY!*'

The chanting gets louder and louder. They want to see their idol.

Johnny sits on the bed and puts his head in his hands. I'm worried about him.

There are too many people in the room. Hotel manager, wardrobe team, a couple of band members, Bill . . . Johnny gives me a pointed look so I politely gather together the overexcited crew and usher them towards the door. Bill looks irritated at the forced exit, but he must be familiar enough with Johnny to know that he needs some space.

I close the door behind them and turn to look at my boss.

'Are you okay?'

He nods, but doesn't speak. He's been like this for weeks and I'm not quite sure what to do other than try to support him as best I can. He seems to have withdrawn into himself. I stupidly thought it might've been me, but that was arrogance of excruciating heights. I'm glad I never told anyone about what happened in Big Sur.

What happened in Big Sur. Ha! What a joke. Nothing happened, Meg, that's the point.

Bess wanted all the juicy details, of which I told her there were none. She's been distant with me, too. It's hard with this confidentiality agreement. Bess doesn't understand it, but I literally have my hands tied. Serengeti-gate was a nightmare. Bess wanted to know why Johnny and Serengeti had split up, but I couldn't even skim the surface, let alone tell her about Johnny shagging that girl . . . Urgh. It still makes me feel ill. Anyway, Bess thinks I don't trust her and there's nothing I can do or say to make her think differently.

Kitty, at least, doesn't question me. She doesn't gossip about Rod, either. If one of us is down about work, it's comforting to know the other understands without being forced to go into details.

My life in England now seems so very far away.

Behind me Johnny lies back on the bed, hands still covering his face. There's such a stark difference to him here, now, compared to how he was with Christian talking about the private jet six weeks ago. He was so excited about the tour then. Now he seems almost numb to it. I wonder if he's depressed. Is this what depression is like? I'll talk to Bill, ask if this is normal for Johnny on tour. The last thing I want is for him to have another breakdown like the one he had years ago. That was well documented in the tabloids. I make a decision to call a doctor when we move to the next hotel.

'Johnny?' I say, quietly. 'Is there anything I can do?'

He takes his hands off his face and tucks them behind his head, staring morosely at the ceiling.

'Johnny?'

He shakes his head so slightly that it's almost imperceptible.

Downstairs I hear a window smash. Johnny raises his head in alarm.

I quickly call security and discover that the fans have started lobbing stones at the windows. We're on the top floor of this seven-storey building so they can't throw as high as that, but as an attempt to rouse Johnny's attention, they've succeeded. They want him to go to the window, to show his face, give them something to get properly hysterical over, but if he does there will be no stopping the frenzy outside. They'll just want more.

'We'll get out of here tonight,' I reassure him.

We're backstage at Vienna's Ernst Happel Stadium. The support act has finished and the lights have gone up on the 49,000-strong crowd. The venue is sold out and the atmosphere is electric.

Johnny is in his dressing room backstage with the door closed. I'm standing with Bill outside.

'Does he always get like this when he goes on tour?' I ask, worriedly.

'Yeah, every time,' Bill answers. 'Don't worry about it, girl, he'll be fine. He always is. One concert in and he'll be kicking down the door of the next venue.'

'Are you sure I don't need to call a doctor?' I ask, for about the dozenth time.

'Doctor schmockter,' Bill brushes me off. 'Don't be bloody ridiculous. I keep telling you there's no need. Stop pestering me, girl!' He cuffs me over the top of the head, good-naturedly.

'I might just check on him,' I say, tentatively, motioning towards the door.

'Be off with you!' Bill growls. '*I'll* do it.'

I look at him, unsure for a moment, but he puts his hands firmly on my arms and marches me away from Johnny's dressing-room door. It makes sense of course. Bill's been on the scene for years; I've known Johnny only a few months.

'Is he alright?'

I turn around to see a concerned-looking Christian. He's here for the first few dates and then he has to go back to London, where he'll hook up with us again to document some more action for his book.

'Bill seems to think so.'

We wander to the communal backstage area, where I'm responsible for maintaining two large tables full of every kind of food and beverage you can think of. Christian homes straight in on a brightly coloured cereal packet.

'Fruity Pebbles, Meg?' He grins at me.

'For you,' I answer. 'And I think you'll find some Skittles over there.' I point.

'You're a top PA,' he says. 'Much better than that Paola lass.'

I laugh. 'I should bloody hope so. She lasted only eight months, didn't she?'

'Was that all?' he asks, surprised. 'Seemed like longer to me.'

'Did you know her well?' I'm still curious about her.

'No.' He shrugs and looks around. 'Where *is* Johnny? He's going to be on soon.'

Johnny's core band members are lounging on sofas on the other side of the room. They're all drinking beer and seem remarkably chirpy for a change.

'Where the fuck is Johnny, man?'

TJ has shouted this question at Bill, who has just emerged from Johnny's dressing room.

'He's coming, he's coming,' Bill reassures them.

'Wonder what TJ's real name is,' I whisper to Christian.

'Tom Jones,' he answers.

'No way!'

'Yeah.' He chuckles.

'Bullshit.'

'I'm being serious! TJ, man, what's your real name?' Christian calls across the room.

'Fuck off,' is TJ's response.

Christian turns back to me. 'I'm telling you, it's Tom Jones.'

I'm laughing when Johnny saunters into the room. 'What are you so happy about?' he asks.

'Hey, Johnny!' TJ and the other members of Johnny's band raise their beer bottles.

Johnny nods at them, then looks at me. 'I would say that you're excited about the gig, but it's not exactly a Kylie concert, is it?'

'This joke is wearing thin,' I reply, and roll my eyes.

He wanders over to the table and cracks open a bottle of whisky, swigging straight from the neck of it.

'Is he always like this when he goes on tour?' I ask Christian, quietly. 'Kind of all distant and unhappy?'

'He doesn't look like that to me.' Christian nods in Johnny's direction. I turn to see him and his band knock back a shot of tequila and crack up laughing as keyboardist Bri starts coughing his lungs up.

'And another!' TJ yells.

'Christian! Come here!' Johnny calls.

Christian looks at me and raises an eyebrow, then walks over to them. I busy myself tidying up the table because I haven't been invited to join their 'shot' gang.

223

'And another!' I hear someone else shout, seconds later, followed by more guffawing.

By the time they make their way stagewards, Johnny and the band are decidedly jolly. So, for that matter, is Christian. He drapes his arm around my shoulders and marches me to the side of the stage. Johnny turns around and clocks us, unsmiling. He makes eye contact with me for a moment, then looks away again as a roadie fixes him up with his electric guitar.

I long for him to be the way he was with me before his Whisky comeback gig months ago. I long for him to be the way he was with me in Big Sur. I don't know what's changed in him since then, but I'm sad we're not as close as we seemed to be getting. I'm trying not to dwell on it.

You can barely hear backstage because of the noise of the crowd – and that's before the concert has even kicked off. They're chanting, banging, and it's like a tribal song as they wait for their hero to emerge.

Then the band walks on and starts to play and they go absolutely bonkers.

Johnny looks at Christian and grins.

'Here we go.'

Spotlights turn the stage bright white and we can barely see him at first, but then we hear the crowd roar as he launches into one of his biggest hits. Christian grabs my arm and pulls me to the back. We can't talk anymore because it's deafening, so he just points at the audience. I look out to see tens of thousands of people jumping up and down as one. It's a phenomenal sight, and right there in front of us, Johnny is strutting across the stage and belting out his songs into the mic.

Everything runs like clockwork back here and it's a hive of

activity. Johnny's same team of roadies have been with him for years and they would know exactly what they were doing even if they hadn't been put through tour rehearsals in LA.

After the first few songs, Johnny bounds backstage, sweat dripping off him. One of his wardrobe girls passes him a towel and he mops his brow and runs it over his damp dark-blond hair. He yanks his black T-shirt over his head, torso rippling for a moment before he drags on a fresh shirt. He doesn't speak to anyone; his mind is still onstage. He strides back out there again.

The cameras recording Johnny's performance for the big TV screens pan the crowd. Christian and I watch as they zoom in on people declaring their love with banners. A girl sitting atop somebody's shoulders tears her shirt open and reveals an enormous bouncing bosom.

'Nice!' I shout to Christian.

'That's nothing!' he shouts back. 'Wait till you see what goes on later!'

I soon find out what he means by that when we go to the communal backstage area after the concert. There are girls *everywhere*. Draping themselves over members of the band on the sofas, hanging by the booze table and eyeing up Mike, Johnny's hot rhythm guitarist. I don't know who they are or where they came from, but they're making me feel distinctly uncomfortable.

Suddenly Johnny enters the room and everyone breaks into spontaneous applause. He walks straight to the booze table and cracks open a fresh bottle of whisky. A group of girls home in on him.

There's one particularly pretty girl with long, wavy blonde hair and an impressive cleavage, and as the night wears on I watch, feeling sick to the pit of my stomach, as she becomes increasingly flirtatious with Johnny. Right now, she has her hand on his chest and is saying something in his ear. He looks over at Christian, who is laughingly telling me about something he saw on TV recently. Johnny comes over.

'Having fun?' Christian asks him.

'What do you think?' Johnny grins.

I stand there like a lemon.

'I've got one for you, mate,' Johnny says, looking back over at the group of girls, who are watching him.

To my enormous relief, Christian says, 'No, thanks.'

'Why not?' Johnny asks, irritated.

'Just not in the mood.' Christian shrugs his shoulders.

'Whatever.' Johnny looks away and swigs from his bottle of whisky. 'Waste not, want not,' he says, glancing back at Christian and winking.

'If you don't need me, I'm going to head back to the hotel,' I say, trying to swallow the bile rising up in my throat.

'No, stay,' he commands.

'Why?' I ask. I can't bear to watch this any longer.

'Because I might need you.' He turns back to the girls. 'More?' he asks the prettiest. She nods, smiling flirtatiously up at him, and tilts her head back. He tips whisky straight into her mouth.

Another hour passes and I'm privy to Johnny getting increasingly wasted. The girls are completely off their trolleys, too. He's stumbling now, and they're giggling and trying to hold him up.

Christian and I, in contrast, are quite sober.

'I'm really bloody tired, now,' I complain to Christian.

'Yeah, I think I'm going to hit the sack, too.'

'I don't know why he won't let me leave.' I look over at

Johnny, who has just wrapped his arm around the blonde girl and given one of her boobs a sneaky squeeze.

'Just go,' Christian encourages.

Johnny stumbles over to us, almost pulling the girl over as he fails to let go in time. They both look back at each other and laugh hysterically.

'Johnny, I am going to go now,' I say, determinedly.

'Me too,' he slurs. 'Bring her.' He indicates the prettiest girl.

'I will,' I answer, although I have absolutely no intention of bringing her. The dirty slapper can stay right where she is.

Johnny stumbles out of the room, leaning on Christian for support. Christian doesn't look very amused. I follow them and make a call, asking for our car to be brought around to the back door.

There are still hordes of fans waiting outside, even though we've been in there for hours and they would have had no way of knowing if Johnny had slipped out through a side entrance earlier. Their dedication is quite something because it's freezing cold and there's a chance of snow tonight.

'Can you do a few autographs?' I ask.

Johnny shakes his head and mumbles something unintelligible so I open the door for him to climb in the car and look back at the now-baying crowds.

'I'm sorry,' I shout. 'I'm sorry, we've got to go!'

It makes no difference to their fury, and as the car moves away, we're pelted by plastic bottles and food wrappers. Christian and I flinch with every hit, but Johnny is oblivious, passed out in the corner.

Chapter 18

I book two hotels at the next city, in case we have to move again, and decide to do this for the rest of the tour. Sometimes we'll need the back-up, sometimes there will be enough security in place so we won't, but it's worth paying the cancellation fee, and chances are the manager will let us out of it in the hope we'll return and stay with them next time.

Right now we're in Amsterdam, four dates in, and after Johnny's initial tour downer, he seems to be well in his stride.

It's early evening and we've got the night off before tomorrow's concert. We played the first of three gigs in Amsterdam last night and the atmosphere was storming. It's Christian's last night before he flies back to London.

There's a knock on the door. Johnny is sitting on the bed, plucking at his guitar strings and I'm sitting opposite him on an armchair. I get up to answer the door.

'Hey, Johnny,' TJ says, nervously glancing at me. 'We're thinking of moseying on down to the, you know, red-light district. You wanna come?'

I immediately tense up, but he replies, 'Nah,' so I relax again, until he says, 'Why pay for it when you can get it for free?' Then he emphasises his comic timing with a few rapid strums on his guitar.

TJ laughs and shuts the door behind him.

'Nutmeg,' Johnny says, sternly, as soon as I turn back to him. It's the first time he's called me Nutmeg in weeks, and warmth rushes through me. 'You didn't bring my girl back for me the other night.'

'Oh,' I reply, and go cold again. 'What do you mean?'

'You know what I mean.'

'Vienna?' I ask, just to be sure.

'Mmmhmm.'

'Sorry, I thought you'd be too drunk to notice.'

'I'm never too drunk.' He winks at me. 'So where does Christian want to go tonight?' he asks, resting his guitar up against the bed.

'I don't know. The Dinner Club or something?'

'Supperclub?'

'Yeah, that's the place.'

'I know it. Sure, yeah, book a table. Join us, if you like.'

'Okay,' I reply, pleased. It's the first time I've been included in their dinner plans since we were in Big Sur. 'Nine-ish?' I ask.

'Yep, cool.'

'Hey, I forgot to tell you, my brother got engaged,' Christian says to Johnny. We're crossing the Prinsengracht canal on our way to the restaurant. Johnny decided he wanted to brave the cold Amsterdam weather and go for a rare walk instead of taking the car. Supperclub is only about half a mile away from the hotel.

'Wow! That's cool, man. Say congratulations from me.'

229

'What's your brother's name?' I ask. It's not really relevant to the conversation, but it's my best shot at being included in it.

'Anton,' Christian replies. 'I have a younger brother, too. Joel.'

'How is little Joel?' Johnny asks.

'He's fine. He's working with Dad now, you know.'

'Is he?'

'What does your dad do?' I ask, as we approach a bridge to cross another canal.

'He owns an electrical shop up in Newcastle,' Christian explains.

'Cool,' I say.

'Actually, it's pretty warm. What with all the electrical appliances turned on, and all.'

'You're so funny, you should do stand-up,' I tease.

'No, that's my older brother.'

'*Is* he a comedian?' I ask, then see Christian's face. 'Stop winding me up, you.'

'Sorry. No, he's an accountant. Hey, did you know the word naive isn't in the dictionary?' Christian glances at me.

'Ha ha.' I play-punch him on the arm. 'I'm not falling for that one.'

I'm walking in the middle of the two guys, Johnny to my right and Christian to my left.

'What about you, Meg, do you have any brothers or sisters?' Christian asks.

'I have one sister, Susan. She's older. Thirty-two. Married. Boring. We don't get on.'

'Why not?' Johnny looks interested.

'She's so full of herself. And I don't like her husband. He's a prat.'

The guys chuckle. 'Tell it like it is, Meg,' Christian says.

'Well, he is. Last Christmas we all went to stay with my parents – they live in the south of France,' I explain. 'And one night, without even asking, he opened up a bottle of wine which my dad had been saving for ages. He guzzled half of it down like it was water and didn't buy a single bottle of booze the whole time they were there. He's such a stingy git. It really pisses me off when my sister doesn't pull him up on it.'

'My brother's girlfriend – well, fiancée now – is a bit like that,' Christian says. 'It drives Mum mad. She always makes herself at home when she comes round ours, but my mum's kitchen is my mum's kitchen, and you'd better have permission even to make yourself a cup of tea or it'll get her back up. And if you're caught rooting around in her cupboards for crisps or anything like that, you're in big trouble.'

I laugh. 'Was she like that with Clare?'

Christian looks a little taken aback at the mention of his ex-girlfriend's name, and I regret being so brazen, but he recovers quickly.

'Yeah, she was a bit.' He humphs. 'That's probably part of the reason she left.'

Johnny and I never did find out why he and Clare split up. Now I'm curious.

'Doesn't sound like much to complain about to me,' Johnny says from beside me. 'At least you've *got* siblings . . .'

I instantly feel guilty and look down at the footpath.

Christian reaches behind me to slap Johnny on the back. 'They're a pain in the arse. You're much better off with me. Well, us,' he says, nudging me.

Johnny looks at us both and smiles. 'So where is this bloody restaurant? Whose stupid idea was it to walk here, anyway?'

*

'Why did you and your girlfriend split up?' I ask Christian, two hours and several glasses of wine later.

'She ran over my dog.'

'No!' I gasp. Johnny sniggers beside me. I give Christian a wry look. 'You don't have a dog, do you?'

'Not since she ran over it, no.' Christian pulls a sad face.

'Stop it! Tell me the truth!' I prod him in the ribs.

'Ow! Stop it or you're going to get hurt,' he warns me.

'Okay, okay! Spill the beans, then.'

'We had a difference of opinion,' he says.

'Oh. About what?' I ask.

'She didn't have a sweet tooth, Megan. Seriously clashing personalities.'

'Okay, I give up,' I say, sitting back in my seat and giving Johnny an unimpressed look. 'Is he always like this?' I ask.

'Afraid so,' Johnny says, and flags down one of the ridiculously good-looking waitresses to order another bottle of wine for Christian and me. He's on the spirits again, so Christian and I have got through two bottles on our own.

'Oh no, I don't think I can drink any more,' I protest.

The waitress looks at the three of us, waiting for a final answer.

'We'll take that bottle,' Johnny tells her. Even in the dim lighting I can see she's on edge. She's trying to be professional and not seem overawed by her customer's star status, but it can't be easy. We've already been interrupted three times by other diners wanting autographs. Johnny signs them, quite happily, even with his mouth full.

'Seriously, I'll fall over if I drink much more,' I inform him.

'We're not going to have a difference of opinion about alcohol consumption, are we, Nutmeg?' Johnny asks, raising his eyebrow. 'Anyway, we'll pick you up, won't we, Christian?'

By the time we get to our next venue, I am positively steaming. I wanted to go back to the hotel, but the boys dragged me to a club and I was too far gone to object. Right now I'm sitting in a darkened booth surrounded by Christian, Johnny and the four members of the band who have joined us following their 'erotic adventure'.

They're stoned now as well as drunk, and are not shy around me regarding what they got up to. If I weren't so drunk myself I'd probably feel sickened. As it is, I'm feeling sickened anyway, thanks to all that wine.

'You alright, Megan?' Christian slurs in my ear.

'No,' I slur back. 'Feel like I'm going to throw up.'

'She's not going to chuck up here, is she?' TJ butts in.

'Want me to take you to the bathroom, Megan?'

'Mmm . . .' I nod my head, although I don't really want Christian to take me. Where are your girlfriends when you need them? 'Actually,' I say, 'I think I'd rather go back to the hotel.'

'Okay.' He gets up and holds out his hand for me. I slowly scoot along the booth seat. Johnny grabs my arm.

'Where are you going?' he asks, annoyed.

'I'm taking her back to the hotel,' Christian tells him.

'Why?'

'Look at her, Johnny, she's wasted.'

I stumble slightly and Christian holds me up.

'She's alright. You're alright, aren't you, Nutmeg?' Johnny tries to sound jolly.

'No,' I shake my head.

Christian starts to lead me away.

'Oh, come on,' Johnny calls. 'The party's only just starting!'

'See you tomorrow, mate,' Christian calls back.

'For fuck's sake,' is the last thing I hear Johnny say before Christian manoeuvres me through the packed club.

I barely remember the taxi ride back to the hotel. The next thing I know I'm outside my room.

'Can't find my key,' I say with frustration, and empty the contents of my bag onto the corridor carpet. Christian immediately bends down to retrieve the key, then picks up my belongings and stuffs them back into my bag while I stagger up against the wall.

'Whoa, you alright, Meg?'

I don't answer. He puts the key in the lock and turns it, helping me into my bedroom.

'Gotta go bathroom,' I say.

Five minutes later he knocks on the bathroom door. 'Meg, I'm worried. Can I come in?'

'Yeah. Urgh . . .'

I'm kneeling on the floor in front of the toilet. I haven't been able to throw up.

'Jeez, let me help you out of your coat – you must be boiling,' he says, before adding, 'I've called room service. They're bringing up some toast.' He seems remarkably sober considering how much he had to drink. But then, maybe that's just in comparison to me.

He makes me eat two slices before sitting me on the bed and pulling back the covers. He kneels down and removes my high heels then leans me forward and unzips my dress. 'You can take it off when I've gone,' he tells me, ever the gentleman.

But like a lunatic I tug it over my head and it gets stuck, so he has to jump in and help me out of it. Luckily, I wore a bra tonight.

He sits on the armchair opposite the bed.

'What are you doing?' I ask, blearily.

'I'm staying with you.' He wriggles around.

'Don't be silly. I'll be fine.'

'Meg, don't argue with me.'

'Christian, I'm okay. Go to bed.'

'No, Meg. Go to sleep.'

'In that case,' I say, groggily shifting over in my bed, 'sleep up here.'

He looks over at me in my nice, king-size bed and doesn't have to be told twice. 'Only if you're sure.'

'Sure I'm sure.' I roll over and close my eyes.

In the early hours of the morning I awake, feeling horribly worse for wear. I groan.

'You okay?' Christian murmurs.

'Why did I do that?' I hold my hand to my head.

'You didn't have much choice. He's very hard to say no to.'

'You manage to, most of the time.'

'It's taken years of practice.' His voice is even deeper than usual. He sounds rough.

I slowly sit up in bed. I really need some headache tablets, but I don't want to get out of bed wearing next to nothing.

'What do you need?' Christian asks, sensing my anxiety.

I tell him.

'Where are they?'

'In my washbag in the bathroom.'

He brings the tablets back, along with a glass of water.

'Get that down you.'

I do as he says and then lie back down beside him. My arm rubs hard against his. I instinctively edge away.

Suddenly he gets out of the bed.

'Where are you going?' I ask, startled.

'I'm going to head back to my room.' He pulls his trousers on. 'You're alright now, yeah?'

'Yes, I'm fine.'

He slips his shoes on and grabs his jacket, heading to the door.

'See you for breakfast?'

'Sure.'

It occurs to me for a horrible moment that Johnny might see him come out of my room and jump to the wrong conclusion. But he doesn't. And when I finally emerge later that morning, Christian has already set off for the airport.

Chapter 19

After Amsterdam comes Zurich, then it's Milan followed by Rome. Each and every stadium is sold out as the European cities begin to melt into one.

I'm not really enjoying myself as much as I thought I would. The combination of travelling constantly and never really knowing where I am with Johnny is making me feel a little apprehensive.

Right now I'm backstage at the Vallehovin Stadium in Oslo. I look over at the table stocked full of drinks. I can't believe how much alcohol has already been consumed on this tour and we haven't even reached the halfway point. Johnny has been getting through increasing amounts of spirits every night. Earlier I voiced my concern to Bill, but he laughed me off.

'This is nothing. You should've seen him seven years ago!'

'I just don't want a repeat of that,' I said.

'I just don't want a repeat of that,' he mimicked me. 'Have a word with yourself, love. Listen to what you sound like, all prim and proper. I thought you were more worldly-wise than that when I hired you.'

I'll keep my mouth shut in future.

Johnny strolls into the backstage area with his guitar.

'There you are! What do you think to this?'

He's been so upbeat these last few days – a complete contrast to how down he was at the start of the tour. Bill was right about that, at least.

He sits down next to me and starts to strum a few notes. 'It's a new intro to "What You Are",' he says.

'What You Are' is one of his greatest hits.

'Why?' I ask. I thought it sounded fine the way it was.

'I'm bored with it.'

'You've only been playing it for the last month!' He rearranged it just before we came on tour.

'Yes, and I'm bored with it,' he says again, stressing each word to really drive home his point.

'Okay, shoot,' I say, not wanting to dampen his enthusiasm.

He starts to play, talking over the top to tell me what he's planning. 'And then the strings will come in here, and I'm not talking the little string section we bring on tour, I want a full-blown orchestra.'

'You want *what*?' Bill says, coming into the room.

'Bill! There you are! Listen to this . . .'

He goes through the motions again with Bill.

'Yeah, sounds good, Johnny boy, but we can't bring a whole orchestra in this late in the tour.'

'Yes, we can,' Johnny replies, still strumming.

'Where are we going to get one?' Bill huffs.

'That's up to you,' Johnny comments. 'But I know you'll manage. It's what I pay you for,' he adds, giving Bill a look.

'Okay, I'll see what I can do.' Bill glares at me. 'But Terrence is going to be pissed.'

Terrence is the tour manager, responsible for organising the whole shebang.

'Don't see, do it.' Johnny's tone is firm.

Bill stomps off. I'm impressed. And I'm delighted. Bill really annoyed me with that 'prim and proper' comment, so I'm glad he's got his work cut out for him.

'I think that sounds really good.' I nod at Johnny's guitar.

'Cheers,' he answers.

It's a testament to how much power Johnny wields in the industry that Bill does manage to find a whole orchestra at this short notice. They're flown in four days later when we're in Copenhagen, with only a couple of days free to get up to scratch before we play at the Olympic Stadium in Munich. I've booked an out-of-use theatre for everyone to rehearse in, and I'm currently sitting halfway back in the seats with a magazine. But I'm not reading, I'm watching. Watching Johnny direct his usual band and backing singers, along with a brand-new orchestra.

Everyone should have had a couple of days' rest between Copenhagen and Munich, and now they have to rehearse instead. But no one seems to mind. When Johnny is 'up' like this, it rubs off on everyone. Including me. I'm filled with a renewed sense of respect for him, for what he's capable of. Which is why it hurts so much to witness the sort of thing I saw last night.

I was in his suite showing him some press cuttings when there was a knock at the door.

'Housekeeping!'

'Do you want me to ask them to come back later?' I ask Johnny.

'No, I could do with some more bubble bath.'

'Bubble bath?'

'What?'

'Nothing. Come in!' I call.

'Housekeeping!' Five more rapid knocks.

'I said, come in!'

Knock, knock, knock!

'That's strange,' I mumble. 'Why doesn't she have a key?' I open the door. Standing there is a cute, petite brunette who looks to be in her late teens or early twenties.

'Housekeeping?' I ask. She's dressed in a maid's uniform, but her face is lit up with such excitement as she attempts to peer past me into the room that I become suspicious. I can't believe she's that thrilled about cleaning out somebody's toilet.

'Are you really from housekeeping?' I ask, warily.

She nods, manically.

'I don't think so.' I begin to shut the door.

'Wait,' Johnny says. 'Let her in.'

He saunters to the door, leaning his right arm up against the door-frame.

'Johnny Jefferson!' the 'maid' says, delightedly.

'Hi.' He grins.

'Johnny Jefferson!' she says again. 'I come in?'

'That's enough, now,' I interrupt. 'Thank you, you can leave.' I try to shut the door but Johnny pushes it back open.

'Don't be such a spoilsport, Nutmeg,' he says, casting his eyes over the girl in the maid's uniform. She's smiling up at him, through lowered lashes.

'I come in?' she says again, this time more sexily.

Johnny pushes the door further back and steps aside for her.

'Johnny!' By now I'm cross, but that doesn't stop the girl from wandering past me into the room.

'That'll be all, Meg.' He dismisses me.

I stand there.

'You don't speak English, do you?' Johnny asks the girl.

'English?' she says, in her strong Italian accent. 'No. I no speak English.'

'Just as well we don't need to talk.' He winks at me and closes the door, leaving me out in the corridor.

I'll never get used to the groupies. Each time I witness him with other women, I feel like a part of me is being chipped away.

'That's sounding good, guys. Let's take a break.' Johnny bounds off the stage and jogs up the aisle. I sit up straighter in my seat.

'Can you get me a sandwich or something?' he asks me.

'Sure.' I grab my coat. 'You want it back here?'

'Yeah. I'm going to crack on. I think that riff needs something else there.'

He's a hard worker, Johnny. I didn't realise it at first, with all the late nights, booze and women, but he is.

I return shortly afterwards with a tuna and mayo roll for him.

'Thanks,' he says, taking a bite standing up. He reaches into his pocket and pulls out a small hip flask, opening it up and tipping it back into his mouth. 'Damn. Out,' he says, handing over the flask. 'Can you top it up for me?'

'Er, sure,' I say, hesitantly. 'What with?'

'Whisky, what else?' He gives me an amused look.

'Do you want me to get you something else as well? Coke? Pepsi?'

'Coke would be good.' He grins at me, cheekily. I don't get the joke for a moment and then it registers. He laughs when he sees my face. 'No, chick, just the whisky would be good.'

241

'What, now?'

'Yes.'

'Johnny, I'm a bit worried about how much you're drin—'

'Thanks.' He cuts me off and nods at the flask in my hand.

I turn around and scuttle back up the aisle and out in search of a local off-licence. I knew I should have stocked up the theatre with the usual backstage food and drinks, but Johnny told me not to bother for rehearsals.

Two days later, I'm backstage at Munich's Olympic Stadium when Johnny appears by my side. He looks even hotter than usual tonight.

'Are you feeling okay?' I ask him.

'Yeah, yeah, yeah, Nutmeg! This is going to be fucking awesome!'

He's really hyper, bouncing up and down on the spot.

A roadie appears with his guitar, but it takes time to hook him up because Johnny won't stay still.

The set is kicking off with 'What You Are', the newly arranged orchestral version, and I'm feeling on edge, even if he's not. It was sounding great in rehearsals, but I bet it's a whole different story when you're playing to an 80,000-strong crowd.

'Don't look so nervous.' He stands in front of me and puts his hands on my hips looking straight into my eyes. My heart flips as he studies my face momentarily and then grins at me. His eyes look funny. Kind of jittery. He's obviously on a high, and it suddenly occurs to me it's probably not a natural one.

'Are you okay, Johnny?' I ask again, this time more guardedly.

'Yeah, yeah, yeah! Chill out, girlfriend!'

He frenetically rubs my hips with his hands and then sniffs, before letting go and bouncing on the spot again.

'Here we go.' He looks out at the stage.

The orchestra start to play and Johnny's band join in as the rearranged song makes its debut. Then Johnny's out there, launching into the first verse, driving the crowd into a frenzy.

At moments like this, I'm struck with the realisation that I know this guy, *the* Johnny Jefferson.

I watch him caressing the microphone with his hands as the song quietens down just before the chorus kicks in. His guitar is hanging behind him on a strap and he swings it round and pounds on it as if his life depended on it. I watch, full of pride, and then I remember that jittery look in his eyes and a feeling of unease settles over me.

He's even more hyper after the concert, and it's the same at the next show in Nice and in the two days off before we play in Barcelona.

I reluctantly mention my concern to Bill.

'And?' he says.

'What do you mean, "and"?' I reply.

'What's the big deal? Haven't we been through this with his drinking?'

'Yes, yes, yes,' I say with frustration. 'And I don't care if you think I'm prim and proper, I'm just worried about him, Bill.'

'Christ Almighty, girl! Give it a rest. Anyway, what do you want me to do about it?'

'I don't know – stop him.'

'Stop him?' He laughs. '*Stop* him? How do you bloody well think I'm going to do that? He's a big boy, you know, girlie. He's not going to do what he's told. Now run along and stop being a nuisance.'

Needless to say, Bill's really starting to piss me off.

It's early December by the time we reach Barcelona. It's the first of three Spanish dates, with the next stop being San Sebastian, followed by Madrid.

We're staying in the city centre and we have the night off before the concert tomorrow night at Camp Nou. I decide to go for a walk, so rug up warm and head out of the hotel.

I've downloaded Johnny's back catalogue onto my iPhone and have been steadily making my way through it. I haven't told him – he'd probably make fun of me – but his music is really starting to grow on me. I put my headphones in now and listen to his voice as I walk around town. Gaudí's Sagrada Família has been lit up with spotlights, and the enormous, ornate church looks spectacular in the dark night. My phone starts to ring as the music in my ears simultaneously dies down.

'Hello?'

'Meg, it's your mother.'

'Hi! How are you?'

'Oh, not the best, dear.'

'Why? What's wrong?' I ask in alarm.

'It's your grandmother. I'm afraid she died this afternoon.'

Regret engulfs me. I loved my gran. I realise I haven't even sent her a single letter since I've been in LA. I feel dreadful. I start to cry.

'Meg, Meg, don't cry, dear. She was so proud of you, you know.'

Which only makes me cry harder.

'What happened?'

'She'd been under the weather. She was in hospital. She fell asleep a few days ago and didn't wake up.'

'Why didn't anyone tell me?' I complain.

'We didn't want to bother you,' Mum explains. 'We know you're busy—'

'Mum! You should have told me! When's the funeral?'

'The day after tomorrow.'

We play in San Sebastian the day after tomorrow.

'I know you won't be able to make it,' my mum continues.

'What do you mean? I have to come!'

But even though I protest, I know that it would be incredibly difficult for me to leave the tour.

'Meg,' Mum chides, 'it's okay. She wouldn't have wanted you to sacrifice your work. I know you have to be there for Johnny . . .'

I return to the hotel to wallow in my misery.

Oh, Gran . . . I feel terrible at the idea of missing her funeral. But the more I think about it, the more I realise it would be a nightmare for me to leave.

I should probably let Johnny know I won't be joining him and the crew tonight. We were planning on going to a bar in the Gothic Quarter.

There's loud music coming from his room and I don't think he can hear me knocking, so I take out my purse and retrieve his spare electronic key card.

Opening the door, I walk into the suite and am instantly struck by the sight of Johnny hoovering up a line of white dust into his nose with a straw. A spaced-out-looking guy with greasy black hair and stubble is lounging back on the sofa beside him.

'Want some?' the guy shouts to me over the music. He leans forward and offers up a small, clear plastic bag.

'NO!' Johnny puts his hand on the guy's chest and angrily pushes him back hard against the sofa.

'Whoa!' the guy says.

'She's not into that shit,' Johnny snaps, pointing a remote control at the stereo and turning the music down.

'Okay, okay, man.' The guy leans forward again and starts to unhurriedly pack away into a leather pouch the silver straw Johnny has just used.

I stand there for a moment, not quite sure what to say or do. I want to turn and run but, remembering Bill's patronising words, I try to stay calm.

'Johnny, I wanted to tell you . . .'

It's hard to keep my concentration and not look at the white lines of powder on the coffee table in front of me. The greasy-haired guy is really putting me off, too, just by his mere presence.

'I wanted to say . . .'

Johnny is still looking furious. I don't know whether he's mad at me for seeing him snort cocaine, or his mate for offering me some.

'I can't come to the bar tonight,' I manage to spit out.

'Why not?' he asks, his green eyes penetrating my dark ones.

'My . . . my . . . I've had some bad news,' I stutter. 'Personal stuff. Okay?' I must look desperate. I really want to leave the room now.

'Meg. Meg!' he calls, as I start to back away.

'I have to go . . .'

He blocks me off at the door.

'What's wrong?' He's looking down at me intently, his hand on the door. I look away. 'Hey! Nutmeg! Look at me!' he demands. 'What is it?'

Apart from seeing the man I have feelings for get wasted every night, come on to groupies and do drugs, you mean?

I have an overwhelming urge to cry again, not just for my gran, but for myself. The last few months have been so intense. I constantly feel confused. Johnny is lovely to me one day, detached and horrible the next. I keep telling myself that this silly crush on him will go away, that it's not serious, but every time I see him flirting with girls backstage I feel like he's causing me physical pain. There's an ache inside me right now as I look up at him.

He puts his hand roughly on my arm. 'Nutmeg, what's wrong?' he demands again.

Then he sniffs. It brings me down to earth with a bump.

'It's my grandmother,' I tell him. 'She passed away this afternoon. I'm just a bit upset about it, that's all.'

'I'm sorry. Is there anything I can do?'

'No. I just need some time alone.'

'Of course, of course.' He lets go of my arm, leaving it cold. 'When's the funeral?' he asks.

'The day after tomorrow.' I quickly tell him that I won't be going.

'Are you sure?'

'Yes, I'm sure.'

I put my hand on the door handle and look at him, waiting for him to step aside. He does. Then I open the door and walk out into the bright corridor.

By the time we reach Paris, just over a week later, Johnny's behaviour has taken a distinct downturn. A couple of days ago, after we'd played in Madrid, I went into his room to wake him up. He was out cold. There were two girls in his bed, also out cold, and puke in one corner on the floor. The room stank. He'd made me promise the previous afternoon to get him out of bed at ten o'clock so he could check out an art gallery in town which closed at midday.

I stood there at the foot of his bed for a minute with my heart pounding before I went back to my room and called him instead. The phone rang out three times before he groggily picked up.

'What you wake me for?'

'You said you wanted to go to that gallery today . . .'

'No.' He grunted. 'Rather sleep.'

I didn't see him at all that day. I called him twice more, but each time he told me he needed to sleep.

Now we're in Paris and he's hyper again. We're playing two concerts here at the Stade de France – the first was last night, the next is tomorrow night – and after that we're heading back across the Channel to do Manchester, Newcastle, Glasgow, Dublin, Cardiff and London.

We're staying in a beautiful, old, five-star hotel near the Champs-Élysées, and I have the night off before tomorrow's concert. My parents have travelled up from Grasse in the south to have dinner with me at the Pompidou Centre. My mum is telling me about my grandmother's funeral.

'Did Susan and Tony go?' Tony is my sister's husband.

'Of course,' Mum says, before realising that might sound slightly insensitive considering I didn't make it.

'Bet she was pissed off with me for not going,' I grumble, looking out of the window at the city of Paris stretched out below us. It's a wet and windy night, but I can just make out the Eiffel Tower off in the distance.

'She said you haven't spoken to her in months.' Mum's voice is stern.

Dad fingers the glass vase holding a single long-stemmed rose in the middle of the table. He hates domestics and there are usually several where my sister and I are concerned.

'I thought you said you were going to call her?' Mum continues.

'Yeah, well, she never called me,' I whinge.

'You're as bad as each other,' my mum decides, ending the conversation by picking up her menu and burying her head in it.

'Did anyone say anything about me not being there?' I persist, hoping in some way to alleviate some of my guilt, but realising it will probably have the opposite effect.

'Everyone understood.' Mum tries to reassure me. It doesn't work. I moodily study my menu.

'This restaurant is rather fancy, isn't it?' Dad attempts to change the subject.

I glance around the room at the giant, rounded aluminium structures. They're like something out of another world, silver on the outside and glowing different colours within. The one closest to us is yellow inside and is hosting a table full of happy diners drinking large glasses of wine.

'What's going to happen to her house?' I focus my attention back on Gran.

'We're going to rent it out,' Dad tells me.

I don't really like the idea of other people staying in my gran's home. I tell my parents as much.

'Well, how would you feel if we sold it?' Dad asks, as the waiter appears with our drinks.

'Worse,' I admit.

'Exactly. Your mother and I were even thinking we might want to live there one day.'

'Really?' I'm pleasantly surprised at the thought of them moving back to England. I disregard the fact that I might be in America.

My phone rings, interrupting our discussion.

'Hello? Meg Stiles?'

'NUTMEG! Where the fuck are you?'

It's Johnny, and it sounds like he's wasted.

'I'm having dinner with my parents.' I try to sound calm. 'I told you that.'

'Get your arse down here, man, we're having a wicked time!'

'Where's "here", Johnny?' I go along with it.

'Where the fuck are we?' I hear Johnny shout. He comes back to me a second later. 'I don't know where the fuck we are.' Then he cracks up laughing.

'Johnny!' I raise my voice. 'Are you okay? Do you need me to send a car?'

'No, Nutmeg, we'll be fine. We'll be FINE!' He cracks up laughing again and hangs up.

I stare down at my phone.

'Is everything okay?' Mum asks, tentatively.

'Yes,' I say, determinedly.

We place our food order, but I'm preoccupied now. When my phone rings I jump, even though I was half expecting it.

'Meg, it's Bill. Where are you, girlie?'

'At the Pompidou Centre. I'm with my parents in the restaurant.'

'I think you should get back here sharpish. Johnny's gone AWOL.'

'What do you mean? He just called me.'

'He called you?' Bill sounds surprised.

'Yes. Just a little while ago.'

'What did he say?'

'He wanted me to meet up with him. But he couldn't tell me where he was.'

I glance at my parents across the glass table. They look worried.

'Well, he's not answering his phone, now,' Bill says.

'Let me give it a go.'

'He's not going to answer it any more if you call than if I call!' Bill snaps.

'Just let me try it. If he doesn't, I'll come back to the hotel,' I insist, ending the call.

I dial Johnny's number. It rings and rings. Come on, Johnny, pick up. As Bill predicted, he doesn't.

'What's happened?' Mum asks.

'Johnny's disappeared,' I tell her, getting to my feet.

'Do you really have to go?' Dad looks disappointed.

'I should,' I say, pushing in my chair. 'Johnny's manager wants me back at the hotel.'

'You haven't even eaten!' Mum points out, frustrated.

'I'm sorry, but this is just the way it is.'

And the way it is, is a bloody nightmare.

'Perhaps we can have a coffee tomorrow?' I suggest, kissing them goodbye.

I wind my way back through the tables and aluminium pods in the restaurant and back down several sets of escalators. Crossing the square to the main road, I hail a cab and head back to the hotel. I go up to Bill's room where I discover there's still no sign of Johnny. I've tried calling him a dozen times on the way back here, but each time it went straight through to answerphone. Earlier it just rang and rang, which means that it's probably run out of battery. Either that, or something might have happened to it. Or to Johnny. I shudder at the thought.

'Where do you think he could have gone?' I ask Bill.

'Fuck knows. But he'd better get back quick. Terrence will go ape-shit if he has to cancel tomorrow's concert.'

'What makes you think he won't turn up for that?' I ask, scared. 'I mean, why are you so worried? He's probably just gone for a walk or something.'

'TJ said he was acting funny earlier.' Bill looks shifty.

'What sort of funny?' I ask. 'Drugs funny?'

'Possibly,' Bill admits. 'But fuck knows what he's mixed to get himself into that state.'

'What do you mean? What state?' Now I'm seriously concerned.

'He climbed over the railings of the hotel balcony and hung off, laughing his bleedin' head off.'

'Holy shit,' I say. His suite is on the top floor.

'What did he say to you again? When he called?' Bill asks.

'He just wanted me to come and meet him. He didn't say where.'

The hotel phone rings and Bill snatches up the receiver.

'Yes! Where? Where is that? Can you get us a car? Okay. We'll be down right away.'

Bill hangs up and grabs his jacket. 'He's down by the river. Some paparazzi arsehole snapped him and alerted the hotel. He must be well and truly fucked up for that to have happened. Normally they'd just get their photo and piss off.'

As we drive through the streets of Paris in the rain in search of Johnny, I stare out of the window at the Eiffel Tower looming way up above the rooftops. The photographer said that he saw Johnny somewhere nearby, and we're just hoping and praying he'll still be there by the time we reach him.

'As long as he hasn't thrown himself into the bloody river,' Bill mutters.

The comment makes me feel slightly hysterical. 'Why would he do that? Why? Has he done anything like that before?'

'Calm down, girlie!' Bill snaps. 'I don't think he's suicidal. But yes, he has been in the past.'

The tabloids had said he was screwed up after the band split, but I hadn't realised it had been as bad as that. I feel like my intestines have tied themselves up into knots inside my stomach.

'Why the hell didn't you follow him?' Bill angrily directs his question at two of Johnny's security team, who we've brought with us.

'He told us not to!' one of them hotly responds.

We cross the river and drive along beside it in the direction of the Tower. I stare out of the window, desperately hoping to see Johnny, but fearing it's a lost cause. He could be anywhere by now.

'There he is!' Bill suddenly shouts.

'Where?' I shout back.

'There!'

I follow Bill's finger to a crowd of people near a bridge. I can't see Johnny, but I can see flashbulbs going off.

Using my A-Level French, I direct the driver to take us as close as he can, then we scramble out of the car and push our way through the hordes.

I freeze. Johnny has his left arm around a down-and-out youth. His other hand is clutching an empty bottle of whisky. He's almost falling over, he's laughing so hard.

'Johnny!' I yell.

'Nutmeg!' He looks obscenely delighted and stumbles towards me, dragging the youth with him. 'Bill!' he shouts, letting go of the guy and the whisky bottle, which smashes to smithereens on the ground. He opens his arms up wide to Bill who, along with the security guys, is trying unsuccessfully to disperse the people

253

who have gathered. Johnny turns back to me and smothers me in a hug, leaning his body weight into me so hard that I almost collapse. He reeks of a combination of booze, fags and vomit. Not a scent anyone will be wanting to bottle and turn into Johnny Jefferson-endorsed aftershave anytime soon.

'Come on, let's get you back to the hotel.' I breathe through my mouth to avoid the stench, and try to drag him through the crowd. Many are still snapping away with their cameras. Johnny, wasted, is clearly a much bigger tourist attraction than the famous 300-metre-high structure towering above us.

'Wait. Wait!' Johnny pulls me back. 'Come and meet my new friends.' He spins around and grabs my hand, pulling me back in the direction of the bridge where there is a group of large boxes, some of which have been covered with plastic and old scraps of material. A homeless community appears to reside there.

'Johnny, I don't think we should.' I tug back on his hand, trying to resist.

'Shame on you, Nutmeg. They're people too, you know.' He cracks up laughing again. 'Listen, Nutmeg, listen,' he says, then shouts at the small group of destitute youths before him, 'Say it! Say it!'

'Heeeeeeeerrrre's Johnny!' one of them responds.

'Listen, Nutmeg, listen to this. Say it again!'

'Heeeeeeeerrrre's Johnny!' the same guy complies.

Johnny turns to me excitedly. 'Heeeeeeeerrrre's Johnny!' he shouts. 'Heeeeeeeerrrre's Johnny!' he shouts again.

Bill and the security team burst through the crowd at that point and drag him back towards the car.

'Quick! Move!' Bill yells at the driver.

'*Vite! Dépêchez-vous!*' I repeat his words in French.

254

Johnny winds down the window and sticks his head out.

'Heeeeeeeerrrre's Johnny!' he shouts at the top of his voice. 'Heeeeeeeerrrre's Johnny!'

Who the hell is this person? I try to take his hand, but he snatches it away and laughs, hysterically.

Racked with anxiety, I dial the hotel's number and ask the manager to call a doctor.

By the time we get to the hotel, Johnny has calmed down considerably, although it's still a trial to get him up to his room and not into the hotel bar as he would have liked. I pull back the bed covers and sheets and prepare it for him, while Bill removes his shoes. The security guys stand by in case they're needed again.

'Come on now, mate,' Bill says, trying to get Johnny to sit on the bed.

'Nutmeg . . .' Johnny holds out his hand to me. 'Come here, Nutmeg.'

I glance at Bill, who nods, and go towards the bed. Johnny takes my hand. 'You're a good girl,' he slurs, and tries to pull me down beside him.

'Johnny! No, mate,' Bill manages to roughly extricate my hand and Johnny slumps back against the pillows, smiling up at me, sleepily.

When the doctor arrives, Johnny is snoring steadily. After checking him over, the doctor determines that he just needs to sleep it off.

Bill slumps down into a chair. 'I'll stay with him. You get some rest,' he says, gruffly.

I hesitate.

'Go!' he insists. 'Got to make sure he doesn't throw himself out of the window before tomorrow's concert.'

'Bill, he can't play in this state,' I say, reasonably.

'You shut it!' He raises his voice.

'Bill, do not tell me to shut it!'

'Don't try to be an expert about things you know nothing about!' He points his finger at me.

I know I won't win this argument so I leave him to it.

Chapter 20

The tabloids the next day speculate that Johnny has lost the plot, that it's a repeat of seven years ago. There are pictures scattered across every publication, some better quality than others. Clearly the general public sold their tawdry holiday snaps to all and sundry.

Christian calls me at eleven o'clock in the morning. 'What the fuck?' he exclaims down the line.

'I know. Disaster,' I confirm.

'I'm at St Pancras. I'm on my way.'

'You're coming to Paris?'

'Yep, I'll be there at three, your time.'

'I'll send a car for you. Fill you in when you get here.'

My parents also ring. They're concerned, having seen for themselves the evidence of Johnny off his trolley.

'Your father's worried about you,' Mum says. 'And I am, too.'

'Don't be worried. I'm fine.'

'We just don't think you're suited to this sort of thing. You'd be

257

much better off where you were, working for that nice architect lady.'

'Mum!' I snap. 'Don't be ridiculous!'

'It's not right!' she squawks.

'I'm not saying it's *right*, Mum, but I'm not going to quit and leave him in the lurch like that! He needs me!'

They want to come to the hotel to see me, but I tell them I'm too busy now. The last thing I need is pressure from my parents to quit my so-called glamorous job.

I've been checking on Johnny all morning. He's still dead to the world. I can't believe Bill hasn't cancelled tonight's concert, yet. I've been fielding calls from journalists all morning, wondering what the score is. I have to keep fobbing them off.

When Christian arrives, I take him up to Johnny's room. Bill blocks us off at the door.

'He's just waking up,' Bill says.

'Can we come in?' I ask.

'Give him some time.' He tries to ease the door shut on us.

'Bill, why can't we see him?'

'A bit more time,' he says, and shuts the door.

'We'll give it fifteen,' Christian says. 'Then we'll go back in there.' We wait in my room in uncomfortable silence.

'I thought I told you to give him a break?' Bill barks at the doorway, a quarter of an hour later.

'Bill, it's okay, mate, let them in,' I hear Johnny say from inside. Bill glares at us and pulls the door open, standing back to let us pass.

'Hey, man.' Johnny gets up and gives Christian a sprightly hug. He turns to me. 'Heeeeeeeerrrre's Johnny!'

I take a step backwards in alarm.

He laughs. 'I'm joking, Meg.'

I mustn't look very impressed because he continues, 'Chill the fuck out, it's not a big deal!' He sits down on a chaise longue and picks up his guitar, strumming a few up-tempo chords. Then he puts his guitar down and grabs at his fags on the table.

I regard him, warily. 'Are you okay to play tonight?'

Bill snorts from behind me.

'Yeah, course.' Johnny grins and lights a cigarette. 'What do you think I am, a fucking pansy?' He taps his fingers rapidly on the table.

'Christ, man, you had me worried.' Christian sighs with relief and slumps down on the chaise longue beside him. Johnny chuckles and rubs at his nose.

I look at Bill, suspiciously.

'Right, that's it. Off you go,' Bill says, urging me in the direction of the door. 'He needs his rest.'

'Wait!' I say.

'What?' Johnny widens his eyes in mock seriousness, then laughs. 'Look at that little face.' He nudges Christian and nods at me. 'Isn't she cute when she's concerned?'

Christian doesn't answer, but fed up with being patronised by Bill and Johnny, I turn on my heel and leave them to it.

The concert does go ahead that night, and Johnny is even more energetic than usual. I watch from the sidelines as he pokes fun at his speculated meltdown. The audience loves it.

'You go and hang out with a few homeless chaps and everyone thinks you've gone fucking bonkers!' he shouts into his microphone.

Christian is standing backstage with me.

259

'What do you think?' I ask him. 'Was he like this last time?'

'I don't know.' Christian shrugs. 'We kind of lost contact for a couple of years so I wasn't around to see it.'

'That's right!' I have to shout over the music now, as the band launches into the next song. 'I forgot!'

'About what?' He quickly turns to look at me.

'Your girlfriend!' I yell.

He nods, then stares back at the stage.

I stand there feeling ill at ease for a minute before telling myself he probably stopped our conversation because of the loud music. Though I know I shouldn't have said anything.

Bess calls me the next day. I haven't spoken to her in weeks, it's been so manic.

'Hi! It's so nice to hear your voice! How are you?'

'Fine, thanks. How are you?' She sounds a little cold.

'Pretty good. Busy. It's just been non-stop since we left LA.'

'I bet,' she says.

There's an awkward pause for a moment as I wonder why she called.

'Are you still coming to London?' she asks.

'Oh! Yes! We get there the week after next.'

'Do you need somewhere to stay?' she asks. Her tone is decidedly detached.

'Um, no, we're staying in a hotel. Thank you, though,' I add.

'Okay.'

Another awkward pause.

'Shit!' I suddenly remember. 'I must get you a couple of tickets to the Wembley concert.'

'Can you spare them?' she asks.

'Of course!' I tell her. 'I'll get you backstage passes too.'

'*Really?*' Now she sounds cheerful. 'That would be so cool!'

I grin. 'I'll bike them to you when we're in London.'

'Oh.' She sounds disappointed. 'Sure. I mean, you must be snowed under, right?'

'Yes,' I say, regretfully. 'Well, you could come to the hotel and pick them up, if you like?'

'Oh, no, it's okay,' she says. 'I'm pretty busy too. But we'll see you at Wembley, right?'

'Of course!' I gush. 'I can't wait. Listen, Bess, I'd better go. There's someone trying to get through. Been fobbing off journalists non-stop since Johnny went doolally a couple of nights ago.'

'Serena's been going on at me to ask you about that,' she says. 'What on earth happened?'

'I'll tell you when I see you,' I lie. 'I really need to take this other call.'

It saddens me that I can't open up to her like I used to. If I had a bad day dealing with a nasty client when I was working with Marie, I could tell her about it. It's completely different now.

I decide to wake Johnny. He should have had enough of a sleep-in by now. He went out clubbing with the crew after the concert last night so I imagine he's still feeling the worse for wear.

He doesn't answer the door so I have to use my key card.

'Johnny!' I call from the entrance to the suite. 'This is your wake-up call!' I add, brightly. No answer. I go in, half expecting to see two groupies in his bed again, but there's just one figure under the crumpled bed covers, just one head of hair.

I look around. The room is a mess. Empty bottles and fag ash line every surface. There's a murmur from the bed.

'Hey,' I say, going over to it. 'Johnny? Are you awake? How's your head?' I pull back the bed covers and then leap back in alarm. A girl with messy blonde hair and smudged eye make-up groggily looks up at me. Her eyes seem to focus suddenly and she opens them wide in shock. She quickly sits up and pulls the covers around her naked chest.

'What the hell are you doing?' she says to me crossly in French.

'*Où est Johnny?*' I ask, trying to keep my emotions in check.

She shrugs and looks shifty.

'I need to know where he is.'

'I don't know,' she answers in English. Then she yawns and relaxes. 'He was here last night.' She gives me a knowing look.

I check the bathroom in case he's in there.

'What sort of a mood was he in?' I call to the girl. 'Was he doing drugs? You can tell me,' I add, coming out of the bathroom and looking at her. 'You won't get into trouble.'

'I think so,' she says. And from the look on her face, she *knows* so. 'What's wrong?' she asks, looking concerned.

'You should go,' I tell her, towering over her at the side of the bed.

She looks up at me, annoyed, for a moment, then lazily lifts up the bed covers and rummages around for a little while before pulling out a lacy black G-string. I feel increasingly nauseous as she unhurriedly turns it the right way around and then wriggles about underneath the covers and puts it on. She climbs out of bed, wearing just her knickers, and hunts out a skimpy red dress. She's only just slipped it over her head when we hear a groan from the other side of the room. We both look at each other sharply, and then race over to where the noise came from. Behind the chaise longue is Johnny, butt-naked and covered in his own puke.

'*Mon Dieu!*' she exclaims.

I kneel down, trying to ignore the sight of Johnny's limp cock protruding from between his legs. I may have dreamed about seeing Johnny naked, but accessorised with his own vomit? I don't think so.

I urgently pat him on the face. 'Johnny. Johnny!'

'Is he okay?' the girl asks, leaning forward. I push her back and reach over the chaise longue, grabbing Johnny's leather jacket and covering up his bits.

He groans again.

'Johnny!'

He opens his eyes and stares at me, unfocused. Then he closes them again.

'Johnny, wake up!' I demand, patting him on his face again. His eyes flutter open and he puts his hand up to his head. 'Ow . . .' he moans.

I need to get the girl out of the room and fast. The last thing we need is her selling her story to the tabloids and I don't want her to be a part of this any more than she already is. I stand up and grab my bag from inside the doorway. I hurriedly walk back to the sofa, pulling two hundred euros out of my purse as I go.

'Here,' I say, handing them over. 'For a taxi. You need to leave now.'

'I don't want your money!' she snaps.

'You need to leave now,' I repeat in French, fanning the fifty-euro notes out.

She stands up, sulkily. 'I don't want them!' she reiterates, glaring at the four notes in my hand.

I pick up a coat I'm assuming is hers and hand it to her. She takes it, then retrieves her black high-heel shoes from underneath the coffee table and slips them on. Johnny groans again and tries to sit up.

The girl glances over at him. 'I hope he's okay.'

'He'll be fine,' I quickly assure her, and usher her out of the room.

By the time I get back around the chaise longue to Johnny, he's flat on his back and out cold again.

Chapter 21

'I'm worried about him,' I say to Christian, nine days later. We're in the lobby of the hotel where we're staying for the Wembley Stadium concert. Christian wants to catch up with Johnny, but Johnny has told me under no circumstances to let anyone into his room. It's six o'clock in the evening and he's still in bed. His behaviour reminds me of how he was at the start of the tour, except this time I know it's down to drugs as well as depression.

I had to enlist Bill's help to get Johnny off the floor when we were in Glasgow the other morning. Even he looked dismayed at the sight of him.

'Do you think he'll be okay for the concert tonight?' Christian asks.

'I hope so,' I reply.

Johnny is not okay by any stretch of the imagination, but Bill insists on business as usual. He plies Johnny with whisky on the way to the venue and tries to get him psyched up by his enthusiasm.

'First gig at the new Wembley Stadium! Going to be a bit different from last time, eh? Eh?'

Johnny doesn't answer. We're sitting in a booth at the back of the tour bus, away from the rest of the band who are boozing it up at the front. Johnny is staring out through the window.

We've used a combination of bus and private jet on this tour so far. The bus is strangely more convenient most of the time, although the jet was not an experience I'll forget anytime soon. If only all air travel could be like that: gourmet meals, champagne on tap and not a queue to be seen.

'Here, mate, have another whisky.' Bill tries to sound cheerful.

Johnny makes no indication of having heard him.

'Come on, Johnny boy.' Bill swigs from the bottle. 'Mmm. Bloody good whisky, this is. Have some.'

'Bill, I don't think Johnny wants any whisky,' I state.

'Mind your own business! I know what's good for him!' Bill snaps.

'Don't speak to her like that,' Christian says, firmly.

'Oh, fuck off the lot of ya.' Bill gets to his feet and plods off down the aisle to join the party at the front of the bus.

'You alright?' Christian asks his friend.

Johnny sighs. 'Yeah.'

'You're obviously not, mate,' Christian says, glancing sideways at me.

Johnny sighs again and turns around to look at us both across the wooden table. 'What's anyone going to do about it?' He reaches over and takes the bottle of whisky Bill left.

'Johnny, should you be drinking that?' I ask, tentatively.

He sniggers and takes a swig. 'What are you, my mother? Oh no, that's right,' he says, sarcastically, '*she's* dead.'

I do a sharp intake of breath.

'You've only got tonight's gig to get through, then you'll be back in LA and able to rest up a bit.' Christian carries on as though he hasn't heard Johnny's last sentence.

'Yeah, and the fucking party.' Johnny gives him a wry look. His wrap party is tomorrow night and everyone who's anyone is going to be there. Select journalists from certain publications are even giving up their Christmas Eves to have a few minutes of interview time with him.

'I hate this fucking business,' Johnny adds.

'Come on, mate, how can you say that?' Christian tries to jolly him up. 'You love this shit. Once you get on stage, you'll be fine. You always are.'

Christian is right, to an extent, but after watching Johnny play every other day for almost two months, right now, backstage at Wembley Stadium, I can see that his heart isn't really in it. His performance is perfunctory. He's not really interacting with the audience, and that's a shame because the British critics are out in force tonight.

A member of the security team brings Bess to me after the show, and I get to meet the ubiquitous Serena at last. She's actually very pretty: short, spiky-black hairdo, olive skin and brown eyes.

I give Bess a big hug and shake Serena's hand. Serena's eyes are flitting around all over the place. I'm sure she's searching for Johnny, but he's nowhere to be seen.

'Did you like the concert?' I ask them.

'Yeah, it was great!' Bess enthuses.

'Really good,' Serena answers, distracted. She flicks her hair

267

back and puts one hand on her hip before letting it fall to her side again. I can see she's trying to act cool, but it would be much more endearing if she jumped up and down on the spot with excitement.

'I think Johnny's in his dressing room,' I say, putting them both out of their misery. 'I'm sure he'll come through soon.'

At that moment, Christian appears.

'Hey, Meg, you want something to drink?' he asks me.

'Sure. Christian, this is my good friend Bess and her flatmate, Serena.'

'Hi.' He shakes hands with both of them. 'Bess . . .' he thinks aloud. 'Didn't Meg used to live with you?'

'Well remembered,' I say. 'Let's all go and get a drink.'

Forty-five painfully long minutes pass and there's still no sign of Johnny. Christian stayed with us for the first half an hour until the small talk wore him out, and the rest of the crew are doing shots on the other side of the room where the groupies have also descended. I'm embarrassed to be here in front of Bess and I really want to go and check on Johnny. I tell her the latter.

'Can we come?' she asks, breathlessly. Serena's eyes light up at the thought.

'Um, not really,' I tell them with regret.

Bess's face is a mask of disappointment and Serena looks severely disgruntled.

'Sure, sure, I know you've got a job to do.' Bess dismisses me.

'I'll see if I can persuade him to come out,' I tell her, heart sinking.

As soon as I see him, I know that he'll be doing no such thing. He's sitting on a chair in his room, smoking a cigarette with the lights off. He's made his way through a bottle of vodka.

I switch the light on. 'Johnny, are you coming out?' I ask, cautiously.

'Another one . . .' He holds the empty bottle out to me. It wobbles from side to side in his hand.

'No,' I say. 'I think you've had enough.'

'Another one!' he says, angrily.

'No.' My voice is firm. 'Come back to the hotel.'

'Fine. I'll get it myself,' he slurs, rising unsteadily to his feet. He stumbles and I rush over to help him. I can barely support his weight. I need Christian!

'Johnny! Sit back down!' I shout. 'I'll get you another bottle if you wait here,' I fib, going to the door.

Christian is in the backstage area, picking the orange Smarties out of a bowl. He has about twenty in the palm of his hand.

'Want one?' he offers them to me.

'No. Christian, I need your help with Johnny.'

He knocks the sweets back in one and swiftly follows me out of the room. Bill is chatting up a couple of groupies near the sofas, and I'm glad he's distracted. I don't want him there. I barely register Bess and Serena standing next to the door.

'Where is it?' Johnny slurs, looking at my empty hands.

'Come on, mate, we'll get you back to the hotel,' Christian says, lifting him up.

'What the fuck?' Johnny asks, pulling Christian's left hand close to his eyes and scrutinising it. The orange food colouring from the Smarties has rubbed off on his hand.

'Smarties,' Christian tells him.

'You and your sweets, man,' Johnny chuckles, drunkenly. 'Get me my fucking vodka!' he shouts.

'Back at the hotel, mate,' Christian tells him, calmly. 'Come on, we've got to go.'

I follow Christian and a stumbling Johnny out of the room and down the corridor to the exit. Then I remember Bess and run back to say goodbye.

'I have to leave,' I tell her, hastily.

'Right, okay,' she says, looking unimpressed but not surprised.

I give her a hug. There's tension on both sides.

'I'm sorry,' I say. 'I'm sorry. I'll call you!' I promise, dashing out of the room.

There's a chasm opening up between us, and Serena is on Bess's side of the bridge. I don't know who is on mine. It should be Johnny, but it sure as hell doesn't feel like it.

Johnny has passed out by the time we get back to the hotel. I take a seat on the sofa in his suite and open up a magazine. I've decided to stay with him to make sure he's okay. Christian sits down next to me.

'What are you doing?' I ask.

'Keeping you company,' he says.

'You don't have to.'

'I know.' He goes over to the kitchenette area and switches on the kettle. 'Tea?' he asks.

'Vodka?' I fire back. 'Sorry, sick joke,' I say. 'Yeah, a tea would be nice.'

'He needs to go to rehab,' Christian says, bringing our cups over to the coffee table. 'Sugar?'

'One, thanks,' I reply. 'I wonder if he will?'

'Bill could make him.'

'Bill's an idiot,' I say.

Christian chuckles. 'He's not.'

'Yeah. He is.'

'He's been there for Johnny over the years.'

'He's been there for the money over the years, you mean,' I say, drily.

'I'm sure that helped. But you're wrong about him.' Christian hands over my cup. 'Fuck, I wish we had some custard creams.'

'Mmm! We could order room service?'

'What, custard creams from room service?'

'No, you wally. Just room service. I don't know, a nice slice of chocolate cake or something.'

'Actually, you know what?' he says. 'I could really do with some proper food. Don't look at me like that. I'm in a savoury mood.'

I gasp, jokingly. 'I can't believe you would defect to the other side!'

'I'm not defecting, Megan. I'm just dabbling.'

Johnny is still out cold in bed when our food arrives. Christian has opted for chicken curry.

'Why *did* you and your girlfriend split up?' I find the courage to ask, digging into my cake.

I'm half expecting him to tell me some silly story about her overfeeding his goldfish or something, but he nudges at his food with his fork, before saying, 'I wanted kids and she didn't.' He laughs, a touch bitterly. 'Not often you hear that, is it? She wasn't really one for commitment.'

I put my fork down in sympathy.

'I wasn't fussed about getting married, or anything,' he continues. 'Not really sure I believe in all that, to be honest. But I did want kids one day. Not immediately, but some day. She didn't want them at all.'

'That's sad,' I say.

'Yeah. Obviously wasn't meant to be. I saw her the other day. Bumped into her in Soho. She was with another guy.'

'That must've been weird.'

'Yeah, it was.'

'Are you still in love with her?' I ask, tentatively.

'No.' He shakes his head. 'But I would have preferred her to see *me* with another girl. You know, see what you're missing out on, kind of thing.'

I smile. 'I know exactly what you mean.' I tell him the story about Tom. 'He's with another girl now,' I say. 'I should probably call him while we're here.' I take a deep breath. 'But I'm not really sure I'm going to have time.'

Christian chuckles. 'No time to make a wee phone call?'

I give him a wry look. 'Yeah, okay, maybe I just don't want to.'

'Are you still in love with him?' He turns my earlier question around on itself.

'Definitely not. But hey, maybe we should both go for a walk through Soho later in the hope that our exes will spot *us* together.'

He smiles at me sideways and holds eye contact for a little longer than necessary. I quickly look away. I hope he doesn't think I want to go out with him in *that* way.

I yawn. 'Are you really going to stay here all night?'

'Probably,' he responds.

'You're good at that,' I say, remembering he did the same for me when I went overboard in Amsterdam.

'Did you take anything other than drink that night?' he asks me now.

'God, no! Definitely not.' At least Johnny knows me better than that. 'Why, did you think I had?' I ask.

'Maybe not on purpose, no,' he says.

'What do you mean? You think someone spiked my drink?'

'It's possible. You were pretty far gone.'

I consider this idea and anger wells up inside me.

'Hey, don't let it get to you now,' Christian tries to placate me.

Easy for you to say that. 'Who the hell would have done something like that?'

Christian shrugs. He glances over at Johnny.

'No way.' I shake my head. 'No way. He would never do that.'

'Who? Johnny?' Christian asks.

'Yes. You just looked at him.'

'Not because I thought he spiked your drink,' he scoffs.

'Oh, okay.'

'Listen,' he says, after an uncomfortable silence. 'Why don't you go off to bed? There's no point in both of us being awake all night.'

'In that case, I should stay,' I tell him. 'I'm his employee.'

'Yeah, and I'm his friend. And blood is thicker than water, and all that stuff.'

'Fair enough.' Not that they're related, but I know what he means.

'Anyway, I haven't got a room at the hotel,' he adds. 'But let's go for breakfast in the morning, hey?' he says to me. 'I'll come and knock for you at nine.'

'You didn't last time,' I point out.

'I will this time.'

At nine o'clock the next morning, there's a knock on my hotel-room door.

'Is he awake?'

'He was just starting to stir,' Christian replies. 'Has quite a headache.'

We go downstairs to the restaurant for a change of scenery and devour some fluffy American-style pancakes with maple syrup.

Afterwards we head back upstairs to Johnny's suite. We're expecting him to still be in bed, so Christian uses the key card he swiped from the bedside table.

We walk into the room and straight away see the bed is empty. Turning the corner, we're greeted with the sight of Johnny snorting cocaine off the coffee table.

'Johnny, what the fuck are you doing?' Christian shouts, rushing over to him. 'You've got a problem, man!'

'Fuck off,' Johnny shouts. 'Don't you dare fucking touch that!' He grabs Christian's hand, which was on the verge of sweeping the coke off the table.

'You need help, bro!'

Johnny sniggers and leans down with his straw. Christian and I watch in dismay as he snorts up a line right in front of us. He sniffs and wipes his nostril, then lounges back on the sofa, bottle of whisky in his hand.

'Meg, can you get me some fags?' he asks me.

'Piss off, you dickhead,' Christian snaps. 'Don't act like this is nothing, because it's not. This isn't normal. You're going to end up in a fucking state just like you did seven years ago.'

'Oh, and you would know about that, would you?' Johnny looks at him, angrily.

'Hey, the fact that I wasn't there is nobody's fault but your own.'

'Yeah, yeah,' Johnny spits. 'I know. If only I hadn't slept with your fucking girlfriend. I know that's why you never introduced me to Clare,' Johnny adds, nonchalantly. 'I would have fucked her, too.'

'You son of a bitch,' Christian says, stepping forward and then stopping. If looks could kill, Johnny would be dead right about now.

'How dare you talk about my deceased mother like that?' Johnny fakes melodrama.

'Fuck you, you arsehole. Stop using your dead mum to get sympathy.'

'Christian!' I shout.

'It's true, Meg. He does it all the time.'

'That's enough,' I say. 'Cut it out, both of you.'

'No, I will not cut it out,' Christian snaps. 'I *know* you, Johnny *Sneeden*. You're a fucked-up son of a bitch. No disrespect to MRS Sneeden.'

Before I know what's happening, Johnny is off the sofa and hurling himself at Christian.

'STOP IT!' I scream, as Johnny shoves Christian backwards into the coffee table. It cracks underneath his weight and cocaine dust flies everywhere. Christian is back up on his feet before I know it and he punches Johnny squarely in the face. Johnny stumbles backwards and swings at Christian. He misses. Christian grabs his coat, gives us both a glare that would stop traffic, and storms out of the hotel room. Johnny slumps down on the sofa. I go to his side. His nose is bleeding.

'Oh, shit!' I say, trying to take his hand away from his face so I can see if his nose is broken. I wouldn't have a clue how to tell if it is, mind.

'Hang on, I'll get you some ice.'

There's none in the tiny fridge so I call room service. Johnny reaches for the whisky bottle and takes a swig from it.

'Johnny, please! You've had enough!'

'Painkiller,' he says to me, glumly.

'Johnny, please,' I say again. 'You need help. You can't meet the press in this state.'

'I'm not going into fucking rehab. Rehab is for pussies.'

'Come on, Johnny. You need a break from all this.'

'I'm not going into fucking rehab,' he repeats. 'You can help me, Nutmeg. You always help me, Nutmeg.' He holds out his hand and grabs mine, pulling me down onto the sofa and looking at me with sorrowful green eyes.

'I can't help you unless you help yourself,' I say.

He snorts with laughter and I frown at him.

'Sorry, sorry,' he says, trying to be serious. 'I can't help you unless you help yourself!' he mimics me, in much the same way Bill did when he called me prim and proper. It really rubs me up the wrong way.

'Fine,' I say, standing up.

And that's when I spot the syringe.

'Johnny, what the hell is that?'

He follows my stare. 'Aw, Nutmeg,' he says. 'I haven't used it.'

'I can't do this. I can't do this, Johnny.' The colour drains from my face as I back away.

'No, wait!' His tone is urgent. 'Meg, I swear to you I haven't used it. I've done everything else, but not that.'

'So why do you have a syringe, Johnny?' I don't know if I believe him. 'I have to go.'

'Meg! Stop! I need you. Don't leave me now. I'm sorry. I know you're right. I do have a problem. This whole tour has been . . . I don't know. I *do* want to sort myself out,' he reiterates, looking at me seriously. 'I'll go cold turkey. Anything. But I'm not going into rehab.'

Chapter 22

I know how Bill is going to react to my plan and I'm too much of a chicken to tell him face to face. I'll call him once we're on the road. But first I need to organise things, which means hiring a car, and calling my parents . . .

'Dad, I need a favour.'

'Sweetheart, we've just been talking about you. What's going on with Johnny? Everywhere we look we see something awful about him . . .'

'Dad, please. Johnny needs help. I'm going to help him.'

'Is that Meg? Let me speak to her!' I hear my mum demand in the background.

'No, Cynthia, I'm dealing with this!' my dad says, firmly.

'Give me the bleedin' phone!' I hear a scuffle and then my mum comes on the line.

'What are you doing? What's going on?'

'Mum, I was just talking to Dad.'

'Your father's otherwise indisposed. You can talk to me,' Mum says.

I sigh. 'Okay. I was wondering if I could borrow Gran's house.'

'What for?' Mum demands.

'I need to take Johnny there.'

'That Johnny Jefferson is trouble! I knew he would be!'

'Mum, you'd never even heard of him until I got this job.'

'I had heard of him!' She gets all uppity.

'Whatever. He needs to get away.'

'He needs to go to Alcoholics Anonymous, from the sounds of it.'

And Narcotics Anonymous, but I don't tell her that.

'He won't go into rehab, Mum. He needs to recoup somewhere quiet. Can you help me or not?'

After they've told me they'll let Gran's neighbour know I'll be collecting the spare set of keys, I head out of the hotel to collect the car. I've hired a Vauxhall Vectra. It's a far cry from Johnny's Bugatti Veyron, but it won't draw attention to us, which is exactly what I'm after right now.

The hotel receptionist is surprised when I settle up the bill early, so we have to be quick about getting out of there in case she alerts any of the tour crew.

My phone buzzes on the way back up to the room. I've been ignoring calls all morning, but now I see from caller ID that this one is from Christian.

'How is he?' he asks.

'He's not going to make the wrap party tonight,' I tell him, coming out of the lift and walking down the corridor.

'What do you mean?'

'He's not well, Christian. He needs to get away.'

'He needs to go into rehab, that's what he needs.'

'He won't. I've already tried that.' I reach Johnny's room and wait outside.

'Put him on. Let me speak to him.'

'I'm sorry, he doesn't want to talk to anyone.' Especially not to you.

'He needs expert help, Meg,' Christian says. 'You can't save him.'

'That may be so, Christian. But I'm going to try.'

After we hang up, I switch my phone off. It can stay that way for the time being. I'll call Bill later.

Bill is predictably furious. We're already on the M1 going north, but I don't tell him that. My parents are the only ones who know where we're going and I've sworn them to secrecy.

Bill demands that we turn around and get our arses straight back to the hotel, but I steadfastly refuse.

'There is no way he's capable of talking to anyone from the press tonight, Bill.' I glance across at Johnny in the passenger's seat. He's leaning up against the door, dark shades on. I think he's asleep.

'That's not your call, girlie! Do you know what a fucking nightmare it will be for me to cancel everyone?' he demands. 'How many important people you're going to piss off? How much this could affect press coverage and therefore album sales in the future?'

'I'm sorry. But it can't be helped.' I keep my voice calm. 'Listen, I've got to go. I'm driving. I shouldn't be on the phone.' I don't tell him I've got my hands-free plugged in.

'DON'T YOU BLOODY WELL HANG UP ON—'

I end the call and switch the phone off again. That's more than enough negativity for now.

'Pretty pissed off, hey?' Johnny murmurs from beside me.

'You could say that.' I indicate to move back into the fast lane.

'Thank fuck for that,' Johnny says.

'What? Thank fuck that he's pissed off?' I ask, confused.

'No. Thank fuck you've speeded up. I could run quicker than this.'

I don't laugh. I'm in no mood for his jokes.

'Where are we actually going?' he asks.

'Scarborough. To my gran's house.'

'The one who died?'

'Yes.'

'Creepy.' He shivers.

'It's not creepy!' I snap.

'Sorry.' He's contrite. 'Is this the same gran who gave you that necklace?'

I'm surprised. Does he remember that from Serengeti's premiere?

'You know, the red sparkly one you wore to whatshername's premiere?' he continues, when I don't answer.

'Yes, I know the one you're talking about. Yes, she is the one who gave it to me.'

The radio DJ starts to talk about a competition to win tickets to Johnny's party tonight. Bill won't have had time to inform the press, yet. He's probably still thinking we'll turn around and come back.

Johnny reaches over and switches the radio off.

'Don't need the reminder, sorry.'

He falls silent after that.

The further we drive from London, the more uneasy I become. What if Bill's right? Am I putting Johnny's career at risk by taking him away like this? What will his record company think of me? What the hell am I doing? Who do I think I am? I'm just a PA for an architects' firm, for crying out loud. What do I know about any of this?

I look across at Johnny. He's twitching in his sleep. I turn my attention back to the road.

It's Christmas Eve and it's like a ghost town in Scarborough. All the lights along the shorefront have been switched off and there's an eerie silence about the place. I start to dread going into my gran's once warm and friendly house.

I take a left and wind up into the narrow roads towards the castle. Parking is a nightmare up here, so we'll probably have to walk a little way. It's a windy night, but thankfully it's not raining, and at least we don't have much luggage. I packed only our bare necessities, and Johnny brought his guitar, which I guess is a necessity to him. The hotel is holding onto the rest of our stuff.

We arrive at Gran's house and sadness washes over me as I look up at the dark windows. I collect the keys from the neighbour's and exchange condolences, while Johnny waits at the front door.

The house is still full of Gran's things – Mum and Dad haven't had a chance to come over and sort everything out yet – and it's strange seeing her beloved photo frames above the fireplace, telling their own story of my family and its history.

'Shall I take you to your room?' I ask, trying to swallow the lump in my throat.

'Sure.'

We keep our coats on for the time being because the house is so cold. Johnny follows me up the narrow staircase. My gran should have three bedrooms, but one is more of a cluttered store-room, so effectively she has only two. I'm not sure how I feel about sleeping in her bed, because my initial instinct is to put

Johnny in the spare room, but then it occurs to me he should really have the larger room.

'Is this okay for you?' I ask, surveying my gran's small double bed. It's still covered in her dark-green bedspread, although it's not as pristinely made as it would be if she were still here. I try to suppress my grief. 'Sorry, I know it's not exactly what you're used to . . .'

'It's fine,' Johnny brushes me off, propping his guitar up against Gran's wooden chest of drawers.

'The heating will kick in soon,' I reassure him.

'Meg, it's fine.'

'Do you want to watch some TV? I can't believe it's Christmas Eve, can you?' I try to sound light-hearted.

'I'll be down in a minute,' he says.

A few minutes later he pokes his head around the door.

'I'm just going to nip out.'

'Why? Where are you going?' I sit up in alarm.

'Just going to pop to the pub.'

'Johnny, what do you mean? You said you wouldn't drink!'

'Chill out, Nutmeg. I'm not going to drink. I need to get some fags.'

'Okay,' I say, hesitantly.

'I never said I was quitting smoking,' he points out.

'No, I know. But maybe I'll come with you?' I start to get up. 'Or I could go and get them for you myself?'

'No, it's fine. I won't be long.'

'Johnny, I think I should come. I really don't want you slip up.' I'm on the edge of my seat now.

'Meg, no,' he says, firmly. 'If this is going to work, you're going to have to trust me. I'll be back in ten minutes.'

The door slams behind him and I slump back on the sofa again. But I can't concentrate. I feel anxious. If something happens to him here, I really am on my own. The thought scares me.

Half an hour later he still hasn't returned, and I am going out of my mind with worry. I try to tell myself that it will be okay, that not much is open and he's probably struggling to find cigarettes, but it's little relief.

Another half an hour passes. Where is he? Maybe he's lost.

But Scarborough isn't a small town. If I go out there now, I could very well be searching for hours. I may never find him at all. Oh God, what if he falls off a cliff into the sea? I killed Johnny Jefferson! That's what Bill would say. I'll be hunted by mad fans for the rest of my life. I've got to do something.

I stand up and put my coat back on, having taken it off only a short while ago. Grabbing my purse and Gran's keys, I walk to the door. But I stop short of actually leaving the house.

What if he's just gone for a walk? What if he comes back when I've gone out? He won't be able to get back inside. I'll probably drive him to drink by doing that. He'll have to go somewhere warm, like . . . a pub. Damn it.

I go back and perch on the sofa for another hour, after which I start to think I don't have any other choice. I can't ring around all the pubs and bars. What would I say? 'Excuse me, is Johnny Jefferson – you know, the international rock star and multimillionaire, the one who's just failed to show up at his own wrap party – yes, *him* – is he slumped in the corner somewhere? No? Never mind, I'll try the next pub.'

Like that's *really* not going to draw attention to us.

I have no choice. I'm going to have to go out and look for him myself.

The night is so dark and cold and I feel like my hands are going to freeze because I've left my gloves in Gran's spare room. Too restless to go back, I plunge my hands into my coat pockets and set off down the narrow roads towards the shorefront. I'm sure I saw an open pub down there, and if I saw it, that means Johnny saw it. So much for trusting him.

He's not in the first pub so I ask the landlord if he knows of another one open. He's disgruntled that his pub isn't good enough for me, so I tell him I'm looking for someone. There's no sign of Johnny in the next pub, either, so I go through that rigmarole again and set off hoping it'll be a case of third time lucky. I despise Johnny for making me walk into these pubs all alone and get stared at by dodgy old men, while I search them high and low. I suddenly realise I haven't been looking in the gents and the thought slams into me that that's probably where he is: kneeling in front of a toilet or laid out in his own vomit. Oh God, do I really have to go back to that first pub and ask the landlord to check for me?

I'm filled with dismay. I'll just check this third pub and then I'll retrace my steps.

I walk into the dark and dingy pub. The ceiling is stained yellow from cigarette smoke over the years, and the patterned red and black carpet feels soggy underfoot. I feel five sets of eyes on me as I look around the room.

'Can I help you, love?' the landlord calls.

'No, thanks,' I tell him, horribly aware of how out of place I seem here. 'I'm just looking for someone.'

Johnny isn't here so I go through a door at the back to a second room. It's empty. I'm about to give up and return to the first pub when the landlord calls out again.

'I think I know who you're looking for.' The old guys sitting at the bar, nursing their drinks, watch me with vague interest. 'He left about ten minutes ago,' the landlord continues.

'Where did he go?' I feel light-headed as adrenalin kicks in.

'I don't know. Had to ask him to leave,' he says, ominously, and from his expression I suspect it was a forced exit.

'Please don't tell anyone he was here,' I beg.

'Why the bloody hell would I do that?' he scoffs. 'He's not famous or anything, is he?' He clocks my expression. '*Is* he?' he asks, incredulously.

'No, of course not!' I shout, running out onto the street and looking left and right. I take a punt on right and hurry back towards the shorefront. I run down to the beach and peer through the darkness. The fairground rides off in the distance are deserted and the amusement arcades and ice-cream parlours have shut up shop for Christmas. Waves crash hard against the shore and it starts to rain. Could this night get any worse? No, don't answer that.

And then I see him.

'Johnny!' I shout, but my voice is engulfed by the elements.

He's zigzagging along the footpath above me. I run back up the steps and after him.

'Johnny!' I shout again. He slowly turns around and sees me, drunkenly wobbling on the spot. 'Oh, what have you done?' I despair.

'Needed fags,' he slurs, trying to suck the life out of one that became a butt long ago. 'Won't let you smoke indoors anymore. Fucking ridiculous.'

'Come on.' I take his arm.

It takes forever and I'm wet and freezing, but we finally make it back to the house. I think of how Gran would roll over in her grave if she could see me like this. She was always very protective.

I start to doubt myself again. Am I crazy to think I can help him? Should I take him back to London?

No, Meg. Persevere.

I get him as far as the front room before he collapses, and I almost cry with frustration trying to get him out of his wet clothes. I put on the electric fire and grab some blankets from upstairs. There is no way I'm capable of getting him up there on my own. In fact, I know I'm going to have to rethink this plan altogether.

By the time he comes round, late on Christmas morning, I have our packed bags and his guitar in the hallway.

Years ago, when I was about ten and Susan had just left for university, my parents took me to stay in a cottage in a remote part of the Yorkshire Dales. I've been scouring the internet on my phone and have found it. I didn't really expect it to be vacant at this time of the year, but I was hoping the owners might be able to recommend somewhere else nearby. I was amazed when they told me it was available and I could collect the keys in a few hours. Some good luck, at last.

'Come on, get up,' I demand, when Johnny starts to stir.

'Where am I?' he groans.

'In Scarborough, Johnny. At my gran's house,' I remind him, unhappily.

'I feel like shit.'

'I'm not surprised after what you drank last night. Merry bloody Christmas, boss. Thanks for going back on your word like that.'

He squints up at me and suddenly seems to remember what happened. 'Whoops,' he says, putting his hand to his head.

'It's not fair, Johnny. If something had happened to you . . . It would be bad enough if you were just an ordinary friend of mine who I was helping through a rough patch. If you fell off a cliff then or drowned in the sea, at least I'd be allowed to mourn in peace. But if something happened to you, the whole bloody world would know about it and I'd be responsible.'

'Don't be so melodramatic, Meg. I wasn't going to kill myself.'

'Don't you *dare* call me melodramatic, Johnny!' Now I'm angry. 'I've gone out on a limb for you!' I pause, then say, 'Maybe this is just too hard. Maybe I should just quit and leave you to it.'

'What, quit your job? Quit working for me?' He starts to sit up.

'Yes.'

'Don't say that.' He looks remorseful. 'Look, I'm sorry, okay? Give me another chance. Don't give up on me, yet.'

I sigh. 'So. In light of recent events . . .' I give him a look. 'There's been a change of plan.'

He stares at me, questioningly.

'We're not staying in Scarborough. There's too much temptation. We're going somewhere in the middle of nowhere, where there are no pubs, no off-licences, and no access to any of the crap you've been getting yourself caught up in. But I need to know if you're with me on this. *Really* with me on this. Because you have to commit, otherwise I'm taking you straight back to London.'

He smirks, but stops short of taking the piss out of my 'psychobabble bullshit', as he'd probably call it.

'Yep,' he says, rising to his feet and reaching for his now-dry T-shirt from the radiator. 'Let's do this thing.'

Chapter 23

We drive west out of town, past houses laced with rope lights, and soon we're in the midst of the greenest of green fields. Flocks of birds sweep and soar high above the bare trees, and the berries on the bushes lining the road are abundant. It's a grey and drizzly day, but it's not too cold. We won't be seeing snow this Christmas.

Johnny is asleep next to me. He's rolled up his leather jacket into a ball and wedged it against the window as a pillow. His tattooed arms are bare so I've turned the heating right up.

We arrive just after three o'clock, while it's still light. I've stopped at a petrol station along the way to stock up on enough essentials and ready meals to last us a week, but I'll need to go to a local supermarket to stock up after that. My cooking will pale in comparison to Rosa's, no doubt about it, but desperate times call for desperate measures.

We collect the keys from the owners of the cottage, who live in a village ten miles away. Johnny stays in the car so he won't be noticed, but they invite us in for a cup of tea and some Christmas pudding. It breaks my heart to say no.

The cottage is much smaller than I remembered, a grey-stone, two-storey building, surrounded by a dry stone wall and situated at the bottom of a large, grass-covered hill. There's a stream running through the garden and a little bridge crossing it. The garden is leafless and muddy, but I remember it in summer when it was full of flowers.

There's no central heating, but the cottage does have gas heaters in most rooms, and in the living room downstairs there's an open fireplace. Upstairs are two small bedrooms and a bathroom. I give Johnny the back room, facing the hill. I take the one facing the road at the other side. I say road, but it's actually more of a track. We really are in the middle of nowhere here.

I put my bags in my room and go back downstairs to unpack the groceries. Johnny appears twenty minutes later.

'Do you want to build a fire and I'll make us a cup of tea?' I ask him.

'Sure.'

He goes through to the living room and I switch the kettle on.

'Actually, Nutmeg . . .' He comes through a moment later. 'I think I might pop out.'

I laugh. 'No way.'

'I just feel like a drive, that's all.'

I ignore him.

'Nutmeg, come on.'

'No, Johnny, *you* come on,' I say angrily. 'You're not going out to get booze. Live with it.'

'Where are the car keys?'

'You're not having them, Johnny.'

'Where are the fucking car keys?'

'I've hidden them,' I shoot back.

'Give them to me.'

'You can keep asking me as much as you like, but you're not getting them.'

Now he's angry. 'Give me the car keys or you're fired.'

'No!' I raise my voice.

He glares at me and starts rooting through the kitchen drawers.

'You won't find them,' I tell him, calmly.

I follow him through to the living room where he starts opening cupboards and searching under ornaments.

'Seriously, Nutmeg.' He turns to me. 'I need them. Please. Where are they?'

'Johnny, NO.'

He picks up one of the ornaments on the mantelpiece, a little white dog with floppy ears. 'Give them to me or I'm dropping this.'

I frown. 'Johnny, don't do that.'

'I'll drop it . . .'

'You're not having them.'

'Fine,' he says, and lets go of the dog. I flinch as it breaks into a dozen pieces on the stone floor.

He picks up another ornament, a young girl in a red skirt.

'Break them all. See if I care. You've got enough money, you can replace them.' I hope he doesn't call my bluff.

'Oh, for fuck's sake.' He bangs the ornament back down on the mantelpiece, leaving it intact. 'Nutmeg, I *will* fire you if you don't give me those car keys.'

'Let me make it easier for you: I quit.'

We glare at each other for a full ten seconds, both of us resolute. Finally he picks up his jacket from the sofa and puts it on. 'Fine. I'll walk to the nearest village.'

'It will take you hours,' I point out. 'You'll get lost and will probably freeze to death.'

'If that's what it takes . . .' He shrugs, expecting me to give in.

But I won't. 'Fine,' I shrug. 'You're getting a bit old and past it anyway. About time you moved over and let someone else have a taste of the limelight. You can live on through your music,' I add, theatrically.

He glowers at me, then storms out through the front door, slamming it shut behind him.

I sweep up the china and then sit on the sofa pretending to read a copy of *Horse & Hound* magazine from 1999, but as the minutes tick by, I become more and more anxious. When the front door opens again, it's all I can do to act unfazed.

'Shall I build us a fire, then?' Johnny asks, standing in front of me.

'That would be nice.' I snap my magazine shut and stand up. 'How about I make us a cup of tea?'

To my amazement, Johnny doesn't lose his nerve again, but the same almost can't be said for me. There have been several times when I've wanted to call Christian – and even Bill. It's the hardest thing I've ever done, watching Johnny experience aches and shakes, cold sweats and even delirium. I ran through to his room the other night because he was screaming, and the look of terror on his face was enough to turn my blood cold. He thought there were spiders climbing all over his body. I eventually managed to calm him down, but afterwards I went back to my room and sobbed my heart out. I had no idea what I was getting myself into.

291

We've run out of supplies, so I drive to the next village to get some while Johnny is asleep, and return to find him still in bed. I've bought just about every type of magazine I could find in the newsagent, including some music titles for Johnny. The news of his disappearance hasn't made the weekly magazine press yet – their offices would have closed for Christmas – but I have a quick flick through the *NME* to see if I can see anything in there by Christian. I can't.

I wonder how he's getting on. I wonder what he must think, us running off like this. I bet he's surprised. I bet he's pissed off, actually. This would have been brilliant fodder for his book and now I've gone and buggered that right up.

Johnny emerges, sleepily navigating the steep staircase wearing a black T-shirt and black leather trousers. It's funny seeing him here like this. I just grabbed what I could find, clothes-wise, but I probably should have sought out some more casual attire for him to wear.

'Good morning,' I chirp. 'Can I get you anything? Scrambled eggs, maybe?'

'Have you been down the shop?' he asks, eyes lighting up.

'Yes, just nipped out.'

'Did you get me some fags?'

'Yes, Johnny.' I sigh, wandering through to the kitchen.

'Give 'em, give 'em, give 'em . . .' He waggles his fingers out at me.

'You haven't run out, yet, have you?' I ask, opening a drawer and retrieving a packet.

'Almost.'

He takes the packet and some matches from me, and lights up, his hands shaking. Then he opens the window above the sink and hangs his cigarette hand out of it. Bringing his fag in for a moment, he takes a drag and leans across the counter to blow smoke out of the window. He's letting all the cold air in, but I appreciate the sentiment of him not smoking inside.

'Why don't we go for a walk?' I suggest, desperate to get out of the house.

'Bit bloody cold, isn't it?' He shivers.

'It will do you good.'

He throws his cigarette butt out of the window and closes it again.

'I got you some magazines,' I tell him.

'Which ones?'

'Oh, a whole stack.'

He follows me through to the living room and riffles through them. 'Cool, thanks.'

'You're welcome.' I smile. 'Now, can we go for a walk?'

He tears his eyes away from an article about the hit singles of the year and looks up at me. 'Are you bored?'

'Might be,' I answer, folding my arms.

'Come on, then.' He casually drops the magazines on the sofa. 'I'll just get my shoes.'

I found a couple of old coats in the cupboard under the stairs the other day and I pull them out now and hand one to Johnny when he returns.

'Fuck off, you're not getting me in that.'

'You won't be warm enough in your leather jacket,' I warn him, still holding his coat out. 'Put this on over the top.'

'Nutmeg, that is a proper flashers' trench coat. I'm not wearing it.'

'Well, I'm putting mine on.' It's a giant, puffa ski-jacket in pink and aqua green with fluro yellow piping.

293

'Jesus, yours is even worse,' he says.

I ignore him and throw his coat on the table, squeezing myself into my puffy sleeves. Then I turn to him and comically gush, 'Mmm, it's really warm!'

He chuckles. 'You look like a right idiot.' Then he says, 'Fuck it,' and puts his own coat on.

I start to laugh, which is a nice feeling after a week of melancholy.

He points at me. 'You shut it.'

He seems so much better now, and the realisation that I was right to bring him here fills me with joy.

We trek out of the house and cross over the bridge. The water is flowing much faster now in winter. I remember my dad and I making little boats out of paper and racing them down the stream. I tell Johnny about it.

'Do you get along well with your parents?' he asks.

'Most of the time, yes.' I smile sideways at him. 'They're not too happy about me running away with you, though.'

'Aren't they? Whoops.'

We're walking along the stream, in the direction of the fast-flowing water. There are a couple of ducks struggling to paddle against the current.

'Should have brought some bread,' I comment.

'I bet you had lots of pets when you were growing up, didn't you?' he asks, amused.

'I had a few,' I admit. 'What about you?'

'Goldfish.' He glances at me. 'I wanted a dog, so much.'

'Weren't you allowed one?'

He pauses for a moment before answering. 'We were going to get one. But then Mum got sick.'

I keep quiet, hoping he'll open up to me more, but he doesn't.

'You could have one now?' I suggest.

'Away too much. Too cruel.'

'Wouldn't do a Paris Hilton, then? Hire someone else to look after a menagerie of animals?'

'Bollocks to that. I'll get a dog when I retire. A proper dog. None of that Footsie shit.'

I laugh. 'You'll be waiting a while, then.'

'You said I was getting old and past it, the other day . . .'

'I was joking!'

'That was a horrible thing to say.' He looks hurt.

'I didn't mean it!'

'Made me feel really awful,' he adds.

'Okay, now you're milking it,' I say. 'Anyway, you told me I was fired.'

'No,' he says, 'you quit.'

I laugh. 'Alright, then.'

'You haven't really quit, though, have you?'

'No, Mr Jefferson. I'll probably still be working for you when I'm thirty. *If* you live that long,' I add.

'Oi!' He shoves me and I almost stumble into the stream.

'You bastard!' I squeal and push him back.

We continue walking for a moment and he lulls me into a false sense of security before nudging me again.

'Johnny!'

He wraps his arm around my shoulder and pulls me in for an affectionate squeeze.

'Who would save me ten thousand dollars on my car insurance if you left, hey?'

He lets me go and I look at him in surprise. I told him that on the way to Big Sur, but I didn't really think he took it in, much less that he would remember it.

'Shall we head back? It's getting dark,' he says.

He builds another fire while I decide to try my hand at making some dinner for us. I pour some olive oil into a frying pan and start to chop onions into chunks, adding them into the pan as I go.

'What are we having?' Johnny comes into the kitchen as I add another chunk of onion to the now-smoking oil.

'Tomato and onion pasta,' I tell him.

He peers into the pan, the contents of which seem to be burning.

'Oh, no,' I exclaim in dismay.

'You've got the heat on too high,' he says, taking the pan off the stove and discarding the charred veg. He wipes the pan out with kitchen towel and puts it back on the stove with fresh olive oil.

'I didn't know you could cook.' I'm actually being sarcastic. I grab another onion from the fridge and start to chop it.

'Don't have to do it very often, but you are making a right balls-up of that. Budge over,' he says, extricating the knife from my fingers and pushing me out of the way.

'Oi!' I shout.

He starts to slice the onion, super-finely.

Now I'm impressed. 'Where did you learn to do that?' The slivers of onion are so fine I can practically see through them.

'Mum taught me.' He pauses. His hands are shaking.

'What, when you were . . .'

'Twelve. A year before she died,' he confirms, glancing at me. 'Wanted to teach me how to fend for myself before I went to live with my no-good dad.' He keeps his tone light. 'Tell you what,' he says. 'You go through to the living room and I'll finish up here.'

'This is very domesticated, Johnny Jefferson.' I look up at him, amused.

'Do you think so, Meg Stiles?'

'I didn't know you knew my last name,' I comment.

'Of course I know your last name, Nutmeg! Jesus, what sort of a boss do you think I am?'

'Sorry,' I say, feeling embarrassed.

'Go on,' he says, pointing towards the living room with the knife.

I obey, going through and sitting down on the rug in front of the fire. I lean my back up against the sofa. Johnny comes through fifteen minutes later. I start to get up.

'Shall we sit down there?' he suggests.

'Sure.' I settle back down.

'I am a crap boss, actually.' He hands me my plate of food. 'I didn't even get you a Christmas present.'

'You didn't have to get me a Christmas present,' I tell him. 'I didn't get you one.'

'Yeah, but you don't have to. I'm your boss. I should have got you one.'

'Don't worry about it.'

'I'll make it up to you,' he promises.

'Just don't fall off the wagon again, that's all the present I need.'

He grins at me. 'You're so cute, Nutmeg.'

I twirl some spaghetti around my fork and try not to drop any sauce on myself as I balance my plate on my lap.

'This is really nice,' I tell him. 'Your mum taught you well.'

He smiles and stares into the fire.

'What did Christian mean when he called you Johnny Sneeden?' I ask cautiously.

It's a while before he answers. 'My mum's surname was Sneeden. I changed my name to Jefferson when I went to live with my dad. That was his surname,' he explains. 'They never got married. Mum didn't even put Dad's name on my birth certificate.'

'Oh, right,' I say, awkwardly. 'Well, Jefferson does sound cooler . . .'

'Mmm,' he agrees, still staring into the flames.

'You feel guilty about it.' It's not a question. 'I'm sure she'd understand.'

He pushes his spaghetti around on his plate for a moment. 'I'm not sure that she would.'

'What was she like?' I ask, tentatively.

'I don't really know. She was just my mum to me. I know that she loved me. I know it would hurt her to see me like this. She always told me not to end up like my dad.'

'What was he like?'

'Drink, drugs, women . . .' He glances at me.

I don't say anything.

'Exactly,' he says, putting his half-empty plate down beside him.

'Why do you sleep with so many women?' It's out of my mouth before I can decide whether or not it's a good idea to ask.

'Why not?' He shrugs.

I look away from him. 'I just don't know how you can do that.'

'It's just sex, Nutmeg.' He glances at me.

'But how can you detach yourself?' I furrow my brow, not understanding.

'Why? Can't you?' he asks, before casting his eyes to the heavens and adding, 'Silly question.'

'No, actually,' I tell him anyway. 'I like sex to mean something.'

'Of course you do.'

'You think I'm naive.'

'Did I say that?'

'You may as well have,' I say.

'Actually, I think you're sweet.' He continues, 'I think you look at life through rose-tinted glasses.'

'I'm not as innocent as I seem.' I'm now a tad annoyed.

'Okay . . .' he says, crossing his legs in front of him and staring at the fire. He clearly doesn't agree.

'I'm not!' I insist. 'Anyway, this is not about me. I want to understand you.'

'Why?'

'I don't know.' I avert my gaze. 'I just do. So how many women have you slept with?'

He chuckles. 'Come on. I'm not answering that.'

'Why not? Can't you remember?' I challenge him.

'Actually, no,' he says, flippantly. 'But even if I could, I wouldn't tell you.'

'Well, can you tell me how many women you've had *meaningful* sex with?'

'That's easy. None.'

I look at him in disbelief. He meets my gaze quite calmly, before explaining. 'You can't have meaningful sex if you've never been in love, can you?' He picks up the glass of water by his side and takes a sip, putting it back down with a look of distaste on his face. 'God, I miss whisky.'

I ignore his comment. My jaw is still on the floor. 'You've never been in love?'

'No.'

299

'Are you serious?'

'Why would I lie?'

'You've been with all those women and you've never fallen for *any* of them?'

'No.'

'But what about Serengeti?'

'No.'

'What about . . . Christian's girlfriend?' I enquire, hesitantly.

'No.'

'Didn't you even have a first love?'

'No, Nutmeg, no, no, no!' He throws his hands up in the air. 'I have *never* been in love!'

'Okay, okay!' Pause. 'That's really sad.'

He laughs. 'Jesus, girl, if I'm not sad about it, why should you be?' He gets to his feet and bends over to pick up his plate from the floor before holding his hand down for mine. He takes them both through to the kitchen.

I can't believe he's never been in love. Maybe I can make him fall in love with me? Yes! That's what I'll do.

Ha!

He returns a moment later.

'Hey, did you know it's New Year's Eve?' I say, suddenly.

'No shit?'

'What shall we do?'

'Get pissed? Joke. Shall we go into town?' he suggests.

I shift, uncomfortably. 'I'm not sure that's such a good idea.'

'Why not? Nutmeg, I'm not going to run into the nearest pub and do tequila shots.'

'No, I know.' I shrug.

'You don't know. But you're going to have to trust me again sometime.'

I stay silent.

'Maybe not tonight, though, hey?' He goes over to the cupboard under the stairs. I sit there, feeling wretched. 'What else is in here?' He rummages around for a bit. 'Only crappy coats?'

'What are you looking for?' I ask.

'Don't they have any board games or something?' He spreads the contents of the cupboard on the floor.

'Johnny!' I laugh. 'Stop making a mess! They're not in there. They're in the cupboard under the window.'

He goes to the cupboard in question and starts rooting around. 'Ah, here they are.' He pulls out a pile of old boxes.

'Are you serious?' I ask, in amazement. 'Board games?'

'Yeah. Why not?'

'Didn't figure you for a board games kind of guy.'

He takes no notice of me and studies the boxes, one by one.

'Snakes and Ladders?'

'What else is there?'

'A jigsaw . . .'

'Right.'

'Trivial Pursuit?'

'Mmm.'

'Monopoly!' he exclaims.

'No.' I shake my head. 'I hate Monopoly.'

'Why? What's Monopoly ever done to you?' he asks, placing the boxes on the table and pulling out a chair.

'People get so bitter with Monopoly. I don't enjoy winning and causing everyone else's misery, and I dislike losing even more. All in all, it's a lose-lose situation.'

He chuckles. 'What do you reckon, then?'

'Jigsaw? What's it of?'

He holds up the box for me to see and raises his eyebrows. It's a picture of a litter of multicoloured kittens in a basket.

I giggle and get up. 'Perfect.'

'Don't you mean, puuurrrrrfect?'

'I can't believe you just said that.'

He chuckles and puts the other games back in the cupboard. I join him at the table and empty the jigsaw pieces out.

'Right, first you've got to find the corners,' Johnny directs me.

I have done a jigsaw before, but I keep quiet and humour him.

'Now we need the edges,' he says, once the corners are in place.

We work quietly for some time, handing each other pieces that we think might fit. Eventually I speak.

'So, are you going to call Christian when you get back to LA?'

'Mmm. Pass me that piece there.'

'This one?'

'Yep.'

I hand it to him and watch him try to press it in. It doesn't fit. He discards it and continues hunting.

'What are you looking for?' I ask.

'A nose,' he tells me. He's working on a ginger cat. 'I will call Christian,' he says, suddenly. 'I don't want to lose touch with him like last time. Anyway, he's still got my biog to write.' He tuts. 'I dread to think what crap he's currently spewing.'

'I bet he's annoyed at me for whisking you away like this.' I also dread to think what Bill is going to do when he next sees me . . .

'Whisking me away . . .' He laughs. 'Don't worry about it. And don't worry about Bill, either,' he says, as though reading my mind. 'I'll tell him I'll fire him if he gives you any grief. If he's got any sense he'll realise I couldn't go on like that. I'm sure I was going down the same path as last time.'

We continue working until we're down to the last few pieces of puzzle. One by one we slot them in. Johnny hands me the last piece.

'Are you sure?' I ask, grinning.

'Yes,' he replies, firmly.

I put it in place and push it gently in.

'Aah,' I sigh, happily. 'There's something very satisfying about that. It's the board game equivalent of giving someone your last Rolo.'

Johnny grins and I think of Christian. He would love that reference.

'Are you tired?' I ask, as Johnny yawns, loudly. He nods, yawning again. He pushes back his chair noisily on the stone floor and gets to his feet. I do the same, only with more care so as to avoid replicating the sound of chalk screeching on a blackboard.

I glance down at my watch. 'Hey, happy New Year!' I exclaim. 'It's twelve-thirty. We missed the countdown!'

'Aah, happy New Year, Nutmeg. He pulls me in for a hug. He's so warm, I don't want to let go. He releases me and holds me away from him, fondly smiling down at me for a moment.

'You do realise we're going to have to go into town to get another jigsaw now, don't you?'

'Tomorrow,' I say. I want to trust him, but I'm scared. I don't want to lose him again. In every sense of the word.

Chapter 24

'You can't go out looking like that.' I laugh. 'It's a small town. The people who *don't* recognise you will think you're bonkers.'

Johnny is wearing his leather trousers and a silver shirt. He's also wearing his requisite shades.

'Come on, then, stylist. What do you suggest?'

I climb back up the stairs and go into his room. I unpacked for him on our second day here, so I open a couple of drawers now and riffle through them. I know he has a sweatshirt in here somewhere, and I swear I brought some dark-blue denim jeans with us. I find what I'm looking for and pull out a T-shirt, too. It smells of cigarettes and wood-fire smoke.

He appears at the doorway, just as I'm about to put his T-shirt to my nose and breathe him in. How embarrassing it would have been if he'd seen me do that!

'Right, here you go.' I quickly get up and hand him his clothes. He starts unbuttoning his shirt. He's standing between me and my escape route so I busy myself pretending to tidy his drawers. I look around just as he's tugging the shirt on over his head and catch a glimpse of his naked torso. Sigh.

I locate the car keys from inside my bumper packet of Smarties ('Clever, Nutmeg, clever') and we go out to the car.

It's New Year's Day and the little town is bustling with activity. We wander along the cobbled streets and peer into shop windows.

'Do you want a sheepskin jacket for Christmas?' Johnny asks.

I laugh. 'No, thanks.'

'A sheepskin rug?'

'No, it's okay.'

'A sheepskin sheep?'

I giggle.

'You're tempted by the sheep, aren't you?' He grins.

'I am kind of tempted, yeah.'

He starts to go inside.

'No, Johnny, I'm only joking!' I call after him.

'You're getting the sheep, Nutmeg,' he calls back.

I quickly look around to make sure no one heard me call him Johnny. We're trying to look inconspicuous. I persuaded him to leave his sunnies off and he's wearing a woolly hat to cover up his hair. He stopped shaving about a week ago, so he's actually got the start of what could be quite an impressive beard if he keeps it up. Not that anyone would expect Johnny Jefferson to be wandering around here, anyway.

Johnny comes back out with a brown paper bag and hands it to me.

'Merry Christmas,' he says, grinning.

'Thank you,' I reply, peering in and seeing the toy sheep. I giggle at the thought of what Kitty would say. Rod got her a car for Christmas last year.

There's a brass band playing in the town square and we wander over there to listen to it.

'Have you ever thought about putting a brass band on any of your songs?' I ask Johnny.

'No.' He glances at me, amused.

'What?' I ask.

He looks away.

'Look, just because I like Jessica Simpson, doesn't mean I can't have an opinion,' I tell him.

'I didn't say anything!' He starts chuckling and I smack him on his thigh. He wraps his arm around me and gives me a squeeze. An old lady standing across from us smiles at me, warmly. To anyone else, we must look like young lovers. I suddenly, desperately, can't bear the thought of ever leaving.

That night, as we're sitting at the table working our way through another jigsaw puzzle, I stare across at Johnny. There's an ache in my stomach sometimes when I look at him, and it's there now. I rarely feel relaxed in his company.

'What are you thinking?' he asks after a moment. I realise I'm still watching him.

'Nothing,' I say, busying myself with the puzzle.

'Not true, Nutmeg.'

'It's very quiet, isn't it?' I try to change the subject.

'That it is.'

'You haven't played your guitar much since we've been here.'

'I haven't played it at all,' he corrects me.

'Why not?'

He shrugs. 'Just haven't really felt like it.'

I slump back in my seat. 'I don't want to go back to LA,' I suddenly find myself telling him.

He mirrors my actions and leans back in his chair, staring across at me with a serious expression on his face.

I expect him to say something, to make a joke, anything, but he doesn't. He locks eyes with me for a while, neither of us speaking. Finally he gets up.

'I'm going outside to have a fag,' he says, delving into his pocket. He shrugs on his jacket and walks out through the front door.

I get up, feeling sick and nervous and not quite understanding why. I go over to the hearth and start to tear pages out of one of the magazines we've already made our way through. I roll them up into balls and prop a couple of logs up against each other on top of them.

Johnny returns a moment later. He joins me at the hearth, adding another log and some kindling. Then he takes his lighter out of his pocket and holds the flame to the paper at the bottom.

'Do you fancy a coffee?' I ask.

'Sure.'

I come back to find him leaning up against the sofa, staring at the fire. I hand him his mug. He takes it without saying anything and places it on the floor next to him. I sit down beside him and also gaze silently at the flames.

He rests his head back against the sofa and turns to look at me. I stare back into his eyes as butterflies swoop into my stomach and flit around the pain.

Staring at my lips, he reaches over and strokes my jaw. Then he slowly leans towards me and pulls me in for a long, slow kiss.

When he releases me, I feel drunk. He leans his head back against the sofa and looks at me.

I'm in shock. I can't speak. Did that really just happen?

'I want you,' he says.

I don't answer. I know I shouldn't. I know it's wrong, that it will only come back to bite me in the future. I know I'll probably lose my job. I know I'm one of many.

I know all that, but I can't resist. Won't resist. I lean into him and he cups my face with his hand and pulls me towards him, kissing me slowly at first and then more passionately. He grabs my waist and pulls me onto him, devouring me with his lips. I feel so giddy I could faint. He unbuttons my shirt and unclips my bra, then tugs his sweatshirt and T-shirt over his head in one go. I put my hands on his chest, then reach down to unbutton his jeans. He kisses me harder, rougher.

He reaches into his back pocket and pulls out a condom. Again I think of the hundreds of other girls who have been here before me, but I don't care. I just want him inside me, physically, because he's already there emotionally.

We make love, there, in front of the fire, and afterwards, lying in the crook of his arm, I gently run my hand over his navel. My eye catches the tattooed inscription near his trouser-line and I lean down to read what it says.

I hurt myself today, to see if I still feel . . .

I glance up at him.

'Johnny Cash lyric,' he explains, propping himself up on his elbows.

'Did you get it done after your band split?'

'About six months after, yeah.'

'Was that your lowest point?'

He nods.

'You wouldn't ever hurt yourself now, would you, Johnny?' I ask, fear rising up inside me at the thought of anything bad ever happening to him.

'No.' He shakes his head and reaches for his shirt, putting it on. Suddenly I feel overwhelmingly sad.

He stands up and pulls on his jeans, then he bends down and retrieves his boxer shorts, casually stuffing half of the fabric into his back pocket. He leaves his shoes in front of the fire.

'I'm knackered,' he tells me. 'Going to hit the sack.'

'Okay,' I say, trying not to sound as upset as I feel.

I want him to invite me to go to bed with him, but I know he won't.

That night I can't sleep. I etch every single, minuscule detail into my memory for fear it will never happen again. I don't want to forget.

The last time I look at my watch, it's five o'clock in the morning. I must have dozed off after that, because when I wake up, bright winter sunlight is flooding through underneath my curtains.

I grab my watch and see that it's ten o'clock. I leap out of bed and pull on some clothes, smoothing my hair down. I feel ill at the thought of what happened last night. Not the making love part, but going to bed alone afterwards. I dread to know what he must think of me.

I head out of my room and see that Johnny's bedroom door is open and his bed is empty. I go downstairs and find he's nowhere to be seen. A mild panic starts to build up inside me as I open the back door and hope to see him standing outside having a cigarette, but he's not there. My head starts to throb as I imagine him driving off in the night while I was still asleep and drinking himself into a stupor somewhere. I rush to the front of the house and look out; the car is still on the driveway. Pulling on my coat, I venture out of the house and down the garden. I hear him before I see him. He's climbed to the top of the hill behind the house and is sitting on the grass, strumming on his guitar. I watch him for a moment, then decide to go back inside. It's another hour before he returns and I still can't rid myself of the nausea I feel inside.

'Are you okay?' I ask, concerned.

'I'm fine, Meg.'

Meg. He just called me Meg.

'But it's time to go back to LA,' he says.

Chapter 25

'Are you free tonight?'

'I think so . . .'

We've been back in LA a week and while there were times on the tour when I longed to be back in my 'own' room, now that I'm here, it doesn't feel like home at all. So when Kitty calls me in the office on Friday morning and invites me to a showcase that night, I have to restrain myself from kissing the telephone handset. I'm so relieved to have some female company again.

A showcase is a way of introducing a hot new act to important people in the industry. The act in question is a four-piece indie band from Britain, which is why Kitty thought I might like to come. I'm not so interested in the band, but I would give anything to get out of the house for the night – and a few free drinks wouldn't go amiss, either. Of course, I have to run it by Johnny first . . .

He's still being distant with me. We haven't spoken about what happened in the Dales and I sometimes wonder if I dreamed it, but no, it was real. It hurts too much not to be.

I start to get up, then sit back down again and click on an open internet page. I hold my breath as I scan through the messages, eventually breathing a sigh of relief.

This week I've seen countless messages on Johnny's MySpace and Facebook pages from adoring girls hoping he's okay. Then on Wednesday I saw a message which turned my blood cold:

> You were the best sex I ever had! Hope to meet up with you next time you're in Italy so we can do it all over again . . .

On Thursday, there was another one like it, only this time the country in question was Spain.

I've been trying to use this reality check to toughen myself up, to move on and get on with my job. Sadly, it just doesn't work like that. I refresh the page and have one last look for new messages before I reluctantly close down the window. I know I'm becoming obsessive. A familiar figure walks past the open office door.

'Rosa!' I call. She halts in her tracks as I swiftly exit the office. 'I'll take that. Need to run something by him.' I detach the coffee mug from her fingers. She reluctantly lets go and plods back to the kitchen.

I'm sure she suspects something has happened between Johnny and me. The other day I walked into the kitchen when Johnny was in there and you could have cut the atmosphere with her Cook's knife. She didn't say anything – but I know she's too shrewd for her own good.

I carefully make my way up the stairs, knocking before entering.

Johnny's face lights up when he sees the mug, then falls again when he sees who's holding it.

'Just leave it there, Meg.' He turns his back on me.

I do as he says and put the mug down on a side table. 'I need to run a few things by you.' I try to keep my voice level, but I feel horribly awkward. I've been storing items up so I don't bother him any more than I have to.

'Shoot.' He doesn't look at me, focusing his attention on the guitar in his hands.

'You have a dentist's appointment . . .'

He plucks a string.

'You have a dentist's appointment . . .'

He plucks another string.

I try again. 'You have a dentist's appointment at three-thirty tomorrow. Johnny, can you stop tuning your guitar for a moment?'

He stops and looks up at me, a pained expression on his face.

'You have a dentist's app—'

'I got that,' he interrupts. 'What else?'

'Lunch with Quentin on Wednesday at twelve.'

'Right.'

'I've also arranged for a private viewing of Marvin Stately's collection. Is Thursday morning okay with you?'

'Who's Marvin Stately?' he asks, frowning at me.

'The artist. You know, the guy with the bald head? Goatie? Specs?' I add, when he still shows no signs of recognition. 'You told me you were interested in buying some of his art when you saw him on TV the other day.'

'Fine. Is that all?'

'Erm . . .'

'Can you—'

'Close the door behind me. Yes, Johnny.' I can't keep my irritation out of my voice. I turn to face the door, then stop.

'Actually, there's one other thing.'

He looks up at me, warily. I tell him about the showcase and he looks relieved when I don't broach the subject of our Dales trip. He needn't worry. I have no intention of bringing it up.

'I was thinking of going to that myself,' he says, eventually.

'Oh. Is that a problem?'

'I guess not.'

'So it's okay if I go, then?'

'Yep.'

'Shall I ask Davey to collect both of us?' I ask, hopefully.

'No. I'll take the bike.'

At least that means he won't be drinking, I try to console myself as I walk back down the stairs to the office to pore over the new messages on MySpace.

Kitty is already there when I arrive. As I approach, she intercepts a waiter holding a tray full of canapés.

'Good timing!' she exclaims. 'Dig in!'

The waiter narrows his eyes.

'No, thanks, I'm not hungry,' I tell her.

'Not hungry?' she screeches. 'They're canapés! There's always room for canapés!'

'No, really,' I say. 'I don't want anything.'

I've barely touched food since we've been back. I've even gone off peanut M&Ms.

'Oh.' She's disappointed. 'I'll just have a couple, then.'

The waiter waits impatiently as she makes her selection before hurrying off to a small group of impossibly skinny blondes.

'So!' She turns to me after she's devoured a California roll. 'Tell me what happened!'

I look around, shiftily. 'What have you heard?'

'Well, the papers have been full of it. Bill kept saying he was in an "undisclosed location", but he wouldn't say where.'

I don't tell Kitty that the location was undisclosed even to Bill. Not that he would have told anyone that. He wouldn't want to lose face.

She continues, 'Charlie was insistent that he was in some remote rehab clinic in Thailand, but I don't know . . .'

'When did you see Charlie?' I ask.

'At Isla's New Year's Eve party.'

'You went to that?' I can't mask my surprise.

'Only because Rod wanted to,' she tells me. 'So was she right? About the rehab location?'

'No,' I scoff. 'We went to the Dales.'

'I haven't heard of that one,' she says, cocking her head to one side.

'It's not a rehab clinic.' I try not to smile. 'It's a place in the north of England.'

'Hang on.' She puts her hand on my arm. 'You just said "we". Did you go with him?'

'Yes,' I reply, uneasily. 'He wouldn't go into rehab, so I took him somewhere quiet to get away from it all.'

'Wowsers.' She looks at me, wide-eyed.

I try to ignore the fact that she just said 'wowsers'.

'Can you tell me anything about what went on there?' she asks, hopefully.

315

'No,' I reply, attempting to sound regretful, but being enormously thankful for confidentiality clauses and the fact that I'm standing with someone who knows all about them.

'Shame,' she says, her face dropping.

'How's Rod?' I ask.

'Fine.' She sighs, her mind clearly still on Johnny.

'And Charlie? What's she up to these days?'

'Still the same,' Kitty tells me. 'Although I heard a rumour that Isla was relocating to Britain to live with her new man.'

'Her new man?' I haven't heard about this. I'm usually so 'up' on celebrity gossip. But I have been out of the loop recently . . .

'She only met him a couple of weeks ago.' Kitty looks unimpressed. 'In fact, it was at the party I told you about. Will Tripping, or something like that.'

'Will Trepper?' I ask.

'That's the one. You know him?'

'Yeah,' I answer with interest. 'He's a really cool British actor. I didn't think he'd be her type. Or vice versa.'

'Well, apparently they're *madly* in love.' Kitty rolls her eyes. 'So Isla's thinking of moving over to England to be with him.'

'Blimey. What's Charlie going to do?'

Kitty shrugs. 'Heaven only knows.'

'I can't imagine her in Old Blighty.'

'Old what?' Kitty looks confused.

'Never mind,' I say dismissively. I've just spotted Lola – the rock chick from that band Spooky Girl. She looks super-cool in a short red dress and black high heels. I remember Johnny admitting his crush on her after that night at the Standard Downtown when I first came to LA. The thought of seeing him with her now makes me feel even worse than it did back then.

'Are you sure you don't want a canapé?' Kitty asks, as another waiter passes. The snooty waiter has been avoiding us since his first Kitty encounter.

'I'm sure,' I answer, distractedly.

'Hey, look! Paola's here!'

That gets my attention. I sharply turn to see where Kitty's looking. 'Where?'

'There.' Kitty nods, trying not to be too obvious by pointing. 'The tall, skinny one with long, dark-brown hair . . .'

'I see her,' I interject.

Johnny's former PA is even prettier than I thought she'd be. She's having an animated conversation with another girl who looks to be about the same age – early thirties, I'd guess. The other girl says something and Paola throws her head back and laughs. She has a beautiful smile.

'Do you want to go and talk to her?' Kitty asks.

'No.' I look away. I may be curious about her, but I have no desire to meet her whatsoever.

I hear a familiar murmur of excitement vibrate through the room and turn to see Johnny at the entrance.

Kitty nudges me gleefully as I watch him make his way through the room to a crowd of young, cool, trendy types.

I can't believe I slept with you.

It seems so surreal, to think that I ran my hands over that chest. That I unbuttoned those trousers . . . I recall the intensity in his eyes as he looked into mine and a shiver goes down my spine.

'Are you okay?' Kitty asks.

'Mmm.'

I tear my eyes away from him and glance behind me to gauge

Paola's reaction. She looks shocked. Her companion says something in her ear and they both immediately look at me.

'Ooh, they've spotted you, then.' Kitty giggles, completely oblivious to how weird this is for me.

I look back at Johnny. He has a glass of what looks like whisky in his hand.

'Oh God,' I say.

'What?' Kitty asks, concerned.

'He's drinking.'

She follows my gaze towards Johnny. 'Darn.'

'He never said he'd stop completely, but I thought . . .'

At that moment Johnny spots me, then he looks past me and freezes. I know he's spotted Paola. Still looking at her, he knocks his drink back in one and takes another one from a passing waiter.

The next thing I know, Paola and her friend have walked out. Kitty, who has witnessed this also, turns to me, her eyes wide.

'It's true, then,' I say aloud. My heart is in my throat.

'What's true?' Her expression is perplexed.

'Johnny slept with Paola.'

Kitty looks over at Johnny. 'How do you know that?'

'I just do.'

I catch a flash of red and see Lola walking in Johnny's direction. He reaches out and grabs her hand as she passes and pulls her towards him, giving her a kiss right on the lips.

He laughs as she pushes him away, unimpressed.

Jealousy courses through my veins like poison. I can't be here. I turn to Kitty. 'I think I'm going to go home now.'

'Are you alright?'

'Yeah. Just don't feel very well.' I'm not lying.

'But you haven't even seen the band play.'

'I know. I'm really sorry.'

'Okay . . .' Kitty tries not to seem too upset.

'Will you be okay?' I ask, guiltily. I do feel bad about leaving her.

'Yeah, don't worry about me. I know plenty of people here. I won't enjoy talking to them as much as I would you,' she concedes, 'but I'm not going to force you to stay if you're not up to it.'

'Thanks,' I tell her, looking back over my shoulder to see if Johnny has noticed I'm leaving. If he has, he doesn't show it.

Chapter 26

Santiago turns up the next day and it's nice to see him after such a long time away. It hasn't really been warm enough to go swimming, but he needs to clean the pool anyway, so I join him out on the terrace to have a catch-up. He wants to know about the tour, but much more than that, he wants to know what happened when Johnny and I went AWOL. I have to be quite careful in what I say. Bill hasn't spoken to me since we got back. If he calls for Johnny, he's super-succinct about getting to the point. Johnny clearly kept his word about threatening to fire him. That, at least, gives me some comfort.

'Where did you go?' Santiago asks.

'We went to a cottage in the middle of nowhere,' I tell him. 'So he could detox.'

'Did you get up to any naughty business?' He gives me a wink.

'No, we did not!' I reply, hotly.

He grins at me, cheekily. 'Where is Johnny, man?'

'In his studio, I think.'

'Do you think he'll mind if I have a smoke?'

'Maybe you should go around to the front, just in case,' I say. 'I'll come with you.'

We wander around to the front of the house and sit under a tree next to the garage. Santiago is wearing long, beige-coloured shorts and a white vest. I'm wearing a red jumper and jeans. It may be winter, but the weather is pretty mild. It's a far cry from Europe.

'Which country was your favourite?' Santiago asks, lighting up and leaning back against the tree. I'm sitting cross-legged in front of him.

I consider his question. 'That's a toughie. Certain countries stood out, but not always for the right reasons.'

'Oh?' He regards me with his dark eyes.

'I loved Amsterdam . . .'

'Kinky,' he jokes.

'Not for that reason.' I laugh. 'No, I loved its canals. It was beautiful, but I did have one bad night there so that kind of spoilt it.'

I think of Christian again and remember how he looked after me. I feel sad momentarily. He hasn't been in contact since we returned. Not as far as I know, anyway. Johnny hasn't said anything. I stare down at Santiago's glowing cigarette in a daze.

'What sort of bad night?' he asks.

'Too much to drink.' I skip over the details. 'I also really liked Barcelona.' Again, I have bad memories of that city because that was where I found out about Gran. *And* it was where I saw Johnny take drugs for the first time . . .

'I'd love to go there,' he comments.

'You should.'

'I haven't even got a passport,' he says.

321

'Then get one!' I laugh.

I loved Paris, too. But again, that was a combination of good and bad. There's been a hell of a lot of that recently. An image flickers through my mind of Johnny kissing me.

'Can I have a cigarette?' I ask Santiago, on an impulse. I haven't had one since my first year of university, but I really feel like one all of a sudden.

He looks surprised, but hands one over, leaning forward to light it. I've barely taken two drags when Johnny walks around the corner towards the garage, clad in his biker gear.

'What the fuck are you doing?' He spots me and strides over, wrenching the cigarette from between my fingers.

'Hey!' I yell.

'You don't smoke!' he shouts, throwing the fag on the ground a few feet away. 'And what the fuck are *you* doing?' He directs his anger at Santiago. 'Get back to work!'

Santiago scrambles to his feet in surprise and hurries towards the back of the house and out of sight.

I look up at Johnny in shock as he scowls after Santiago. Then he looks down at me and gives me a look of such disgust that I almost fall backwards. He storms off towards the garage, not saying a word.

'Oi!' I shout after him.

No reaction.

'Johnny!'

He heads into the garage.

Now I'm angry.

I get up and follow him, opening the side door and banging it closed behind me. He spins around at the sound.

'Do you mind?' he asks, loudly.

'As a matter of fact, I do,' I reply. 'What the hell is your problem?'

'Leave it, Meg,' he warns, turning around to his bike.

'No, I will not leave it, Johnny. You can't screw me, ignore me and then give a shit if I smoke or not.'

He straddles his bike and turns on the ignition, then kicks the bike into life.

'Johnny, I'm trying to talk to you!' But the sound of the engine drowns my voice. I angrily reach over and turn off the ignition. He grabs my wrist, hard.

'Let me go!'

He doesn't. He looks at my lips as I struggle under his grasp, then he flings my wrist away at the sound of footsteps passing on the gravel outside the open garage door. I turn to see Lewis, one of Johnny's security guards, going about his business. The next thing I know, Johnny has turned the ignition back on and kickstarted the engine. He takes his helmet off the handlebars and pulls it over his head before squealing out of the garage. I fold my arms in front of me and watch him go.

'What was that about?' Santiago asks when I appear around the side of the house.

I shake my head at him and don't answer, before going inside and sliding the glass door shut behind me.

That night I lie in bed, wide awake. I went through today in a daze, unable to concentrate on anything, unwilling even to scour MySpace and Facebook for messages from groupies.

Johnny, Christian, Paola, Kitty . . . Faces and names rush through my mind as I try to piece together the jigsaw puzzle inside my head.

What happened with Johnny and Paola? Why did she quit her

job? Or was she fired? Did they definitely sleep together? Was it just the once? Did she fall for him? Stupid girl, I think, before remembering I'm in the exact same position. It's humiliating to think that she was there before me. If, indeed, she was.

Oh God. The dull ache inside me is ever present. I can't get rid of it. I'm sure Johnny almost kissed me in the garage. I know that I wanted him to. I also know that he's a bad boy, and I have *never* been attracted to them. So why can't I stop thinking about him?

Because I want him to fall in love with me. I want to be the one who changes him.

I picture myself walking down the red carpet with him; dining out with him; being gracious towards the paparazzi. I'd never complain about his bike messing up my hair. We'd get a dog. I'd look after it. Rosa would like me again because she'd realise that I was the real deal – not just some silly slapper like all the rest of them.

I *am* different. I'm sure I am. Who else cares for him like I do? He confides in me. He told me about his mum. He laughs with me. Well, he used to. And he will do again.

I hear a sound outside my door and lift my head from my pillow, startled.

'Hello?' I call.

The door opens and reveals Johnny's silhouette in the doorway.

'Johnny?' I ask, confused.

He strides towards the bed and I struggle to sit up in time before he pulls the covers back. The cool air hits my skin. I'm barely dressed, wearing only a skimpy, cream camisole top and knickers.

He climbs onto the bed and kneels above me. I'm breathing so hard it sounds like I have a megaphone pressed to my lips. His jeans are coarse against my bare skin. I unbutton his shirt and slide my hands inside as he kisses me, hot and passionate. His tongue tastes of cigarettes and alcohol, but I don't care. He reaches down and frantically unbuttons his jeans, then pushes my knickers aside before taking me, rough and urgent.

I can't catch my breath for a long time afterwards as I lie there, in his arms, anticipating his departure back to his own room. Even when he falls asleep and his breathing slows to a steady rhythm, I'm full of dread, waiting for him to wake up and leave me again.

I must doze off eventually, because when I finally come to in the early hours of the morning, I open my eyes to find him lying on his side, quietly watching me. I don't smile, and neither does he. He undresses me, this time taking it slowly.

I *will* change you. I *will* make you love me.

Afterwards he smiles at me, his expression soft.

'Are you on the pill?' he asks.

'No.' I immediately feel worried.

'Don't worry, I always use condoms,' he says. 'But you should probably get the Morning After Pill.'

'Okay, I will,' I say. 'I'll get it today.'

He clearly isn't concerned about my sexual history. He folds his arms behind his head and stares up at the ceiling.

'I didn't like seeing you with Santiago,' he says.

'I wasn't doing anything,' I tell him.

'I didn't like it.'

I prop myself up on my elbow and put my hand on his stomach. He glances at me then back at the ceiling. I run my finger along the tattoo of the Johnny Cash lyric.

I hurt myself today, to see if I still feel . . .

He reaches down and takes my hand, bringing it up to his lips. 'I never thanked you,' he says.

'Thanked me? For what?'

'For taking me to the Dales. For looking after me. You know you are special to me, right?'

Happiness bubbles through me as I nod back at him. Then the nerves appear. I know I shouldn't ask, but I can't restrain myself.

'Johnny,' I say, hesitantly. 'What happened between you and Paola?'

He drops my hand and looks at me, sternly. 'I don't want to talk about it.'

'Johnny, please. I saw her there on Friday night. I know she saw me, too. What happened? Why won't you tell me?'

I sound like I'm whingeing, but I can't stop the words from coming out.

'I'm not talking about this,' he says, sitting up in bed. 'Not to you. Not to anyone.'

He climbs out of the bed, still naked, and picks up his boxer shorts, slipping them on.

'Where are you going?' I ask, trying not to sound desperate. I don't want him to leave me again.

'I've got to get back to work.'

'It's Sunday,' I say. 'Do you really have to?'

'Yes.' His reply is firm. 'Albums don't write themselves, Nutmeg.' He grins at me and I relax back onto the bed at the sound of my nickname, watching him collect his clothes and walk out through the door.

Chapter 27

I don't want to freak him out, so I try to act completely normal around Johnny from then on.

'Have you heard from Christian?' I ask, when I go into the studio on Monday to show him a couple of crazy fan letters.

'That is fucking hilarious,' he says, perusing one letter from a 35-year-old woman who claims she can sing his debut solo album backwards while standing on her head. She'd dearly love to demonstrate in person.

'Get her in,' he says.

'Really?' I ask in surprise.

'No fucking way, Nutmeg. Get a restraining order,' he jokes, passing the letter back to me. 'Yeah, I have, actually.'

'Have what? Oh! Christian! Have you really?' I ask.

'Yeah. We spoke a couple of days ago. He's coming over at the end of the week.'

'Brilliant!' I beam.

Johnny looks at me, curiously.

'What?' I ask.

'Nothing.' He reaches down for his guitar.

'How's it all going?' I nod towards his instrument.

'Good,' he says, starting to play.

'That sounds great,' I tell him, then remember back to the early days when I thought he'd written something by The Smiths.

He stops playing and puts his guitar down, while I'm on edge, fearing I've just made the same mistake again.

'Not finished yet,' he tells me, reaching for the mug of coffee I've just brought up to him.

That's a relief. 'Well, I guess I should get on.' I head for the door.

'Nutmeg.'

I turn around again and look at him, inquisitively, as he puts his mug back down.

'Come here,' he says, beckoning me with his finger.

I look at him, unsure.

'Come here,' he says again, leaning back in his swivelling chair.

I walk back to him. He takes my hand and pulls me onto his lap.

I gasp.

'Fancy a quick shag?'

'Hey!' Christian says, coming into the office to greet me when he arrives on Friday. I get up from my desk and go round to give him a hug.

'How the hell are ya?' he asks.

'Good!' I grin up at him. Johnny emerges behind him and winks at me.

'How's he been treating you?' Christian asks, motioning towards his mate. 'Given you too much grief?'

'No.' I shake my head, feeling my face heat up. Christian looks down at me, amused.

'So where are we off to tonight?' Christian turns to Johnny.

'Aren't you jet-lagged?' I ask, surprised.

'Yeah. But we all know he's going to drag me out anyway. May as well get in there first.'

Johnny shrugs. 'Dunno. Viper Room, perhaps. Want a bevvy by the pool, mate?' he asks Christian.

Christian nods and follows him out of the office while I put in a call to the Viper Room.

They seem totally normal with each other. I love it how blokes can just sweep things under the carpet like that.

My Facebook and MySpace obsession has steadily got worse this week. I saw a message on MySpace yesterday from that Asian babe, Nika, asking if Johnny wanted to hook up again. I deleted it, and then it occurred to me that it would have been smarter to reply and pretend to be Johnny, telling her I wasn't interested.

A message flashes up on MySpace – it's a flier inviting Johnny to a Spooky Girl gig tonight. My finger moves on autopilot towards the delete button. I already got rid of one of these Spooky Girl fliers earlier this week, but this time I stop myself. What if Lola asks Johnny about it next time she sees him? Hmm. In that case I'll just 'forget' to mention it.

I click onto my emails and start replying to messages until I come across one from Bess:

Hey, how's it going?

Is that it? Talk about keeping it simple. I should write back to her, but there's so much to say. And obviously I can hardly say anything.
 I reply with:

Good

I'm tempted to leave it there and press Send. Well, she kept it brief, didn't she? For a laugh, I continue writing:

Actually, it's bloody fantastic. Johnny and I are going at it like rabbits. He's the best shag I've ever had. Even better than you'd imagine!

I chuckle to myself and press Delete.
 Holy shit! I just pressed Send instead! Fuck, fuck, fuck!
 I quickly type out a new message:

OBVIOUSLY that was a JOKE!

Bugger, now I have to write back properly.

All is well. I'm in LA again after the whole disappearing-act thing. It was really nice to see you in London. And meet Serena.

Liar.

I'd love to go out with you both next time I'm in town.

Liar, liar. Pants on fire.

How are things with you? Did you have a good time at
the Wembley concert? Sorry I had to dash off like that,
but you've probably heard what happened. Anyway, I
guess I'd better get on with my work . . .

I yawn and press Send, then slump back in my seat, bored.

A memory comes back to me of Bess and I singing karaoke at
my leaving party and I catch myself. To my surprise, a lump forms
in my throat. How can I have grown apart from my best friend so
quickly? And not just Bess. I've barely been in touch with anyone.

I remember when I first started working for Johnny. How much
I wanted to send her a picture of his bare chest, out by the swimming pool . . . How much I thought she'd squeal her head off . . .
I remember how often she used to ask me if she could come and
stay. The answer, honestly, was always going to be 'no'. It would
never have worked.

'I'll have a double whisky. What are you two having? Want a
bottle of Bolly?'

Christian and I glance at each other, warily.

'What?' Johnny snaps. 'When did I say I was never going to
drink again?'

It's a rhetorical question, so I ignore him and reply,
'Champagne would be great.'

'Why did you leave Scarborough?' Christian asks. We've just
been filling him in on what happened after he last saw us. I suppose we should leave out the sex . . .

Johnny starts to relay the story, but I can't resist chipping in and
telling it from my point of view. The waitress arrives with our drinks.

'Bastard wouldn't let me smoke so I told him to piss off,'

Johnny says, taking his glass before it even hits the table and knocking it back in one.

'Another, please,' he tells the waitress, putting his empty back on her tray. 'Will you two stop looking at me like that?'

'Johnny!'

'Hey, man! How's it going?' Johnny's glare transforms into a grin when he sees who's interrupted us. I vaguely recognise the guy from Serengeti's premiere party.

'Cool, dude. Long time no see. Hey, are you coming to Spooky Girl later?'

Dammit!

'No? I didn't know they were playing?'

'Yeah, dude, at the Whisky. Come along! Lola said she put you on the guest list.'

I wait with baited breath.

'Sure.'

Bollocks.

'Hey, Laurence,' Johnny continues. 'This is my friend Christian from back home, and this is Meg, my PA.'

Laurence leans across the table and shakes hands with both of us. 'Come along too, man. The more the merrier.'

The Whisky is familiarly dark and grungy. Johnny has been spotted by a few people, but they're leaving him alone. This crowd is way too cool to stalk a celebrity.

I watch with envy as Lola struts across the stage like a supermodel, belting out Electropop tunes. She's wearing high-waisted gold hotpants and black tights. You'd have to be a real stunner to carry off that outfit, and she does. I feel unbearably boring in my skinny jeans and black top.

I glance at Johnny. His attention is focused on Lola. I look past him and see Christian smile at me. I smile back, but feel sick inside. I really want to go home. And I really want Johnny to come with me.

When Christian goes off to the bar, I turn to Johnny. 'Are you going to tell Christian about us?' I ask.

'No!' He looks back at me, horrified.

'Why not?'

'It's none of his business.'

After the encore, I adopt a bright and breezy tone. 'Shall I call Davey? Get him to pick us up?'

Johnny shakes his head. 'Nah. I'm going backstage. You two alright, here?'

'Sure,' Christian replies, but his friend is already striding towards the backstage door. I look after him in dismay.

'You happy to be back in LA?' Christian turns to me. 'Meg? Hello?'

'Sorry?'

He repeats his question.

'Yeah, it's good.' It would be a darn sight better if I didn't feel so tense about Johnny the whole time.

'Must've been a bit of a toughie looking after Johnny in the Dales like that.'

'It wasn't too bad,' I reply, distractedly. Where has he gone? Is he with Lola?

I remember his words earlier in the week:

You know you are special to me, right?

I try to let them comfort me now.

After half an hour of standing at the bar making small talk, Christian says, 'I don't know if he's coming back, you know.' He rolls his eyes at me, jokingly, but I'm not seeing the funny side.

'Shall I text him and check?' he asks.

'Yes, good idea.' I watch eagerly as he gets his phone out. He texts Johnny then puts his phone back in his pocket and carries on talking.

'Has he texted you back?' I ask after a minute.

Christian pulls his phone out and checks. 'No. So anyway . . .'

I can't concentrate. I ask him to check again after another couple of minutes. Still no reply from Johnny. I hate how insecure he's making me feel.

Christian yawns. 'I'm wondering if we should shoot off.'

'No, er,' I stammer. 'I don't think so. We should wait for him.'

'He's a big boy, he can fend for himself.' Christian smiles and puts his empty glass down on the bar top.

'No. I think . . . Maybe he'll expect Davey to be here.'

'We'll send Davey back for him.' He shrugs.

'Um . . .' I shift from foot to foot. What is wrong with me?

'Are you alright, Meg? You seem a bit antsy tonight.'

'No, I'm fine!' I hurriedly assure him. 'I guess, well, you must be jet-lagged . . .'

'Very.'

'Let's go, then.' I cast another longing look at the backstage door and follow Christian out of the venue.

Chapter 28

'Where did you go for so long?' I'm trying not to sound upset, but I'm not sure I'm doing a very good job of it.

I heard Johnny come home at three o'clock in the morning. He didn't come to my room as I'd hoped, but he didn't have anyone with him either, so at least I could sleep easier after that.

'Just hanging out, you know.' Johnny reaches into the cupboard and pulls out a glass, filling it up with apple juice.

We're in the kitchen. It's Saturday early afternoon and he's only just surfaced. Christian is in the office, working at the spare desk.

'Was Lola there?' I ask, casually.

'Of course.'

I say nothing, opening up the fridge, looking inside aimlessly and closing it again.

Johnny leans back on the kitchen countertop and regards me. 'You're not jealous, are you?'

'No!' I exclaim.

'Good.' He puts his three-quarters-full glass in the sink and saunters out of the kitchen.

I drink the rest of his juice and, for want of something better to do, wash up his glass instead of putting it in the dishwasher. I look at the kitchen clock. It's almost one-thirty. I should go and ask if Christian wants any lunch. He must be starving.

I walk towards the office, but stop outside when I realise Johnny is in there with him.

'Good night last night, mate?' I hear Christian ask.

'Yeah, ace.'

'Get your rocks off with Lola, did you?'

Johnny chuckles. 'Not yet.'

'Don't worry,' Christian sounds amused. 'I'm sure she'll succumb to your charms before long. They always do.'

I back away from the door, feeling like someone has punched me in the stomach. My wedge heel buckles and I stumble, almost toppling to the ground. I cry out in shock.

'Meg!' Johnny appears at the doorway, looking startled to see me. 'I didn't know you were there. Are you okay?' he asks, concerned.

'Yes, I'm fine,' I tell him, hurriedly, trying not to limp. 'I . . . I was just about to ask if you wanted me to get some lunch.'

'Lunch?' Christian calls. 'What is there?' He appears at the doorway, behind Johnny. 'What's wrong?' he asks, when he sees my face. 'You look as white as a ghost.'

'Nothing,' I say. 'Um . . .' I stand up straight and try to focus. 'I think there's a chicken casserole and Rosa also left some soup.'

'What flavour?' Christian asks.

'Erm . . . Vegetable, I think.' I glance at Johnny.

'Bread?' Christian asks.

'What? Bread, yes, bread. There is bread, yes.'

Christian laughs. 'You're not very with it today, are you, Megan?'

Johnny scratches his chin.

'I'll go and put the soup on.' I turn and walk back to the kitchen.

'What's wrong with her?' I hear Christian ask. I don't hear Johnny's reply.

'So what time does this party kick off, then?' Christian asks Johnny a short while later, when we're all in the kitchen.

Party? What party?

'We'll probably head there at around nine,' Johnny tells him.

'Are you coming?' Christian asks me.

'Whose party is it?'

'Some record exec guy. Isn't he, Johnny? Loads of celebs going. Should be a blast.'

'Oh, I know the one.' I glance at Johnny, but I can't work out if he minds if I join them or not.

'Have you got other plans?' Christian asks, sensing my hesitation.

'No . . .'

'So come, then,' Christian says, casually. 'I need someone to keep me company while this one is off chatting up laydees.'

I look at Johnny through narrowed eyes. Bugger it.

'Okay, then,' I tell him.

The party is being thrown by Daniel Steinbeck, one of the head honchos at Johnny's record company. His house is up in the hills, not far from where we live.

Christian is driving and taking the corners fast. I can hear Johnny's sharp intakes of breath and have been trying to stifle my giggles.

The paps are out in force when we arrive, camera bulbs

flashing through the windows at us as we drive through the gates into Daniel's private residence. Just like Johnny's pad, this place has incredible views over the city, with a swimming pool at the front. It's a warm night, so we make our way through the beautiful people to the outdoor area. The music is pumping, but it's not as loud outside.

Johnny lights himself a cigarette and looks around for familiar faces.

'Back in a tick,' he says, distractedly. He walks off, leaving me alone with Christian.

'Hey,' I say. 'Hey! There's my friend, Kitty. Kitty!' I call.

'Meg!' she squeals from the other side of the pool. 'I didn't know you were coming?'

'I didn't know I was coming either until a few hours ago.' Seeing her immediately makes me feel better about Johnny abandoning us.

'Me too!' She glances at Christian.

'Kitty, this is Christian, Johnny's friend.'

'Hi! Really nice to meet you.' They shake hands. 'Are you from England, too?' she asks.

'Yeah, Newcastle.'

Kitty nods and smiles, blankly. 'Is Johnny here tonight?' she asks us.

'Yes,' I reply. And it would be nice if he came back and joined us.

'Charlie's here, too,' she says.

'Oh, great.' I roll my eyes.

'Who's Charlie?' Christian whispers, conspiratorially.

'Isla Montagne's PA,' Kitty explains.

'Shit, she's not here, is she?' Christian asks.

'Yes, why?' Kitty replies.

'Better keep her away from Johnny. She's bonkers. She went a bit doolally over him a year or so ago.'

'*Really?*' Kitty loves a bit of gossip.

'I probably shouldn't have told you that,' Christian says. 'Don't say anything.'

Kitty grins. 'Don't worry, I won't. Anyway, she's over him now I'm sure.' She looks at me. 'She *is* moving to England.'

'Really? What's Charlie doing?'

'She's resigned.'

'No shit?'

'Why is Isla moving to England?' Christian butts in.

'You tell him,' I say to Kitty. 'I'm just going to nip to the ladies' room. He's a journalist. Give him an exclusive!' I wink at Christian and make my way indoors.

Christian shouts after me, 'I'm not that sort of journalist!'

It's even more crowded inside. I look around for Johnny, but can't see him anywhere. Nor, for that matter, can I see the bathrooms. I peek my head into a room, hoping to spy one or the other. As I turn around to exit it, I come face to face with Charlie.

'Argh!' I shout.

'I heard about what you did.' Her tone is snide.

'What?'

'Johnny. Detoxing.'

'Oh, right. Yes.'

'You could have killed him!' she erupts.

I'm astonished. '*I* could have killed him? What the hell have you heard?'

'Withdrawal from alcohol has to be treated properly!'

'Come off it,' I mock. 'Going cold turkey hasn't ever killed anyone.'

'Are you out of your mind? You're not supposed to go cold turkey when you're an alcoholic. You're supposed to be weaned off the booze with drugs.'

Is that true? Oh. 'What makes you such an expert?' I ask, backtracking.

'My stepmother was an alcoholic,' she informs me.

I picture a young Charlie, growing up without her real mother, having to live with an evil alcoholic stepmother instead. I almost feel sorry for her.

'Well, I wouldn't really say he's a proper alcoholic. And anyway, he's better now,' I say, sullenly.

'He doesn't look better to me . . .'

She nods behind me. I turn in time to see Johnny plonk an empty shot glass down on a tabletop and slap a cool-looking indie-rocker guy on his back. Oh, God. I turn back to face Charlie.

'Do you know where the bathrooms are?' I ask, melancholically.

'Over there.' She points.

'See you later, Charlie,' I say, hoping that the opposite will be true.

I come out of the bathroom to witness Johnny doing another shot. Should I go over to him? Try to stop him? I watch in despair as he grabs a bottle of vodka and swigs straight from the neck.

No. It's too late for intervention. He's too far gone.

I rejoin a laughing Kitty and Christian.

'You okay?' Christian's face falls when he sees mine.

'Johnny's doing shots inside.'

His shoulders slump. 'Nothing we can do about it, Meg.'

I cast my eyes longingly indoors.

'Meg,' he says. 'I think you should let it go.'

'I *have* let it go,' I reply, irritated.

Kitty looks uncomfortable standing next to us.

'Good,' Christian says, bluntly. 'I'm going to the bar. Are we sticking with cocktails?'

'Sounds good!' Kitty enthuses.

I nod, half-heartedly.

'He's lovely!' Kitty gushes as soon as Christian has walked off. My stomach tightens. 'Has he got a girlfriend?' she asks.

'No,' I reply, sharply. 'Actually, I don't know. Maybe he does,' I add, looking away.

'He really likes you,' she says.

I look back at her quickly. 'What do you mean? In what way?'

'You know, in *that* way.'

'What makes you say that?' I ask, stomach still tight, but not unpleasantly so.

'Just the way he talks about you.'

'Really?' I don't believe it. 'What have you been saying?'

'Just the tour and a few things like that. How you both like kiddies' cereal.' She grins.

Christian returns, struggling to carry three glasses. 'Hurry! Take 'em!' Kitty and I laughingly do as he says. Then I adopt a serious expression.

'I can't believe you told her about our Pebbles addiction.'

His face becomes grave. 'I thought it was best to face up to it, Meg. It's the only way we can combat it properly.'

'But I'm not ready to give it up, yet, Christian. It's too soon.'

He puts his hand on my arm and looks into my eyes. 'I know. It will be okay.'

Kitty giggles and gives me a cheeky grin. I sneakily pull a face at her then look past her to see Johnny on the other side of the pool, coldly watching us. I'd forgotten about him for a moment. I mouth, 'Are you okay?'

Christian glances at me then over at Johnny, just in time to catch him striding back indoors. My heart sinks.

I don't enjoy myself after that, and I know I'm bringing the mood down. It's so hard keeping it together when I have no control over what Johnny does. I tell the others that I fancy a wander inside. I'm sure Christian knows I'm going after Johnny.

He's not in the first room I look in, or the next. I finally find him after five minutes of searching. He's sitting on a sofa, and a bikini-clad girl is sitting astride him. He looks up and sees me, but acts like he hasn't, taking the girl's hands and pulling her into him, tighter. He reaches around and spanks her bottom, hard, and she responds by slapping his chest, playfully. Then he runs his hands through her long, brown hair and pulls her in for a snog.

Darkness clouds my vision and I think I'm going to faint. I back away, clutching my throat. I have to get away from here. I rush back through the crowd and past the swimming pool, barely registering the two A-listers I spot along the way. I run out of the gates, not caring that I'm leaving Christian and Kitty behind. The paparazzi straighten up and take notice when I appear, then relax back into conversation with each other when they realise I'm a nobody.

I hurry down the road, tears streaming down my face. I'll walk home from here. I'm pretty sure I remember the way.

But after ten minutes, I start to doubt I know the right way after all. Everything looks the same, and I wasn't really paying attention in the car. My feet are killing me in these heels and I'm tempted to take them off, but there are cactus plants on the side of the road and, knowing me, I'll step in some prickles or broken glass, and end up bloody and bruised, as well as tear-streaked and desperate.

How could he do that to me? He saw me standing there and kissed her anyway. I thought I meant more to him than that. These last few days . . . He's been so nice to me. I thought he cared about me. I thought . . . I know it's crazy, but I did think that there might be a future . . . How could you be so idiotic, Meg? Oh God, what am I going to do now? Where the hell am I?

The tears fall heavier and I'm suddenly struck by the stupidity of my actions. I think I'm lost. I picture a rapist or murderer spotting a helpless girl on the side of the road and snatching me away. That would teach Johnny! That's my first thought, my second is, holy shit, I'm scared now.

I'll call Davey. Dammit, I've left my bag back at the party! This is the worst night ever!

Headlights appear around the corner and I jump back, trying to hide behind some bushes. The car slows down. Oh fuck, oh fuck, oh fuck, this is it. Can I run in these heels? Maybe they won't see me. Argh, they've pulled over!

'Meg!'

It's Christian.

'Christian!' I cry, coming out from the bushes.

Another car appears around the corner. Christian leans across from the driver's seat and opens the door. 'Get in, quick!' He's parked dangerously.

I climb in and close the door behind me, then wipe away some of my tears. He checks his rear-view mirror and pulls away from the kerb.

'What happened?' he asks, glancing at me.

I shake my head.

'Meg?'

'I can't talk about it.' My voice is croaky from crying so much.

When we get home, he tries again, but not before he's sought out the medicine cabinet and has helped me apply plasters to my blistered feet. We're sitting on the sofa in the living room.

'It's Johnny, isn't it?' he says.

I don't reply.

'I knew it.'

'What do you know?'

'He can't fucking help himself, can he?' He sounds angry.

I look at him, unsure if he really knows what's going on. I'm reluctant to say anything, just in case.

'When did it start?' he asks.

'When did what start?' I ask, cautiously.

He looks a little impatient. 'When did you start sleeping together?'

Okay, so he knows, then. 'In the Dales,' I answer.

He glances away from me at the blank television. 'That figures. And tonight? What happened?'

'A girl,' I answer, tearfully. 'In a bikini.' What she's wearing is not strictly relevant, but it feels so to me.

He nods, glumly. Finally he looks at me. 'He won't change, you know.'

I reach over and smooth my plasters down.

'He won't, Meg.'

'Okay, okay!' I snap.

He falls silent.

'You won't put it in the book, will you?' I ask, suddenly fretful.

'Of course not!' he admonishes me.

I take a deep breath then relax a little. 'Good. Shall we watch some TV?'

'Sure.' He glances at his watch. It must be after midnight, and he's probably knackered, but I appreciate the company. I know I won't be able to sleep until Johnny comes home.

Christian tries to stifle his yawns for going on two hours until finally we hear the door open. We both sit up, on full alert.

We hear the girls before we see them. Johnny appears around the corner, walking backwards as though enticing his prey into his lair. Two girls follow him, giggling and holding hands. I recognise the girl in the bikini – she's had the decency to put some more clothes on – and her 'friend' is slim and blonde and also very pretty.

'What the fuck are you doing?'

I jump at the sound of Christian's fury. So does Johnny. He spins around and spies us on the sofa together. His initial shock swiftly changes to nonchalance.

'What does it look like?'

The girls glance at each other apprehensively.

Christian speaks. 'It looks like you're about to have a three-some and force your brilliant PA to quit her job.'

Johnny looks taken aback. He stares at me. 'Did you tell him?'

Before I can answer, Christian speaks again. 'Mate, I found her in a right state. She was trying to walk home. She rushed out of the joint after seeing you getting up close and personal with, I presume, one of these two.' He gives the girls a dirty look. 'She didn't have to tell me. I mean, Jesus, Johnny, didn't you learn your lesson after you fucked Paola?'

My stomach lurches.

'Sorry, Meg,' Christian says. 'But you should know what he's capable of.'

345

'Shut the fuck up, Christian,' Johnny warns, malevolently.

'No, I will not. She was a nice girl,' he says to me. 'He could have had something special with her, but the second he started to fall for her, he screwed her over. Just like he's doing to you, now.'

'Shut up!' Johnny says, angrily, storming over to the sofa and pointing at Christian.

The girls are now looking very uneasy.

'Shall we go?' one of them asks.

'Yes!' Christian shouts.

'No!' Johnny shouts at the same time.

They shift from foot to foot. Clearly the thrill has gone out of their threesome.

Johnny is breathing hard and fast. He's still pointing at Christian. 'If you have a problem with the way I do things around here, you can fuck off home.'

'With the way you do things around here? Have you heard yourself, you arrogant prick? You know what, maybe I will fuck off home. And maybe I'll take Meg with me.'

Johnny laughs, hollowly. 'Fine. Go.'

He turns and puts his arms around both the girls and guides them up the stairs.

As soon as Johnny's door has closed behind them, Christian comes over and kneels in front of me. I'm shaking.

'Are you okay?' he asks.

'I don't feel very well,' I tell him in a small voice.

'Come here.' He tries to put his arms around me, to comfort me, but I pull away. I don't want to be touched.

'Is it true? Is that what happened with Paola?' I ask.

He nods, grimly.

346

'He told me he's never fallen for anyone,' I say.

'That's probably the truth. He fucks them over before it gets that far.'

'Is that what he's doing with me, do you think?' My tone is hopeful. I *want* him to be falling for me. It doesn't really sink in that I'm probably going to lose him over it.

'I don't know.' He pauses, then says, 'Meg, why don't you come back with me? To the UK?'

'I don't *want* to go back to the UK!' I cry.

'Okay!' he says, surprised.

I sniff. 'You're not really going to leave, are you?'

He considers my question for a moment before answering. 'Yes. I am. I'll catch a flight tomorrow.'

'No! Don't go!'

'I will. It will teach him a lesson. Anyway, I've enough material now. I just have to finish writing it up.'

'You won't write anything about this, will you?' I ask, anxiously.

'Meg, I've already told you I won't.'

I hear muffled noises coming from Johnny's bedroom and remember what's going on in there. I'd forgotten for a moment.

Christian looks at me with concern. 'You're going to get hurt so badly if you stay.'

'I'm already hurt, Christian,' I reply. 'But this –' I motion upstairs – 'this is just sex. It's going to take a hell of a lot more than this to push me away.'

He stands up and points the remote control at the TV, switching it off. Then he turns to me and says, sadly, 'I knew you were going to say that.'

Chapter 29

I take Christian to the airport the next day, just to get out of the house. We don't talk about last night. In fact, we say very little. When I return, I find Johnny sitting at the outdoor table by the pool, staring down at the view.

He jumps when he sees me. 'I thought you'd left,' he says in a monotone voice. I can't read his expression.

'What, and taken your Porsche with me?' I laugh, oddly amused.

He studies my face, before asking, 'Where's Christian?'

'Oh, *he's* left,' I say, flippantly. 'But I'm still here.' I sit down opposite him and put my sunglasses on top of my head. 'Good night last night?'

'Are you alright, Meg?' He looks at me, cagily.

'Not really.' My voice is cheery. 'But I'll get over it. Now, do you want some lunch? I'm starving!'

'No . . . Thanks . . .' He's looking at me like I've grown little green horns and am currently head-butting the table.

'Okay, then.' I get up and go indoors.

I carry on this pretence of not actually giving a shit for a few days, going about my business as though I'd never actually slept with a rock star. Finally, on Wednesday, Johnny cracks.

'Meg, will you stop this? It's driving me nuts.'

He's come into the office to check what time he's supposed to be meeting with his record company.

'What's driving you nuts?' I look up at him, calmly.

'This.' He throws his hands in the air. 'You. Stop acting like nothing's happened.'

'What do you want me to do, Johnny? Cry? Scream? Quit?' I stress the last word.

'No. I don't know,' he says, frustrated. 'I've gotta go. See you later.'

He walks out of the room and I carry on with my work, feeling strangely elated.

Later that day he comes back into the office.

'Meeting go okay?' I ask.

'Yeah.' I can see he's distracted. 'What did Christian say to you?' he asks, furrowing his brow.

'What do you mean?'

'You know what I mean.'

My laugh is brittle. 'I don't actually. You'll have to spell it out.'

'Forget it!' He storms out of the room in a huff.

I'm quite enjoying this.

The next day he's back in the office again.

'Do you have that Kitty chick's number?'

My heart skips a beat. I try not to let it show. 'Sure.'

I find it on my phone and scribble it down on the back of a business card. When I don't ask why he wants it, he divulges the information himself.

'She's pretty hot. Thought I might take her to that showcase tonight.'

You arsehole! I want to scream. 'She's already going.' I call his bluff. 'With her boyfriend,' I add, hoping he won't see through me.

He looks down at the number. 'Shame,' he says, wandering towards the door.

I carry on tapping away at my keyboard, trying not to let my anger overcome me.

'For fuck's sake,' he exclaims, turning around and leaning on the doorframe. He flicks the business card in the bin.

'What's wrong?' I ask.

He runs his hands through his hair and stares at me, before dejectedly slumping down in the black Eames chair beside my desk.

I swivel my chair around to face him. He leans forward and rests his forearms on his thighs, staring up at me.

'I heard from my dad last week,' he says.

'*What?*' Now he's got his reaction. 'I thought your dad was dead?'

'No,' he says. 'He lives in Essex.'

I cross my legs and fold my arms across my chest. 'What did he say?'

Johnny shrugs and looks down. I wait, patiently. I'm not playing this game. If he wants to tell me, he can tell me.

He looks edgy. 'He's found a woman. Wants to get married.'

'Oh, right,' I say, intrigued.

'Wants more money,' he adds, a touch bitterly.

'Hmm . . . Are you going to give it to him?'

'Yeah,' he says. 'Not like I can't spare it, is it?'

I nod. 'True. Does he ask for money a lot?'

He leans back in his seat and puts one foot up on his other knee. 'He doesn't have to. He's got a monthly allowance. Got his house.'

'Which you bought for him?'

'Yep.'

Considering his dad is supposed to be a no-good so-and-so, I would have thought Johnny would want nothing to do with him.

'You seem surprised,' he says.

'I am surprised,' I tell him.

'Why?'

I take a deep breath. 'I can't work you out, Johnny Jefferson. You're so . . . transient.'

He raises one eyebrow at me. 'I've never been called that before.'

I say nothing, steadily meeting his gaze.

He reaches over and strokes my leg. I flinch.

'Don't do that,' I warn him.

He looks at me, forlornly. 'I'm sorry, Meg.'

Now I'm lost for words.

'Christian was right, you know,' he continues.

'Right about what?' I ask, warily.

He leans in again and takes my hand. I'm so stunned about his apology that I let him.

'I don't want you to leave.' Adrenalin pumps through my veins. 'Come here.' He tries to pull me to him, but I shake my hand free.

'No, Johnny. No!'

He strokes my leg again, strokes my arm, strokes my cheek.

'Stop it,' I say, with less ferocity.

'I need you,' he says. His eyes are fixated on my lips.

I hold my breath, unable to resist any longer as he leans in to kiss me.

'Come upstairs,' he says, pulling me to my feet.

Afterwards, as I lie in his arms, and he gently runs his rough fingers across my naked back, I try not to think of what went on in this bed just a few days ago. I prop myself up on my elbows and smile at him.

I care about you, Johnny Jefferson. However hard you make it for me.

'I need you too, you know,' I tell him.

Something comes over his face. It's like a mask.

'What's wrong?' I frown at him.

'Nothing.' He looks annoyed. 'I should probably get ready,' he says, climbing out of bed.

'Ready for what?' I'm confused.

'The showcase?'

'Oh. Are you still going?'

'Of course.' He walks towards his en-suite. 'Don't bother with Davey. I'll take the bike.'

I don't bother asking if he'll also take me. I know that look. I'm being pushed away again and the realisation fills me with grief.

I don't hear him come home that night. Full of worry, I mention it to Samuel.

'He must be in bed,' he says. 'He rocked up at about two o'clock in the morning.'

'Did he?' I'm amazed.

He was quiet when he returned, then. Maybe it will be alright after all. I go into the office and carry on with my work. At about eleven o'clock, I hear footsteps outside the office, heading towards the kitchen.

There he is, I think to myself. When he doesn't come to see me after a few minutes, I decide to go and find him.

As I approach the kitchen, everything starts to feel like it's moving in slow motion. Johnny is not in the kitchen, but a girl is. And I recognise her voice instantly.

I arrive at the door to see Rosa put two mugs of coffee on the table.

'Thanks,' Lola says, picking up both mugs and turning to see me. She starts, spilling a little coffee. She's wearing one of Johnny's shirts. It comes down to her thighs.

'Meg!' She laughs. 'I didn't see you there. Sorry, Rosa,' she apologises, as Rosa gets to her knees with a sponge.

'No harm done,' Rosa says.

Lola grins at me, sheepishly. 'How are you? You didn't make the showcase last night?'

'No,' I say, shortly.

'Don't worry, you didn't miss much.' She smiles.

I don't smile back.

'Well, okay, then,' she says, going to move past me with the coffees. 'I'm just going to take this up to him.'

I step aside for her.

'Do you want me to call a car for you?' I finally find my voice. I want her out of here.

'No, thanks,' she replies, gratefully. 'Johnny said he'd give me a ride. *If* I can stomach it again.' She rolls her eyes at me good-naturedly and starts to walk towards the stairs. 'Jeez, he rides that bike fast, doesn't he?' She's not really expecting an answer. 'Didn't matter when I'd had a few, but today it could be a different story.

Anyway, see you later,' she calls over her shoulder, before momentarily turning her lips down when I don't respond. I watch her reach the top of the stairs and try to open Johnny's bedroom door with her hands full. A second later the door opens. I hear Johnny chuckle as she goes inside.

I glance behind to see Rosa quietly watching me. I rush into the office and close the door.

Not her. Anyone but her. She's his perfect match. She's so cool, so talented. She doesn't take any crap from him. He respects her.

I sit there in a daze for hours, unable to work. At three o'clock, there's a knock on the door. I look up as it opens; it's Rosa.

'I've got to head off early today,' she says.

I nod, blankly.

'Are you okay, honey?' Her tone is sympathetic.

I don't speak.

She comes into the room and closes the door behind her. I watch as she makes her way to my desk.

'Come here.' She motions for me to get up. I do as she says and she engulfs me in a warm, cuddly hug.

Suddenly I miss my mum. I miss Bess. I miss everyone and everything about my home, my real home. I try to stifle the tears, but they come anyway.

'There, there,' she says. 'It's okay.'

'I'm sorry,' I sob.

'Don't you say sorry to me!' she admonishes me.

She doesn't tell me it's my own fault. She doesn't tell me that she warned me. She would have witnessed this exact same scenario with Paola, and she saw it coming a mile off, but she lets me cry, and she does her best to comfort me. Eventually, she breaks away.

'I do have to go, honey. It's my daughter's school play tonight.'

'Of course.' I try to smile at her. 'Wish her good luck from me.'

'I will.'

I don't see Johnny that night. I'm sure he's stayed at Lola's, and it kills me to sit in that big, lonely house on a Friday night and imagine what my friends are getting up to in London.

The next day I hear him come home, but I stay up in my room for hours, thinking. Eventually I go downstairs.

I look out of the glass, the city of LA sprawled out before me in the hazy afternoon sunshine. But I can't appreciate the view now. Johnny is sitting on one of the sunloungers. His dirty blond hair is partly obscuring his face, but I can see the lit cigarette dangling from his mouth, the bottle of whisky by his side. He's playing his guitar, and I watch as the muscles in his tattooed arms flex with the movement. I feel like there are invisible strings coming out of my stomach, close to my heart. They are attached to him. Wherever he is, I am pulled. I try to cut the strings, but they reconnect themselves to him. Oh God, it hurts so much.

I need to get out of here.

Tears prick my eyes as I walk determinedly into the office. I call Johnny's travel agent and book myself a ticket on the next available flight to London. Then I ring Davey and ask him to collect me at three. My flight isn't until this evening, but I'll wait at the airport. Anything is better than waiting here. And I know there's a risk of changing my mind if I stay for much longer.

I collect my suitcase from the store cupboard in the laundry and carry it up the stairs. I pull my clothes out of the wardrobes, barely bothering to fold them before laying them in the case. My eye catches the toy sheep that Johnny bought me in the Dales. It sits on a shelf in the open wardrobe, watching me as I pack up my belongings. When my case is full, I stand and stare at the toy.

No, I decide, and bend down to zip up my case. It can stay where it is. I imagine Johnny walking into my room and opening the wardrobe, his heart sinking as he realises I've gone.

The truth is, Rosa or Sandy the maid will probably find it and toss it in the bin, but I like my scenario best.

I scribble out a short note for Rosa, struggling to think of what to say.

I have to go. I'm so sorry, but I think you know why. I did enjoy working with you and I will miss you. I wish you and your family all the best. Please give my love to Lewis, Samuel, Ted and Sandy . . .

I leave it in the kitchen, behind the toaster. Johnny won't see it there, but Rosa is sure to on Monday.

Suitcase by my side, I glance out of the window. Johnny is no longer on the sunlounger. I look around, but I can't see him. Maybe it's for the best.

The buzzer goes. It's time.

As Davey drives me through the gates, a familiar green truck pulls up.

Santiago! I forgot about Santiago.

'Hold on!' I tell Davey, and jump out of the car.

'Hey, Meg,' Santiago says.

'Santiago, I'm leaving.'

'Leaving? Why?' he asks, shocked.

'It just hasn't worked out,' I tell him.

'Man, I'm so sorry. Who am I going to chat to on Saturdays, now?'

'You'll just have to get on with your work instead.' I grin and he grins back at me.

I grab a pen from his dashboard and scribble my Hotmail address on a piece of old cardboard. His truck is full of junk food wrappers. 'Email me!' I hand him the scrap.

'I don't have an email address,' he says, regretfully, looking down at it.

'No way?'

He shrugs.

I laugh. 'They are free, you know?'

'Okay, I'll get one,' he says, but instinct tells me we won't stay in touch.

Suddenly I hear a roar come from behind the gates. I can barely breathe as Johnny appears on his bike, black metal glinting in the bright sunlight.

'See ya round.' Santiago raises one eyebrow at me, then glances at Johnny, before driving through the open gates.

Johnny flips his visor up. 'Where are you going?'

'I'm leaving, Johnny.' I try to keep my voice steady.

'What, just like that?'

'Just like that.'

We stare at each other for a moment, neither of us speaking. I'm vaguely aware of Davey waiting in the car behind me.

Johnny nods, curtly. 'Okay, then.'

He flips down his visor and revs up the engine, wheel spinning off down the road, leaving a trail of dust in his wake.

I don't know what I expected. For him to stop me from leaving, beg me to stay, tell me he made a mistake?

But no, in the end he's the one who cuts the strings.

Later, on the plane, I stare out of the window, trying not to cry. I only lasted six months in this job – even less than Paola – and now I'm going home a failure.

Sadness presses into me, devastatingly, silently. I fold my arms across my chest and squeeze, tightly, trying to dispel the pain. It doesn't work. I feel like it's crushing me, and no one can help me release the pressure. I can't talk about what happened with Johnny to anyone. Apart from him, Christian is the only person who knows about us, and that makes me feel unbearably, excruciatingly alone.

Chapter 30

'Mum says you lost your job.'

'I didn't lose my job, I quit,' I patiently explain to my sister down the phone.

I'm sitting on the sofa at Bess's place. It's been my bed for the last month. Serena was away for the first two weeks, but she's back now, and it's kind of crowded. I need to find somewhere else to live, but I just can't get motivated yet.

After watching daytime TV and working my way through several bags of Haribo Kiddies' Mix, I finally got off my arse a week ago and found a job. My first port of call was Marie, my old boss. She spent the first couple of minutes going on and on and on about her brilliant new PA, which did nothing for my self-esteem, I have to tell you. When I finally got a word in edgeways to inform her I was out of work, it rendered her speechless with guilt.

'Do you know what?' she said finally, trying to be helpful. 'I've just finished a job for the owner of a private members' club in Soho. He said he was looking for staff. I can give you his number, if you like.'

Marie thought he meant clerical staff, but when he told me he needed waitresses, I thought, 'Why the hell not?' I'm fed up with looking after one person all the time. Okay, so with waitressing, you're looking after a whole bunch of people, but at least it's not personal. They come, they tip and they leave, and that's just the way I like it.

'I can't believe you never called me!' Susan complains.

'Well, you never called me, either,' I tell her.

'I didn't want to bother you. Mum always said you were so busy.'

'I *was* busy,' I admit. 'Anyway, I can talk now. What have you been up to?'

'Why did you lose your job?' she asks, going back to Johnny.

'It just didn't work out,' I say.

'Come on, tell me what happened . . .'

'You know what, Susan, I couldn't tell you even if I wanted to. I signed a confidentiality clause.'

Big mistake. Now she thinks something did happen and spends the next few minutes trying to get it out of me.

'Tony's angry you never got him a signed album,' she says, eventually, referring to her annoying husband.

'I didn't know Tony wanted a signed album.' I sigh.

'You would have done if you'd called . . .'

Here we go again. Oh, it's great to be home.

I haven't heard anything about Johnny in the press. He's been surprisingly quiet. Probably holed up at home having sex with Lola. I shudder at the thought.

It was difficult not being able to come clean to Bess. She was a little cold with me at first. She's still distant, to be honest. I don't know how we'll ever get around that.

I hang up finally and slump back on the sofa, pointing the

remote control at the telly to turn the sound up. The living room is a mess. It isn't easy living out of a suitcase for this amount of time. I'm sure I must be annoying Serena now, but she's got a guilt complex about whether or not she should move out and let me have my old room back. I'm not sure that I want that. I do need to get my own place. I've even thought about buying a studio or something – I saved up a decent chunk from working with Johnny which would do as a deposit – but I don't know. I might go travelling. I haven't made up my mind yet.

Plenty of celebrities come into the members' club where I work. It's odd being on the other side, looking at them and knowing all about the worlds in which they live.

I'm at work at the moment, and am just returning to a table with an expensive bottle of red wine. There are two men dining together, one older, one younger. I see the older man surreptitiously slide a small clear plastic packet across the table to the younger guy, who I recognise as a presenter from a children's TV show. I deliver their wine, then go and find my manager. We have a strict 'No Drugs' policy here.

'Excuse me!' I turn at the sound of an American accent. 'Can we get a bottle of water, please?'

I try not to look surprised to see Isla Montagne sitting at the table in front of me, next to Will Trepper, the cool British actor she moved here to be with.

'Sure. Still or sparkling?' I ask.

'Still.' She looks at me through narrowed eyes. I ignore her and turn away.

'I recognise you,' she says a short while later, when I bring her water.

'Do you?' I act innocent.

'Yes. Did I know you in LA?'

'No,' I say.

'Hmm. I'm sure I've seen you somewhere.'

I pour the water and take their order. When I return later with their food, she bolts upright.

'Johnny Jefferson's PA! That's it, isn't it?'

I glance around to make sure no one heard her. In the clear, I nod.

She leans back in her seat, looking pleased with herself. 'I knew it! What are you doing working here?' she asks, snobbily giving my black and white uniform the once-over.

'I felt like a change.'

A customer sitting a few tables away indicates that he wants the bill. Relieved, I excuse myself and get back to work.

Later, when the club has emptied out and I'm tidying up for the night, Isla calls me over again to her table. She and Will have been huddled up in a corner couch for the last couple of hours.

'I need a PA, if you're interested . . .'

'Um, thank you, but I wasn't very good at it.'

'I don't believe you.'

'Why not?'

'Because Charlie was jealous of you.' She laughs a tinkling laugh.

Now I'm curious. 'Whatever happened to Charlie?'

'She went to New York to look after her mother for a bit.'

'Her stepmother?' Poor Charlie, having to look after that evil alcoholic.

'No, her real mother.'

'I thought her mum was dead?'

'What on earth made you think that?'

'I don't know, actually. Is her real mum the alcoholic, then?'

Isla looks at me like I'm a bit dim. 'No,' she says, speaking slowly. 'Her real mother broke her leg in a skiing accident last month. I think I remember Charlie saying her stepmother does have a drinking problem, but Charlie hardly ever sees her. Her mother got a massive alimony payout when she and her daddy got divorced years ago, hence why Charlie's such a spoilt brat.' Isla laughs that tinkling laugh again.

'Oh, right.'

'So,' she says, 'what do you think? Wanna get out of this joint and come be my PA?'

Will Trepper is looking up at me with sparkling blue eyes. I'm kind of tempted. But not that tempted.

'Thank you, but, like I said, I wasn't very good at it.'

Isla rolls her eyes and looks at Will. He shrugs. 'Whatever,' she says. I go back to clearing tables.

Later that week, Isla reappears at the members' club.

'Hello again,' she says.

'Hi,' I answer. 'What can I get you?'

'I spoke to Johnny,' she says, off-handedly.

My heart starts to beat, double time.

'He said you were a really good PA.'

I gulp. 'He did?'

'Yes. He was pretty surprised to hear you were working here.'

I don't say anything.

'So what do you think? Want to come work for me?'

'I already told you—'

'That you were a crap PA, yes, yes, I know,' she fobs me off. 'But now that I know you were *lying*, the offer's still there.'

I sigh. 'Look, I really appreciate you asking and everything . . .'

'Are you *really* going to turn me down?' she challenges me.

I meet her eyes for a moment, aware that my manager is watching me from the bar area.

'Yes,' I reply, turning away.

'What was that about?' my manager asks me later.

'Nothing.'

'She didn't look too happy to me, Meg. I suggest you tell me what that was about so I can undo any damage you've done,' he says, pedantically.

'She offered me a job,' I tell him, which makes him start in surprise. 'I turned her down,' I add, and don't wait to see his reaction before getting back to work.

It's only later, when I'm sitting at 'home' on the sofa, that Isla's words start to sink in.

Johnny knows where I am.

I've been trying so hard not to think of him. I've avoided conversations that involve him, magazines and newspapers that may feature him. I've even walked out of French Connection because they started to play one of his songs. And now . . . Now . . . He knows where I am. He could come and find me if he wanted to.

My heart aches at the thought of it.

Stop it, Meg! He's a bastard! I feel like slapping myself across my own face to snap myself out of it.

That's a life that you left behind. He's not coming for you. No one's coming for you. MOVE ON!

But my throat begins to swell up and before I can stop it, I start to cry.

Dammit! Where are the bloody tissues when you need them? I go into the bathroom and pull on the toilet roll, trying to stifle my sobs. It's after midnight and Bess and Serena are asleep. I blow my nose and return to my so-called bed. But as soon as the tears stop, they start again. I sob, silently, into my pillow.

'What's wrong?' I hear Bess's concerned voice from above the sofa.

Obviously not sobbing that silently, then.

'Nothing,' I tell her. 'Go back to bed.'

She comes and joins me on the sofa.

'Meg, tell me what's wrong.'

'I can't!' I wail, then shoot a worried look at Serena's (aka my) bedroom door.

'Don't worry,' Bess says, 'she wears earplugs. And snores like an elephant,' she adds, cocking her head to one side.

'How do you know what a snoring elephant sounds like?' I ask, tearfully.

Bess grins at me. 'You almost sounded like your old self then,' she says, before her face falls. 'Sorry, I didn't mean anything by that . . .'

I look down at my hands. Do you know what? Fuck confidentiality clauses!

'You can't tell anyone what I'm about to tell you,' I warn.

'Of course not!' Bess hisses.

'Seriously. I could get sued . . .'

'Meg, shut up.'

'Okay . . .' I take a deep breath, and tell her the whole sorry story. She does squeak the odd, 'Oh my God', but on the whole is remarkably restrained.

'And so here I am,' I say, finally.

She shakes her head at me in wonder. 'I can't believe you had sex with Johnny Jefferson!' she exclaims for the zillionth time.

Her reaction would have made me laugh a month ago. Now I just feel sad.

'How the hell did you keep it quiet?' she asks.

'I wanted to tell you. I so wanted to tell you. But I couldn't.'

'Yes, you could've,' she says, pulling a face at me.

'No, Bess, I couldn't . . .'

'Yes. You. Could. Have,' she says again.

I sigh. 'I was worried you'd tell Serena and she'd go and sell the story to *heat* magazine or something.'

She berates me. 'I wouldn't have told Serena! She can't keep a secret for buggery! She's a bit annoying, to be honest.'

I giggle. 'Really?'

'Yeah.' She nods. 'Makes a mean spaghetti carbonara, though. Nice change from burnt beans on toast.'

Now I laugh.

'I knew I'd have you laughing again.' She smiles at me. 'You've been depressing the hell out of me since you got back.'

'I'm sorry.'

'Don't worry about it. Are you okay?' She hands me another couple of pieces of toilet roll and I dab my eyes.

'I will be. Doesn't feel like it right now, though. God,' I sniff. 'I only lasted six months. Even bloody *Paola* lasted eight months!'

'Don't beat yourself up about it,' Bess says, nonchalantly. 'He fell for you much quicker than he fell for her. If anything, I'd say you should be feeling pretty damn smug, right about now.'

Huh. I really hadn't thought of it like that.

Chapter 31

I'm still on edge, a week later, when I come into work for the afternoon/evening shift to see a blond-haired guy sitting at a table, facing a wall. I know almost instantly that he's not Johnny, but it's that split second beforehand that worries me. I'm clearly not over him. I'm clearly nowhere near over him. Even though he treated me terribly, I'm still thinking he might come for me. It's stupidity of the highest degree.

So it's because I'm so jittery about every blond-haired customer that I don't even notice the dark-haired one until I'm standing right in front of him.

'Christian!'

'Hello, Meg.' He smiles up at me.

'How did you find me?' I ask in surprise, before adding, '*Did* you find me? Or are you just here by chance?' Please don't let it be the latter. That would be embarrassing.

'Johnny told me you were working here.'

'Johnny? Did he?'

'Yes,' he says, calmly.

'What are you doing here?' I ask, hoping that doesn't sound rude.

He shifts a little uncomfortably before answering. 'I wanted to see . . . I wanted to see if you were okay.'

Out of the corner of my eye I notice my manager. 'Can I get you anything?' I ask, taking out my notepad. 'My manager is watching me,' I mouth.

'Ah, okay. Yes,' he says, perusing the menu. 'I'll have the . . . Hmm, what's good?'

'I can thoroughly recommend the roast chicken. The chips are the best.'

'Actually, I'd better just grab a coffee.' He snaps his menu shut and I hold out my hand for it. 'Can you chat later?'

'I'll try to come back when he's on his fag break,' I whisper.

Half an hour later, as promised, I go back to see Christian.

'So what are you doing? Apart from working here. Where are you living?'

'With my friend Bess,' I tell him. 'On her sofa. Do you remember her? You met at the Wembley concert.'

'That's right,' he says.

'It's crowded,' I continue. 'In fact, I've just started looking around for a flatshare. So if you hear of anything . . .'

He nods, thinking for a moment.

'Anyway, sorry, I'm rabbiting on. What about you? What have you been up to?'

At that point my manager comes back into the room. I glance over at him, immediately on edge.

'Your manager back already?' Christian asks.

'Mmm.'

'Tell you what, I have to shoot off now anyway. Got a meeting

368

with my publisher.' He raises his eyebrows, faking importance. 'But I wanted to know if you'd have dinner with me sometime?'

'Dinner?'

'Yeah, you know, just to catch up. See how you are . . .' he adds.

'Um, sure, okay,' I say, uneasily. I don't want him to get the wrong idea.

'When are you free?' he asks, unperturbed.

'Er, tomorrow's my night off.'

'Perfect. Where are you living? Want to go somewhere local?'

'London Bridge. But I don't mind travelling. Where do you live?' I ask, interested.

'Belsize Park,' he says. 'North London.'

'So let's meet centrally, hey?' I grin. 'Bar Soho?'

'Eight o'clock?'

'Done.'

Christian gets up, chucking some money down on the table. 'Oh, and I got you something.' He hands over a paper bag. 'It's nothing,' he adds, quickly. 'Look when your manager's not watching you,' he whispers out of the corner of his mouth.

'Eek. Okay. See you tomorrow!'

I open the bag when he's gone and can't help but giggle. It's full of Pick 'n' Mix sweets.

'Does Johnny know you're having dinner with me?' I give Christian a wary look across the table. He leans back in his seat.

'No,' he says, shortly. 'Do you want him to?'

I scratch my head. 'No. I don't know.'

'I haven't really spoken to him much since we last caught up.'

'In LA?' I ask. 'After that night?'

'Yep,' he says, tapping his fingers on the table.

'I feel bad,' I say.

'Why?' He looks confused.

'For causing a rift between you two.'

'Don't be ridiculous, Meg. Nothing's changed. Not really. We'll be the same as ever next time we catch up. No, I've just been too busy writing to get in touch with anyone. Except you,' he adds.

I smile at him, not feeling uneasy anymore. In fact, not feeling anything except completely comfortable.

'Fuck,' he mutters, suddenly.

'What?'

He glances sideways. 'My ex has just walked in.'

I follow his gaze to see a tall, curvy brunette with wavy hair talking to a waiter. She's with a broad-shouldered, olive-skinned man.

'Are you okay?' I ask Christian. He nods, but I can see he's anything but.

'Shall we do that thing?'

He grins at me, knowing exactly what I'm talking about. 'Go on, then.'

I reach across the table and put my hand on his. We both lean in and gaze into each other's eyes, adoringly.

'Christian,' I say, 'thank you sooooo much for my present. It was incredibly thoughtful.'

He smiles back at me, lovingly. I can see he's trying not to laugh. 'Meg, you deserved it.' He reaches across and strokes the corner of my lip. 'You've got a little ketchup . . .'

'Have I?' I giggle and pick up my napkin.

'Clare! Hello!' I hear him say, and look up to see his ex standing next to the table.

I beam up at her.

She glances down at me and smiles, frostily. 'Hello, Christian.'

'Clare,' he says, warmly, 'this is Meg. Meg, Clare.'

'Nice to meet you!' I gush, shaking her cold hand.

'Hi.' She looks awkward. 'This is Boris.'

'Hi, there,' Christian says, jovially, shaking Boris's hand.

'We're just having a bite to eat,' Clare says.

'Well, what do you know. So are we!' Christian enthuses, and I kick him under the table. Don't be too OTT, mate.

'I recommend the burgers,' he says.

Clare gives him a haughty look. 'I'm a vegetarian, remember?'

He laughs. 'Oh, shit, sorry. Of course you are. Well, have a good one!' he says. 'You too.' He grins at Boris, who as yet hasn't said anything.

Boris nods and puts his arm around Clare's waist, ushering her towards a table where their waiter is patiently holding menus. Christian stares after them.

'Christian,' I say, firmly.

'Mmm?' he answers, distracted.

'Eyes on me. Don't give the game away.'

'Right, yes, got it.' He refocuses his attention. He flexes his hands and picks up his knife and fork, before putting them down again.

'You haven't lost your appetite, have you?' I ask, concerned.

He takes a deep breath. 'Have a bit,' he replies.

I push my bottom lip out. 'Do you want to go? They do really good desserts, here . . .' I try to tempt him.

'Maybe we could go and get an ice cream in Leicester Square instead?' he suggests.

'Ice cream? In this weather?' I ask, then slap my hand on my forehead. 'Sorry, I forgot who I was with for a second. Yeah, let's.'

'That was a bit weird,' he says, a little while later, after we've walked hand in hand out of the restaurant.

I rub his arm. 'Are you okay?'

'Yeah,' he says.

'Had you really forgotten she was a veggie?' I ask.

'Nah.' He shakes his head and grins at me.

'Oh . . . Good one,' I say, impressed.

'Cheers.' Still grinning, he adds, 'Thanks, by the way. Really appreciated that.'

'I'm sure you'd do the same for me.' I smile, thinking of my ex, Tom. And then suddenly I'm remembering Johnny. My smile drops, just as Christian glances at me.

'So where do you want to live?' He changes the subject.

'I don't know,' I answer. 'Anywhere, really. As long as it doesn't take me too long to get to work.'

'And are you going to carry on working there?'

'Yes,' I reply, a touch defensively.

'Did Isla Montagne really offer you a job?' He looks at me sideways.

'Yeah, she did.' I smile. 'Johnny said I was a good PA, apparently.' I roll my eyes, trying to seem unbothered.

'Well, you were,' Christian says. 'Much better than that Paola lass.' He jokingly repeats the joke he made when we were on tour.

'In every way, do you reckon?' I say, before clamping my hand over my mouth. 'Sorry, that was really inappropriate.'

He chuckles, but doesn't say anything.

Much later, after we've eaten ice cream, wandered the streets, stopped for coffee and chatted the night away, Christian and I stand deep in the heart of Tottenham Court Road tube station, between both platforms. He's going north on the Northern Line; I'm going south.

'You know what?' he says to me. 'I have a spare room, if you want it.'

'Er . . . Really?' I ask, surprised.

'Yeah.'

'Were you thinking of renting it out?' I check.

'No,' he admits. 'But if you're as good a flatmate as you are a PA, I don't reckon I can go wrong.'

'Well, you'd have to ask Bess for a reference on that one,' I say, before adding, 'Actually, don't. The living room's a mess. Oh – should I have admitted that?'

He chuckles. 'Why don't you come round for tea sometime? Check it out?'

'Okay. When?'

'Are you free any time this weekend?'

'Sunday afternoon. Would that work?'

'Great.'

He scribbles his address on a pad, just as a tube train rushes down the line behind me.

'That's me!' I say, grabbing the piece of paper and reaching up to give him a peck on the cheek.

'See ya, Megan.' He smiles at me.

Christian's flat is stunning. It's a maisonette in a large, white, Georgian terrace. The lower ground floor features a living room to the front with a huge bay window, and a kitchen and dining room to the back, with French doors leading out to a small garden. Upstairs there are two bedrooms, a large bathroom and a small office.

'It's beautiful,' I say, for about the dozenth time. I'm actually wondering how the hell he afforded to buy it, especially as super-expensive Hampstead is only a short walk up the hill. It occurs to me that maybe Johnny helped him, but almost as soon as that thought comes to my mind, Christian explains.

'I got very lucky on the property market,' he says.

'Oh? How do you mean?'

'I bought a small studio in Islington as soon as I got a job after uni. Made a bit of money on it.'

'Enough to buy this?' I ask, surprised.

'No, but enough to buy a one-bedroom and do it up. And then a couple of years later I made enough to upgrade again, and again a couple of years after that. Like I said, I was pretty lucky.'

'Doesn't sound to me like you were lucky,' I say, impressed. 'Sounds like you were smart.'

He smiles down at me. 'So what do you reckon? Want to move in?'

'I would *love* to. But are you sure? If you've never rented your room out before . . . Don't you want your own space?'

'You forget I used to live with my girlfriend,' he says. 'And actually, I hate living alone. I'm a company kind of guy.'

'Me too.' I smile. 'I've been thinking about buying a studio flat, but I think I'd get lonely.'

He asks me how much I used to pay at Bess's and we agree a monthly amount, bills not included. Then he walks into the kitchen and puts the kettle on. I go and stand by the French doors, looking out into the bare winter garden. It's very neat and tidy. I bet it's beautiful in the spring. Happiness surges through me at the thought that I'll be here to see it for myself.

'Do you get out in the garden much?' I ask, after he's handed me a mug.

'Yeah, a bit. Quite like gardening, actually. You?'

'I haven't had a garden since I've been living in London, but yes, I really like the idea of it.'

'Well, I've got me bulbs planted and me shrubs pruned,' he says, in a jokey Farmer Joe-style voice. 'So in a couple of weeks, it'll be boooootiful out there.'

I laugh. 'You idiot.' I sip my tea. 'So when can I move in?'

Chapter 32

All I have to do is throw the odd item back into my dishevelled-looking suitcase and zip it up again, so I'm able to move in on my next day off. Bess is sorry to see me go.

'No! Do you have to move out?'

'I can't carry on sleeping on your sofa forever . . .'

'Yes, you can. Anyway, it's half your sofa, remember,' she whines.

'Bess, you can have it,' I say, generously, then laugh. We actually found it on the side of the road a year and a half ago. It was in pretty good nick.

'Bloody North Londoner,' she mutters, before giving me a big, cuddly hug and grudgingly promising she'll come and see me soon.

Christian cooks us Mexican fajitas on the night I move in, and it reminds me of Rosa and the meal she made me on the first night I stayed at Johnny's.

'What are you thinking?' Christian asks, so I tell him.

'What do you think Johnny will say when he finds out I've moved in with you?' I ask.

'Don't have to tell him if you don't want. He's only ever been to my place once, anyway.'

I don't say anything. I don't want Christian to know I *want* Johnny to know where I am.

The phone rings, so Christian excuses himself and gets up to answer it. He takes the phone through to the living room and collapses down on the sofa, crossing his legs up on the coffee table. It's his mum, from what I can gather.

'Sorry about that,' he says, when he returns to the table. 'My mum's freaking out about my brother's wedding.'

'Anton, right?'

'Yeah.'

'Why's your mum freaking out?'

'Just the usual wedding crap. People haven't RSVP-ed, the cake maker has gone out of business, Vanessa's dress isn't ready yet . . .'

'Vanessa?'

'My brother's fiancée,' Christian explains.

'When's the wedding?'

'In a couple of weeks.'

'Are you his Best Man?'

'No, I'm not, actually. Cheeky git has asked a mate from university. He doesn't want any other groomsmen.'

'Oh. Are you disappointed?'

'Nah. Bloody thankful I don't have to do a speech, actually. I'll be able to get hammered instead.'

He sighs and leans back in his chair, rubbing his stomach.

'That was really nice.' I get up and start to clear the table. 'You're a good cook.'

'Not as good as Rosa,' he says, getting up. 'But I'm not too bad.'

'Could Clare cook?' I ask, following him into the kitchen.

'Yeah, but she was only into vegetarian rubbish. So I had to fend for myself,' he adds, melodramatically.

'How long did you live together?' I ask, as he starts to load the dishwasher. I hunt out clingfilm and cover the salsa and sour cream bowls with it.

'Couple of years? Something like that.'

Christian groans and rolls his eyes. 'That's the other thing my mum was stressing out about. Me not having a date to take to the wedding.'

'You don't have to have a date!' I exclaim.

'According to my mum I do.'

'I'll go with you,' I say, jokingly.

His eyes light up. 'Would you?'

'Er . . .' I wasn't expecting that. 'I guess I could.'

'That would be brilliant!' he enthuses.

'I won't have to pretend I'm your girlfriend or anything, though, will I?'

He chuckles. 'No, don't worry about that. Mum's just worried about the seating plan. But she'll be delighted to meet you at last,' he adds.

'At last?' I query.

'Oh,' he says. 'Well, I told her about you.'

'Did you?' I ask, gleefully. 'Why?'

'Just said you were keeping me company in LA. She still gets a bit worried about Johnny's influence on me. Never forgave him after the whole shagging-my-girlfriend malarkey.'

I chew on my bottom lip.

'Anyway, that would be brilliant. Thanks for that!' he continues, rinsing out a sponge and taking it to the table. I follow him.

'No worries. Now I just need to find a dress.'

'That one you wore to whatshisname's party in the hills would be fine.'

'What one? The blue one?'

'Yeah. That was really nice.' He pauses wiping over the table and glances up at me.

'Thanks,' I say, surprised. 'But any excuse to go shopping, hey? In fact, I might pop up to Hampstead in the morning and have a look around.'

He's so sweet to me. So thoughtful. I watch him go back into the modern open-plan kitchen and rinse the sponge out again, before wiping over the countertops. He's wearing a black, long-sleeved T-shirt and dark-blue jeans, and maybe it's just the colour, but I swear he's slimmer than I remembered him.

I wonder if Kitty was right about him. Liking me, I mean.

Kitty! Christ. I keep meaning to check my emails, but I haven't been near a computer for weeks and I left my iPhone in Johnny's office. I didn't feel right about keeping it.

'Hey, would you mind if I borrowed your computer to check my emails?' I ask Christian.

'Sure,' he says, and leads the way upstairs to his office. He opens up his laptop and logs in, then moves aside for me.

I pull up his chair and sit down, logging onto Hotmail. But there's nothing there. Only junk mail. I remember I never actually gave Kitty my personal email address, only my work one. I take a deep breath and start to type out a message. Explaining why I quit is going to be difficult. She'll definitely think something dodgy has gone on, especially considering it's taken me so long to write to her. I apologise for not getting in touch sooner, and then gloss over the details as much as I can, saying I missed

London and wanted to get back here. She'll know there's more to it than that; I just hope our mutual understanding of confidentiality clauses prevents her from prying too much.

I borrow Christian's computer again the next day to see if she's replied. She has.

> THERE YOU ARE!!!!!!!!!!!!! I can not BELIEVE you left without saying goodbye!!!!!!!!!!!! The CPA world has been going gaga over your disappearance. Everyone thinks you slept with Johnny.

Argh!

> You didn't, did you?!!!! Don't suppose you could tell me, even if you had . . . And what's this about you living with Christian? Has he asked you out, yet? You mark my words, Miss Stiles, he will before long.

I scan the email, looking for another mention of Johnny, but there is none, just some news about Rod's latest film deal, a recent premiere Kitty went to and the dress she bought on Melrose Avenue yesterday. I pause for a moment and check my feelings. Nothing. I don't miss LA. Even walking around Hampstead this morning in the rain didn't make me miss LA. I'm glad to be home.

'Hey,' Christian says, coming into the office.

'Sorry, do you need to use your laptop?' I ask, getting up.

'No, no, stay where you are. I just need to get my manuscript.' He lifts a thick wad of A4 paper off the top of a filing cabinet.

'Ooh.' I open my eyes wide. 'Is that your book?'

'Yeah,' he says, looking down at it.

'The finished version?'

'Yep. Well, almost. I'm just having a last read-through.'

'Wow,' I say.

'Do you . . .' he starts.

'Yes?'

'Do you want to have a look?' he asks, tentatively.

'I would love to! Are you sure?'

'Um, not really,' he admits, with a half-hearted chuckle. 'But yeah, go on, tell me what you think.'

I hold out my hands for the weighty manuscript and look down.

Johnny Be Good
The Official Johnny Jefferson Biography
by Christian Pettersson

'Cool! I like the title . . .'

'Thanks. My brother came up with it.'

'Anton?'

'No, Joel.'

'I hope you bought him a nice present to say thank you.'

'I'm going to!' He throws his hands up in the air. 'Jeez, you're as bad as my mother.'

I laugh. 'Where's your surname from?' I saw it on the business card he gave me months ago, but didn't really take it in.

'Sweden,' he says.

'Really?' I realise I don't know that much about Christian.

'Yeah. It's where my dad's from.'

'You don't look very Swedish . . .'

'What, blond hair, blue eyes kind of thing?' He laughs. 'That is such a cliché, Megan. But you're right, anyway. I take after my mum.'

'Can you speak any Swedish?' I ask, intrigued.

'Bilingual.'

'No shit?'

'No shit,' he confirms.

'That's brilliant! Oh, I wish my parents had brought me up to be bilingual!'

'Where are they from?' he asks.

'England,' I say.

He laughs. 'Nutcase.'

For a minuscule moment there, I thought he was going to call me Nutmeg.

'Anyway,' I stand up. 'I've got to get ready for work. Can I read this later?' I hold up the manuscript.

'Sure,' he says. 'I'll leave it in your room.'

It's after midnight by the time I get home and, as promised, *Johnny Be Good* is waiting for me on top of my bed. I eye it as I get ready, and then finally, exhausted, I climb under the covers and pick up the first few pages. I'll just read one chapter for now.

Hours later, I haven't been able to tear my eyes away. They're red and sore, but I cannot put this book down for the life of me. Reading about Johnny in such detail . . . The groupies, the drugs, the gigs . . . And then there's the personal side to him. The deeper side. His talent for music. His presence when he walks into a room.

As promised, there's no mention of our liaison, but Christian has written about me, and it's the weirdest thing, reading about myself in the third person. I'm not in the book much, but I do feature as Johnny's PA – and more importantly, his friend.

Tears well up in my eyes as I gently place the last page down on top of the stack. I miss him so much. Will I ever see him again? Face to face? Or am I destined to read about him in the press forever, like all of his other fans? I can't bear the thought of it. I can't.

Chapter 33

'You may now kiss the bride . . .'

Everyone breaks into spontaneous applause and I look at Christian and beam. I love a wedding.

'I am so sorry,' he whispers in my ear a short while later, during a reading by one of Anton's colleagues.

'Don't worry about it! I keep telling you it's fine.'

'I swear I told my mum we're not together. She obviously doesn't believe me.'

I laugh again. Poor Christian. We turned up at his parents' house this morning to discover his mum had put us in his old room. Together. Christian had told me he'd sleep on the sofa, but it turns out his uncle is also staying at the house. And his Swedish cousins. There are five of them.

'I should have insisted on going to a hotel,' he moans.

'You did try,' I reassure him. 'But if I remember that phone call correctly, she wasn't going to be swayed. It's fine!' I whack him on his leg. 'Not like we haven't shared a bed before, is it?'

'True,' he concedes.

I like Christian's family. They're good fun. The Swedish contingent is particularly hilarious. His dad is currently knocking back red wine like it's going out of fashion, his face as pink as a prawn, and his hair as yellow as the sun. Anton and Joel are the same. As for Christian, I see what he means when he says he takes after his mum. She's tall and attractive, with black curly hair and dark-brown eyes. She reminds me a little of a gypsy, but I'm not about to tell Christian that, even if I do mean it as a compliment.

'What was Johnny's mum like?' I ask, out of the blue.

'Tall, skinny, blonde. And very warm and friendly. She and my mum were good friends, actually.'

'So she knew Johnny when he was a boy?'

'When he was just plain old Johnny Sneeden, yes.' Christian smiles.

'What does she think about the way he's turned out?'

Christian's lower lip turns down and he shrugs. 'Okay, I guess.'

'Does she think his mum would be disappointed?'

'Nah. His mum loved him to death. She would have been proud of him for sure.'

'Johnny doesn't seem to think so,' I say, sadly.

'I know.' Christian leans back against a wall and stares out at the dance floor.

'I got fuck-all sleep with that racket going on. What about you?' Christian asks me the following morning, when we're lying side by side in bed. His dad and the Swedish army drank most of the night away downstairs in the living room.

'Your dad puts even Johnny to shame,' I say, then giggle nervously as I wait for Christian's reaction. But he just laughs.

'Do you fancy a cuppa?'

'I don't know if I dare.' I remind him of the time he told me his mum's kitchen was his mum's kitchen and no one else was allowed in it.

'She'll be down there by now, anyway. Has probably laid out a right old spread to try to impress you.'

'She doesn't really think we're together, does she?' I ask again.

'I honestly think she does. Especially after this.' He motions to the double bed we're sleeping in. 'Make the most of it. Her homemade fruit toast is a dream. If she's trying to keep up appearances, she will have made some. Come on, let's go.'

'I can't go downstairs in my PJs!'

'Yeah, you can. You look fine. Come on.'

I follow him, reluctantly.

The smell of freshly baked bread hits my nostrils the second we exit Christian's bedroom. I look at him with delight. 'Mmm!'

'Wait till you try it,' he says.

'Good morning!' his mum chirps. I don't think she drank much last night. His dad, on the other hand, is nowhere to be seen. 'Would you like a cup of tea, Megan?'

'Yes, please,' I answer.

'It's just Meg, Mum,' Christian tells her.

'Well, you call her Megan,' she replies, defensively.

'Only for a joke.'

'What's funny about that?' she asks.

Christian turns to me. 'I don't suppose anything is funny about it, actually. Why *do* I call you Megan?'

'I dunno.' I shrug.

'Meg it is, then. Mum, get us some fruit toast, pllleeeaaassssssee!' He sounds like a little boy. In fact, I can just picture a young Johnny sitting at the table beside him.

'Oh, you . . .' she scoffs, but puts four slices in the toaster regardless. 'So Megan – Meg,' she corrects herself, 'what do you do now? Christian says you're no longer working for Johnny, is that right?'

'That's right. I'm waitressing at a private members' club at the moment.'

'Mmmhmm. And what was it like, working with wee Johnny?'

I try not to smile at the use of 'wee'. Johnny is anything but.

'It was good,' I say.

'Mum, don't pry,' Christian warns.

'What? She can tell me if she wants to!'

'She doesn't want to, Mum,' he says. 'She's just being polite.'

'You're not just being polite, are you, Megan? Meg?'

'Um, no?' I try.

'So when did you two meet?' she asks us both, and I breathe a sigh of relief at the change of subject until I realise which path she's going down.

Christian casts his eyes upwards. 'Mum! Cut it out. Meg and I are not going out together!'

She sniffs. 'Well, I think you make a lovely couple.'

As February turns into March and the daylight hours gradually become longer, I settle back into London life with a sense of calm. I love living with Christian. He's so lovely, so relaxed. We eat together whenever work allows, and we like nothing more than going down to our local and sitting at a corner booth, catching up over a couple of pints. In fact, as time goes on, we become even more like boyfriend and girlfriend. Without the sex, obviously. Although I have thought about it. The more I get to know him, the more attractive Christian becomes. And he is a nice guy, the type of guy I normally go for. But I still can't get Johnny out of my head.

Even now I'm avoiding reading any press about him. And I haven't seen Isla at the members' club since the time she asked me to go and work for her. Kitty tells me she's fled back to LA, broken-hearted. Rumours are rife that she found Will with another man. I don't know whether or not I believe it.

Kitty keeps me up to date with all the LA gossip. I'd almost rather she didn't, but there's not a lot I can say without her getting suspicious about Johnny all over again. Luckily she says very little about him. If he's still with Lola, the press haven't picked up on it.

One late afternoon, I'm sitting at home watching TV after working the morning shift, when there's a knock on the door. We rarely have visitors, but have been known to hear from the odd salesman, so I'm tempted to ignore it completely. The knock comes again, this time more frantically. I get to my feet, annoyed at having my *Richard & Judy* viewing session interrupted, and go to answer it.

Peering through the peep-hole, I swear my heart stops momentarily when I see Johnny standing there.

'Quick! Open up!' he urges, behind the closed door.

I do as he says. It's only when I close the door behind him that he jolts in shock and stares at me.

'Meg?' His tone is guarded, almost as if he thinks he's seeing things.

'Hi, Johnny.' I pray my voice won't shake.

'What are you doing here?' he asks.

'I live here.'

'You *live* here?' he asks, in astonishment. 'What, with *Christian*?'

'Yeah.' I laugh at the look on his face. 'Not like *that*, you moron. As friends.'

'Oh.' The relief on his face is palpable. Which is nice.

'Christian's not here,' I say. 'He's up in Manchester on an assignment.'

'Oh, right. Can I?' He motions towards the kitchen.

'Sure, of course.' I lead the way. 'Do you want a tea or coffee?'

'What else have you got?'

I look at him, patiently. 'What are you after? Booze cabinet's over there.' I point. I'm sure Christian won't mind if Johnny helps himself. I get out a glass and put a couple of chunks of ice in it. I know Johnny will opt for the whisky, and this is the way he likes it best. I hand him the glass so he can pour the caramel-coloured liquid into it himself.

'Cheers, Nutmeg,' he says, casually. I jump at the sound of my nickname and he looks up at me. It just rolled off the tip of his tongue, but I can see now that even he found it weird.

He waits in the corner of the kitchen while I make a cup of tea. I'm nervous, but I'm trying not to show it. I don't know what to say.

'I thought I was being tailed.' He speaks eventually, explaining why he turned up at the door in a panic.

'What, by the press?'

'Paps, yeah.'

'What are you doing in the UK?' I ask.

'Dad's wedding.'

'So soon?'

'Mmm.'

'When is it?' I lead the way to the sofas and mute the sound on the TV.

'Actually, I might go outside for a cigarette,' he says. 'Come chat to me?'

It's cold outside, so I grab my coat and pull my gloves out of my pockets, sliding them on. We sit on the bench at the end of the garden and Johnny lights up. To my surprise, he offers me his cigarette packet.

'You don't smoke, do you?' he asks.

'No,' I say, waving them away. How strange.

He pushes them back into his pocket and takes a long drag, staring back at the house. I pull my knees up in front of me and wrap my arms around them, trying to keep warm.

'So when is your dad's wedding?' I ask again.

'This weekend just gone.'

'Was it okay?'

'Bit strange,' he admits.

'In what way?'

'Ah, just . . .' He glances at me, those green eyes sending a shockwave through my system. 'Felt a bit on show.' He flicks his ash onto the muddy garden bed.

'Was it a big wedding?'

He laughs, hollowly, before answering. 'Yes. Turns out Shelley – my dad's woman – has a lot of *friends* . . .' The way he says 'friends' implies he means anything but.

'All there to see you, hey?'

'Mmm,' he answers, wryly.

He glances at me again. My arms are still wrapped around my knees. 'You cold?'

I nod. He pats the bench space next to him, so I edge a bit closer. He puts his whisky in his other hand, along with his cigarette, and puts his now-free arm around my shoulder. He rubs my arm with his hand, vigorously.

'Brr, Nutmeg, it is a bit cold, isn't it?'

My stomach is tying itself up into knots and I'm anything but comfortable. I try to steel myself. 'Shall we go inside?' I ask, glancing at him, but we're so close I have to look away again.

'Sure,' he says, removing his arm and stubbing his fag out on the ground.

Calm down, Meg, calm down, I tell myself as I lead the way back indoors. I look up to see Johnny watching my face in the reflection of the French doors and am reminded of the time in LA when I first met him. I reach for the handle to open the door.

We take off our shoes because they're muddy and then Johnny takes a detour via the booze cabinet.

'Are you still working at that members' club?' he asks, joining me on the sofa in the living room.

'Yep,' I reply.

'Didn't take Isla up on her offer of a job, then?' He raises one eyebrow at me.

'No.' I look away at the TV. It still has the sound turned down, but I can see they're doing a feature on weddings.

'Huh. That looks a bit like Vanessa's dress,' I comment out loud.

'Vanessa?'

'Anton's fiancée. Well, wife now.'

'Anton? Oh! Christian's brother. Fuck!' he exclaims. 'I forgot to send a card.'

'You can still send one now,' I suggest.

'Yeah, I suppose I could. Don't have his address, though.'

'Send it to his parents' place. Do you have that one?'

'Somewhere, yeah.'

'Want me to get it for you?'

'Could you?' He smiles, sheepishly.

I go upstairs to the office, returning a minute later with the address written down on a piece of paper.

'Thanks,' he says, looking down at it for a moment.

'Have you got a new PA?' I ask, convinced he's thinking about how I used to do this sort of thing for him all the time.

'No.' He shakes his head.

Ha!

'When do you think Christian will be back?' he asks.

I look at my watch. 'I don't know. I think he said he was catching the seven o'clock train so could be another hour or two yet.'

He gets to his feet and folds the piece of paper up, stuffing it into his back pocket. 'I should probably head off, then,' he says, retrieving his shoes from inside the French doors.

I get up, too, and walk him towards the door. 'Where are you staying?'

'Soho Hotel.'

'Just around the corner from where I work,' I say in surprise.

'I know.'

We look at each other for a moment.

'Want me to call a car for you?' I ask, feeling awkward.

He chuckles. 'No, it's alright, N— Meg. I'll catch a cab out on the main road.' He opens the door and looks out.

'All clear?' I ask.

'I think so. See ya, then.'

'Bye.'

I watch as he makes his way up the narrow steps from Christian's private entrance to the street above. He looks left and right and then glances down at me and raises his hand in a half-wave, before stepping out of sight. I close the door, feeling empty inside.

Chapter 34

'Hey!' Christian beams at me when he walks into the kitchen with his overnight bag. 'Did ya miss me?'

'Nah,' I tease.

Actually, I did.

'How was your assignment?'

'Good. Much easier than I thought it was going to be.'

He was writing something about the music scene in Manchester. God knows what. It all goes right over my head.

'Have you been outside?' he asks in surprise, spying my shoes by the door.

'Yeah.' I try to sound casual. 'Johnny was here.'

'Johnny?' He looks taken aback.

'He came to see you.' I explain how he thought he was being followed. 'Wanted a fag so went into the garden.'

'Decent of him,' Christian says, and I'm not sure if I detect sarcasm. 'What did he want?'

'I don't know,' I reply.

He stares at me. 'You okay?'

'Why wouldn't I be?' I don't mean to sound defensive.

He wanders through to the living room.

'Been at my whisky too, has he?'

Johnny's empty glass is still on the coffee table. I've been reluctant to wash it up since he left.

'I hope that's okay.'

'It's fine.' He sighs and slumps down onto the sofa. 'Chuck us the phone, will you? I'd better give him a bell.'

I try to seem casual as I hand over the phone and wander back into the kitchen, but I really want to be around for this conversation. After a few minutes of listening without hearing Christian's voice, I go back through to the living room.

'Not there?' I indicate the phone.

'Going straight through to voicemail,' he confirms.

'Oh, right. I might go and check my emails. Is that okay? You're not wanting to do any writing tonight, are you?'

'No, it's fine. Go for it.'

I climb the stairs and head into the office. My emails contain nothing of interest, and after a few minutes of sitting there, staring into space and thinking of Johnny, it occurs to me I could call Bess and tell her about seeing him again. I pick up the phone and instantly hear Johnny's voice down the line.

'Why didn't you tell me she was living with you?'

'I didn't think you'd care,' Christian replies.

'Well, I do,' says Johnny.

I hold my breath, listening.

'In what way?' Christian's tone is suspicious.

'You fancy her, don't you?' Johnny says. 'I mean, the way you've gone on about her in the past . . . And now this. Getting her to move in with you. Are you two shagging each other or something?'

'Piss off.' Now Christian sounds annoyed.

The fax machine behind me starts to whir, noisily. Argh!

'What's that?' I hear Johnny ask.

'I don't know,' Christian responds.

I gently press the red button and put the phone back down in its cradle, more confused than ever.

Later that night, after Christian has gone to bed, I finally speak to Bess.

'Did Christian say anything to you about it?' she asks.

'No. And I didn't want to ask because that would have given away my eavesdropping.'

'Do you think he *does* fancy you?'

'I don't know,' I reply.

'Do you fancy him?'

'No. I don't think so. I mean, sometimes I look at him and think he's really attractive, and I wonder *wh*y I don't fancy him . . .' I try to explain.

'Well, that's obvious,' she says. 'Johnny.'

I have to laugh.

'What?' she asks.

'Can you believe *I*, of all people, have fallen for Johnny Jefferson?'

She giggles. 'It is pretty funny. Remember how I used to tease you all the time? You denied it and denied it, and all the time you *did* want to get into his pants!'

'Oi!' I laugh.

'And what about that email you sent me from LA?' she suddenly screeches. 'You *had* been shagging him!'

'I know,' I answer, shamefaced. 'I pressed Send by mistake.'

'I still can't believe you've gone to bed with Johnny Jefferson,' she says in wonder. 'It really sucks that you can't tell people about it.'

'I wouldn't want to, even if I could.'

'Why, because that would cheapen it?' She giggles.

'Yeah, actually. It would.' I don't like her thinking this is some kind of joke. It's not. This is my heart we're talking about.

'Sorry,' she says. 'It just seems so surreal.'

'Don't worry about it.'

I wait on tenterhooks for Christian to mention Johnny during the next couple of days, but he says nothing. I start reading the tabloids again, surfing the internet . . . All in the hope of catching some news about him. He's consuming me again. Every part of me. And I don't like it. I feel like I have to free myself of him all over again.

As the days become weeks, I catch the odd snippet about Johnny in the press. He's back in LA, back to his old ways, drinking in bars, pulling groupies. It doesn't hurt as much as I thought it would, and eventually I find I can go whole days with barely a thought about him.

One afternoon, in early May, Christian comes home after a meeting with his publisher.

'I bumped into Clare today,' he says, casually putting one foot up on his opposite knee. We're sitting in the garden.

'*Did you?*'

'Yep. It was fine.' He grins at me. 'Didn't feel a thing.'

'That's brilliant,' I tell him. 'Really good. Is she still with that Boris bloke?'

He shrugs. 'Dunno. Didn't ask.'

'Really? Now *that's* impressive.'

'I thought so,' he says, flippantly. 'She asked about you, though.'

'Did she?' My eyes open wide. 'What did you say?'

'I said we were living together.'

I start to giggle.

'Not like that,' he chides. 'I told her you were just my flat-mate.'

'Oh, right,' I say, feeling my face heat up.

'Told her you were too hung up on Johnny Jefferson to give any other lads a look-in.'

'You didn't!' I'm horrified.

'No, not really.' He grins.

I slap him on his thigh.

'You are, though, you know.' He glances at me.

'What, too hung up on Johnny?'

'Yeah.'

'Do you think I'm going to end up sad and alone?' I joke.

'Yeah.' He laughs, hollowly. 'You probably will.'

We both fall silent. After a while, I sigh and get up.

'Meg . . .'

He grabs my hand and I look back at him, startled.

'What?'

He gently pulls me back down to sit beside him. I look at him, nervously.

'What?' I ask again.

He lets go of me and runs his hands through his dark, indie-boy hair. 'Forget it,' he says, looking down at the bright yellow tulips in the flower bed. He sounds frustrated.

'Tell me,' I say.

He looks back at me suddenly, intensely, and I'm surprised to feel my heart flip.

'I care about you,' he says.

'I care about you, too,' I reply, cagily.

'No. I *care* about you. Too much.' His dark-brown eyes still meet mine, and I want to look away, but find that I can't.

'Meg . . .'

He runs his fingertips down the curve of my waist. When I don't stop him, he leans in closer. I don't pull away, but I don't move in towards him, either. He kisses me, slow and gentle.

He tastes nice . . . Sweet . . . I like him so much, I *want* to fancy him the way I fancy Johnny.

Johnny. You know it will never work. You have to move on.

I kiss Christian back, harder, desperate to feel the passion I felt with his friend.

Christian is perfect for me. He's lovely, he's intelligent, he's mature, he wouldn't mess me around. I like him so much.

But do you love him?

No.

Do you love Johnny?

Don't think about that now.

'I really want to make love to you,' Christian says. His breathing has quickened.

'Okay.' I nod.

The earth doesn't move, but it's loving, it's tender, there's no feeling of dread afterwards.

He holds me in his arms and strokes my hair, and I try so hard not to think about the man who brought us together.

'Are you alright?' he asks.

I look up at him and smile. 'Yeah. That was nice.'

'Just "nice"?'

'*Really* nice,' I say. 'Want to do it again?'

He chuckles. 'Why not?'

Chapter 35

'I'll bring you back some Pebbles,' Christian promises, giving me a kiss on the lips.

It's eight o'clock in the morning. He's flying to LA tonight and I'm just leaving for work. We won't catch each other this evening.

'Say hi to Johnny for me,' I call over my shoulder, then stop and turn around. 'Actually, don't,' I decide.

'Really?' he asks.

'Yes.'

He looks relieved. 'See you next week,' he says.

He's going to LA to meet with Johnny about his book. Johnny has final copy approval, so this will be his last chance to read over the finished product and make any amendments before publication.

Bess comes round that night to keep me company and watch a chick-flick.

'How's it all going?' she asks.

'Really good,' I say.

'So you're definitely attracted to him now, then?'

'Yes.' I laugh. 'It would be a bit weird me sleeping in his room every night if I wasn't.'

It's been a month since Christian and I first slept together. And it *is* going well. I do really like him.

'I'm happy for you,' Bess says. 'He's a nice guy. What does his mum think?' she asks. I filled her in about the wedding debacle back when it happened.

'He hasn't told her yet,' I say. 'Too soon.'

'Fair enough.' She grabs a bowl of popcorn from the coffee table and starts to chow down on it. 'So,' she says offhandedly, 'are you over Johnny, then?'

'Yeah,' I say. 'I think I am.'

'Good. What about him being done for drink-driving, hey?'

'*What?*' I bolt upright.

'Oh, you don't know?'

'No! What happened?'

'Last night. He was on his motorbike. There are pics of him being pulled over in today's papers.'

'I haven't read them. Bloody hell. Is he in jail?'

'He's out on bail, apparently.'

'God. What an idiot.'

'I'll say. Shall we watch this movie, then?'

'Sure,' I reply, but my mind is elsewhere.

Christian calls me from LA to touch base the next day. I ask him about the drink-driving incident.

'Yeah. It's a bit of a pain, actually. My publisher wants it covered in the book. Reckons it will be a nice end point.'

'How are you going to manage that? I thought it was going to the printers soon?'

'It's supposed to be, yes. They're pushing back the publication date a little so we can get in the court hearing and any jail time, if necessary.'

'When is the court hearing?'

'His lawyers are trying to get one, asap. He's got them working overtime.'

'How's Johnny about it? Is he okay?'

'Pretty pissed off, as you can imagine,' he says. 'Reckons the cops were out to get him.'

'They probably were.'

'Yeah, well, what do you expect when you're out drinking and doing drugs every bloody night? He's as bad as he was when we were on tour, you know . . .'

'Is he?' I ask, nausea creeping up on me.

'Afraid so. In fact, I'm going to change my flight and come home Thursday, instead.'

It's Tuesday, now.

'Why? Had enough?'

'Yeah.'

I feel pity for Johnny being left on his own, but I know I can't say that to Christian.

'Do you want me to change the flight for you?'

'No, it's okay. Johnny's PA can do it.'

My head throbs. 'Johnny's PA? Has he got another one?'

'Yeah. Some Danish woman. Not very attractive. Not a patch on you, gorgeous.'

'Aah.' I feel warm again. 'Have you told Johnny about us?' I ask, tentatively.

'Not yet,' he says. 'But I was planning to tonight. If that's okay with you?'

403

'Yes,' I decide. 'That's fine.'

'Meg,' he starts.

'Yes?'

'I love you.'

I pause before replying. 'I love you, too.'

In the late hours of Thursday night or the early hours of Friday morning, I'm not sure which, someone starts pounding on the door downstairs.

The knocking keeps coming, so I go downstairs to the front door and look through the peep-hole.

It's Johnny.

I flatten myself up against the wall. What is he doing here? Oh God, I'm in my crappy PJs. What should I do?

'Meg, open up!' he whispers, loudly.

I hurriedly smooth my hair down and wipe the sleep from my eyes. I glance down at my outfit. Urgh. Okay. I'm opening the door.

He rushes past me, into the corridor.

'What's wrong? What are you doing here?' I look back outside in alarm, wondering if he's being chased. He pushes the door shut and tries to take my hands.

'Meg, Meg, Meg,' he says, over and over again. He's drunk.

'Johnny, stop it. Where's Christian?'

'Meg,' he moans, taking my arms in his hands.

'Johnny! Where's Christian?' I ask in alarm. 'Is he okay?' Panic rises up inside me as I start to imagine he's here to deliver bad news.

'He's fine, he's fine!' He cups my face with his hands.

'Where is he?' I demand.

'LA!' he shouts, frustrated.

'What are you doing here?' I shout back, equally frustrated and more than a little confused.

'I had to see you,' he says, desperately.

I push him away violently. 'He told you, then.'

He looks at me in anguish.

'I get it.' I'm angry. 'You don't want me until *he's* got me. Is that right?'

'No . . . I miss you, Nutmeg.'

'My name is MEG.'

He looks hurt. 'Don't say that.'

'How did you get here before Christian?' I ask. His plane's not due until the morning.

'Jet.'

I assume he means his private one.

'Meg, please . . .' He comes towards me again.

I put my hand up to stop him. 'Haven't you hurt him enough?'

He looks bewildered.

'He loves me, you know. He *loves* me,' I repeat, hoping it will sink in.

'Nutmeg . . .' He runs his thumb down the side of my neck.

'Stop it!' I bat his hand away. 'Why are you doing this? I'm *happy*, Johnny. I *like* Christian!'

'There!' He practically shouts, pointing at me. 'You said "like"!'

I step backwards. 'I *love* him,' I say, determinedly.

He shakes his head and leans back against the corridor wall, opposite me. We still haven't made it further than the front door.

'You said "*like*",' he says again, this time more slowly. 'You *love* me.'

'I do not!' I bite back. 'I *love* Christian and I don't even *like* you! You've been a wanker to me since the first day we met!'

'I have not!'

'You have!' I yell, crossly, before suddenly remembering the neighbours.

I must calm down. 'Go home, Johnny. I'm not doing this again. You're jealous and you're drunk, and I don't want anything to do with you.'

His shoulders slump, dejectedly, and he leans his head back against the wall and gazes at me.

Don't look at me like that, I think to myself.

'I'll go to rehab,' he says, simply.

'You'll what?'

'I'll go to rehab,' he repeats.

I'm flabbergasted. 'You would do that? For me?'

He shrugs. 'Yeah.'

'Oh, I get it,' I say, sarcastically. 'You're going to have to go to rehab anyway, right? Is that the deal your lawyers are putting together?'

He looks shifty.

'Argh!' I push him in the chest. 'Go, go, go!'

He grabs my wrists. 'I love you.' His tone is urgent.

I stop struggling and stare at him in shock.

'Please . . . Meg . . .' He puts his hands on my waist and tries to pull me in.

My chest hurts. I can't go through this again.

He starts to kiss me and I melt into him, just like I used to.

No.

NO!

I pull away and push him backwards again. Then I open the

door. 'Leave. I love Christian. You won't hurt me again. GO!' I shout.

'I'm coming back for you,' he warns, stepping outside. 'After rehab. I'm coming back.'

I slam the door in his face and run upstairs to sob my heart out.

'Where is he?' Christian demands hours later. 'Was he here?'

'Yes,' I reply. 'He's gone now,' I hurriedly tell him, when I see the look on his face. 'I told him to leave.'

He drops his bags on the floor of the living room. I'm sitting on the sofa in my PJs. I haven't had the energy to get dressed this morning.

'Are you okay?' he asks, coming to join me.

'I'm fine.'

Actually, my eyes are red and puffy from crying so much, but I'm hoping Christian will see what he wants to see.

'He went mad when I told him,' Christian says, looking away.

'Shit!' I exclaim, seeing the side of his face. It's tinged red and blue.

'He punched me.' He lets out a half-hearted laugh.

'He *punched* you?' I ask in disbelief.

'Yeah.'

'Oh, no, you poor thing!' I touch his face gently and he flinches. Compassion wells up inside me.

He meets my eyes. 'You told him to leave?'

'Yes,' I reply.

He smiles at me, softly.

'Come here,' I say, and wrap my arms around him and bury my face in his neck.

I feel safe again.

Chapter 36

As predicted, the judge remands Johnny to rehab for six weeks. The press are all over the story like a rash, and I can't go anywhere without hearing or seeing something about Johnny Jefferson.

He got into trouble for breaking the terms of his bail and fleeing the country for a couple of days. The judge let him off lightly because his dad, of all people, swore an affidavit to say he'd been poorly. He said Johnny had flown over in a panic to see him.

No one knows it was actually me he came to see.

I don't tell Bess about Johnny's visit. And I don't tell Christian he kissed me, either. I just try not to talk about it. Or think about it. But the latter is easier said than done.

Late at night his words haunt me.

I'm coming back for you . . .

He won't come back for me. He just won't. He was drunk. He was angry. He was reacting to a situation he couldn't control.

I love you . . .

He didn't mean it.

Work is really starting to get to me. I want a new challenge, but I'm not quite sure what. Even now I'm not ready to be someone else's PA. I'm still considering the idea of going travelling. Christian hates it when I bring it up.

'Don't go travelling.'

'Why not?' I ask.

'I'd miss you.'

'Come too!'

'I can't.'

'Why not?'

'I have to work.'

He's not lying. His publisher is so happy with Johnny's biography that he's been given a two-book deal – to write fiction, this time.

Christian is ecstatic. It's what he's always wanted.

The day Johnny is allowed out of rehab, I'm glued to the TV like the rest of the world.

I watch him walk out of the centre in his dark glasses and silver shirt, looking forever the rock star. He climbs into a car, which I suddenly recognise as Davey's. I feel a pang as I watch him drive Johnny away.

Christian has decided it might be for the best if he speaks to Johnny about his rehab experience on the phone instead of in person. He thinks it might be too soon after what happened. He's probably right.

The footage of Johnny walking out of the centre is being replayed on the television. They've got some commentator talking about it, claiming to be an expert about what Johnny is going through.

I fold my arms tight across my chest. I hope he's okay.

Christian is upstairs, watching the footage in the office. He needs peace and quiet to concentrate and make notes.

I need peace and quiet to think.

The phone rings, making me jump.

'Hello?'

'Meg, it's Bess. Are you watching it?'

'Yep.' I cast a glance at the TV.

'How do you feel?'

'Okay, I think.'

'Do you reckon it will last?' she asks.

'I doubt it. He'll be back to his old ways before long.'

'Bloody good publicity for his new single, though, hey?'

'That's for sure.'

They've been playing Johnny's new single on the radio for a few weeks now. It's tipped to go straight to Number One.

'Well, I just wanted to check you're okay,' Bess says.

'Thanks. I am,' I tell her.

But as the days pass by, I feel increasingly on edge.

Christian keeps asking me what I'm thinking and why I'm so quiet, and I have to lie and tell him I've got a stomach ache or period pains or something. He buys it, most of the time, but I usually have to offer up more cuddles to put his mind at rest.

Do I *want* Johnny to come back for me? I'm happy with Christian. Do I *want* to feel confused all over again?

But I *am* confused. I'm always confused. It's out of my hands, now, anyway.

I put make-up on every day, just in case. It's stupid, I know, but

I want to look my best in case he comes. You know, for when I turn him down again.

One afternoon I arrive back at the flat after working the morning shift. I've walked down the narrow outdoor stairs and have my keys in the front door before I see him. He's standing in the far corner behind me, out of sight of anyone walking above on the street.

'Jesus!' I squeal. 'You scared the life out of me!'

'Shh,' he says, approaching slowly. 'Can I come in?'

I can tell immediately that he's sober. I feel light-headed. He follows me inside.

'Christian's not here,' I say, leading the way through to the kitchen.

'I know,' he replies. 'I called him earlier.'

'Oh. Okay. Do you want a tea or coffee?' I ask, half expecting him to opt for whisky instead.

'Tea would be good.'

'It worked, then?'

'Rehab?' he asks. 'Yeah.'

'Not going to relapse?'

'I hope not,' he says. 'But every day as it comes.'

I nod and turn away to get a couple of mugs.

'Thanks,' he says, as I hand over his tea and he hesitantly takes a sip.

I watch him. 'What are you doing here, Johnny?' I ask, finally.

'I said I'd come back for you.'

My heart beats so loud I worry it might pierce my eardrums.

'I told you, I'm with Christian.'

'I'm aware of that,' he answers, indifferently.

I stare at him, frustrated.

411

'You know it would never work, don't you?'

'Why not?' he asks.

'We're not suited to each other,' I say. 'Lola's more your type.' I shoot him a loaded look.

'No, she's not,' he says.

'Whatever happened with her?' I can't help but ask.

'Nothing after that night.' He puts his mug down on the countertop.

I don't know whether or not I believe him. The crazy part of me wants to.

But there was still that night. Still all the other women who have been there before me – and since. I'd always wonder if he was comparing me . . . How I measured up . . . I don't think I could handle that.

And is he even capable of being faithful? I'd love to believe he is, that I would be enough for him, but I haven't been so far, and the memory of Lola and all the other girls is still so raw. It's a hopeless situation.

'What do you want?' I ask again. Be specific this time.

'I want you to come back to LA with me.' He folds his arms.

'I can't go back to LA with you.'

'Why not?'

'I don't want to be your PA again!' I raise my voice.

'I don't want you to be my PA again, either. I've got a perfectly good one as it is, thanks.'

I look at him in surprise. 'What do you want, then?'

'I want you to come back to LA with me as my *girlfriend*, Meg. Come and live with me.'

Thoughts rush through my head. Red carpets . . . Glitterati . . . Everything and anything I could ever want.

412

Except Christian. I want Christian.

He may not be a world-famous rock star. He may not have the female population of the world falling at his feet. But he cares for me. He's a good guy. The type of guy I've always gone for – at least, before I met Johnny. But I'm still the same person I was back then. Despite the world I've been living in – drink, drugs, sex – I haven't changed. And neither has Christian.

I *do* love him. I love him so much.

'I can't.' I turn to Johnny, resolute.

He nods. 'I just want you to think about it.'

His words do something to calm me, bizarrely. I sigh. 'Okay.'

'Cool.' He picks up his mug again.

'You seem different,' I say, carefully.

'I am different.'

'But you're still happy to steal your best friend's girl?'

'I'm not happy about it,' he replies, nonchalantly. 'I've never been happy about it. But you were my girl first.'

He meets my eyes quite calmly. God knows how. I feel anything but calm.

'I like your new single,' I say, trying to keep the conversation light.

'Thanks. I hope you like the next one more.'

'Why?' I ask, intrigued.

'I wrote it for you.'

I look at him in amazement. 'You wrote it for me? When?'

'Up in the Dales. I started it then,' he says. 'Finished it when we got back. It's the second single released off the new album.'

I'm stunned. 'When is it coming out?'

'In a couple of months,' he says. 'But you can hear it tomorrow if you come back to LA with me.'

'I can't come back to LA with you,' I tell him again. 'Will you stick around for a bit?' I ask, glancing down at my uniform. 'I might go and get changed.'

'Sure,' he says.

I walk upstairs and go into my bedroom. I can't focus. My head is a jumble of thoughts.

I pull some jeans and a shirt out of my wardrobe. I'm just sliding my arms into the shirt when I hear a noise behind me.

'Johnny, what are you doing here?' I exclaim, wrapping the shirt around my chest.

'You're not sleeping in Christian's bedroom, then?' He gives me a wry look.

'Yes, I am,' I reply. 'But I keep my clothes in here.'

He walks towards me.

'Don't,' I say.

He reaches me, his stare intense.

'Don't,' I say again, putting my hand on his chest to stop him coming any closer. My knees feel weak.

He takes another step, pressing my hand hard into his chest. I freeze, barely able to breathe. And then he's kissing me.

My willpower is shot. I kiss him back.

He pulls my shirt off my body, caresses my breasts, runs his hands down my back . . . His touch becomes more urgent, more frenzied, as he pushes me down on the bed and kisses my neck. I reach down to unbutton his jeans, Christian far from my mind. Right now it's just Johnny.

I'm addicted to him. And no rehab centre is the world is going to be able to cure me.

Afterwards I lie on the bed beside him, a film of perspiration covering my body. I look up at the ceiling, at the frosted green-glass lampshade that Christian bought me weeks ago in Camden Market.

Guilt washes over me.

Oh God, what have I done?

I get up and pull my clothes on. Johnny props himself up on his elbows and watches me. I don't look at him.

'You'd better go,' I tell him, once I'm dressed.

'Meg . . .' he says, gently.

'You need to go,' I repeat, more forcefully. 'Christian will be home soon.'

He collapses back on my bed and looks up at me, sadly. 'You're not coming to LA, then?'

I stare down at Johnny and shake my head, slowly. 'I can't. I can't do that to him.'

'What about me?' he asks.

'What about you? You'll be okay,' I tell him. 'You always are.'

He gets out of bed. 'I'll give you three months,' he says, tugging his jeans on.

'Three months?' I look at him, perplexed.

'That's how long I'll wait for you.'

A lump forms in my throat and I bite back tears.

'But no longer, Nutmeg. After that, I'm letting you go.'

'Okay,' I say. 'Okay.'

Epilogue

I'm in the kitchen, staring out of the window at the garden. The leaves are just starting to turn. Christian is in the living room, working on his book. He's listening to his iPod, lost in another world, another place.

A song comes on the radio. It's been at Number One for a month. I listen for a moment, right up until the point the brass band kicks in and Johnny's voice soars into the chorus. Then I lean over and turn the radio off.

I trace my fingertips across my tummy and whisper, 'That's Mummy's song.'

He can't hear, yet. And I know in my heart it's a 'he'.

I just don't know who he's going to look like.

Acknowledgements

First of all I really want to thank everyone who read my debut novel, *Lucy In The Sky*. I was blown away by the sheer number of people who went to the trouble of reading it – not least my husband's amazing 91-year-old grandma – and your enthusiasm, encouragement and feedback have meant more to me than anything.

Thank you to the brilliant Suzanne Baboneau, who is the loveliest editor I could ever wish for. I adore working with you. Thank you to Nigel Stoneman – you definitely are the best in the business, mate. And thank you to everyone else at Simon & Schuster for really getting behind me and my books. I sincerely appreciate all your hard work.

Many thanks to Helen Brookes, Angela Mash, Miranda Ramsay and Lauren Libin (the quintessential Facebook nut) for their suggestions and help with various forms of research.

Thank you to the mothers of (in order of appearance) Louie, Ash, Aidan, Zoe, Tahlia and Millie, for never failing to ask at our weekly catch-up sessions how the writing was going.

And thank you – always – to Bridie Tonkin and Naomi Dean for their continued love and support.

MASSIVE thanks to my brother Kerrin Schuppan, who came up with the title for *Johnny* as well as *Lucy* – I owe you big time. Now, bro, can you start thinking about the next one? It's about . . . Oh, I'll tell you later.

Thank you to my parents, Vern & Jenny Schuppan, for going above and beyond in so many ways I would have to write another book if I were to list them all here. (But Mum, this time make people buy their *own* books, otherwise you'll need to take out a second mortgage . . .)

And thank you – so much – to my husband, Greg Toon, who has now read TWO chick-lit books for me and has been such an incredible sounding board for every part of this novel-writing lark. Thank you for the ideas, design input, constructive criticism and all your advice. You have always believed in me and I couldn't have done it without you.

But most of all, thank you to my son, Indy, for sleeping just enough hours in the day in his first few months of life to enable me to finish my book. Love you, little one.

Simon & Schuster and Pocket Books proudly present

Paige Toon's sensational debut novel

LUCY IN THE SKY

Available to buy in bookshops now!

ISBN 978-1-84739-043-1

Turn the page to read a sample chapter of

Lucy in the Sky . . .

Prologue

London to Singapore

Friday: Depart London Heathrow at 2105
Saturday: Arrive Singapore at 1750
Duration: 12 hrs 45 mins

'*Ladies and gentlemen, would you please fasten your seat belts, stow away your tray tables and put your seats in the upright position. All electronic equipment must be turned off during take-off and landing, and mobile phones must be switched off until you're safely inside the terminal at Singapore International Airport, as this can interfere with the aircraft navigation systems . . .*'

Oh, bugger it, I think I've left my phone on. Bollocks! It's in the overhead locker. I weigh up my options: ask the fat bloke next to me to move or cause a possible plane crash? Fat bloke? Plane crash? Better not risk it.

'Excuse me, please.'

He looks confused.

'I've left my phone on.'

Grunting unhappily, he nudges at his skinny wife to move.

Then, huffing and puffing, he hauls himself from his seat. Now all he has to do is edge sideways and we'll be home and free. Argh, this is taking forever! Wonder if he'd be quicker in an emergency? I'm starting to regret my decision to have a window seat.

Path cleared at last, I quickly locate my phone in my bag and see that a text message has come in. My finger hovers over the off button, but that tiny blinking envelope is far too inviting. Nope, I can't resist. Aah, it's from James.

HI LUCY! JUST SHAGGED JAMES IN UR BED. THOUGHT U SHOULD KNOW. 4 TIMES THIS MONTH. NICE SHEETS! XXX

It doesn't compute. I don't understand. It's from James. What does he mean, just shagged James . . . Oh, no. My stomach feels like it's plummeted 10,000 feet but the plane hasn't even taken off yet.

An air hostess hovers in the aisle. 'Miss, would you take your seat, please? The aircraft is about to depart.'

I can't. My feet are frozen to the spot. I look at her in alarm, my grip tight on the phone.

'You need to turn that off.' Her tone is steely as she nods towards the phone's glowing screen.

'Please. I just have to make—'

She shakes her head, slowly, adamantly, and Fatso heaves a heavy sigh. I feel the weight of dozens of pairs of eyes staring at me as I stagger, stunned, into my seat. The whole row quakes and judders as my hefty neighbour manoeuvres himself back in beside me.

'Miss. Your phone.'

I glance up at the unsmiling air hostess, then back down to my mobile. The message screams out at me.

HI LUCY! JUST SHAGGED JAMES IN UR BED.

But I have no choice. With her beady eyes watching me like a hawk, my finger slowly presses down on the little red button. There's no nuclear explosion. No one dies. The light on the phone merely dims and my heart sinks.

James has cheated on me.

And the slag had the gall to text me from his mobile phone.

The plane is taxiing to the runway. Outside the window it's a cold and windy English winter night. I'm on my way to Australia for the wedding of my two best friends, Molly and Sam. And some summer sunshine . . .

But right now I don't know how I'll ever be warm again. I feel like someone has ripped out my intestines and replaced them with shards of ice.

My gorgeous sandy-haired boyfriend has been having sex with another girl.

The image of him in bed with someone else slams into my mind. Someone else running her fingers through his hair. Someone else gazing into his blue, blue eyes. Someone else writhing up against him, their bodies bathed in sweat . . .

I think I'm going to throw up. I rummage around the seat pocket in front of me and manage to find a sick bag. But the feeling passes and I force myself to take a couple of deep breaths. Oh, God, this is a thirteen-hour flight! I don't know how I'm going to cope.

The plane lurches forward and forces me backwards into my

seat as it zooms off down the runway. Suddenly we're in the air, and we're climbing, climbing, climbing, and leaving the lights of London far behind us. Then abruptly there's cloud and it all goes dark outside.

My mind whirrs into action. Who is she? Have they been seeing each other long? How many times have they slept together? Is she better in bed than me? Is she slimmer? Taller? Sexier? Does he love her? Oh, God. Oh, God. How could he do this to me?

Nausea rockets back through me and this time I really do throw up.

'Urgh.' Fatso flinches in disgust, while his anorexic wife peeps at me nervously from behind his great hulk of a frame.

Ding. *'Ladies and gentlemen, the captain has switched off the fasten seat belt sign and you are now free to move around the cabin . . .'*

'Excuse me.'

It's uncanny how much quicker my neighbour moves when the stench of vomit is filling the air. Sick bag in one hand, phone in the other, I edge out and begin to walk uphill to the toilet as the aircraft continues to climb. As soon as I'm inside, I lock the door and empty the revolting contents of the bag down the pan, before rinsing my mouth out with water. The diamond earrings that James bought me for my twenty-fifth birthday last October glint back at me in the mirror.

'Hey, baby . . . Lucy, wake up . . .'

'Urgh.'

'Happy birthday.' James smiles, kissing my forehead. I wrestle myself awake and look at him, deep blue eyes peering eagerly into mine.

'I'm so tired. What time is it?'

'Six thirty.'

'James, six thirty? I don't have to get up for another hour!'

'I know, but I have to go into work early. I wanted to give you this.'

He places a silver gift box on my stomach, on top of the downy duvet. Looking at his expectant face, it's impossible not to forgive him for the early morning wake-up call. I sit up in bed and smile at him.

'I hope you like them.'

Them? I lift off the lid to find a black velvet box. Nestling inside is a pair of diamond solitaire earrings.

Now I'm awake.

'James, these are beautiful! They must've cost a fortune!'

He flashes me a mischievous grin and takes the box, carefully lifting the earrings out.

'Will you put them on? I want to see what they look like.' He hands them to me, one by one, while I fasten them to my earlobes. Then he leans back and nods his approval.

'Stunning. They suit you.'

I climb out of bed excitedly and go to the wardrobe mirror, while James flicks the bedroom halogens on. The earrings immediately sparkle, white diamonds perfectly set off against my dark hair. They're heavy, but I love them so much I don't think I'll ever take them off.

'Thank you.' I turn back to him, tears welling up in my eyes. He holds his hand out to me and I crawl back under the covers and into his warm arms.

'Do you really have to go into work early?' I ask, as he starts to kiss my neck.

'Nah. Well, not this early.'

'You little sod . . .'

He grins and undresses me until the only thing I'm left wearing are the diamonds on my ears . . .

I switch my phone back on, needing to read that message again, whatever the consequences. I look at the time it came in: 9 p.m. I tried to call him on my way to the departure gate at Heathrow. He didn't answer. Now I know why. I crouch over the pan and throw up again.

Fatso is sitting in the aisle seat when I get back, and grumbles about me being up and down all night.

I ignore him, while his wife smiles at me apologetically. 'Are you alright, love?' she asks, as soon as I'm seated. The small act of kindness breaks me. I answer 'No' in a small voice, and the floodgates open.

It's the worst flight of my life. I can't eat, I can't sleep, I can't concentrate on any of the films. I take a sleeping pill and as I curl my legs up underneath the window, and in between terrible dreams and recurring pins and needles, I manage to doze off. Every time I wake up, stark reality hits me and I check the time on the digital flight chart to see how much longer I have to wait before we arrive in Singapore and I can call him.

Ten hours and fifty-one minutes . . .

Seven hours and thirteen minutes . . .

Four hours and twenty minutes . . .

It's agony. What if he doesn't answer? No, I can't think about that right now.

James and I met at a party in London three years ago, introduced by a friend of a friend. He was already working as a corporate lawyer, while I was barely out of university. I didn't even fancy him at first. Fairly tall at six foot, well built with shortish, sandy blond hair, he was still wearing his dark grey work suit with a white shirt unbuttoned at the top. He'd taken his tie off so he didn't look *too* City Boy. But his cheeky smile reeled me in. That and his blue, blue eyes.

On our first date he took me to the Oxo Tower, where we drank champagne looking down over the city of London and the boats on the Thames. We made love four days later in a flat that he shared in Clapham with a South African bloke named Alyn. Two months after that, I moved in and Alyn moved out. Some people thought we'd moved too quickly. I couldn't move quickly enough.

James paid the lion's share of the rent while I pulled warm pints in a pub most evenings and did work experience at Mandy Nim PR, a public relations firm which promotes everything from vodka to lipgloss. After eleven weeks – one week short of the time I'd given myself to find a 'proper job' – I was lucky enough to be in the right place at the right time and landed a junior position there. Now I work as a senior PR and my friends tell me I've got the best job: taking home all the freebies I could ever dream of.

Thinking about it now, even in those early days James would often arrive home later than I did after my shifts down the pub. Were all those late nights at the office really necessary? Surely he wasn't cheating on me back then . . .

No. No. It's not possible. I just don't get it. He would *never* cheat! Would he?

Oh, Christ, I don't understand. Maybe there's been some mistake with that text. Maybe his friends sent it! That could be it. Maybe he was down the pub and they grabbed his phone when he went to the Gents. That's possible, isn't it?

But in my heart of hearts I know that's simply not true.

Fatso is guffawing at some joke on the TV screen. His wife whimpers in her sleep. I wonder if she's getting a better night's kip sitting upright in a chair than she would at home in bed where the gravity of his body weight must pull her in. She looks fairly peaceful.

I stretch my legs out under the seat in front of me and flex my feet. I'd like to go for a walk up and down the aisle but I can't be bothered going through the rigmarole of getting out past Fatso again.

Oh, bugger him! I ease myself up and over his sleeping wife. 'Don't get up!' I whisper loudly as he looks at me in surprise. I tread carefully, toes nudging aside his flabby flesh that was spilling over onto the armrests. Finally I'm free.

I pace the aisles for a couple of minutes before starting to feel self-conscious. Eventually I go and lock myself in one of the toilets. I look tired, drawn. My eyes are red and puffy.

Oh, James . . . I love you. I don't want to lose you. This flight is taking forever. I've never gone so long without being able to use my phone. I sit down on the toilet seat and start to weep with frustration.

What am I going to do? The thought of moving all my stuff out of our flat . . .

Our lovely, lovely flat. We bought it last summer. It's in Marylebone, just off the High Street. It's only a small one-bedroom, but I adore it.

For a short, sharp moment, anger surges through me. No. *He* should move. Bastard! If he's been shagging around . . .

But my rage soon dissolves back into despair. Where would I go? Would he move in with her? I couldn't even afford the mortgage on my own. If I moved out, would she move in? What would I do with all my stuff? How would we divide our CDs? DVDs? Who would get the sofa? The TV? The bed? Oh, no, the bed. Please don't let me think about it.

There was a night back in January, when I woke up at two o'clock in the morning to see James at the foot of the bed taking off his suit trousers, seemingly trying not to fall over. He'd told me he was working late, but the stench of cigarette smoke and alcohol filled the air. I pretended to be asleep because I didn't want to talk to him when he was drunk. The next morning he denied he had a hangover, even though his face was practically grey. He insisted he'd had only two drinks after getting his work done. I don't know why he lied. It was obvious that he went out and got hammered. But sometimes it simply isn't worth arguing with him.

Just the other evening I was searching through the kitchen cupboards for my box of chocolate cherry liqueurs. I knew James hadn't eaten them because he doesn't like them, but I asked if he knew where they were, anyway.

'No,' he'd replied.

'I can't find them anywhere.'

'Oh, shit, that's right, I gave them away.'

'You what? Who to? There were hardly any left!'

'A tramp.'

'A tramp?' I asked in disbelief.

'Yeah.'

'Oh, please.' I shook my head.

'It's true! He was rummaging around the black bin bags on the pavement downstairs and making a right mess. I ran back up and grabbed the first thing I could find to get him to bugger off.'

'James, cut it out. Where have you put them? Stop winding me up.'

'Lucy, I'm not joking. Why would I lie?'

'I don't bloody know. Anyway why would you give liqueurs to a tramp? He might've already had a drinking problem and there's you encouraging it.'

'Yeah, it probably wasn't very smart, was it?' he relented. 'But I wasn't really thinking.'

What a load of bullshit. There is no way he gave away my chocolate cherries to a tramp. I bet the bitch he's been shagging scoffed them.

I get back to my seat feeling nauseous, and the smell of the greasy food on the trolley coming through the cabin doesn't help. I won't be eating anything. I don't think I'll ever be able to eat chocolate cherry liqueurs again, either.

Which is just brilliant.

Who the hell is this slag? Someone he works with? A memory suddenly comes back to me of James's office Christmas party a couple of months ago. He left me chatting to one of the firm's secretaries as he went to get us something to drink. Ten minutes later he still hadn't returned so I set off to find him. He was standing by the bar talking a little too intimately, I thought at the time, to a tall, slim brunette. Their body language was close, and I remember feeling a white stab of jealousy. But when he glanced up and saw me he didn't look guilty. 'Lucy, there you are! I was just talking to, er, Zoe here.'

Later, when I asked him about her, he told me he was embarrassed because he almost hadn't remembered her name. She was new, he said, and didn't have many friends. He thought she seemed nice, but she wasn't his type. I asked, of course. I always ask.

I feel a shift in the atmosphere and look at the digital flight chart: only twenty-five minutes to go. A wave of nerves soars through me, followed by a quick throb of nausea. Seconds later the captain makes the announcement about landing. I fasten my seat belt, stow away my tray table and put my seat in the upright position. As other passengers switch off their electronic equipment, I clutch my mobile phone tightly – Singapore International Airport terminal is only minutes away . . .

Singapore

Singapore International Airport
Stopover time: 2 hrs 10 mins
My phone is in my hand as I walk through the gate towards the airport terminal. I can see that it's busy up ahead so I do a U-turn and push back through the throng towards the emptying gate. Then I'm dialling his number and it's ringing, ringing, ringing . . .

Voicemail.

I don't believe this! I've waited thirteen bloody hours to make this call. It's just after ten in the morning in England – where the hell is he? I'm not sure I want to know. I press cancel and try again, but then the sickness in the pit of my stomach engulfs me and I slump down into a seat and bury my head in my hands.

'I wish I could come with you. I'm going to miss you so much,' he murmurs into my hair as he holds me tight.

'I wish you could come too.'

'No Aussie blokes are allowed within a foot of my beautiful girl-friend. I'm issuing them all with a restraining order!'

'As if, you nutter.'

'I love you, Lucy. Call me as soon as you get there. And call me tonight before you board the plane.'

'I will do. I love you too.'

He kisses me tenderly, then opens the door before pausing and looking down at my suitcase.

'Baby, how are you going to manage that? Are you sure you'll be alright?' he asks anxiously.

I tell him that I'd planned to go to work as usual in Soho, then come back here later this afternoon to collect my suitcase and catch a cab to Paddington. I'm taking the Express to the airport.

'I've got a better idea,' he says, coming back inside and closing the door. 'Why don't you catch a cab to work and take your suitcase with you, then taxi it to Paddington later? That way I can carry it down the stairs for you now.'

'Oh, James, it's too expensive. Honestly, I'll be fine.'

'No, it's not. I'll pay, don't worry about that. Come on, are you ready?'

I waver, as he looks at me with concern. I haven't tidied up the flat after my panic packing but I don't suppose that matters.

'Well . . . okay.' I smile at him gratefully. 'Thank you.'

His face lights up as he takes my suitcase and leads me down the stairs.

I press redial.

'Hello?'

'James!'

'Lucy! Hey, where are you?' he asks me warmly.

'Where were you? I've been trying to call!'

'I was in the shower.' He sounds confused at the angst in my voice.

'With her?'

'Sorry?'

Suddenly rage swells up inside me.

'Were you in the shower with the bloody BITCH you were SCREWING last night who had the NERVE to text me from YOUR MOBILE PHONE?'

Silence.

'JAMES?'

'Lucy, what are you talking about?'

'You know what I'm talking about.'

'Lucy. I categorically do *not* know what you're talking about.'

'The girl, James, the girl you shagged last night. She texted me from YOUR MOBILE PHONE!' But my rage is losing momentum.

Now he's exasperated. 'Lucy, what the— I can *assure* you, I did NOT shag anyone last night. I had a couple of Friday-night drinks with the boys from work and then I went home to bed.'

'But—'

'ALONE.'

'So who sent—'

'I still don't know what you're going on about! *What* text?'

'I got it at nine o'clock, before take-off. It said, "Hi Lucy! Just shagged James in your bed. Thought you should know . . . Four times this month—"'

'Those fuckers!' James angrily interrupts.

'What?'

'It must've been the lads, trying to wind you up. They'll have nabbed my phone when I went to the bar.'

Tears spike my eyes and I take a few deep breaths as I realise he could be telling the truth.

'Lucy?' he asks gently. 'Are you alright?'

'No! I'm not! I threw up on the plane!'

'Oh, God. Lucy, I'm so sorry.'

'It's okay,' I sniff. 'It's not your fault.'

After a moment he speaks softly. 'Baby, you should have known. I would *never* cheat on you. I missed you so much when I came home last night and you weren't there. I can't believe you think I'd do that. It makes me pretty sad, actually.'

'James, I'm sorry. I didn't understand. I didn't know *what* was going on!'

'Hey, it's okay. It's okay. I love you.'

There are people heading down towards the gate next to me now so I dry my eyes and speak quietly into the receiver. 'I love you too. I'm sorry for doubting you. I was just really confused.'

'Don't worry. If one of your friends did that to me, I'd hit the bloody roof! But look, Lucy, promise me you won't let this spoil your holiday. You're going to have such an incredible time.'

When we finally hang up, the relief is so overpowering I actually laugh out loud. A few passengers queuing by the gate turn to stare. I realise I must look a right state, so I head off in search of the nearest ladies' loos.

It's a hot and humid Saturday evening in Singapore and when I packed my hand luggage, I had the intention of making the most of every warm minute. In the cramped toilet cubicle, I change out of my jeans into an emerald-green summer dress and swap my trainers for cork-soled, black strappy wedges. Back out in front of the mirror I tie my just-below-shoulder-length chestnut curls into a high ponytail and splash my face with cold water. I'm not wearing any make-up, but I do apply some moisturiser and cherry-flavoured lip balm.

Feeling much more normal, I set off looking for Singapore Airport's outdoor swimming pool. One of my work colleagues,

Gemma, told me about it. I don't want to swim, but there's an outdoor bar area and I sure as hell need a drink. I've got an hour and a half to kill before the flight to Sydney.

The humidity hits me the second I walk through the electric doors at the end of Terminal One. I decide on a bar-side seat and order myself a cocktail, trying to ignore the terrible Singaporean pop music blasting out of the stereo. Excitement suddenly surges through me. I'm going back to Australia!

The last time I saw Molly and Sam we were all sixteen and still at high school. I can hardly believe that was nine years ago. Molly and Sam were on-again-off-again back then – something which caused me a lot of heartbreak. I had the most overwhelming unrequited crush on Sam, and every time he got together with Molly or cooled it down, my heart would sink or soar accordingly.

I'm so relieved neither of them ever found out how I felt. But life goes on, and now I can honestly say I'm thrilled that my two friends are tying the knot.

At least I think I am, although that could all change when I see Sam again. I sincerely hope not. What is it with first loves that you supposedly never get over?

As soon as Molly called me with the news of their engagement, I knew I'd have to go back. I left Australia when my English mum married for the second time. It seemed a bit silly, her walking out on my drunkard dad in Ireland and taking me to Australia when I was four years old, only to meet an Englishman and move back to England again twelve years later. I cried and cried at the time. It felt like leaving was the most soul-destroying thing in the world. But it's amazing how you adapt. I love England now. I love the city where I live and work and I love going home to Mum and Terry's house in Somerset. I also love having two brothers – well, two stepbrothers – Tom, who is twenty-one, and Nick, who is eighteen. It was lonely growing up with just Mum and me.

There are kids with armbands splashing in the pool. A young couple appear at the top of the stairs. They're both wearing jeans and carrying backpacks and they almost immediately wipe their brows. I'm glad I packed my dress.

I think I'll have another cocktail. 'Excuse me. Could you tell me what this is again?'

'Singapore Sling, madam.'

That figures. 'Another one, please.' The bartender nods and gets to work. What's in them, I wonder, grabbing a menu from further down the bar. Grenadine, gin, sweet and sour mix and cherry brandy . . . Mmm.

This Singaporean pop music is actually quite catchy. James would laugh if he could see me now, drinking cocktails and tapping my feet.

Maybe he did hide my chocolate cherry liqueurs as a joke. I still don't accept his story that he gave them to a tramp.

Okay, here's the thing about my boyfriend. He is prone to the occasional crazy white lie. But I genuinely believe he doesn't mean any harm. For example, at the party on the night we met, he told me his mum was once offered £10,000 to sell her chocolate cake recipe to the boss at Mr Kipling. He no doubt assumed I'd forget, but a few months later I went for afternoon tea at his parents' house and his mum, a tiny little sparrow of a thing, happened to be serving chocolate cake.

'Is this the infamous recipe?' I asked her knowingly, and she replied, 'Oh, no, dear, this is from M&S. I burn everything I bake!'

When I questioned James about it later, he cracked up and asked me where on earth I'd got that idea. I told him and he denied it, laughingly insisting I must've dreamt it. I don't know, maybe I did.

There have been other lies, which I know I didn't dream – some of them quite inventive. Like the one about his grandpa snogging Marilyn Monroe when she sang for the troops in Korea. I found out from James's dad later that the old guy didn't even fight in the Korean War, and anyway Marilyn had just married Joe DiMaggio at the time. I Googled it and everything.

But his mum selling her chocolate cake recipe to Mr Kipling . . . That's my personal favourite. Little ratbag. Sometimes I think James could be an actor. But no, he's far too good as a lawyer.

And he really is. He was promoted six months ago and got a massive pay rise. That's how he could afford to buy me those earrings for my birthday. Knowing James, though, even without the promotion he would have saved up for six months to get them for me. He spoils me rotten. I get flowers at least once – sometimes twice – a month and he's always taking me out to dinner and buying me presents. My friends think I'm ludicrously lucky.

There's a high-pitched buzzing and I can hear a plane taxiing by. It's noisy, as if we're going through a car wash. I watch as a balding forty-something man makes his way down the steps into the swimming pool, his pot-bellied stomach shuddering with every step. Three young guys are sitting at a table on the other side of the bar, drinking beers. One of them looks over at me and then turns back to his mates and says something. All three turn round and grin.

I feel so much happier now. Damn it, I'm going to have another one.

'Singapore Sling?'

'Yes, please.'

I'm feeling a little tipsy. I know you shouldn't really drink on your own but, bugger it, I'm on holiday. And I've been through a lot in the last, how long has it been? Fifteen hours or so? I wonder if I'll laugh about this in years to come. It's starting to seem pretty funny now – but I imagine the three Singapore Slings help.

The thought of poor James going home to an empty flat, sleeping in an empty bed and missing me . . . I wish he could've come to Australia as well. If he hadn't received that promotion he would have asked for the time off, but at the time I was booking my flights, he felt it was too soon. I really wish Molly and Sam could meet him.

There's a couple in the spa and they're kissing. The balding forty-something is doing breaststroke and he keeps copping an eyeful every time he swims past. You don't very often see guys do breaststroke, do you? I kind of wish I had my swimming costume with me now, but then I wouldn't be here, swinging my wedge-clad feet on this lovely high bar stool.

'Would you like another, madam?'

Is he *flirting* with me? That was definitely a twinkly grin. Can you have twinkly grins or is it just twinkly eyes and cheesy grins? I mean cheeky grins. God, I'm pissed.

This is definitely, definitely my last one. Whoa! Almost slipped off my stool. What time is my flight again? There's a TV screen with the flight times behind the bar and I struggle to make out the numbers. No, I'm not looking at you, pal. Where's my flight? Sydney, Sydney, Sydney – ah, there it is. Last Call.

Shit, does that say Last Call?

Bollocks! I slide, almost fall, from the stool and, practically tripping over my wedge sandals, make for the exit. Then I realise I haven't paid. I rush back, see the relief on Twinkly Grin's face after he must've figured I was doing a runner, throw down my credit card, will him to get a wriggle on and then turn and run. Where the hell is Gate C22?

Singapore to Sydney

Saturday: Depart Singapore at 2000
Sunday: Arrive Sydney at 0650
Duration: 7 hrs 50 mins

Oh dear, those air hostesses do not look happy. They've called for Lucy McCarthy twice over the tannoy in the last ten minutes as I've zigzagged my way here. I try to apologise for being late but 'sorry' comes out like 'shorry' and it doesn't help that I'm unable to walk down the plank in a straight line.

Did I just say plank? I meant aisle, of course.

The other passengers are looking at me. Yes, yes, I've had a couple of drinks, but what am I, a total freak? Ah, here's my seat. Window again, fab. Yep, you'll have to move. And I'm not so drunk that I can't see you raising your eyebrows at each other, either. Bet you thought you had a nice empty seat next to you – too bad! I think I'll take my carry-on bag with me to my seat this time.

I plonk myself down and try to locate the seat belt from under my bum. Blanket . . . No. Pillow . . . No. Where is the bloomin' thing? Ah, seat belt. I tug, tug, tug at it. Why won't it budge? Oh, okay, that seat belt belongs to the man next to me. Sorry, mate. I've found mine. Click. I do feel woozy.

'*Ladies and gentlemen, would you please fasten your seat belts, stow away your tray tables and put your seats in the upright position . . .*'

Yeah, yeah, heard it all before. Blahdeblahdeblah.

'*. . . mobile phones must be switched off until you're safely inside Sydney International Airport . . .*'

Yep, I know that bit too. Been there, done that. Oops, I haven't switched it off yet actually.

Can't . . . quite . . . reach . . . bag . . .

Seat belt . . . too . . . tight . . .

I eventually unclick myself and grab my bag, finding my phone. No messages, thank goodness. I switch it off and chuck it back into my bag. Then I buckle myself up again and breathe a nice big Singapore Sling sigh of relief.

My tanned legs are peeking out from underneath my sundress and I admire them happily. I do like this fake tan – it's a nice, natural-looking one. But it is *such* a pain in the arse having to use old sheets on the first night that you apply it. And then you have to wash them and put your good ones back on again . . . So it's two loads of laundry in two days. Well, I had to leave James to deal with the washing this time as he hurried me out of the flat.

NICE SHEETS!

The memory barely registers before my stomach freefalls and I ask myself: how the hell did James's blokey friends know about my shitty fake-tan sheets?

Oh, no . . . They didn't know. Because they didn't send that text.

I hurriedly unbuckle my seat belt and reach for my bag, giving the seat back and the person in front of me a big, solid head-butt. I fumble around for my phone and switch it on.

HI LUCY! JUST SHAGGED JAMES IN UR BED. THOUGHT U
SHOULD KNOW. 4 TIMES THIS MONTH. NICE SHEETS! XXX

'Miss – you need to turn that off.'

What, do they have eyes in the back of their bloody heads?

'I can't! I have to make a phone call!'

'Miss, the other passengers on this flight have already been held up enough, don't you think?' She looks at me meaningfully. 'So you'd better turn that off, right now.'

'Is there a problem?' Another bitchy air hostess arrives to join the party.

'No, Franny, we're alright here. This young lady was just about to turn off her phone.'

With a deep fury bubbling away in my very core, I comply. Power trip over, they smugly sashay off down the aisle. I'm tempted to hurl my phone at the back of Franny's frickin' head.

That lying, cheating son of a bitch. I'm going to kill him.

The plane takes off and I'm so full of rage that I barely notice. The forty-something man and his wife/girlfriend/mistress (most likely) next to me shift uncomfortably in their seats. And while I'd like to think I have a certain amount of self-control, at the moment I'm not entirely sure I do. It's just as well I've been given a window seat – I'd probably be rampaging down the aisle, screaming like a banshee, if I could get out. I can't handle another eight hours of this.

The sun is setting as we start our journey through another night. It calms my mood somewhat and it occurs to me that I haven't actually eaten anything since leaving London yesterday evening. Four cocktails on an empty stomach – oh, dear. I suddenly have an urgent need to go to the toilet. The people next to me are only too eager to oblige, standing up and eyeing me warily as I squeeze past them.

The nasty fluorescent light in the bathroom flickers on. I clock my diamond earrings in my reflection and seriously consider tearing them from my ears and flushing them down the toilet. Ha! Knowing how the bastard lied through his teeth to me, they're probably not even real. Lucy in the sky with cubic fucking zirconia. That'd be about right.

The air hostesses have started to serve drinks at the top of the aisle. I figure they can back up into Business Class and let me take my seat so I walk up towards them. The older one, Franny, nods at the younger one, who swivels round and spots me before turning back to Franny with an almost imperceptible shake of her immaculately groomed head. Then the bitches make me wait back by the toilets while they carry on serving the entire cabin with their frosty, false little smiles until finally they reach me and I'm able to pass. I am livid, but I won't let them see they've got to me. I get back to my seat and realise I haven't even been given a drink.

Franny and her evil counterpart are serving food now. The chicken stir-fry is slimy and unappetising, but I'm famished so I eat it all. Even the fake-cream sponge goes down nicely. The alcohol is starting to wear off and I find I'm exhausted, although I'm still so mad at James I can barely breathe.

So he lied about cheating. I can't believe I actually apologised for suspecting him! How dare he? The image of him in bed with another girl comes to me once more, but I channel my anger back fast and strong. I can't deal with those sick nerves again – anger is much easier to handle.

I need to go to the loo again. The air hostesses have already cleared our dinner trays, but they're still working on the seats behind us. The curtain that divides Economy and Business Class is tied back and the Business Class toilets are tantalisingly close. What the hell, I think, and walk up the aisle.

It's much nicer in here. They've even got hand cream and flowers.

There's a knock at the door. What now? I wee as quickly as I can while the knocking increases in urgency and volume, and then unlock the door. Surprise, surprise, it's Franny's frosty friend. She must have seen me come in here. I haven't even had time to use the hand cream yet – damn.

'Miss, these are *Business* Class toilets – the Economy Class toilets are at the other end,' she tells me condescendingly.

I motion to the passengers in Business Class and say, 'I don't think anyone here really mi— Wait. Are those *telephones*?'

An Asian businessman has a phone to his ear and this phone is attached by a cord to the back of the seat in front of him.

'That's certainly what they look like, don't they?'

I look at her desperately. 'I need to make a phone call.'

'I'm afraid you can't. They're for Business Class passengers only.'

'No, you don't understand. I *have* to make an urgent call.'

'I'm sorry, but there is nothing I can do. You need to take your seat now.'

I should've known better than to piss off an air hostess.

She determinedly guides me back to my seat as I look over my shoulder in desperation at the phones. I don't care that there's only a few hours left of this flight. I want to call the son of a bitch and scream at him NOW. I *will* use that phone.

An hour later, when all the other passengers are either sleeping or watching the in-flight entertainment, I hoist myself up in my seat and climb over my dozing neighbours, carefully treading on their armrests so as not to wake them. I lift back the curtain dividing us and Business Class and step through. The Asian businessman is sleeping, so I creep over to him. Carefully taking the phone from its mount, I scrutinise it. No! It looks like it needs a credit card.

'Miss! What *are* you doing?'

The businessman jolts wide awake at the sound of the air hostess's shrill voice and stares at me, startled. He shouts something I can't understand and, before I know it, the phone has been wrestled out of my grip by Franny and I'm being frogmarched up towards the front of the plane.

In the kitchenette area she turns to me and says with icy-cold hardness: 'You'd better listen to me long and hard. First, you rocked up late and drunk. You were lucky that we didn't refuse you passage on this aircraft—'

'I wasn't that drunk,' I interrupt.

'Enough! This is the one and only time I am going to tell you. If you don't go back to your seat and calmly stay there for the duration of this flight, you will be banned from ever flying with this airline again. DO YOU UNDERSTAND ME?'

A red flush has crept across my face and I nod my assent. Mortified, I make my way back to my seat. Again I climb up and over the sleeping passengers, all the time watched closely by Franny. When she's satisfied that I've been put firmly and literally back in my place, she turns and leaves, shaking her head in disgust.

After a few minutes of sitting there with my face burning, I decide I'd better watch a film or something – anything to try to take my mind off my situation. I won't be moving again.

An hour later, when they're bringing the breakfast trolley through, I barely look up, and when we finally land I can't meet their eyes as I walk out through the door. They don't say anything which may cause a scene in front of the other passengers, but I know they're delighted to see the back of me. I just hope they're not on my return flight. But right now, of course, there are other concerns on my mind.

POCKET
BOOKS

Lucy in the Sky
Paige Toon

A lawyer.   A surfer.   A 24-hour flight.   The frequent liar
points are clocking up and Lucy's got choices to make . . .

It's been nine years since Lucy left Australia. Nine years since
she's seen her best friend Molly, and Sam, the one-time love
of her life. Now her two friends are getting married. To each
other. And Lucy is on her way to Sydney for their wedding.

Life for Lucy has moved on. She's happily settled with James,
her gorgeous lawyer boyfriend, with their flat in London and
her glamorous job in PR. Surely there's no reason to expect
this two-week holiday in the sun will be
anything out of the ordinary?

But just before take-off, Lucy receives a text from James's
mobile. She can't resist taking a look . . . and, in one push
of a button, her world comes crashing down . . .

'I loved it – I couldn't put it down!' MARIAN KEYES

ISBN 978-1-84739-043-1
PRICE £6.99

POCKET
BOOKS

Drop Dead Beautiful
Jackie Collins

The bestselling author of *Lovers & Players* returns
with her twenty-fifth dynamic new novel and her best-loved
character, Lucky Santangelo . . . so get ready
for a scandalously wild ride!

Lucky is back with a vengeance – every bit as strong, sexy and
seductive as ever. But Lucky is older and wiser now – and
she's hot to reclaim her power position in Las Vegas by
building a magnificent billion dollar hotel complex.

Max, Lucky's rebellious teenage daughter, is every bit as
outrageous as Lucky herself. Max is hard to control, especially
when she takes off to rendezvous with a stranger
she meets on the Internet.

While Lucky is busy building her hotel, she is unaware that
a deadly enemy from her past has surfaced. A person determined
to take everything from her, including the family
that she holds so dear.

Internationally bestselling author Jackie Collins marks
her twenty-fifth novel with another dazzling page-turner,
packed with desire, sex, revenge and love.

ISBN 978-1-84739-315-9
PRICE £6.99

POCKET
BOOKS

Certain Girls
Jennifer Weiner

Readers fell in love with Cannie Shapiro, the smart, sharp-tongued, bighearted heroine of *Good in Bed* who found her happy ending after her mother came out of the closet, her father fell out of her life, and her ex-boyfriend started chronicling their ex-sex life in the pages of a national magazine.

Now Cannie's back. After her debut novel – a fictionalized, no-holds-barred version of her life – became an overnight bestseller, she dropped out of the public eye. Happily married to the tall, charming diet doctor Peter Krushelevsk, she has settled into a life that she finds wonderfully predictable – filled with knitting in the front row of her daughter Joy's drama rehearsals, volunteering at the library, and taking Over-Forty yoga classes with her best friend Sam.

As preparations for Joy's bat mitzvah begin, everything seems right in Cannie's world. Then Joy discovers her mother's novel, and suddenly finds herself faced with the story Cannie hid from her all her life. When Peter surprises his wife by saying he wants to have a baby, the family is forced to reconsider their history, their future, and what it means to be truly happy.

Radiantly funny and tender, *Certain Girls* is an unforgettable story about love, loss, and the enduring bonds of family.

ISBN 978-1-84737-019-8
PRICE £11.99

SIMON &
SCHUSTER

Ursula's Story
By Sandra Howard

From the author of the acclaimed *Glass Houses* comes a
captivating new novel: the story of a woman whose marriage
break-up makes headline news, while she tries desperately to
keep her family together and forge a new life for herself . . .

Ursula's story opens on the morning of her ex-husband
William's wedding. The press call her first thing, demanding
she share her innermost feelings with the world at large. Her
three children cannot restrain their excitement. After all, it
isn't every day that their father marries a government minister,
and the Prime Minister and half the Cabinet
are to be among the guests.

Ursula, herself embarked on a shaky new relationship
with Julian, a local antiquarian bookseller, sees how hard
their 11-year-old daughter Jessie has taken the break-up.
Her father's favourite, she has put up walls, closed doors
and turned to Julian for support. But Julian himself is hard
to read, his absences from their lives ever more prolonged
and unexplained. Are Jessie's defences strong enough to
protect her, when a threat to her life catches
Ursula completely off-guard?

ISBN 978-0-7432-8556-8
PRICE £12.99

POCKET
BOOKS

The Birds and the Bees
Milly Johnson

Romance writer and single mum Stevie Honeywell has only
weeks to go to her wedding, when her fiancé Matthew runs
off with her glamorous friend Jo MacLean. But Stevie knows
exactly how to win back her man. By undergoing a mad
course of dieting and exercise, she is sure things will
be as sweet as nectar again before very long.

Likewise, Adam MacLean is determined to win back his
lady. All he needs to do is convince Stevie to join him in his
own cunning plan – a prospect that neither of them finds
attractive, seeing as each blames the other for the
mess they now find themselves in.

But when her strategy of self-improvement fails dismally,
Stevie finds that desperate times call for desperate measures.
She has no option but to join forces with the big Scot in a
scheme that soon reaches heights neither of them could ever
have imagined. So, like a Scottish country jig, the two couples
change partners but continue to weave closely around each other.
And Adam and Stevie find they have to deal with the heartbreaks
of the past before they can deal with those of the present. When
Adam's crazy plan actually starts to work, the question is: just
who will he and Stevie be dancing with when the music stops?

ISBN 978-1-4165-2591-2
PRICE £6.99

POCKET
BOOKS

These books and other **Simon & Schuster** and **Pocket Books** titles are available from your local bookshop or can be ordered direct from the publisher.

Please send cheque or postal order for the value of the book,
free postage and packing within the UK, to
SIMON & SCHUSTER CASH SALES
PO Box 29, Douglas Isle of Man, IM99 1BQ
Tel: 01624 677237, Fax: 01624 670923
Email: bookshop@enterprise.net
www.bookpost.co.uk

Please allow 14 days for delivery. Prices and availability
subject to change without notice